PATRIOT LIES

A JACK WIDOW THRILLER

SCOTT BLADE

Black Lion Media

PUBLISHED BY BLACK LION MEDIA.

ALSO BY SCOTT BLADE

The Jack Widow Series

Gone Forever

Winter Territory

A Reason to Kill

Without Measure

Once Quiet

Name Not Given

The Midnight Caller

Fire Watch

The Last Rainmaker

The Devil's Stop

Black Daylight

The Standoff

Foreign & Domestic

Patriot Lies

The Double Man

Nothing Left

The Protector

Kill Promise

1

THE OLD MAN on the park bench was outside, freezing on a cold October night.

It was typical for him. October. August. January. July. None of it mattered.

Every night, he slept somewhere that didn't belong to him. He slept wherever he was. Sometimes he was in the same place as the night before. And sometimes he wasn't.

The locations changed, but two things remained the same. The exact time of year meant nothing to him, all but one day, his daughter's birthday. He always remembered the date and the year she was born, but he never knew if he was on that exact date or not. He didn't know because he couldn't keep up with what day of the week *he* was in.

He knew the current month was October. He recognized October by the cold setting and the leaves changing colors.

The second thing that never changed was that he was drunk. He drank himself to sleep every night. He was a man trying to forget.

An empty bottle of Old Crow Whiskey lay out sideways on the brick sidewalk below him. The last drops streamed back and forth, slowly, across the inside of the bottle, like a carpenter's level.

The old man had drunk most of the bottle, but not alone. He'd shared it with other homeless men. One of them he knew by face. One he knew by name. And three of them he had never seen before in his life and would never see again.

The three he didn't know were friendly enough. They drank with him that very night. They helped him to the park bench and left him there. It was one of his nightspots, a good spot, too, because it was nestled in a tree-covered nook in the park that was often well-hidden and overlooked. A pedestrian passing by on the street would miss it unless he was looking for it.

The night trees weren't the same as the day trees. Technically, they were the same trees, but not to him. The night trees whistled in the wind. They swayed heavily, making creaking and rocking sounds like growing pains, all in the night's stillness.

Cars barely passed along the four streets that surrounded Lincoln Park.

Everything was quiet in a way that made him think of the open desert nights in Iraq.

The bench was all metal, painted deep red. It was hard and cold and not long enough to support a tall man. Luckily, the old man wasn't tall. He stood five-foot-nine and a half, when he wasn't hunching over. That half-inch used to be very important to him, when he cared what people thought. Those days were long gone. And it showed.

He let his beard grow wild to where even his friends from twenty years ago wouldn't recognize him. He'd let his pores clog. He hadn't showered in days. He couldn't remember the last time a razorblade had touched his face. He couldn't remember the last time he had brushed his teeth or combed his hair or laid hands on a bar of soap.

Not to mention, he couldn't remember the last time a woman had touched him. No woman would touch him now. He knew that for sure. Now, all he got were dirty looks and people avoiding him.

Lincoln Park wasn't his first choice for spending a cold October night. He usually rotated between the back of a 7-Eleven on Benning Street or the Kingsman Field Dog Park on Tennessee Avenue or one of the ten churches in less than ten square blocks or the back alley of a yoga studio over on Tenth Street, past the Maryland Avenue overpass.

But not tonight.

Tonight, he slept in Lincoln Park. Not planned. He had gotten drunker than usual. It was just the way things worked out. He'd ended up there by a series of events that seemed random, like every other day of his life. Nothing had been planned. There was no predestined reason for him to be drinking with the other homeless guys. Nothing seemed out of the ordinary.

Early that night, he'd met a guy, got a ride, and found a bottle of booze, which he shared with other homeless guys. He got drunk, too drunk, and now here he was, sleeping on a park bench. It was all a typical night, except this time he spent it with drinking buddies and a full bottle.

His drinking buddies numbered five guys. There was the one he knew by name, the one he knew by face, and the three he didn't. When you're homeless, you take all the drinking buddies you can get—random or not.

The five of them gathered around a trashcan fire to stay warm. Autumn nights in DC could be relentlessly cold. Not like winter nights, but still he risked catching a cold; at worst, he could freeze to death.

The five homeless guys stood around and bullshitted about bullshit and not much else.

Within forty minutes, he was buzzed. Within two hours, he was piss-drunk. Thirty minutes after that, he was fast asleep on the park bench. His homeless drinking buddies were gone. The trashcan fire burned out.

He was alone.

The old man slept for nearly an hour before the black Cadillac Escalade pulled up to the curb on East Capitol Street from North Carolina Avenue. Both one-way streets were marked with clear one-way markers.

The Escalade's engine ran and purred under the hood. There were four guys in the truck. The driver left the engine on and hopped out with the rest, shutting the doors behind them.

They wore all black. Black jackets. Black pants. Black boots. They matched, like a secret private security force.

The first guy led the way into Lincoln Park and over to the homeless guy on the bench. He walked as if he knew the way in advance, like he had been there before, like he had rehearsed it at this exact location.

He approached the old man's position as if he knew exactly where the old man was perched, like there was a tracking beacon on him.

The second guy followed the first guy. The third and fourth guys followed halfway over to the old man, and then they branched off, walking toward different entrances to the park. Three of the guys formed a perimeter, as if they were guarding against anyone coming in or going out.

The first guy led the way to the bench and pointed out the sleeping homeless guy to the second guy. Then, the second guy turned and faced away as if he were standing guard. He stuffed his hands into his coat pockets to look like just a guy standing around.

All four men carried firearms in concealed hip holsters under their clothes. All four holsters' safety buckles were unsnapped. All four firearms were chambered with a nine-millimeter bullet. All four weapons were well-oiled and well-maintained. All four weapons had been fired before. All four men had killed before.

The first guy walked over to the sleeping homeless man on the bench. He carried a brand-new bottle of Clyde Brothers' Whiskey. The price tag was two hundred bucks, far more than a cheap bottle of Old Crow.

The first guy couldn't use the Old Crow, not that there was any left to use. He needed a flammable whiskey. Old Crow wouldn't do the job. Not the right way, even if it was a full bottle.

It's a myth that any old bottle of alcohol will make a good accelerant. It's true that alcohol is highly flammable. The right bottle of alcohol makes for the perfect Molotov cocktail. But most cheap alcohol is cheap for a reason. There's not much pure alcohol left in a cheap bottle of whiskey. Not enough to do the job that the first guy needed it to do.

To get the most bang for your buck, you need a cask strength whiskey. Bottom-shelf whiskey is watered down, which reduces its strength and its cost.

Cask strength isn't the highest proof nor the strongest alcohol content in a whiskey, but it burns well enough. Cask strength whiskey will catch on fire and burn just right.

The first guy stood directly over the homeless man, watching him sleep, listening to him snore. The homeless guy snored with his mouth wide open.

The first guy looked up. He looked left, looked right. Making sure no one was watching.

He saw no one, just his guys.

The wind gusted around him. It brushed through Lincoln Park. It whistled through the crevices and ridges over the Emancipation Statue, a life-size memorial that portrayed President Lincoln, standing over the last enslaved man to be captured under the *Fugitive Slave Act of Missouri*.

All around, the first guy heard nothing over the wind noise, except the usual weeknight sounds of Washington, DC.

Horns honked far off in the distance. Sirens wailed, but far away. Mechanical motor sounds rumbled along the city streets. Tires rolled over pavements. Worn brake pads hissed. A dog barked to the south. But no one was around. No witnesses.

The first guy tore the seal off the top of the Clyde Brothers' bottle and pulled out the cork. He tossed them both to the ground. He held the bottle out at full arm's reach and tipped it upside down, spilling the contents all over the snoring homeless man.

The alcohol gushed out, drenching the homeless guy and the bench beneath him in whiskey.

The homeless man was so drunk that he didn't wake up to the liquid dousing him all over. Not at first.

It wasn't until the first guy doused the bottom fourth of the bottle all over the homeless guy's face that he woke and reacted.

He half-leaped up and waved his hands over his face as if he were being waterboarded.

The homeless guy's eyes popped open in time to see the first guy standing over him, emptying the bottle of whiskey all the way until there was nothing left but glass and the label.

"What? What the hell're you doin'?" the homeless guy asked.

The first guy finished pouring the bottle over him. Then he tossed it over his shoulder. It landed off the track into some bushes. The bottle didn't break.

The homeless guy stayed lying on the bench. Frantically, he wiped the whiskey out of his eyes and spat some out of his mouth.

He squinted, staring up into the starry night above. Things were blurry, as if he were looking through a glass of water.

He saw the first guy standing over him. The first guy's features were all covered in shadows and blurred.

"What the hell's going on?" the homeless guy asked.

The first guy reached his free hand into his coat and came out with something palm-sized. He balanced it in his hand and pressed on it with his index finger. Then he swiped left. It was a smartphone.

"What're ya doing?"

The first guy said, "Hold up a second, Commander."

The homeless guy's eyes widened, as if he saw someone he thought he knew, but he couldn't see the guy's face, and he didn't recognize the voice. But the first guy had called him *Commander*, like people did back when he was a commander in the Navy.

"Who are you?" the homeless guy asked.

The first guy ignored him and said, "It's time."

"Time for what?"

The light from the smartphone's screen lit up the guy's face. The homeless guy's eyesight improved, and he focused. He looked over the first guy's face. He saw a clean-shaven chin and deep blue eyes, and not much else to speak of. The first guy's face was average and unremarkable. It was strangely forgettable. In a police lineup, he would blend right in. No one would identify him in a crowd. Besides his eyes and a pair of broad shoulders, everything else about the guy was average, like he was built for spycraft—an average-looking guy with no memorable traits made him someone who could pass through crowds with no problem. Witnesses would never remember enough details to describe him. There was nothing to remember. He was a vague man walking.

The guy was in his late forties. He had broad shoulders, with a lean lower half like a marathon runner, and short black hair, sprinkled with gray.

"Do I know you?" the homeless guy asked. He legitimately wasn't sure. Part of him glimpsed some vague recognition from a deep past that he tried to forget.

The first guy didn't answer. He clicked a button on the phone's screen, and the phone rang—once. Someone answered it on the other end of the line. The first guy put it on speaker.

He said, "Found him, sir."

The first guy reversed the phone and faced it to the homeless guy.

The phone's bright screen lit up the homeless guy's face. Blue back light bounced off the homeless guy's unkempt beard.

The first guy stared at him.

"You look like shit, Commander."

The homeless guy reached up for the phone as if he was going to take it, but the first guy jerked it back.

"Don't touch!" the first guy shouted.

The homeless guy stayed laid out where he was, like he was. He didn't budge. He didn't move. He just stared up at the screen. The first guy moved it in closer to the homeless guy's face.

The homeless guy stared at the screen until he realized that someone on screen stared back at him.

The face was familiar. He knew the eyes. They were dark brown, not black, but they were just as soulless as the last time he'd seen them—twenty years ago. Unlike the first guy, these were not eyes he would forget. He saw them nearly every day in his dreams—his nightmares. They were eyes from a dead past that he wished would stay buried. He thought about that face often. He tried not to. He tried to forget it. He wanted to forget, wanted never to see it again, but here it was, staring back at him.

The first guy stared at the homeless guy from behind the phone's back light and asked a question.

"This him?"

The voice on the screen replied.

"Turn his head to profile. Let me get a good look at him."

The first guy barked an order at the homeless guy.

"Turn your head!"

The homeless guy did nothing.

The first guy reached a gloved hand out and grabbed the homeless guy's beard on the left side and jerked his head to face the right—hard.

The homeless guy struggled, but it was useless.

The first guy barked, "Stop!"

The homeless guy stopped fighting back and gave in.

The voice on the screen ordered, "Show me his eyes."

The first guy jerked the homeless guy's head back to center, released his beard, and reached up to his eye sockets. He got a grip on one of the homeless guy's eyelids and pulled it open wide as far as it would go. In any other human being, the whites of the eyes would've been what showed up, but not here. The homeless man's whites were too bloodshot to be called *white*.

All that was visible were pupils, irises, and blood-red veins throughout his eyes.

The voice on the phone said, "He's piss drunk."

The first guy said, "Yes. Part of the plan. It's how we got him alone."

The homeless guy said, "What? What's going on?"

The voice on the phone said, "Hello, Henry."

The homeless man said, "Who?"

"Henry Eggers. I know it's you."

"No one. No one calls me that anymore. Henry Eggers is dead now."

Eggers looked at the face on the phone. He lifted his head off the park bench's metal armrest and squinted his eyes, trying to focus on the face on the phone's screen.

Both the face on the screen and the first guy waited a long moment until they knew for a fact that Eggers recognized the face on the screen.

They knew because terror swept over Eggers' face.

The face on the phone asked, "You remember me, Henry?"

Eggers said nothing.

The face on the phone said, "Yeah. You remember me. I found you. Can you believe it? It wasn't easy. Finding you was hard. And I've got the resources to find anyone. Anyone, Henry."

Eggers swallowed and said, "I didn't know you were looking for me."

"I've been looking for you for a little bit of time now. Months, in fact."

"How are you?"

The face on the phone's screen ignored the question.

"Henry, you look like shit."

Eggers said nothing.

The first guy said, "He smells like shit too."

The face on the phone asked, "What's happened to you, Henry?"

"I'm between jobs right now."

"Funny."

Eggers paused a beat. For a reason nothing other than he was completely blank on what to say next. Finally, he spoke.

"To what do I owe the pleasure?"

The face on the phone stared at him, hard. Then he spoke.

"I've got to ask you a question."

"Okay."

"Answer honestly, now. This'll all go a lot easier for you. No lies. Understand?"

"Okay."

The face on the phone asked, "What did you do with your money?"

Eggers stayed quiet, but his eyes opened wide. They darted from side to side as if he was tortured by old, unforgotten memories.

A solid minute went by. The face on the phone knew it because he had been watching the time on his phone.

"Henry!"

"What?"

"Where's the money?"

Eggers paused. He tried to grip the bench and pull himself up, but the first guy plunged four solid fingertips into Eggers' chest, shoving him back down on his butt.

"Stay!" the first guy barked.

"Answer the question!" the face on the phone demanded.

Eggers cleared his throat and said, "I don't know."

The face said, "Henry, where's the money?"

Eggers said nothing.

The face said, "Last chance."

The first guy reached into his pocket and pulled out a Zippo lighter. It looked both expensive and familiar to Eggers. It looked familiar because it was. One time, long ago, the lighter had belonged to him. It was a gift from a commanding officer he had back in his Navy days.

An engraving on the polished silver casing read his full name and rank and nothing else.

Eggers said, "I'm not Henry anymore. You don't need to worry about me. I'm one of the forgotten people now. Like a ghost. I'm nobody."

The face repeated, "Where's the money?"

Eggers said, "I don't got it."

The face on the phone called out for the first guy by name.

The first guy pulled the phone away from Eggers and stared at the face on the screen.

The face said, "He's useless. Do it."

The first guy smiled. Eggers saw it in the light from the phone.

Eggers was drunk and ancient, but once upon a time, he had been somebody. Those old instincts might still be there somewhere, down deep. He hoped they were. He hadn't thrown a punch in more than twenty years. The last time he was in close quarters combat, he'd been more than a decade younger and ten pounds heavier, but it was all muscle. Now, he was a shriveled shell of that guy. He was a husk of someone who used to be a highly-trained sailor. He hoped the muscle memory was still there.

Eggers reached down and mustered the strength and the nerve to go for it. He exploded to action and slapped the back of the phone in the first guy's hand and slammed it into his face.

The first guy, not stunned, but surprised, stepped back a foot, unfazed. The effort wasn't the most powerful thing ever, but it had served its purpose.

Eggers didn't need to engage in a one-on-one boxing match with a guy twenty-five years younger than him and built like a brick house. He only needed to surprise him, buy himself a few seconds to get up and run.

Eggers rolled off the bench and stumbled to his feet. Everything was hazy. The darkness and the city lights beyond seemed to blur together like a watercolor painting with the colors running from being left out in the rain.

Eggers might've been drunk-beyond-drunk, but he had experience in this. He knew how to maneuver in the dark, in a state of intoxication. Eggers had been drinking away his regrets for long years. He knew how to live in that world.

He scrambled away from the first guy and took off running.

The first guy reacted. He dropped the Zippo and reached down and jerked a SIG Sauer P226 out of a concealed hip holster.

He pointed the gun at Eggers' back as he ran away.

The face was still on the phone.

He barked, "Don't shoot him!"

The first guy stared through the iron sights. Both of his eyes were wide open. He had Eggers lined up. He could've squeezed the trigger. But he didn't.

"No bullets!" the face on the phone ordered.

The first guy lowered the gun and said, "Roger."

The first guy called out to the other three guys.

"He's heading on foot to Thirteenth Street!"

Eggers ran as hard and as fast as he could, which was to say not quick at all.

He saw Thirteenth Street's lights just ahead of him. He saw a taxi pass on the street.

"Help!" he tried to call out. But his voice sounded hoarse from not having used it in a long time.

He tried again.

"Help!"

Another car drove by.

He kept running. The exit from the park was right there. The street was so close. He almost made it, but he didn't.

Instead, he felt instant pain in the back of his head. He heard a loud, echoing shatter so close it was like it was inside his skull. The next thing he knew, he was on the ground.

He was dazed, more dazed than he ever felt drunk.

Eggers rolled his head to the side and put a hand down on the brick walkway. He pushed himself up and turned to see what hit him in the back of the head. It had been a full bottle of Clyde Brothers' Whiskey, but now it was an empty bottle. It was a broken, empty bottle, shattered all over the brick from hitting him.

The first guy had thrown it at him.

Eggers looked up, while the first guy approached him from the park bench. A gun was in his hand and pointed right at Eggers' face.

Eggers tried to push himself up and stand on his own feet, but then he saw three other men. They came from three different directions around him. They were all dressed in black, looking like they were up to no good, which they were.

No one came up from behind him, from the street, but that made no difference now. He would never make it to the street, and he knew it.

Two of the other guys reached under his armpits and scooped him up to his feet. They kept their grips locked on him. They pulled both of his arms out to his sides as if they were going to put him up on a cross.

He got a look at one of the other guys. He was a massive, bald guy. He had fists like concrete blocks.

The bald guy stood nearby with a gun in his hand. Not a SIG Sauer P226, like the first guy's, but a Glock 34. The thing Eggers deduced about them at that instant, which he should've recognized before, was from their guns.

Special Forces operators are usually trained in as many weapons as possible. The different divisions of the US military service all have their own unique standard-issue weapons. The Army used to have the M1911, back in the day. Then they upgraded to the M9 Beretta for a long, long time. But recently—he couldn't remember the year exactly—the

Army had switched to the SIG Sauer P320 after it won a "Modular Handgun Systems" competition.

The thing that Eggers recognized about the weapons these guys carried was that if there was a shortlist for preferred weapons by Special Forces operators, they would both make the cut.

His brain coupled the choice of weapons with the way they were dressed and the way they placed themselves in a perimeter, along with the face on the phone. And he knew—they had been Special Forces in their pasts.

The first guy lowered his weapon but kept it in hand at his side.

He approached Eggers and raised the phone's screen to face him again.

Eggers looked at the face that stared back at him.

"Henry, I'm sorry it's come to this. Take care of him."

The face said nothing else and hung up. The screen went black.

The first guy slipped the phone back into his pocket.

He said, "Hold him tight."

Eggers felt two of the other men wrench out his arms, holding him locked in place.

The first guy twisted back at the waist and rotated fast and forward. He whipped Eggers across the face with his pistol.

The gun *cracked* across Eggers' lower jaw. Teeth splintered. He spat out two. Blood trickled out of his mouth.

He wanted to beg and plead, but he didn't. The old sailor that he used to be was still there, down deep in his core. Sailors don't beg or plead. They stand tall.

He pushed his feet down into the brick and tried to stand up tall.

He spat out blood toward the bald guy.

"Tough now, are you?" the bald guy asked.

Eggers stayed quiet.

The first guy hit him again with the pistol and then a third time—both across the face. The third one was flat on Eggers' forehead. He felt nothing after that. The blow was hard and dazed what was left of him to daze.

The first guy said, "Drag him back to the bench."

The others lifted Eggers off his feet and took him back to the bench. They forced him to lie flat like he had been when he was asleep.

One of the other guys took out a zip tie and forced Eggers' wrists between the bars on the armrest of the bench. He ziptied his wrists around it.

The men all backed away.

The first guy reached into his jacket pocket and pulled out a pack of cigarettes. He took one out and returned the pack to his pocket. He knelt and scooped up the dropped lighter. He flicked open the top. He stuck a cigarette into his mouth, struck a flame, and lit it. He returned the Zippo to his pocket and puffed away on the cigarette.

He smoked it until it was half–gone. Then he stared down at Eggers and asked a question.

"Want a cigarette?"

"I don't smoke."

The first guy nodded and puffed one last time. Then, he said one final thing to Eggers.

"Hooyah, brother."

The first guy took a long step back. He looked into Eggers' eyes, a taunting, sinister look that would haunt Eggers for the rest of his life.

Eggers struggled against the zip tie and the park bench's metal, but it did not free him.

The first guy took the smoked cigarette out of his mouth and tossed it onto Eggers and the bench. The whiskey that covered his body lit up instantly.

The cask strength whiskey did as advertised. It burned and burned.

The other three men gathered around the first, and they all stood around and watched Eggers burn to death.

After he was dead, the first guy took the cigarette pack out again and spilled a bunch of the cigarettes out on the ground, and he dug a store-bought cheap lighter out of his pocket and struck it twice, so it seemed used, and he dropped it over the cigarettes. He did all of this so the cops would find them. He kept the Zippo. Couldn't leave that behind. It was easier to trace back to his boss.

The cops wouldn't look close enough and wonder how Eggers lit his own cigarette. They'd figure he'd used a match, or they might find the cheap lighter.

One of the others cut the zip tie around Eggers' wrist, avoiding the flames as best he could, but the fire was hot. He couldn't get a grip on the zip tie's remains. It fell somewhere into the flames.

The first guy said, "Forget it. It wouldn't make a difference."

The four men left Eggers' body to burn out on its own. They walked back to their SUV and hopped in. They drove off, following the street signs to their next destination as if nothing was out of the ordinary.

2

Jack Widow didn't know why he stepped off the bus in Washington, DC. He felt like he'd just been there recently. That's how DC is for anyone who's ever lived there. You leave for years and then return, and soon enough, you're ready to leave again.

But he hadn't been there in about a year. He'd once known a girl in DC. Her name was Kelly Li, but by now she would've made Secret Service Agent.

Widow had stayed with her for a few days last year, until they both realized the thing that always comes up for him. His life was all about forward motion. And she was about her career. Careers are for people who are figuratively going places. Jack Widow was literally going places.

On his last day in DC, she took him to the same bus depot he'd just stepped away from.

Li had asked him a question.

"Where will you go?"

Widow told the truth.

He shrugged and said, "Wherever I want."

And those had been the last words he spoke to her. They hugged and kissed goodbye like star-crossed lovers at the end of the final act, never to see each other again.

Beyond his memories of Agent Li, Washington DC held a certain reverence for him. There's a kind of nationalistic veneration the capital holds for every American who ever served in uniform. The city is filled with monuments, representing the foundations of an imperfect country with fantastic root ideologies. Democracy was the experiment; when it would come out of the experimental stages remained to be seen.

Widow was an American and a former SEAL. He stood tall and proud, as he stared out over the city.

The city has evolved into the most crime-ridden place on earth, if you factor in the political crimes of backstabbing and lies.

Before Widow noticed the DC architecture, he felt the brisk wind brush over him. He tucked himself further into a Havelock coat he'd bought somewhere along his trip north a couple of weeks earlier. He'd picked out a coat that was navy blue because the sailor in him couldn't help himself. No one had ever proposed that you can take the Navy out of the sailor.

Under the coat, Widow wore a warm green plaid shirt and blue jeans. Both were warm enough to keep him comfortable in the windy capital.

Gazing upon the majestic monuments, Widow was filled with a sense of patriotism and pride. There was a lot of patriotism in a city filled with lies.

DC wasn't on his mental itinerary. Then again, nothing much was, but also, everything was. The only item that never budged was coffee.

Widow wasn't an impulsive man, not like most people. From the outside, it looked like he didn't have a plan, like he lived impulsively. He traveled from place to place, seemingly at random. But he had a plan. It just wasn't a detailed plan. Life was too beautiful to make detailed plans. Detailed plans were for building houses—things with walls—or for prison escapes. Widow's life was no prison. Not the way other people lived—normal people.

Learn to roll with the punches, but you also have to learn to surf the waves. Live life to the fullest. Pretty simple. That's why it makes for such a good bumper sticker.

Widow's plan was to wander, to roam, to be free, and to see and experience all the riches the United States' landscape offered. He did this according to his own code of honor instilled by the Navy SEALs. Essentially all SEAL codes—minus the ones that have to do with combat—boil down to *do the right thing*.

Widow stepped off a Greyhound bus that had started back in Portland, Maine, passed through Boston and New York City, and had now arrived in DC.

There was no plan. The reason he got off in DC was a simple line switch.

He stepped off a bus with the most detailed plan of the day, which was to step onto another bus and keep on going. But at that moment, he felt hungry.

The Greyhound Bus Depot was on Massachusetts Avenue, down the street from the Capitol building, basically in front of the National Mall. He could see the White House just a few blocks west.

He remembered there was a café he liked over on Seventh Street. He hadn't been there in nearly a decade. It was just a simple café, but the coffee had been so good that he remembered it.

Widow stared at the other passengers from his bus, walking over to the bus they were supposed to ride next.

Americans of all ages and shapes and sizes transferred their luggage from the bus he came in on and wheeled them over to the new one.

The driver waited by the rear of the new bus, helping the elderly and the unable-bodied to load their luggage underneath the back it.

Widow glanced left and glanced right. He fished in his pocket and pulled out his bus ticket and stared at it. He had bought a ticket that still had six hundred twenty-two miles on it. The final destination was Columbus, Ohio.

He flipped the ticket. On the back, it read, in all capital letters: NONTRANSFERABLE.

Widow's stomach rumbled, and he yawned, feeling sleepy. His back cramped from sitting upright for hours on the bus.

He looked at a large, double-sided outdoor clock that jutted out from the main building in the bus depot. The time was eight in the morning. He knew the café's location was about a thousand feet from where he was. It should be a five-minute walk without interruption, maybe ten when he factored in street crossings and busy early morning DC streets and working pedestrians in suits, headed wherever they were headed.

Widow turned right and moved to the street. He tossed the bus ticket in a waste bin before heading southeast to the café.

3

THE WALK to the café should've taken five to ten minutes—tops, but it didn't. It took nineteen whole minutes because on the way, Widow turned right onto East Capitol Street and got stuck in a crowd being diverted north by police.

The crowds were backed up. He had to wait to cross the street for a whole five minutes even though the crosswalk was green three times while he stood there on the corner.

Most of the surrounding pedestrians didn't seem to notice. Many of them were buried in their phones, either talking on them or swiping across the screens.

Something new that Widow has seen all over the place were devices called *wireless earbuds*. It seemed everyone had them now.

All around him, people talked, conversing with the open air and not each other. Not a single person was talking to anyone around them.

Widow saw wireless earbuds jammed in their ears. It reminded him of the day when Bluetooth first came out. By technology standards, that was a lifetime ago.

Finally, a uniformed police officer signaled for Widow to cross the intersection. It pissed off the driver in a taxicab who was there waiting. He honked at Widow like it was his fault that the cop let him cross instead of letting the cab go.

The uniformed cop shot a fiery look at the cab driver.

"WAIT YOUR TURN!" the cop shouted.

He looked at Widow and signaled again for Widow to walk.

The people around him crossed, brushing past him; most didn't even look up.

Widow crossed the street and saw that ahead of him were more people, some coming back the way he'd come, others standing around, bottlenecked. The sidewalk was congested.

Widow stepped out of the flow and went left. He headed north for two minutes and circled around to the next street up and back down the way he wanted to go.

He avoided the bottleneck, but still had to push through the crowds of pedestrians. He headed down Thirteenth Street Southeast for several blocks and turned right and then past the Marine Barracks, which he had passed before. He came to a fork, turned right again, and saw a tiny, charming café. It was the same one he was looking for, only it was different. There was a different name, a different sign above the door.

Widow opened the door and made his way inside.

The café he remembered used to have a wait staff that came over to the table and handed out menus and took drink orders. That was gone now.

Now, it was just another coffee house with staff called *baristas* behind the counter.

Widow took his place in the back of a short line, staring at a menu hung up on the wall. He ordered a triple espresso and not a coffee. He figured he could use the boost.

He paid and picked up the espresso at the end of the counter. He scanned the room for a table to sit at, but their only tables were occupied. He had to settle for a cozy chair next to a fireplace that might or might not have been real.

He sat and kept the espresso cup balanced on his knee, taking sips every few minutes.

Across from him was a guy young enough to be in college, which Widow figured was a good guess since his face was buried in a law textbook.

Widow tried to stare out the window closest to him, but all he saw was the crowd of people shuffling along the street.

Over to Widow's right was a table with today's *Washington Post* scattered about and abandoned. He gazed around in case the owner was still in proximity, but there was no one within reasonable distance of the paper.

He scooped up the first section and started skimming through. It didn't take long before he found an article that piqued his interest.

Buried three pages in was a little square about what had happened across the street. It explained exactly why the cops were blocking the park and holding up traffic on the street.

The title was: *Homeless Veteran Burns Self to Death in Lincoln Park.*

There were two photographs. One was of a bench in Lincoln Park. That image was noted as *stock photo*. And the second was of a bald man, but not bald by choice. The man in the photo had recently shaved his head and face. The man in the photo was not smiling. He wasn't frowning. He was looking firm, distinguished. Widow knew the look because he had taken a similar photo once.

The man in the photo wore his Naval officer service uniform dress whites. He held his uniform cap down by his side. The American flag was to the guy's right, and the Navy flag was to his left. Both hung off short flagpoles in an ugly hallway that Widow recognized. It was Officer Training School in Newport, Rhode Island.

Widow had been there himself.

He read the article. Apparently, a homeless veteran drank himself into a stupor and lit himself on fire right in the middle of a public park. An anonymous source from the Metro Police Department concluded that the vet fell asleep with an open bottle of whiskey and a lit cigarette in his mouth.

Obviously, the thing that piqued Widow's interest was that the homeless man was a Navy vet. And not just any kind of Navy vet. He was a former Navy SEAL. His name was Henry Eggers. It took dental records to identify him.

The article didn't go into detail of Eggers' SEAL missions. It couldn't. They were still classified.

The article mentioned that no living relatives had been found so far. But an open wake was scheduled that night at a church off Connecticut Avenue.

Widow noted the time.

The end of the article listed Henry Eggers as Retired Navy SEAL Commander Henry Eggers—survived by no one.

Eggers and Widow had some things in common that hit home for Widow.

Eggers was Navy like Widow. And Eggers retired at the same rank as Widow had ended his career, which was an O-5 Commander.

They had both served in the SEAL teams. Even though Widow served a double life as an undercover agent for the NCIS during his SEAL tenure, that didn't change the fact that Widow bled SEAL blood, same as Eggers.

If the guy was homeless, and the cops couldn't locate any relatives, then attendance at the wake was probably going to be pretty dismal.

Widow took another sip of his espresso and laid the paper down on his lap. He stared out the window at the crowd of people.

He wondered why the cops were still at the scene of the crime if a wake had already been planned, if the whole scene was nothing more than an accident. Maybe there was a lot more to clean up. Or maybe they were still investigating, even though the paper said it was concluded. That happened. Someone on the police force would tell a reporter the conclusion before a case was over so the reporter could feel like they got a scoop. Sometimes the money from journalists to sources was just too good to pass up. Sometimes it was all about being a hotshot.

Likely, Eggers had burned himself alive. It happened all the time. Obviously, the scene provided enough evidence to make that conclusion. Obviously.

But Widow wasn't very good at letting things go without a closer look. It was just not in his nature.

Widow took another sip from his espresso and thought. He had wanted to spend only the afternoon in DC, but he couldn't help feeling compelled to at least go to Eggers' wake. Being that Eggers was all alone, and he was a fellow sailor, Widow felt he owed it to him on a level that civilians wouldn't understand.

4

THE CHURCH WAS off Connecticut Avenue on a short service road aptly titled Gate Road, probably because the grounds of the cathedral were surrounded by a black wrought-iron fence. The grounds were vast for being in the heart of DC.

The church was a mid-sized building with old gothic architecture. He counted a dozen gargoyles and numerous stained-glass windows depicting religious images. The whole thing was built out of huge stones. The church's front door was a massive oak block with a metal loop as the handle. It was pulled wide open, welcoming passersby into the fold.

Widow pulled up in a yellow cab, which cost more than twenty-five bucks with the tip factored in. Taxis were always expensive, but now with Uber and other ride share apps, he figured they were marking up their prices to keep the whole endeavor profitable.

Widow wasn't going to switch over to Uber. You needed a smartphone and apps and credit cards on file for all that. He wasn't a fan of smartphones because they come with GPS, which helps the users find places but also helps other people find the users.

Widow was the kind of guy who didn't like to be found.

He paid the fare and stepped out of the cab onto the curb. He looked over the grounds and walked the perimeter before entering the church. He strolled along the sidewalk, heading counterclockwise until he was back at the driveway up to the church.

Off the service drive, back on the nearest major street, there were three parked cars, all randomly within view. These included a white Honda Civic, a red Ford Taurus, and a black Cadillac Escalade.

He could see the rear end of the Civic and the front end of the Taurus. Both were empty. He could tell that from where he was. But the black Escalade had tinted windows. It was parked facing the church.

Expensive vehicles having tinted windows was no big deal, but this one had a tinted front windshield—illegal in the District of Columbia—which meant the vehicle was probably a government ride, hard to tell without seeing if there was a government plate on the back.

Widow figured it was government, which made sense because they were parked in front of a federal building.

He turned back to the church and saw no one walking the grounds or the small cemetery at the back half of the church.

Widow stopped out front and saw only two vehicles parked in a small parking lot next to the entrance to the church. One was the church van, and the other was a black Mercedes that looked new.

He entered the drive and walked to the entrance.

Inside, he saw a lobby through the open door and walked inside. The first walls he saw were the same stone as the church's exterior. A huge clock hung on one wall. The numbers were Roman numerals instead of digits.

Widow noted the time was fifteen past seven o'clock at night.

Instrumental church music played over well-hidden speakers. The rhythm echoed and hummed. There was a low, monk-like chanting beneath the instrumentation.

If they were saying something, it was in Latin. Widow didn't understand it.

A little farther in the center of a grand foyer, a sign stood up on a metal rod. The letters were moveable. It read: *Henry Eggers Wake.*

The lettering representing Eggers' rank and being retired Navy weren't there. Widow could've been bent out of shape about it, but he wasn't. He had no stake in Eggers. He only felt obligated to walk into the wake since the paper had not mentioned family. He suspected that a homeless vet with no known family wouldn't have many guests at his wake.

To the right was a table covered in white cloth. There were some candles on it and an open sign-in book with a pen book-marked between the open pages.

Past that were more candles and foldable metal chairs, lining the room from one corner all the way to the wall behind Widow. The chairs were all empty.

Widow wondered if the church staff always prepared for visitors like this. The thought made him also wonder if Eggers' insurance paid for the whole event. He wondered if Eggers was getting a military funeral and burial plot, a three-volley salute from an honor guard. These things were often up to the family of the deceased. Sometimes, servicemen would skip all the ceremonial military acts for various reasons.

The wake being at this specific church meant there was some connection between Eggers and the church.

Suddenly, a figure stepped out of the gloom. A man. He might've been standing there the whole time. The lighting was low and somber. There were plenty of shadows to hide in.

The man wore a polo shirt under a black blazer. He had a black peacoat folded up next to where he sat on the bench.

 He had thin-rimmed glasses on. He smiled at Widow and walked over to him.

"Hello, hello," he said. He stepped a little closer to Widow than Widow liked and offered a hand to shake.

Widow took it.

The man said, "I'm Pastor Richards. This is my congregation. I'm so sorry for your loss."

Widow nodded along and shook the man's hand.

"Jack Widow."

"It's nice to meet you, Mr. Widow. Again, I'm very sorry for your loss.

"Thank you."

"We're glad to see you. You know, we weren't expecting anyone to come. The papers said that Mr. Eggers had no family to speak of."

Widow nodded along.

"Well, please sign in."

Richards pointed at the book on the table.

Widow nodded and withdrew his hand. He sidestepped and walked over to the book. He stared down at it. The two white pages were ninety-nine-point nine percent blank. But one name was signed right on the first page, the first line.

Michael Aker.

Widow scooped up the pen and signed his name on the next line down. Afterward, he dropped the pen back into the crack of the open pages and turned.

Richards stood right there behind him.

He said, "You can go in and pay your respects."

"There's a casket and body?"

"The casket is closed. The body isn't there. It's just for show. But we're guaranteed by the police that they will hand over the remains day after tomorrow. That's why the funeral isn't until Friday."

"Of course. Makes sense."

"But there's another guy here. Maybe you know him?"

"Maybe."

Richards stepped back and pointed the way for Widow to go past the narthex and into the nave of the church.

Widow nodded and walked in.

There were pews on both sides of him. He walked up the middle of the church to the crossing.

A casket was placed in front of the pulpit. It was closed. An American flag was draped over it.

Widow stepped up to it and bowed his head, as if he were saying private words to Eggers' coffin, in case Richards was watching him.

He stared back up, spun around, and walked back the way he'd come. He wasn't sure what to do next. He supposed he could simply take a seat and hang out a while. Perhaps fifteen or twenty minutes would be a respectable time for him to stay. Then he could leave before it was too late.

He knew there were buses leaving at eight and nine o'clock. Otherwise, he would have to stay overnight in the city.

Widow walked back toward the pews. He saw a guy seated in the very back. The guy watched Widow and then stood up slowly, as if he had recognized an old friend.

The guy was probably in his late forties or early fifties. He wore a dark suit with a yellow tie. It was loosened at the neck.

His hairline was fighting gravity and time, and not doing a bad job of holding the front—so far.

He stepped out into the aisle and waited for Widow to reach him.

Widow glanced at the empty seats, but couldn't sit down now. They'd made eye contact. This guy was determined to talk with him. Widow walked right up to the guy and stopped a few feet away.

Pastor Richards was still in the lobby. Widow saw him in the distance.

Widow said, "Hello."

"Hi. I'm so glad you're here."

"Do I know you?"

"No. No. Of course not."

The guy reached into his inner coat pocket and pulled out an expensive-looking wallet. An expensive gold watch peeked out from under his sleeve.

Widow glanced at the guy's shoes. They also looked expensive.

The guy opened his wallet. A bunch of credit cards flashed at Widow. The guy pulled out a business card from behind the deck of credit cards.

He flipped his wallet closed with one hand and held out the business card with the other. He handed it to Widow.

Widow took it and stared at the front. There was a name printed on it, along with an address, phone number, and a web address.

Widow held the card and read off the name.

"Michael Aker. Attorney."

"That's me. I do estate planning and contracts, mostly. But other things too. If you ever need an attorney."

"Doubt I will. But I'll keep the card. Thanks."

Widow pocketed the card into the Havelock and stared at Aker, who grinned back at him.

Aker asked, "How do you know the deceased? You his son?"

"I don't think so."

Aker's grin flattened out, and he looked at Widow in confusion.

"I never knew my father. Doubt it was him."

Aker said, "Oh. Then you were friends?"

"Nope."

"You military?"

"Yes."

"Ah. So, you were in Eggers' unit or something?"

"Doubt it. I have no idea what *unit* you're referring to?"

"You weren't in the Navy?"

"I was in the Navy."

"What did you do?"

Right then, Widow told the truth before he realized it. When it came to lies, he had been out of practice for a while.

He said, "I was a cop and a SEAL."

Suddenly, Aker's eyebrows furrowed, and an expression of intense interest came over his face.

"You were a cop? Like a military cop?"

"I was in the NCIS."

"Wow! You must have a lot of stories."

Widow stayed quiet.

"Did you know Eggers?"

"No."

"Huh. Why are you here? You hear of him or something?"

"I read about him in *The Post*. This morning. It said he didn't have any known family or friends. Said he was in the Navy. I had to come. Couldn't let a man who served in uniform not have a single visitor."

Suddenly, Aker's grin completely vanished, and his cheeks fluffed out.

"I see. You came out of obligation?"

"Duty. I came because it's not right for a vet to not have a single person come to their funeral or wake."

"So, then you're just a stranger?"

"More like a brother."

"I don't understand. I thought you said you weren't related to him."

"I didn't say I wasn't related to him, but I'm not."

"Still not understanding."

"I'm not related to him. Never met him. Don't know him. But he served, and therefore, he was my brother."

"I see. That's cool."

Aker paused a long beat. Then he said, "Thank you for your service."

Widow just nodded.

Aker asked, "You know of anyone who knew Mr. Eggers?"

"I don't. Like I said, I never heard of him till yesterday. What about you? Why're you here?"

"I'm Mr. Eggers' lawyer."

"Don't think he needs a lawyer now."

"I'm his estate lawyer. That's what I do. Estates. Remember?"

"Why does Eggers have an estate lawyer?"

"Everyone needs one. Someone should handle your affairs when you die. Someone should make sure your will is legal and carried out after you die. You know? Someone has to make sure your estate is divvied out to your inheritors as you've requested in writing."

Widow said, "And you're here to do that for Eggers?"

"That's right."

"But I read he was a homeless man."

"Yes. Unfortunately, he lived an empty lifestyle. Sad, really."

"Sad for anyone. No one wants to be homeless."

After Widow said this, he realized technically he was homeless, and he chose to be.

Aker cleared his throat.

Widow asked, "What? You disagree?"

"Mr. Eggers wanted to be homeless."

"How's that?"

"He chose to live this way."

"He did?"

Aker shrugged and said, "I assume he did, because he was a multimillionaire."

"How's that?"

"That's why I'm here. I told you I'm an estate attorney. I'm here to make sure that Eggers' heirs and not the government get his fortune."

"His fortune?"

Aker swallowed and glanced back over his shoulder like he was making sure that the pastor couldn't hear what he was going to say next. He leaned into Widow and motioned for Widow to do the same.

Widow took a step forward and listened.

Aker whispered, "Mr. Eggers had fifty million dollars in stocks."

5

FIFTY MILLION DOLLARS.

That was more money than Widow had ever seen in his life. He tried to imagine it. What could be bought with fifty million? *Anything.* A mansion on the sea. A huge yacht. A small fleet of yachts. A used third-generation F-35C fighter jet. Hell, maybe a used fourth generation. A brand new, off-the-line, fifth-generation would cost more. Widow recalled seeing data where the Navy spent more than eight million on a new fifth-generation F-35C Lightning.

Widow said, "Fifty million dollars buys a lot. Why the hell was the chief sleeping on park benches?"

"Chief?"

"Eggers."

Aker nodded and said, "That's the fifty-million-dollar question, isn't it?"

"So, you're here looking for his heirs?"

"Yeah."

"If that's true, then he must *have* an heir?"

"He does."

"*The Post* said he had no family."

"None that they know of. But he does—a daughter. I came here hoping someone would show up who knew her whereabouts. When I saw you, I was hoping you were a relative."

"Sorry. I never met Eggers."

Aker stared down at the floor.

Widow asked, "No idea where the daughter is?"

Aker looked back up at him.

"None."

"Did Eggers not leave a clue?"

"He didn't know where she was. They haven't spoken in years."

"What's her name?"

"Maven."

"That's uncommon. It'll narrow your search. Did you try an internet search for Maven Eggers?"

"Yeah. I tried everything. Facebook. Google. All that stuff."

"Background check?"

"Of course."

"Where from?"

"Internet service."

"You won't get much from those."

"Really?"

"Probably not. Those services rarely offer any special techniques beyond doing a public register search, something Google would've done when you searched her name, anyway. They're just glorified search engines that comb all free public databases."

"So, how can I find her?"

"Lots of ways."

Aker asked, "Like what?"

"FBI, for example."

"Will they help me?"

"No. Probably not. Not unless you know who to ask."

Aker said nothing.

Widow asked, "Don't you have a PI on payroll?"

After he asked, Widow remembered that Aker's business card didn't list a firm or his title in a firm. There was nothing like: *Michael Aker. Associate Attorney. Smith and Smith,* which made him think there was no official PI, but he was wrong.

"Yes. I have a guy. Other than that, I'm a one-man show. I also have a part-time secretary."

Widow said, "You should get your PI on the case."

Aker nodded, and Widow watched as his expression turned to one a person might get when a light bulb goes off in his head.

He grabbed Widow by the shoulders—excited, as if they were old friends.

Widow looked down at Aker's hands.

Aker said, "Oh!"

Then he saw the look on Widow's face and jerked his hands away.

"Sorry. I just had an idea."

Widow stayed quiet.

Aker asked, "Why don't you join my guy?"

"You want me to work for you?"

"Sure! Why not? Two heads are better than one. Or three heads, in this case."

Widow thought about the question for a moment.

"Nah. I'm sorry. I don't live here. I'm moving on. Tonight."

"I can make it worth your while."

"It's not about the money. I don't need money. I don't stay in one place very long. I've got no investment in what happens here."

"But don't you want Mr. Eggers' estate to go to the proper heir?"

Widow said nothing.

Aker said, "I'm sure his daughter will appreciate it! We can charge a finder's fee."

"Like I said, it's not about the money."

Widow paused a beat, and then he added, "Where did he get these stocks?"

"I can't divulge the company they're in. Legal thing. Not unless you were a relative or on my payroll. Then I could tell you."

Widow thought for a moment, and he thought hard about the offer. Fifty million dollars in secretive stocks was an intriguing mystery that he'd like to solve. But what he wanted more was to take a shower and be on his way, get the grime of DC off his body and his soul.

He reached out his hand to Aker. They shook.

Widow said, "Sorry, but I'm not for hire. Good luck."

Widow pulled his hand away and turned and walked back through the church and into the lobby.

Pastor Richards came out of the shadows once again and stepped out in front of Widow.

"Are you leaving already?"

"I am. Thanks for what you do here."

Richards offered a hand to Widow. Widow took it and shook it.

Richards said, "Sorry for your loss."

"Thank you."

Widow pulled his hand away, and Richards stepped aside and back into half-shadow.

Widow walked back out through the church's heavy open door and down the long drive, back to the street. He needed to hail another cab, but saw none.

He looked right and looked left. The street was one-way, coming in from the right. He turned in that direction and walked on, into the direction of oncoming traffic flow, hoping he would run into another taxi.

6

THE GUY with the forgettable face sat in the passenger seat of the Escalade parked down the street from the church.

In the driver's seat was another one of his guys, a thick bald guy with a long beard. He had a little gray and a lot of auburn in the beard.

He lifted a cold cup of coffee from out of the cup holder and drank from it, set it back into the cup holder. Behind the cold coffee cup rested a Glock 34, which belonged to the driver. He liked the Glock 34 issue because he preferred the longer barrel. Plus, he had large hands and felt the handgrip was better for larger hands. It wasn't true, not necessarily, but he liked it for that reason—true or not.

The two men were both armed. The guy with the forgettable face had his Glock 19 in its holster.

They both watched as a tall stranger whom they'd never seen before came strolling out of Eggers' wake and down to the street in front of the church.

They had watched him pull up in a taxi, get out, and walk the perimeter like he was casing the neighborhood.

The guy with the forgettable face held up a smartphone. He had the camera app on. He pointed the camera at the tall stranger. He watched the screen and saw the tall stranger as a small, out-of-focus figure on screen. He switched to video mode and used the fingers on his free hand to zoom in all the way until he could get the best angle on the stranger's face. He recorded the whole thing as a video.

He tried to get the stranger's facial features on camera as best he could.

The stranger was his complete opposite—especially his face. The stranger's face was very memorable. It was rugged as all hell—unshaven, ungroomed, and defined. Beyond the face was a different story altogether.

The stranger had thick, dark hair that fluttered in the wind like a thick forest of bamboo trees. With the hair, and the ruggedness, the stranger fit all the designations of a pretty boy, only he wasn't. That was obvious. He was too rugged, too weathered, too rough. The stranger had jagged edges. He carried himself in a way that kept him from being anybody's ideal target.

If the guy with the forgettable face was in the business of mugging people, the stranger in front of him would've been the last victim he would ever pick. If a client came to him with a bag of cash and a photo of a target to assassinate, the man with the forgettable face would've asked the client to double the money. The higher the risk of danger, the higher the fee.

The stranger knew how to handle himself. There was no question. He had a specific swagger. It was the same as that of the best Special Forces guys he'd ever met.

Not to mention, the stranger was big. He was tall and lean but had broad shoulders and thick, long arms. The stranger was built somewhere between an NFL linebacker and an ancient Viking.

The driver stared at the stranger.

He asked, "Who you suppose that is?"

The guy with the forgettable face said, "No idea."

"He's at the guy's funeral. He must be somebody."

"It's a wake. The funeral comes after."

The driver said nothing to that.

He asked, "What do we do about him?"

"Nothing. Let him go. He's probably nobody."

They watched as the stranger stopped outside the church's driveway and looked to their left and then right. Traffic came in from their left. They watched as the stranger decided and turned to their left and walked against the flow of the road traffic.

The guy with the forgettable face turned off the camera. They both kept their eyes on him, watched him as he walked back up the street and was lost to sight.

The two men turned back to the church.

The driver looked at his watch.

"I don't think anyone else is going to show up."

The guy with the forgettable face said nothing.

"How much longer is this going to go on?"

"Are you bored?"

"I'm starving."

The guy with the forgettable face ignored that.

He said, "We need to find out who the other guy is."

"I can just go ask him."

"Don't be stupid!"

"I'm sorry. Just hungry."

"You mentioned that. You can eat after. Just pay attention."

"Don't worry. I wrote down his license plate."

"We stay put. Till it's over."

The driver crossed his arms, stared straight ahead, and said nothing more.

7

Night rolled around. Widow sipped a fresh cup of coffee that he'd purchased at a service station across the street from the bus depot. He had watched the attendant make a fresh pot. At first it was too hot to drink, so he left the lid off and watched the hot steam rise, leaving brief contrails hanging over his cup like the back of a flying jet. After a couple of minutes, he replaced the lid and sipped from the cup.

Widow sat on a bench near the street, but far from the other passengers waiting for the same bus to arrive as he was. He bought a one-way ticket to Pittsburgh, a straight shot in terms of not having to make a transfer to get there. That was good. The only problem was the bus didn't leave for another ninety minutes, giving Widow extra time to kill.

The one thing about military life that Widow did not miss was the copious amount of downtime. Much of a military person's life is spent waiting around for something to happen. He was grateful for the skill of patience that all the waiting around had instilled in him.

Widow would've bought a paperback book from the gas station, but he perused their selection and found nothing but trashy romance novels, which weren't his thing. He didn't like to fantasize about romance just before a seven-hour night ride on a public bus. It just didn't seem like a good idea.

He considered buying a magazine. He even picked up a copy of a gun magazine and flipped the pages, looking at the new models of handguns coming out. This entertained him for ten seconds before he got bored with it.

Widow knew weapons. He liked weapons, but he had never been a gun nut. He couldn't imagine reading a magazine dedicated to the next generation trigger of a whatever. For him, a gun needed to fire when prompted and wait safely until needed. A trigger needed to trigger a reaction when squeezed, causing a bullet to fire out of the barrel—and nothing else.

Salivating over photos of weapons in a gun magazine wasn't his thing. He wasn't the target audience for that.

Of course, he skipped right over the Hollywood magazines. He had no interest in which celebrity he didn't know was dating another celebrity he didn't know.

He did pause over the trashy tabloids. It was hard not to. The tabloids had figured out how to grab attention long ago. One was titled: *Is the US President Really a Secret Alien?*

And it had a photo of a little green man, an alien with big bug eyes and green skin, dressed in a suit and tie with an American flag pin on his collar.

How does anyone buy these? he thought.

He sped past the women's magazines like *Cosmo*. He definitely wasn't the audience for those.

He examined the newsmagazines for a good while, but they were eighty percent articles about politics, and he wasn't in the mood to read about how one side was right, and the other was wrong. He liked having a sunny disposition, but these articles were often designed to infuriate.

These days everyone seemed on edge about something. Widow preferred to stay out of it altogether. He focused on his daily life. Let the pointy heads in Washington worry about the political mess of the world.

Widow picked up a copy of the *New York Times* for a moment. But then he saw a copy of the same *Washington Post* he had seen at the coffee shop earlier. He felt compelled to read the article about Eggers again. Maybe he'd missed something.

Fifty million dollars. That was a lot of money. The whole thing gnawed at him like a pest. Some part of him couldn't let it go. It was more than honor. It was his sense that something wasn't right.

Widow couldn't shake it.

He had picked up the *Post* instead of the *Times* and paid for the paper and the coffee. Now he was seated, waiting for his bus.

The Post was folded flat on the empty bench space next to him. He angled it close to the edge to get the most light, which shone down from a vapor lamp high on a pole in the depot's parking lot.

He held the coffee in one hand and laid a flat hand on the bottom of the paper to keep the night wind from blowing the pages up.

He reread the same article. Nothing had changed. Eggers burned himself up in his sleep. He was extremely intoxicated and fell asleep with a lit cigarette in his mouth. According to the article, an anonymous source inside the Metropolitan Police Department guessed that was what had happened based on the scene of Eggers' death.

Widow paused. That word stuck out at him. *Guessed.* The source claimed they *guessed* what had happened.

Widow stared at the word like it might peel off the page, and a different word would be underneath, but it didn't. It stayed where it was.

He took a pull from his coffee and scooped the *Post* up off the bench seat and held it up one-handed. He stared at the article, reading the whole thing again. The whole article was exactly the same as it was when he'd first read it earlier. This time, it was his interpretation that changed. The word *guessed* changed everything.

Once upon a time, Widow had been an undercover cop. He worked with cops of all kinds. He knew that whenever the cops *guessed*, it meant that was what they were going with, and they weren't looking past it.

Someone, probably a uniform cop, looked over the scene and ruled it an accidental death, right there, on the spot. There was no need for an overwhelmed police budget to stretch any further, so they could send out an overworked homicide detective to look over the scene.

Why open an investigation into the death of a homeless vet no one cared about?

Widow's blood boiled. That was the way it was for a lot of guys coming out of the service. Not most, but a shameful number ended up on the streets, addicts of all manners of drugs.

He had no illusion about it.

That's what MPD had done. They didn't give Eggers a second look.

Widow knew it to be true just by looking at the evidence right there in front of him. Other than the word *guessed*, one more thing jumped out at him. It wasn't written about in the article. It was right there in the stock photo. The image was in the background.

Widow pulled the paper close to his face and stared at it. He double-checked what he thought he saw. And he was right.

Faint and blurry and small on the page, he saw outside of the park's perimeter, hanging off a pole, just in line with a traffic light. There was a traffic camera. It pointed at the street, recording the passing cars. Presumably, it was all on a closed-circuit system, stored in MPD some place. Primarily, these CCTV systems were used for getting the tag numbers of cars that broke traffic laws, mostly running red lights, but they could also be used by police to investigate crime scenes. For example, the cameras were often used to identify getaway vehicles from bank robberies.

Widow knew the MPD hadn't even bothered to check the ones around Lincoln Park the night Eggers supposedly burned himself alive.

The camera was pointed at the street, but he could tell the lens also picked up the main entrance to the park and much of the front of the park.

If the bench in the stock photo was the same bench that Eggers died on, then that camera had a view of it from a distance. Not close enough to make out a man's face, but certainly enough range to see if Eggers really lit up on fire with no help from anyone else.

If it was the wrong bench, the camera would still be useful. A man and bench on fire would be a big enough spectacle for the camera to have seen something.

Plus, where there's one CCTV camera, there are bound to be others. Lincoln Park was surrounded by roads. There was probably a half-dozen cameras along that route.

The police should've pulled the footage and looked. Probably they could've ruled Eggers' death a definite accident.

For Widow, guessing wasn't good enough. The photograph gave him doubt. Back when he was an investigator with the NCIS, a shred of doubt meant something had been missed. A single chance was too much for him. Widow didn't settle for an answer. He made sure. When he put a guy away for murder, he made damn sure he had the right man.

Widow memorized the name of the journalist who had written the article, in case he might need it later. Then he set the *Post* back down on the bench next to him.

The bus ticket to Pittsburgh was in his pocket. He knew that if he took it out and flipped it to the back, he would find the word *nontransferable*.

He couldn't keep the ticket and redeem it later. It would be no good later. It was only good for tonight, and only for the one-way trip to Pittsburgh, the Steel City.

He could get on the bus and keep going. According to the laws of physics, it was possible. He was made of flesh and bone. He could step foot onto the bus and take a seat and sit back, and the bus would deliver him to the Steel City.

On a personal level, it was impossible.

Widow was a man who carried nothing. But if he got on that bus and just left without looking into the shred of doubt that ate at him, then he would carry Eggers' face with him the rest of his life. It would forever haunt him.

He needed to know for sure.

Widow wasn't the kind of guy who let wrong deeds go unpunished. It wasn't his way. *Looking the other way* wasn't in his DNA.

If there was a wrong deed here, then he needed to know. He needed to hunt for the answer. He needed to make it right.

Widow stared up at Washington DC's night sky and spoke to himself—one word.

"Dammit!"

8

WIDOW GRABBED a bite to eat at a hole-in-the-wall sports bar. A football game played on TVs mounted all over the place. They were all different brands from different eras, like a network of Frankenstein TVs, strung up on the walls over the years.

It was a night game. Penn State was winning. Widow was good with that for no particular reason.

He sat in a booth, not at the bar. The bar was good and toasty from a heater vent that blasted down on his table from over-head. Before he sat down, he took off his Havelock and draped it over the empty seat next to him. He rolled up his sleeves and then made himself comfortable in the seat. He liked the table because it was high. It wasn't jammed on top of his knees like tables at other establishments he had been to before.

The room was dark. He still had the same *Washington Post* from earlier, folded back to the article about Eggers. He sat at the booth and ate a cheeseburger with fries, and drank coffee. The photograph of the bench in Lincoln Park stared back at him.

At the bar, a touchdown was scored on the TV, and the bar patrons got loud. Some cheered. Others shouted in defeat. After a few seconds, the uproar died back down to low, ambient bar noise.

Widow glanced at the TV. It went to a commercial. He glanced at the entrance, which began with a heavy, wooden door. Widow saw the door open, and a new patron stepped through.

The new patron was a lone man, about average height, average size, only all of it was on a muscular, wiry frame.

He wore cowboy boots and black slacks with a dark coat and dark sweater underneath.

The guy stepped in with a bit of swagger, as if he knew the place. He stepped up to the bar, looked around, apparently trying to spot an empty seat. Then he turned and casually walked in Widow's direction.

Widow eyed his copy of the *Post* again, scanning for something new to read other than the article about Eggers.

The new guy sat in a booth near Widow, angling himself so he could see the game on one of the TVs over the bar. He slipped off his coat and pushed up the sleeves of his sweater.

The waitress walked over with a menu and set it in front of the guy. She asked if he wanted a beer. He ordered coffee, black, which got Widow's attention more than he already had.

Great minds think alike, Widow thought.

A moment later, the waitress returned with a hot coffee for the guy. She asked if he wanted any food. He told her to leave the menu, that he would order something later.

She left him. He sipped his coffee and watched the game.

Widow went back to studying the paper.

Several minutes passed, and the waitress came back through on patrol. She refilled Widow's coffee. Then she topped off the stranger's.

Widow noticed.

The guy looked at Widow, watched his coffee get refilled, and watched him take a pull from it.

The guy smiled at Widow and said, "I see you like your coffee, same as me."

"I don't know if anyone likes coffee the same as me. But you get a bronze medal for drinking coffee in a bar."

The guy took another pull from his coffee and nodded.

"A bronze? I already got one of those."

"Really?"

"Got a Silver Star too."

Widow nodded, impressed.

The guy asked, "What about you? You obviously served before."

"That obvious?"

"It is."

"I got a few medals."

"What's the highest?"

Widow paused a beat. He didn't like to talk about medals. A general rule of thumb for SEALs was not to boast or talk about the specifics of their medals. He couldn't say the same for enlisted sailors, but that's how it was for him.

Widow had been out of the Navy for a long time.

In his career, Widow had been nominated for the Medal of Honor, never received it, although that might have been because the Navy blocked his nomination. The Medal of Honor is the highest medal awarded to military service members.

The brass was concerned about exposing him because the Medal of Honor was awarded in a private ceremony, which at first didn't seem like anyone would find out. The only thing was that the Medal of Honor was bestowed by the sitting President of the United States. That little detail made the whole affair an event with White House reporters. The whole ordeal would have raised too many questions.

Widow didn't mention that. The next most prestigious medal down was the Navy Cross, which he was awarded a single time. He didn't mention that one either. But he decided it wouldn't hurt to mention a more well-known medal that didn't give away too much about him.

He said, "I got a Purple Heart once."

"Really? Where?"

Widow's Purple Heart and Navy Cross and other military ribbons and other military keepsakes were stuffed in his old locker in the basement that didn't exist on a blueprint inside of NCIS headquarters in Quantico, Virginia.

But that's not what the guy was asking.

"I got it overseas."

"Can't give away the exact location?" the guy asked. He paused a beat as if for dramatic effect.

He asked, "You a *water ninja*?"

Widow hadn't heard that one in over a decade. And the last time he heard it was when he was learning SEAL slang. Usually, people said *frogman*, except elite Marines. They usually called him a *frog hog*, like they competed with SEALs. No one competed with SEALs. No one else was even in the same league with SEALs. Not in Widow's opinion.

In Widow's opinion, and the same for every other SEAL he'd ever met, SEALs were in the stratosphere. The most elite Marines didn't even get off the ground in comparison.

Of course, all of that might've been his personal bias toward the Navy.

Widow said, "I was a sailor."

"I'll take that as a *yes*."

Widow didn't respond to that.

The guy said, "You look too wet behind the ears to be a land-lover. That's for sure."

"What about you? You a jarhead?"

The guy's expression turned to surprise, as if he was shocked that Widow knew.

"How'd you know that? Have we met before?"

Without looking at the guy, Widow said, "Your tattoo. Inner left forearm."

The guy turned his arm and stared at his tattoo.

Widow said, "It says *KAM*. You must've been a *Kick Ass Marine* way back when. That's what it stands for, right?"

The guy cracked a smile.

"I still am a *Kick Ass Marine*."

"You still in the Corps?"

"No. It's more of a *once a Marine, always a Marine* kind of thing."

"That sounds right. Every jarhead I ever knew was that way."

The guy pointed at Widow's rolled-up sleeve, at Widow's own ink.

"You got plenty of ink there yourself."

"I do."

"Any of that Navy inspired?"

"Some of it."

"I like your American flag tattoos. Never saw that done like that before. Those full sleeves?"

Widow nodded.

"Must've cost a fortune."

"It wasn't cheap."

Suddenly, cheers erupted from the bar, along with some disdain. It was equal to the last outburst when one team scored a touchdown; only this time, the eruptions were reversed, and the original cheerleaders became the disdained, and vice versa.

The guy looked up at the TV. He banged a fist on the tabletop.

"Damn it!"

Widow asked, "Your team losing?"

The guy paused a beat, breathed in and out like he was trying to calm himself down.

He said, "They just lost."

"Game's not over yet."

"It's a twenty-point spread with two minutes to go."

Widow glanced at the TV. He squinted his eyes. He could see the screen. He saw the score was plastered at the top right-hand corner, but he couldn't read the numbers from that distance. Although, he had perfect vision, the TV was too far away.

He said, "You can see that from there? That's some good vision."

The guy smiled back at him.

"Yeah. Guess what I did in Camp Lejeune for ten weeks?"

"You were a Scout Sniper?"

"That's right."

Widow didn't blink, didn't take a gulp, but that's what the guy was used to. Widow was sure because Marine Scout Snipers were among the deadliest snipers in the world. No question.

Widow stayed quiet, and the guy gulped down the rest of his coffee. He stood up from his booth and fumbled through his pants pocket. He came out with cash and lifted his empty mug. He trapped the money under the cup.

He turned to walk away, but stopped. He looked back at Widow.

He did something weird and a little cryptic. He did one of those finger guns with a wink and a noise like a gun shooting in Widow's direction. It might be a goodbye that a fraternity brother might do to another fraternity brother.

The guy said, "Nice talking to you. Good night, sailor."

Widow said, "Same to you."

The guy said nothing else. He turned and walked, weaving between tables and past patrons. He exited back out the same heavy, wooden door where he'd come in, turned, and vanished.

Widow stuck around a little longer. He finished his food, paid the bill, and left his change as a tip. And he abandoned the *Post* under his plate and walked to a hotel down the street.

DC had motels that would've been cheaper, but he didn't want to pay for a taxi out of the area. He wanted to stay close to where Eggers had died. He wanted to be close to the crime scene if it was a crime scene. The tradeoff was paying premium for a hotel.

He stayed at a hotel chain everyone knew and got the cheapest room he could get, which was more than double what he was used to paying, but he didn't argue.

In the room, he checked all the light switches and the fan in the bathroom and the faucets. He checked for both hot and cold water. He checked the complimentary hotel soaps and shampoo and towels.

Widow turned down the bed and kicked off his boots. He dumped himself down on the bed, dead center. He picked up a phone on a nightstand next to the bed and checked for a dial tone. Following the instructions a recorded voice gave him, he clicked the nine button to dial out. Then he dug into his pocket and pulled out Aker's card. He stared at it as if he had forgotten the phone number, which he hadn't. He dialed the number fast and accurately, which always surprised him because Widow had long, thick fingers like chair legs. Plus, he'd once known an English girl who called him a *klutz*. That was a statement that he never denied.

Klutz or not, he somehow hit the buttons correctly and in the correct sequence.

The phone hummed a beat and then dialed and rang. He waited.

It went to voicemail.

"This is Jack Widow. From the church. I've reconsidered our conversation. I'm still in town. Call me at..."

Widow glanced at a phone number laminated to the phone's base and read it out to the voicemail.

"I'll be at Lincoln Park first thing in the morning. Probably around oh seven hundred."

He said nothing else. He hung up the phone and stood up and took a whiff of his underarm to judge whether he smelled.

And he did, not terrible, just like a guy who'd walked outside all day. He needed a shower.

He took off the rest of his clothes, tossing them over a desk chair. He strung his socks over his boots.

Widow stretched out tall, allowing his muscles to pull and expand, and his bones to crack. Once he felt everything reset, he adjusted back to the body's default stance.

He went into the bathroom and tested to make sure the hot water was indeed hot. And it was. He returned to the main room and scooped up his clothes and took them into the bathroom, everything but the Havelock and the boots.

He twisted the hot faucet for the sink and used a tiny bar of hand soap to scrub his clothes clean. After all was said and done, he wrung out the flannel, the undershirt, his underwear, blue jeans, and socks. With the undershirt and flannel, he pulled hard on the sleeves to stretch them out. Clothes with sleeves had a bad habit of not being long enough for his limbs.

In the end, he hung everything up to dry as best he could. Most of it was draped over the sink, toilet, and windowsill.

Afterward, he took a shower, scrubbing himself from top to bottom, bottom to top, and he hopped back out, killed the water, and toweled off.

The hotel provided only one set of towels. He supposed he was supposed to request new ones every single new day.

The bath towel barely tucked and stayed on him. It hung off his hips. Widow had a well-defined waist and what a SEAL buddy of his called the *V-cut*. It was the ab definition that angled down to Widow's hips. It was the kind of muscular definition that men and women spent decades in the gym to acquire. Widow had it naturally.

Olympic athletes would have the same thing, not from years of lifting weights and putting them back down or starving themselves to death. Widow's muscular definition was built by doing the same constant activity that the Olympic athlete does. He did what he loved; he moved every day, all day.

Widow walked—a lot.

The only times he wasn't walking was when he was sitting to eat, riding on a bus or train or in a stranger's car, or when he was asleep.

It was all simple math. Move the body. Feed the body. Keep the body.

Widow grabbed the flannel and stretched it out flat and draped it over the shower rod. Hanging it there would help to dry it faster and keep it wrinkle-free. He did the same with the blue jeans.

Widow wiped the fog from the shower off the mirror and stared at himself. He looked clean. It was a big improvement. He smiled and stared at his teeth. They were tinted a bit from all the coffee. He needed a new toothbrush. He'd lost his last one somewhere.

Thinking about that, he took note that he also needed toothpaste. The hotel didn't provide any, which it should've, with the price he'd paid. He might as well grab some shaving cream and a razor while he was at it.

Of course, all that would have to wait until the morning because all his clothes were wet, and he couldn't go out naked.

He should've thought it through, but he hadn't. A man of leisure thinks things through a lot less than a man with a plan.

For tonight, Widow would just lie in bed, watch TV, and sip coffee until he fell asleep.

He returned to the room and scanned it once more and saw something that wasn't cool, something he hadn't noticed before.

There was no coffeemaker.

9

IN THE MORNING, Widow woke with the sun and then snoozed. He went back to sleep, a perk of the unemployed bachelor's life. His eyes reopened just before seven in the morning. He sat upright and stared at the motel phone. The little light on it was dark. No missed calls. No messages.

He dressed and sat back down on the bed. He picked up the phone and redialed Aker's number from memory.

The phone rang. He got the voicemail again.

He left another message.

"Aker. I'm headed over to where Eggers died. If you get this, meet me there. If I miss you, leave a message with the front desk."

At the end of the voicemail, he rattled off the name of the hotel where he was staying and read out the number printed on the phone.

Widow hung up and headed out the door. He stopped dead in the doorway because he'd almost forgotten the room card.

The door came equipped with a card reader that served as the lock. Nobody used keys anymore. He couldn't recall the last time he'd been to a hotel with keys.

He took the card, left the room, and exited the parking lot on foot.

Out on the street, Widow walked to Lincoln Park like a man out on a stroll. He passed the hole-in-the-wall bar with the heavy wooden door and the café where he'd had coffee, where he stopped for a moment. He thought about going in, but decided he would do that afterward, just in case Aker didn't show up and he wanted to wait around.

The streets were better than the day before. The police were no longer holding up the street or pedestrian traffic. The cars on the street moved along their way, and the people on the sidewalks did the same. Plus, it was a windy Saturday morning.

Widow tucked his hands into the pockets of his Havelock and kept on moving. He scanned the streets. He noticed the one-way direction of traffic and the signs that designated it. He noticed the various CCTV traffic cameras mounted up on traffic poles. He looked at the streetlights.

He walked to a corner and stopped at a crosswalk. The light changed for pedestrians to cross. He looked both ways even though the street was one-way. It was a force of habit, but also a good practice.

Widow crossed over. He didn't enter Lincoln Park, not right away; instead, he did like he had at the church and walked the perimeter, scanning everything he could while making it look like he wasn't scanning anything at all.

Widow kept his hands tucked into his pockets. To passersby, he was just a guy out walking, enjoying the morning air. He was nobody, a ghost.

Cars and trucks and SUVs passed on the street. Though the number of pedestrians was lower than the day before, plenty of people passed by him. Some were on their phones, talking to someone else on the other side of the connection. Others stared at their phones, probably deep in a text conversation or glued to their lives on social media.

He passed couples holding hands, kids walking alongside their parents, and government workers still doing whatever they did, going wherever they went.

There were no signs of cops or anything out of the ordinary on a DC Saturday morning. Everything was habitual. Everything was systematic. Everything was routine.

After a while, he realized he was the only person looking around at everyone else. The people he passed, the people in their cars that passed him, and the people leaving and entering the buildings across the street. None of them looked at him.

Washingtonians had a thing for minding their own business.

Lincoln Park was basically a big rectangle-shaped park. It was right smack in the middle of rows of residential and commercial buildings, all brick. The landscape comprised clean one-way streets and waist-high wrought iron fences. Beyond many fences were pristine hedges and trees.

The surrounding area appeared to be planned and designed around the park.

The park wasn't fenced off. It was wide open, but the trees were so enormous and plentiful that they acted as natural barriers, guiding park-goers to the entrances and exits.

He could see directly through the park in some places but could not in others. The trees squared around the park on all sides, creating long blankets of dark shadows that Widow couldn't see into, not from the distance he was standing.

Interesting, he thought.

Widow walked and traced the perimeter until he could see where he had started from. He stopped on a street corner and looked up at the nearest CCTV camera and then back at the park. He looked at the nearest building and recalled the *Post's* article from memory. He recalled the photo and the bench and the camera's placement. He hoped the bench in the photograph was the same in the stock photo, or, at least, the actual bench that Eggers died on also had a CCTV traffic camera pointed at it.

He looked up at the closest camera and angled it in his mind and concluded that it was the same one from the stock image. But that didn't mean the bench in the image was the same. He had to go into the park to figure that out.

Widow turned away from the camera and found the nearest entrance to the park and entered. He came in and looked left, looked right, and turned left. He walked around, studying everything he could, all the little details, and all the big-picture details.

The foliage on the trees was something to behold, something quite stunning. The leaves on the trees were stunning. They had turned colors the month before in September and were now peaking. Some had fallen already. Most remained.

Red and orange colors littered the ground from the fallen leaves. They crinkled under Widow's boots.

Widow was surprised how dark it got once he was in the park. Sunbeams streamed from the sky and filtered through the leaves in the trees, creating a festive and eerie autumn atmosphere.

Long, dark shadows were cast all over the grounds and sidewalks.

Dogs and their owners passed him by. He saw dogs lying around in the grass, next to their owners, panting from just having played catch.

He saw young lovers lying around, talking, and enjoying the early morning autumn weather. He saw one guy sitting in the grass, back to a tree, and reading a book. It made Widow a little jealous. He would love nothing more than to do the same thing. But he knew he wouldn't be able to concentrate until he had answers.

He continued on his way, ambling through the park, taking the sidewalks, and then following the footpaths. He looked left and looked right. He passed statues, all of which were monuments to American history. The only one he stopped to study was a statue of ole honest Abe himself.

Widow stared up at it and wondered if Abe was taller than him. Widow stood flat-footed at six foot four. He didn't know how tall Abe had been. He was sure he could google it if he had access to Google.

The thought flew away because right then he saw where Eggers had died. No question.

The scene where Eggers took his final breath was a sliver of the park. It was tucked near a corner of deep hedges and tall trees, taller than others he'd passed by, like these were older. They stood tall the way trees in the wilderness stand, proud and grand. They were taller than some of the neighboring buildings.

This was the right spot. There was no mistaking it, because the metal park bench had police tape strung around it. The grass beneath the bench was charred black at the center and yellow on the outer rings of a large, burned circle.

There was a long, curving brick walkway that cut into two paths. One led out past the trees toward another exit. The second led over to the bench.

Widow took the second and walked to the bench. It was off the beaten path a bit, which Widow figured was why Eggers had chosen it. It was secluded, as secluded an area inside a park could be. Anyone stumbling across him wasn't stumbling across him. They would have had to look for him there.

In this area, Eggers could sleep through the cold night in complete peace. Even patrolling cops, if there were any, would miss him back here, unless they'd already known of it. And Widow figured they wouldn't have.

He stepped back and looked to the right over a cluster of hedges, and saw another exit out to the street. It was less pronounced than the others, appearing as a forgotten portal into and out of the park.

Widow made his way back to the bench and stopped short of the police tape and the circle of burned grass surrounding the bench.

The police tape was bright yellow. It was strung from the bench out and down to several plastic stakes in the ground that held the tape down, preventing the gusty wind from blowing it all away.

There must be a subsection of a section of police literature somewhere in the MPD's police handbook regarding police tape and procedure that indicated it was supposed to set a larger perimeter than the one he stared at. But that might've been only for crime scenes and homicides.

The MPD had already written off Eggers' death as a fiery accident. They didn't view it as a crime scene at all. So, the police tape was more useless than anything else. It was merely a formality. Therefore, he doubted anyone was going to come back for it—ever.

Some of it was already hanging loosely off the bench anyway, as if someone had ripped it. He imagined kids playing in the park and stealing a section.

Perhaps they were playing and thought how cool it would be to take off with police tape.

Widow gave the police tape the same amount of respect and ignored it. He stepped over a low section of tape and stared at the bench.

At first look, Widow saw nothing that would answer questions. He saw exactly the same thing as the first responders who came, the same as the beat cop left behind to linger over the body while the morgue workers took their time coming to pick it up, and the one MPD detective who came by to sign off on the whole thing as an accidental death.

Widow figured the MPD detective would've called the fire department to see if a fire investigator was available. But then again, maybe he wouldn't. Why bother that extra effort for a homeless man that nobody cared about?

Even if a fire investigator was called, what would he do any differently? He would probably take a short look over the scene and see exactly what Widow saw.

Widow stepped to the bench. The seat was charred. Whole sections of black paint had turned to ash. He saw plenty of ash and dust on the seat and the armrests and the dead grass beneath.

Suddenly, the thought occurred to him that the dust and ash might not be from the bench. It could be from Eggers. It could be some of his remains.

Widow turned and looked up at the skyline just over the fencing surrounding the park. He scanned for cameras. The bench he was at wasn't the same as the one in the stock image. That was clear. But he saw two cameras of interest. He saw them through the trees. One pointed at a down angle toward the street. That one would probably not get a clear picture of Eggers' death, but the second one was above it. It looked like it was angled high enough to get a look at the street corner beyond, which gave it a partial angle right over Eggers' bench.

Widow looked at the high camera and followed it down. He imagined the cone of view from it. His vision was obstructed by more foliage and trees that surrounded the park. But he remembered the entrances from the street right there. Maybe the camera had picked up foot and vehicle traffic at the time of Eggers' death. If something more sinister had happened to

Eggers other than accidentally burning himself to death, maybe those cameras could tell a story.

Of course, he figured the MPD, or the fire investigators would've seen them by now. But then again, maybe not. If they were ruling it as accidental death, why would they bother?

It could be worth a look, he thought.

Widow turned away from the cameras and stared at the bench. He took a step back and to the left, angling the white beams of sunlight that filtered through the tree canopies so that he could look at the bench from different angles.

Macabrely, he saw something he hadn't noticed before. From this new angle of light, Widow saw a distinct outline of the space between outlined-human legs right on the bench. It was made in soot and charred steel.

It was a charred outline of Eggers' legs. Had to be.

Just then—he didn't know he was doing it—but Widow saluted the bench.

Widow returned his hand back down by his side and stared at the whole bench. He stared from side to side, armrest to armrest.

He breathed in slowly and heavily and released the same way he would if he were taking a medical examination, trying to take deep breaths for the doctor.

He turned and walked slowly across the brick walkway. He carefully watched each step he took. He saw multiple shoe prints and scuffs all over the place, in the dirt, and on the walkway. They meant nothing. There was no telling how many cops and firemen and EMTs and pedestrians had come through since the body was removed.

Widow walked a little farther than a beat cop would have. He traced the walkway halfway to the exit between the trees and stopped. He looked down. The brick walkway was also covered with early morning frost. It was white, so white he almost missed something important, only he didn't miss it. Right there between the cracks, he saw something small and jagged and white and red.

He knelt and stared at two broken teeth. Both were jammed down in loose cracks. Someone had lost them abruptly, certainly against their will. He knew that because the roots were mostly still intact, but covered in dried blood. The teeth had been knocked out.

Just then, Widow wished he had an NCIS forensic kit. He would have had one if he were still in the NCIS and drove an NCIS vehicle. But he wasn't, and he didn't.

For now, the teeth weren't going anywhere. So, he left them where they were and marked the spot mentally in his head. Then, he looked over the area all around the teeth. He found more dried blood on the brick, easily missed if he hadn't been looking for it.

He stood up and stepped off the walkway onto the sleet-covered grass and inspected the walkway ahead. He walked all the way to the trees and the exit and stopped. He found something else. Some of it was on the walkway, but most of it was in the grass.

He found broken glass everywhere. He looked at it. It all seemed to go together like puzzle pieces.

It had been a bottle before it was shattered into hundreds of shards.

Judging by the number of shards and the small sizes of the pieces, Widow figured the bottle had been thrown at something or someone, hard too. To smash it that much meant that it was most likely thrown full force by a powerful arm.

Widow searched for something to identify the bottle. He searched on one side of the walkway and then the other until he found something. It was part of a label. The glue on the back of the label held part of the glass bottle together.

It was a bottle of Clyde Brothers' Whiskey.

Widow had never heard of it. He took the label, peeled away the shards of glass on the back as best he could, and put the label in his coat pocket. He wasn't worried about fingerprints because the label had been printed side down in the dirt and grass and sleet. Any fingerprint that might've been there would be contaminated by now.

Widow stood up and walked the rest of the length of the brick walkway to the exit. He made it to the street and looked left and looked right.

Traffic was going one way. He saw a black Cadillac Escalade parked off to the side of the street. It was a block away. The windows were tinted.

He recognized it from the church the night before.

He glanced at it and glanced away, not making a big deal of it. But he saw something interesting. The engine in the Escalade was running. He saw exhaust coming from the tailpipe at the rear of the vehicle, which meant that someone was inside it.

Presumably, the engine was running because the heater was on inside the cabin.

The idling Escalade, plus the teeth, plus the broken glass, plus the fifty million in stocks that Eggers had left behind all just added up to something more going on here than just another dead homeless guy.

Widow turned around and reentered the park, fully aware that whoever was in the Escalade was watching him.

He took one more pass over the walkway. He would have to get those teeth. He didn't want to touch them because the blood was probably still identifiable.

Widow walked back to the bench and gave it another look over. Then he saw something else that he had missed the last time. It must've been a change in light, or a change in angle, because this time he saw it.

Not only was there a charred outline of Eggers' legs, but he could also make out what looked like Eggers' arm, maybe. It was raised above where his head would've been. It was an awkward position to lie in.

Widow couldn't imagine that position being very comfortable. Being that he had slept on public benches before, he knew they were already uncomfortable enough. You wanted to make them as comfortable as possible. Park benches were not big, comfy beds, which were always comfortable even when they weren't.

Then Widow noticed something else. He'd almost missed it.

Underneath the armrest, underneath where Eggers' head would've been when he died, Widow saw something in the charred grass. He knelt and reached into the grass, moved the remaining scorched blades aside, and grabbed it. He wasn't worried about prints for the same reasons as he hadn't been with the broken glass. When he felt it in his pinched fingers, he pulled it up out of the grass and into view.

It was burned and warped, but identifiable. He was staring at a used zip tie.

The tie was clipped.

It meant that Eggers was murdered. Someone had zip-tied him to the bench and lit him on fire.

10

WIDOW LOOKED AROUND and saw no convenience stores in sight. He was too afraid to leave behind the evidence he'd found long enough to go walking, searching for a place where he could buy unused zip-lock bags to put the teeth in.

If the Escalade parked down the block was the same one from the church and the guys inside it were watching him, then chances were they were the same guys who had done this to Eggers. Probably.

He didn't want to risk going away, buying a zip-lock bag somewhere, and then returning to find all the evidence gone. So, Widow returned to the teeth, knelt, and scooped them up out of the crack.

He did it fast and slipped the teeth into his coat pocket, opposite from the bottle label and the zip tie.

He wished he owned a cell phone. This was one of the few times it would come in handy. He could've used the camera to photograph everything.

Widow went back to his hotel. He needed to call Aker. They needed to chat.

He headed out of the park and walked back down the street. He glanced at the Escalade. It was still parked. The engine was still running idle.

He wasn't sure if whoever was in it had seen where he was staying or not.

He didn't recall seeing any black Escalades following him the night before or parked in the hotel's parking lot. But that didn't mean it wasn't a surveillance team.

There could've been another player in another car, maybe one that wasn't so suspicious.

Maybe they had seen where he was staying the night before, but they didn't make a move because he knew nothing yet. But now that he was carrying evidence, that might change.

Widow was a formidable fighter; he knew it. But he was unarmed. Guys who drove around in black Escalades with tinted glass everywhere were not unarmed. He knew that, too.

Widow walked along the sidewalk, heading the wrong direction from his hotel. He kept walking along the sidewalk, with traffic, on the same street that the Escalade was parked. Then he crossed over to the other side, their side of the street. He stopped at a corner and looked in every direction like he was lost and searching for a path to take. Then he turned right. He continued along the sidewalk, walking casually, meandering. He kept checking the reflections from windows of parked cars and glass from the windows of nearby apartment buildings. He looked to see if the Escalade was following him.

He walked to the next block, waiting at the crossing. No cars were coming, but he turned and looked every direction just so he could glance back and see if the Escalade was there.

This time it was. It drove slowly, the minimum limit. It followed another car. And behind it was a car that was tailing close enough to hit the bumper if the Escalade hit the brakes.

They were following him. No doubt about it. The night before they must've seen him, clocked him, made the proper notes of his existence. Maybe they even got a photo of his face. Then they'd let him go.

Widow walked on until he came to an alley. He glanced down it and saw the right opportunity.

Suddenly, he turned and took the alley, vanishing from their sightline for a moment.

Once he was behind the buildings, he took off sprinting all the way to the end of the alley, which forked into two separate drives back to the streets. Widow turned right again and got lucky. He saw a woman buzzing herself into an apartment building, and he ducked into the closing door right behind her.

The lady had thick, blonde hair. She had her teenage daughter with her. The teenager was probably thirteen, maybe closer to twelve than fourteen. They carried groceries.

They stopped at the bottom of the stairs and stared at Widow.

He said, "Sorry, ladies. Didn't mean to startle you."

They stared at him blankly.

Widow saw the concern on their faces. The building wasn't very large, which meant they probably knew all the tenants. And they didn't recognize him, which meant he didn't belong.

A large stranger who looks the way he looks following two smaller females into a door off an alley—what would anyone think?

Naturally, they showed fear. He knew all the signs: the sudden look of surprise that turned to concern, the fidgeting hands, and the shaking knees.

The mother slowly reached into her purse, one-handed. Widow presumed she was reaching for a can of mace or a cell phone or possibly a handgun.

He said, "Is either of you Ms. Daniels?"

The mother's hand stopped cold inside the purse. Whatever she had been grabbing for in there was already in hand.

Widow saw the muscles in her forearm tighten as her hand gripped something. He guessed it was a can of mace or the handle of a firearm. Until she pulled it out and sprayed him in the face or shot him in the face, he couldn't be sure just by watching her wrist.

The mother shook her head but didn't give a verbal response.

The teenage daughter asked, "Who's that, mister?"

"It's my real estate agent. I'm here to check out the building."

The teenage daughter asked, "Are you moving into old man Hogan's apartment? He died in there, you know? Your real estate lady is supposed to tell you that. It's the law."

"Hogan? He died in the unit? I didn't know that. Thanks for telling me."

"Your real estate lady is supposed to tell you."

Widow nodded along.

"Thanks for telling me! That's good to know. Some people aren't as honest as you are. It's a good trait to have. Never lose that."

The mother finally spoke.

"The unit is on the top floor. You'll have to take the stairs. The lift is busted."

She signaled at a lift behind Widow in the foyer with a glance. She never took her hand out of her purse. The other hand was carrying a heavy brown paper bag filled with groceries. Widow saw produce sticking out the top.

Widow asked, "Oh, cool. Do you ladies need help with the bags?"

The mother said, "No! No, we can handle it. Why don't you go outside and wait for your agent?"

"Oh, I prefer to wait in here. I like to get a look at the quality of the building first."

Widow didn't give the mother the opportunity to reject him.

"It's not a good sign; the elevator is broken. How long has it been down?"

The teenage daughter said, "For two weeks!"

"Two weeks?"

The mother said, "It's an old building. The elevator, although it has a sticker in it that says it's up to code with a date on it and official city inspector seal and all, it's as old as the building."

"Really?" Widow asked. He opened his palm and made an imaginary pen with his other hand. He mimed like he wrote it down on the pad.

"That's going into my notes. Thank you for sharing. Any other issues with the building?"

Just then, Widow heard a vehicle passing the front door. It was the Escalade. He slid on his feet to the right so that he was out of the line of sight of the window glass on the front doors.

The Escalade's engine roared in the tight space between the brick walls in the alley. He heard it but didn't look back.

The teenage daughter said, "Mrs. Moore on the second floor has too many cats."

"She does? Well, that might not be copacetic for me. I'm allergic to cats," Widow lied.

The teenage daughter asked, "What's copacetic?"

"It just means it may not be good with me. Because of the allergies."

The teenage girl nodded along like she understood, which she only half did.

Widow could hear the Escalade's engine still humming as if they were there, waiting, watching him, but they couldn't see him. He was sure.

A moment later, the engine roared as the driver gassed the Escalade and they drove off, turning left, from the sound of it.

The mother said, "We appreciate your offer to help with our bags, but we can make it."

"Of course. Then I'll just wait down here until Ms. Daniels arrives."

Widow looked at the teenage daughter.

He said, "Thanks for the info!"

"I'm Silvia. This is my mom. Hope to see you around the building."

"I'm sure you will. Be safe now."

Widow waved them off. The mother led the way up the stairs. She never took her hand off the mace can or the gun in her purse.

11

WIDOW WAITED another five minutes in the foyer. He ducked into a nook for the building's mailboxes and waited there for the sound of the Escalade's engine, in case it returned through the alley.

It never came back through.

Widow checked the porthole on the door before exiting. Nothing. He stepped back out into the alley and into the morning sunlight.

He saw no sign of the Escalade or whoever was inside it.

He cursed himself for not getting a plate number. He didn't dwell on it. Whoever they were, they would show up again—no doubt about that.

Widow went into the alley. The Escalade had gone right, so he turned left and retraced his steps the way he had come.

Widow found his way out to the street and thought about returning to his hotel to check to see if Aker left him a message, but he decided against going back to it just yet.

The guys in the Escalade might be gone, and they might not. He was certain that they weren't watching him right then, but that didn't mean they weren't tracking him somehow.

He thought of the teeth in his pocket. As sci-fi as it sounded, he had heard of the CIA using tooth implants to track their agents in the field. He had no idea if it was true or not. He hoped not. It sounded clever because what enemy force would think to check a guy's teeth for GPS chips? But if the word ever got out, then every bad guy on the planet would pull out the teeth of anyone they suspected of espionage.

Widow shook off the thought and went back to the park. He turned and walked the streets, following the same route as the day before. He checked his six and kept his head on a swivel, looking for any sign of surveillance. He saw none.

He glanced in each commercial store he passed: cafés, restaurants, a bookstore, an insurance agency, a law firm, and a multi-office complex. He was looking for something in particular. It was something that was a relic of the twentieth century.

Then, right as he passed a grocery shop, he saw it in the corner of his eye. He entered the grocer and walked over to a short hallway with two doors, leading into two public bathrooms, men's and women's restrooms. In between was a public water fountain, but after both restrooms, there was a public payphone.

Widow stuck his hand into his pocket and fished out a quarter. He was lucky because he only had the one.

He slipped the coin into the box and listened to a dial tone. At first, he almost dialed the hotel to check for a message, but then how would he return it? So, he just dialed straight to Aker's phone.

The phone rang, and he got an answer.

"This is Michael Aker, attorney."

"Aker, It's Jack Widow. We met last night at your client's wake?"

"Mr. Widow. I just left you a message at your hotel. Did you get it?"

"No. I probably won't be going back there."

"Okay. Well, I had called you back to say that I'm very interested in your help to find an heir for Mr. Eggers. We'll need to do this on the up and up. So, you'll have to work with my guy. He's a licensed PI in DC, Maryland, and Virginia. And pretty much all the neighboring states."

"Just a head's up; there's more to it than just finding an heir."

"How do you mean?"

"I'll explain in person. Where are you?"

"I'm at home right now. I was just saying goodbye to my kids before heading out the door."

"Where's your office? I'll meet you there."

"My office is in North Bethesda. Where are you? I never heard of the hotel you were staying at."

"I'm in Capitol Hill."

There was a pause.

Aker said, "Do you have a car?"

"No car. I can take public transportation."

"No. Don't do that. My office is nearly an hour away from you with DC traffic and all. I'll have my PI pick you up. We'll need him."

"Okay."

"Where are you exactly?"

"Tell him to meet me in front of this café nearby."

Widow gave him the name of the same little coffee shop where he'd gone nearly twenty-four hours earlier.

"Okay. He'll meet you there. His name is Tunney."

"What does he look like?"

"He's an older gentleman. Gray hair, but lots of it. He's probably my height, but he's got a little belly. He's retired FBI."

"Okay. Good enough. I got it."

"Okay. He'll meet you there. I'm guessing it'll be twenty minutes."

"Good. See you soon."

Widow hung up the phone without waiting for any more from Aker. He turned and walked out of the grocery. On the sidewalk, he looked both ways, up and down the street. No sign of the guys in the Escalade. Unless they had gotten out and were watching him on foot, which would've been the right move if they knew where he was, which they didn't. He was pretty sure, anyway.

Widow walked on to the café to wait for this Tunney guy. Occasionally, he checked his six and maintained readiness in case the guys in the Escalade were smarter than he figured them for.

12

It didn't take twenty minutes for Tunney to show up in front of the café, as Aker had predicted. It took forty-one minutes. That was fine with Widow because in the extra time, he drank two large coffees, which was the catalyst that sent him for a pit stop in the men's room once before Tunney showed up.

Widow came out of the men's room to find a gray-haired man sitting in his seat when he stepped out.

Widow walked back to his table.

"You must be Tunney?"

The guy had the thick gray hair that Aker mentioned and a bit of a retirement gut, but he also dressed like a retired FBI agent-turned PI. He wore a gray suit and no tie. The suit was sleek, but worn and probably machine-washed many, many times. A PI working in DC probably couldn't afford to dry clean every suit he owned, Widow figured.

The gray-haired man said, "I am. It's Brigs Tunney. And you must be Jack Widow?"

"Brigs Tunney. That's quite a name."

"So is Jack Widow."

Tunney stood up from Widow's chair and offered a hand to shake. The effort exposed a shoulder holster rig under Tunney's right arm, meaning he was left-handed.

The weapon in the holster was a Smith and Wesson Revolver Model 686 Plus, which was a fat weapon. His had a black rubber grip and chrome everything else. Widow knew none of this because all he saw was the grip. But he figured it was a gun comparable to a .38 Police Special because Tunney was as police-looking as they came.

Widow took Tunney's hand and shook it. He added a warm smile to the mix to show that he was friendly.

In Widow's mind, it was better to be friendly with a man who could legally carry a concealed weapon than not be.

"You got huge hands, Widow."

"A gift from my father, I suppose."

"You suppose?"

"Never met him."

"You adopted?"

"No. Raised by a single mother. Just never knew my father. He left before I was born."

"Sorry to hear that. It happens more often than it should."

"It's okay. It doesn't affect me one bit. Besides, I don't think he abandoned us. I think he never even knew of me."

"Oh. That sucks."

Widow shrugged.

Tunney pulled his hand away and left it by his side.

"So, you ready to go?"

"Let me get one more for the road."

"Let me get it for you," Tunney said. He reached into his back pocket and pulled out a thick wallet. Not because it was filled with dollar bills, but because it was stuffed with pieces of paper. At first, Widow thought they were receipts. Some people kept all that stuff for tax write-offs. But when Tunney opened his wallet all the way at the register to get out cash, Widow saw many of the scraps of paper were actually handwritten notes. Maybe they were case notes that Tunney wrote to himself.

Widow got a refill of the same large black coffee, only it was from a fresh pot. He put a lid on it this time because they would be in a moving car.

Tunney ordered a small coffee, black. Which told Widow he was definitely retired law enforcement. It wasn't the black coffee alone, but all the other aspects of Tunney combined with the black coffee.

The guy looked like a stereotype of a retired FBI agent. The only thing missing was a metal flask with alcohol in it. There was still time for that to appear. Maybe he had one stuffed in his inside coat pocket.

After they got their coffee, Widow followed Tunney out of the café. They walked to a silver BMW parked in front of a meter. The meter had no coins in it.

Tunney noticed Widow saw the meter with no coins.

"The meters don't work here. They should take them out. It's all done by app now. On your phone. See that sign?"

Tunney pointed at a sign nearer to the parked car in front of his.

He said, "You just key the number from the sign into an app on your cell phone. They debit my card for the parking."

Widow nodded.

Tunney got into the car, and Widow followed suit and got in on the passenger side.

Tunney fired up the engine, revving it up like he had just gotten the car and wanted to hear it purr. Then he backed up and took off. Minutes later, they were on the freeway, heading to North Bethesda.

Widow watched the street signs, his habit, marking that they were going in the right direction.

After several minutes of nothing but road noise and early eighties rock music playing on the radio, Tunney finally spoke.

"So, you knew Eggers?"

"Never met him."

"Really? How do you know where we can find his daughter?"

Widow didn't answer that. Instead, he told Tunney the whole story. He told him about getting off the bus, going to café for coffee, reading about Eggers in the paper, and going to his wake out of a sense of brotherhood. He mentioned his curiosity about the large value of the investments that Eggers left behind.

They drove along the freeway. Traffic was full but steady. DC drivers seemed to all agree. They were all eager to get somewhere. Some drove fast. Some drove more slowly, but all seemed in rhythm. There weren't any weak links.

Tunney asked, "Are you sure you're not trying to get your hands on the money for yourself?"

"How the hell would I do that?"

"I don't know. Maybe you couldn't resist it. Maybe you heard fifty million dollars and hung on to see if you could get it."

"No. I don't care about the money."

"Is that right?"

"Yeah. That's right."

"It's a lot of money."

Widow nodded but said nothing.

Tunney said, "Aker said you were a drifter."

"That's a word for it, I suppose."

"Imagine what a drifter could do with fifty million in the bank."

"The same things I do right now. I suppose. Maybe I'd be able to stay in nicer hotels. But other than that, it would make little difference in my life."

"You have no interest in being fifty million dollars richer?"

Tunney glanced over at Widow more than once to gauge his reaction.

Widow said, "I'm already wealthy."

This time, Tunney glanced at Widow with a sideways expression.

"How you figure that?"

"I have everything I need. Being rich is a state of being."

"Wealth can only be accumulated by the earnings of industry and the savings of frugality."

Widow thought for a moment. It showed on his face. He looked out the window, seeing the riders in the next car over. He turned back and looked over to Tunney.

"Who said that?"

"John Tyler. He was the ninth president. You know?"

"It doesn't matter about money; having it, not having it. Or having clothes, or not having them. You're still left alone with yourself in the end."

Tunney glanced over his left shoulder, clicked on the turn signal, and changed lanes. He faced forward.

"Who said that?"

"Billy Idol."

"The rocker? You into Billy Idol?"

Widow shrugged and said, "Not particularly, but it's relevant."

"How you figure?"

"He's playing on the radio."

Widow reached down and pointed at the radio.

Tunney smiled.

"So he is."

A long minute passed, and Tunney switched lanes again, back to the lane they started in because he'd found himself behind a slow driver in the fast lane.

Widow said, "Tyler wasn't the ninth president."

"Who was?"

"Harrison."

"Didn't he die in office?"

"He barely made it a month after being sworn in."

"Wasn't it typhoid fever?"

"And pneumonia."

Tunney nodded along and asked, "You're able-bodied and smart. Why the whole drifter thing? Isn't that kind of played out? I mean, the veteran returned home who wanders the countryside like a nomad has been done before."

"Everything has been done before."

"I guess so."

"It suits me. In the Navy, all I did was go from place to place, not knowing anyone, always being a stranger in a strange land. I lived so many double lives throughout my career, being a nobody to no one is a part of who I am, I guess."

"What do you mean *double lives?*"

Great, Widow! Widow thought. He'd let part of the cat out of the bag. He saw no reason not to be honest with Tunney, as honest as he could be without saying he was a double agent, working for NCIS, but being an active SEAL in the Navy.

"I worked for NCIS. I did undercover work."

"You pretended to be someone you weren't to get the bad guys? That sort of thing?"

"You could say that."

"I did a little of that myself."

"Really?"

"Not exactly. I never went undercover myself. But I worked a couple of operations where we had undercover agents in place. Dangerous work."

"It can be. I always felt safe enough," Widow lied.

He'd never felt safe doing it. Not once. He traveled, worked with, and fought alongside SEALs. And even though ninety-nine percent of them were heroes and the best men he ever knew, there was still that one percent that he had to investigate, get close to, and take down. Going undercover among a bunch of misguided drug dealers wasn't the same as infiltrating the world's most highly trained military operators. Not one bit.

Tunney said, "It's nice to know you, Widow. I hope we can find this guy's daughter fast. Imagine the look on her face when she learns she inherited fifty million dollars."

Widow actually hadn't thought of that. Not till Tunney just said it. He glanced at the side mirror and saw his own eyes.

Again, he thought, *fifty million dollars.*

Widow glanced at the clock on the BMW's radio. They had been on the road for thirty minutes, with thirty to go.

He asked, "Tell me about yourself, Tunney."

"What do you want to know?"

"Whatever you want to share."

Tunney stared through the windshield at the road. Widow saw his eyes behind his sunglasses.

Tunney said, "I'm from Virginia. Born and raised. My parents were the typical nineteen-fifties family type. Mom was a stay-at-home housewife. And my old man was a coal miner. We lived in a small town."

"You didn't want to be a coal miner?"

"No way! I got out of there as soon as I turned eighteen. And that wasn't fast enough. I joined the Army for several years. Till I met my wife."

Widow did the math in his head.

He asked, "You fought in Vietnam?"

"I did. That's where I met my wife."

"Really?"

"Yeah. She was the love of my life."

"Was?"

"She's been passed on now for nine years. Cancer."

"Sorry to hear that."

"It's okay. She took it like a warrior. She made little fuss in the thirty-six years we were married, and she didn't make any at the end. She was a great woman. They don't make 'em like that hardly anymore. You find one, Widow, you hold on to her."

Widow stayed quiet, but a couple of faces flashed across his mind. He had known more than one great woman in his day. Maybe he was lucky because he could sit and count many great women.

Tunney asked, "What about you? You got a woman? I'd imagine not, with the way you live."

"There's no one currently, but I'm always open to meeting one."

The female faces that cycled through Widow's mind stopped on one, like cherries in a slot machine. The face that stopped was Kelly Li of the United States Secret Service. He figured it was only because he had just seen her several months ago, and it was there, in Washington, DC.

He remembered the last day he saw her. It went down about like they always went down. His life led down one road, and hers led down another. All of it was understandable. He didn't need to explain any more than she needed to.

Li had a full life and career ahead of her. Why should she give all that up for him? And why should he give his life up for her?

Widow stared out the window again. He stared at gray clouds to the east, rumbling in from the Atlantic Ocean, and he wondered: *Would he have stayed if she asked him to? Would he have given up everything if only Li had asked?*

Stay with me, she could've said.

Be with me, she could've asked.

What if one of the others he had known had asked?

He thought about it and asked himself if he would've stayed. He didn't know.

Tunney noticed Widow had gone into a daydream. He continued to talk about himself.

"And then I worked with the Bureau for twenty-five years."

"You retired early then?"

"When Phuong, my first wife, got sick, I took a lot of leave. After she died, I took more time off. Eventually, I just didn't want to go back. So, I took an early retirement and got my licenses. Now, I do this."

"Are you remarried?"

Tunney said, "I am. She's great! Too good for me!"

He paused a beat and, like he couldn't help it, he added one more thing to that fact.

"We're not talking right now, though. Husband and wife stuff. You know?"

Widow didn't respond to that.

He asked, "How do you like being a private investigator?"

"Hours are better. Usually. But the pay sucks."

They both laughed.

After several more minutes of driving, Tunney flipped the turn signal on again, only this time it was to exit the freeway.

Widow looked over and saw they were exiting for North Bethesda.

Off the exit ramp and onto a local street, Widow watched the buildings and suburbs around them go by.

"Looks like a nice area."

"You ever been to Bethesda before?"

"Can't say I have."

"If you think this area is nice, go see Massachusetts Avenue Heights or Berkley."

"They're better than this?"

"Houses in those neighborhoods go for millions."

"Really?"

"Yeah. The cheapest ones probably don't crack below a mill."

"I guess the only thing that rich people are more afraid of than the poor is leaves."

Tunney glanced at Widow quickly.

"Leaves?"

"Yeah. Rich people are so afraid of leaves they're always hiring guys with leaf blowers to go around and blow them away. You never heard that joke before?"

"Nope."

Widow shrugged and said, "Maybe it's a Southern thing."

They drove the rest of the way in silence until Tunney turned into an office building's parking lot.

"This is it," Tunney said. He wound through a parking lot in the front, looking for a space.

They circled the same lot twice before they found someone pulling out. Tunney waited and then took the space.

They both got out, and Tunney locked the car with a press of a button on his electronic key.

Tunney said, "That was lucky. I hate parking in the garage. It's tight. Come on. This way."

Widow followed behind Tunney. Because of the way the sun was angled, Tunney literally walked in Widow's shadow all the way to the office complex's entrance.

Inside, there was a security desk with one security guard sitting behind it and another patrolling one who had just walked up.

"What's with the security?" Widow asked.

"There's a big law firm on the top level, and one federal judge has an office on the third floor. This is DC. The security feature enables the owners to jack up the rent. Don't worry about it."

Tunney walked over to the guard behind the desk. He took out a building badge and showed it to the guard, who acknowledged it and waved them both through.

Widow followed Tunney past the guard desk and down a long hallway to the end, where they came to a set of elevators.

They got on one and rode it up to the third floor.

Widow asked, "Aker isn't a part of that big law firm you mentioned then?"

"Aker? No. He's on his own."

They got off on three and walked down to the end of the hall, past offices, until they reached a single office door in the back corner of the building.

A sign posted on the door read Aker's full name with his credentials at the end. It was all pretty simplistic.

The first room Widow and Tunney stepped into was a waiting room, set out in front of a secretary's station, which was just a desk and two filing cabinets, plus a few bookshelves with law books and a few fiction books.

The law books looked boring. Widow's eyes homed in on the fiction section, which comprised nearly forty books. Widow recognized them all.

It was the complete John Grisham library.

Widow had read some of them. He liked them. As his eyes traced them he noticed they were in order from year published, starting with *A Time to Kill*.

Widow thought about Eggers, a man who had served in the same uniform that Widow had, and someone setting him on fire.

The thought ignited something in him, and the title of the first book registered in his mind.

A time to kill, indeed, he thought.

Beyond the secretary's desk, there was an open door. Widow saw Michael Aker standing in the middle of the room. He was facing in the other direction. He slid a bag off his shoulders and slipped out of a suit jacket. He straightened out the jacket and hung it on a hanger and hung it up on a coat rack.

He turned and saw Widow and Tunney.

"Widow, you made it."

Tunney said, "Sorry we're late."

"That's okay. I just walked in myself."

He beckoned the two men into his office. Tunney entered first and Widow followed.

Tunney took a spot next to another bookshelf and leaned against it. He took gum out of his coat pocket and slipped a piece into his mouth. Widow saw it was nicotine gum.

"I'm glad you changed your mind," Aker said to Widow. "Please have a seat."

Widow took a seat in front of the desk.

Aker walked over to a temperature control panel on the wall and fooled with buttons. The whole thing was digital. He flipped through the setting until he found what he was looking for, which must've been heat because Widow heard it kick on and felt hot air blast the top of his head.

"What changed your mind?"

"I guess in a way I never changed it. I always knew I would help. Soon as I read Eggers retired at my rank and was in a similar position in his platoon."

Aker nodded along like he understood, but Widow knew he didn't. He was the kind of guy who had skipped the Navy recruiter stations at the job fairs at whatever high school he went to. Aker was a born lawyer. Widow didn't know him well, but he knew how to read people, and Aker was always destined for a job that required years of book learning.

Nothing wrong with that. Every bee colony that has ever existed couldn't thrive without the worker bees, the same as it couldn't thrive without the soldier bees.

Tunney was different. He caught on to what Widow was implying right at the start.

He asked, "You a frogman?"

Another slang for Navy SEAL. That was two in twenty-four hours for Widow.

Widow nodded.

"Frogman?" Aker asked.

"Widow was a SEAL."

"Oh. Like a Marine?"

Tunney shot Aker a sideways glance. Same as he had Widow back in the car, only this one had a punch to it.

"No. Not like a Marine. SEAL is a special operator."

Widow said, "It stands for United States Sea, Land and Air Teams. It's a special operator fighting force."

Tunney said, "They're the best of the best. Best in the world."

Aker asked, "At what?"

Tunney said, "At everything."

"We do whatever's necessary to save lives, defend America, defeat or disrupt the enemy overseas."

Aker nodded and asked, "Like Green Berets?"

Tunney said, "They wish they were as good as the SEALs."

Widow stayed quiet.

Aker said, "So, you want to help us find Eggers' daughter out of a sense of duty? Is that how it is?"

"Not exactly."

The answer surprised Tunney, who had already probed Widow about his interest in the fifty million dollars in stocks.

Aker asked, "Then what exactly is your interest?"

"It is out of a sense of duty, but not in helping you find his next of kin."

Tunney asked, "What then?"

"It's out of a sense of justice."

Tunney asked, "Justice?"

Aker asked, "What kind?"

Widow turned in his chair and looked back over his shoulder.

He asked, "We're all alone here, right?"

Aker said, "Yes."

Widow said, "I believe Eggers didn't light himself up by accident."

"He did it on purpose?"

"No. I believe he was murdered."

13

"MURDERED?" Aker asked. His jaw dropped and his eyes hung open wide.

Tunney had a similar expression.

Widow said, "Yes. I believe I've found evidence."

"What kind of evidence?" Tunney asked.

Widow reached into his coat pocket and pulled out the cut zip tie, the label for Clyde Brothers' Whiskey with the broken glass stuck to the back of it, and the pair of bloody teeth. He laid them all out on Aker's desk.

"What the hell is that?" Aker asked, pointing at the teeth.

Tunney answered.

"Looks like bloody teeth."

"They are," Widow said. "I found them in a crack in the walkway near the bench where Eggers burned alive."

"Are they his?" Aker asked. He fanned out the fingers of both hands on his desk and leaned in to take a closer look.

Widow said, "I don't know. Just found them."

Tunney said, "They look knocked out. That's why the blood pattern."

Widow said, "That's what I thought."

"They could be anyone's. They don't have to be Eggers."

Widow said, "I found them a few yards away. Removed teeth will last forever, but not blood. The blood is dried on them, but I would guess it's only a couple of days old. Maybe three. Possibly four. I wouldn't put the bloodstains older than that. According to the *Post* article I read, Eggers died the night before last."

Aker nodded along. He made a disgusted expression as he stared at the teeth.

Tunney was now on his feet, no longer leaning against the bookshelf. He neared the end of the desk and peered down at the teeth.

He reached into his pocket and pulled out a stainless-steel fountain pen. It looked like the same pen that Widow had seen a thousand times before. Often agents in the NCIS or FBI and other law enforcement agencies had guys who carried nice pens like that. They were often gifts from loved ones or from a boss for a job well done. And often they were engraved.

This one might've been engraved, but Widow didn't see it.

Tunney used the pen's tip to separate the teeth from each other. Then he stuck the pen under the remains of the zip tie and lifted it up so they all could see it.

The plastic was melted a bit and charred. It was definitely snapped in one place, as if it had been cut by a knife or other sharp object.

Tunney stared at it.

Aker asked, "What's that?"

"It's half a zip tie."

"Zip tie?"

Widow said, "Eggers couldn't have accidentally lit himself on fire because Eggers was restrained to that bench."

Tunney looked at Widow. No reaction on his face, no surprise, but Aker stared at him with disbelief in his eyes.

Aker mumbled, "He was murdered?"

Widow said, "I don't know. But I'm going to find out."

Tunney said, "We're going to find out."

Widow nodded.

Aker said, "We have to call the police."

Widow said, "The police have already ruled his death an accident. They completely overlooked this evidence."

Tunney said, "DC is often the murder capital of the US. Metro is spread thin."

"That's no excuse."

"I agree, but I'm just saying they missed it. We should give them the chance to correct their mistake."

Widow said, "I'm okay with that. Just know that my interests lie in the truth, in justice being served. I won't stand in their way if they want to step up and do the right thing. I also won't hold my breath while they shuffle this off to the back burner."

Tunney nodded.

Aker repeated, "We should call them."

Tunney said, "I'll take Widow over there. We'll bring the evidence and explain the situation."

Aker paused a beat, and then he asked, "Will they want to put a hold on the inheritance? I mean, won't they want to tell me to stop searching for Maven Eggers until they wrap up whatever investigation they might do?"

Tunney said, "Doubt it."

"Won't they see it as a motive? I mean, it is the motive, right? Fifty million dollars?"

Tunney said, "Might be."

Widow said, "I'm not so sure."

"Why?"

"Because what? Maven Eggers found her homeless father, burned him alive for the inheritance money, and then forgot to make herself known to the world so she couldn't receive it?"

The two men looked at each other and then at Widow.

Widow said, "The money is a factor, but if Maven is the direct heir and she had her father killed for the money, then where the hell is she? No. It doesn't add up. She'd be here now, trying to get the money."

Tunney said, "Unless someone is using her to get the money. Maybe she's hiding out from them."

Widow said, "Maybe. I'm not saying the money isn't a clue. It's got to be an element in the whole thing. It's too much money for a homeless man to have in stocks and not be tied to his murder. I'm saying that I'm not sure it's the motive."

Aker asked, "So what do we do?"

"We look at everything. Where did the money come from? What's the story with it?"

Tunney added, "We need to go to the cops first. I can take Widow. I got some friends there still."

Widow said, "For now, I say we keep the circle of people who know what we suspect to a minimum. Because there's one more thing."

He told them about the black Escalade, about the tinted windows, about seeing it at Eggers' wake and then on the street at Lincoln Park. He told them about the chase it gave.

Both Tunney and Aker stared at him with a bit of hesitation and a bit of skepticism and a bit of fear that he was telling the truth.

Widow said, "One more thing. There are traffic cameras along the streets. And there's one in particular that I think might've recorded whatever happened at that bench. Can we get hold of that feed?"

Tunney said, "I don't see why not. We can certainly make it a condition with some of my buddies in Metro. We can offer them what we got for what they got. They'll go for it."

Widow said, "Good."

Aker's face changed to something different. It was excitement.

Widow could see the wheels in Aker's head turning. He was now seeing this whole thing as a mystery similar to the ones in his Grisham thrillers: *A struggling DC lawyer gets a dead client and discovers conspiracy and murder.*

Aker said, "Okay. I guess we go to the police and keep doing our part."

Tunney said, "Widow and I can keep looking into it. If the cops give us any shit about it, we can just claim it's part of our search for the heir."

Widow nodded. He didn't care what they called it. He wouldn't give up or just hand it off to the cops. If actions spoke louder than words, then the MPD had already said enough to him with their lack of actions so far.

He wouldn't let a fellow sailor and SEAL's murder roll away unavenged.

Aker said, "Widow, stick with Tunney. As I told you before, he's licensed in the surrounding states and you're not. So, whatever he says goes. His credentials will get you into places that you otherwise couldn't get into."

Of course, there weren't many places that Widow couldn't get access to. But he didn't argue.

Tunney said, "Give him a phone."

Aker nodded and stepped back from the desk. He dumped himself down in his desk chair, which had wheels. Then he wheeled himself forward just a little. He ducked down and went into the bottom drawer and pulled out a packaged smartphone. It wasn't a name brand, but some kind of cheap knockoff.

Aker opened the packaging and took out the phone. He had to put in batteries and a SIM card that was in the same package. He set the whole thing up and got onto the phone to follow automated instructions that turned it on. After several long minutes, he was done. He handed the phone to Widow.

"I programmed my number and Tunney's into the phone. It has internet if you need it. It's all paid for, so don't worry about that."

Widow took the phone and checked it the same way he would an untested weapon. He clicked the screen on and off button and sifted through the features.

In the end, he nodded and thanked Aker.

Widow asked, "Now that I'm officially a part of your team, I need to know where that money came from? How did Eggers get that investment stock in the first place? What kind of stock is it? Is it one thing?"

Finance wasn't one of Widow's strong suits. As long as he always had money to get food, buy coffee, and keep moving forward, he never really thought that much about it.

Aker said, "The stocks all began with one company and grew from there. It's a single stock and pays dividends."

"To whom?"

"What?"

"Who gets the dividends?"

"Eggers."

"How? What? Is it all in a bank account somewhere?"

"No. The dividends are paid out and then reinvested. So now, his portfolio is more diversified."

"Diversified into other stocks?"

"Right. But the bulk of the earnings is still from the first stock he bought."

"If he's been sleeping on the street for more than ten years, then who does the investing for him?"

"It's an investment banker at a firm."

Tunney stepped into the conversation and said, "Can you send us the name of the investment banker, the firm, and the original stock purchase?"

Aker said, "The stock code is SHG on the New York Stock Exchange."

Widow asked, "SHG? What does that stand for?"

Both Aker and Tunney shrugged.

Aker said, "I've got no idea. Look it up on your phone. I don't play the stocks."

Widow said, "Follow. Or invest. Or watch."

"What's that?"

"You don't *play* stocks. You invest in stocks. No one *plays* them."

"Whatever. I don't invest in stocks. So, I've got no idea what code stands for what."

Tunney moved on, looked at Widow, and said, "Okay. Let's get going."

Widow took his new smartphone, forgot to look up SHG, and stood up.

Tunney said, "Better take the teeth."

Widow nodded.

Aker put a hand up to stop him.

"Hold on."

He reached into a top drawer and pulled out an open package of tissues and pulled a couple out, handed them to Widow.

"Probably better to pick that stuff up with these."

"Thanks," Widow said, and he took the tissues.

He wrapped the teeth up together in one and then the glass and label in a different one, followed by the zip tie in a final one. He stuffed all of it back into his coat pockets.

Widow nodded at Aker and followed Tunney out of the office and back down the elevator to the lobby. They exited the building, got into Tunney's BMW, and drove out of the parking lot.

14

WIDOW AND TUNNEY had a near hour-long car ride again, back to where they came from, because DC's Metro Police Department headquarters was less than two miles from where Eggers had died.

The two men shared more small talk for some of the drive, but after that Tunney made a phone call and got hold of one of his old cop friends from his FBI days. He told the guy what they had, how it all started, and that they were coming in now. He also asked the guy if he could provide some quid pro quo and share some information back with them.

Widow listened to the whole phone conversation without a say in the matter, because Tunney put the guy over the car's internal speaker system.

At the end of the conversation, the guy hung up.

Widow said, "You didn't mention the guys following me around this morning?"

"I didn't think it was a good idea."

"Because it makes me sound crazy?"

"I don't think it's relevant."

"You don't believe me?"

"We don't have any proof. So why tell them?"

"I'm the proof. I told you it happened."

Tunney said, "But why tell them? We're about to drop a bunch of circumstantial evidence on them. No reason to give away the store."

Widow stayed quiet and stared out the window at the same route he had seen earlier from Lincoln Park out to Aker's office, only in reverse this time.

They rode in silence the rest of the way. Tunney cranked the radio up a little higher and played the same eighties rock station from earlier.

They finally got off the freeway and drove onto Indiana Avenue. It was apparent that Tunney knew exactly the roads to take and how to get to the Metro Police Department with no help, because he knew exactly where to go and where to park.

Tunney parked the car on the street. They got out and Tunney locked the car with the press of a button.

They walked a long way over grass and frost to grand concrete steps with a large mural and past it until they saw a large square.

DC architecture was quite something to behold. They were surrounded by buildings that looked like they were from ancient Rome, except they had modern attachments such as windows with glass and revolving doors.

While standing in the square, staring at it all, Widow almost missed Tunney veering off to the right.

He called back, "This way."

Widow turned and followed.

They entered through glass partitions and stepped into a grand lobby with shiny tiled floors and twenty-foot walls, plastered with accolades, all surrounding a giant American flag posted at the center of one wall.

The inside didn't disappoint Widow. All the law enforcement department headquarters in DC were designed more like cathedrals than office buildings.

They walked through the lobby, passing uniformed cops and pedestrians. Many of them wore suits.

They arrived at a desk with a line for both checking in and getting information.

Tunney said, "Let me call my buddy and tell him we're here. It'll make this faster."

Tunney stepped away and called his old contact.

A minute later, he was back, smiling.

"He'll come to get us."

Several minutes after that, a man about the same age as Tunney came walking out from a hallway beyond the information desk and through a security checkpoint. He stepped over to Widow and Tunney. His hand was out for Tunney, and he wore a smile on his face.

"Brigs, you look like shit."

Tunney's friend was a plainclothes detective; that was clear. He had a silver suit jacket with a five-day-worn tie underneath and black pants.

Tunney had a retirement gut, but not that bad. The detective had it in spades, and he was still on the job.

Tunney said, "I look like shit? Look at you!"

The two of them chuckled and shook hands heartily like long-lost brothers reuniting.

Tunney asked, "How's Alexus?"

"She's good. You should come to the house for dinner one night."

"She still doesn't know how to cook."

"She's gotten better. I'm still alive."

"Barely!"

The two men continued to shake hands for a minute like it was a game to see who could last the longest, like the staring game.

In the end, Widow cleared his throat. Tunney pulled away first.

He said, "Tom, this is Jack Widow. He's the one who discovered the new evidence."

"Widow, this is Tom Kidman."

Kidman offered his hand to Widow to shake. Widow took it and shook it, although not as heartily as when Kidman and Tunney shook hands.

Kidman said, "Good to meet you, Jack."

"Just Widow. No one calls me Jack. I was Navy for sixteen years. Last names first is a way of life."

"Okay, Widow. You can call me Tom, if you like. Or Detective."

They stopped shaking hands.

Kidman looked Widow over from his shoes and then back up to his face because it was easier to go that route than it was to start from *his* eye level, which was Widow's chin, and try to scan up and then back down a long track, just to return lost somewhere in the torso.

Kidman said, "You're what my grandson would call a *big dude*."

Widow nodded and ignored the comment. Instead, he asked, "Hey, you know what SHG stands for?"

Kidman's face looked puzzled.

"No. What's it stand for?"

"No idea. I hoped you'd know."

Kidman just shook his head.

Widow forgot again that he could just Google it.

Kidman said, "Okay. Let's go."

He turned around and waved for them to follow.

They followed and stopped at a security station with a step-through metal detector. A uniformed cop stood out in front of the entrance to the metal detector, blocking the way to walk around it. And a second uniformed cop stood on the other side of it, waiting for people to pass through.

To the right, there was another desk before going through the security station.

Kidman led them over to the desk first. He got them both visitor passes in laminate hanging from cords.

"Both of you have to keep these on at all times. Okay?"

Widow slipped his on over his head and let it drop so that the word *VISITOR* was prominently displayed. Tunney did the same.

Before crossing through the metal detector, Kidman looked at Widow and asked, "You carrying?"

"No."

Kidman looked at Tunney.

Tunney said, "You know I am."

Kidman said, "Turn it over."

"I have to?"

"Yeah. Afraid so. Don't worry. You'll get it back when you leave."

Tunney turned his weapon over to the guard at the desk and signed a document. Widow and Tunney followed Kidman back through the metal detector and past the guards to a set of elevators. They went up one level and through another corridor until they came to a huge bullpen that took up the rest of the floor.

Widow saw police detectives all over the room. They were on phones, on computers, or talking back and forth to each other.

Widow liked the sounds of busy cops.

He smiled, but no one saw it.

They stopped inside the doorway.

Kidman turned to Tunney and pointed at a young detective in glasses at a lone desk. He stared at a computer screen.

"This way," Kidman said. He led them to the detective hovering over the computer screen and stopped.

The detective looked up.

Kidman introduced the young detective as Shaw. He introduced Widow, Tunney, and Shaw to each other.

Shaw stayed seated but showed that he was paying attention.

He asked, "You guys got some evidence for me about the homeless man in the park?"

Widow said, "Eggers was his name."

"Right, Eggers. So, what do you have?"

Tunney took over and told Shaw everything, minus the black Escalade and Widow's theory that something more sinister was going on.

At the end of Tunney's explanation, Widow took out the tissues with the wrapped-up evidence and dumped them down on Shaw's keyboard, which made him stand up so fast his glasses nearly slipped off his face. They hung at the end of his nose by the time he was on his feet.

The tissue concealing the teeth unraveled first, and the bloody teeth showed up.

"Jesus!" Shaw said and jolted up from his chair.

Tunney put a hand on Widow's chest and spoke first.

"Sorry about my associate. He doesn't get around people much, but he's a damn fine assistant PI."

Widow said nothing to that.

Shaw pushed his glasses back into place and took a breath and asked a question.

"Are these Eggers' teeth?"

Tunney said, "We don't know. But we think so. We found them at the crime scene."

"Crime scene? We already ruled it as an accidental death."

Widow started to speak, but Tunney kept his fingers on Widow's chest as a way of telling him: *Let me do the talking.*

Widow didn't like it, but he knew when to shut up. Right then, the faster this went, the faster he could get on with finding the guys in the black Escalade.

Tunney asked, "Who ruled it as accidental death? You?"

"I did."

Tunney spoke, showing the same level of frustration that Widow would've shown. Only he kept it civil.

He said, "We found these teeth and the zip tie and the broken bottle all at the crime scene. Did you not think to do any detective work?"

Shaw looked stunned and a little ashamed.

He said, "I don't see how this strip of plastic, or the bottle mean anything."

Widow brushed Tunney's fingers off his chest like he was tapping into a wrestling match.

He said, "It's a zip tie. Someone restrained Eggers to that bench and set him on fire."

Shaw looked up at Widow.

"Sorry, I just see plastic. I can't do anything with this. But the teeth. That's something."

Tunney asked, "How long for you to test the blood on the teeth? Maybe it'll match Eggers'."

Shaw turned back to his desk and bent over to look at the teeth.

"I don't think the blood is usable. Maybe. I won't know till our forensic guys look."

Tunney said, "Still, you can match the teeth to Eggers' dental records?"

Widow said, "That's how they identified his body, according to the *Washington Post*."

Shaw nodded. There was a look on his face.

Widow asked, "What is it?"

"Eggers was missing two teeth. There was no indication that it had been done when he was in the Navy."

Widow said, "Those are his teeth. I'm sure."

Shaw stared at the teeth.

Kidman said, "Okay. On face value, the teeth suggest someone pulled out his teeth before he died."

Widow said, "Or knocked them out."

Kidman nodded and said, "That is enough for us to reopen the investigation."

Widow asked, "What about the bottle?"

Shaw asked, "What about it?"

Tunney asked, "You think the bottle was used to knock the teeth out? Is that why it's shattered?"

Kidman said, "Maybe that why it's shattered. Maybe it was thrown at Eggers?"

Widow said, "I didn't bring it in to suggest it was the weapon used to knock out his teeth."

Shaw asked, "Then why bring it in?"

"Because of the label. The brand."

Kidman leaned over Shaw's shoulder and looked down at the label on the desk. He read the label aloud.

"Clyde Brothers' Whiskey. Never heard of it."

Widow said, "Everyone knows that alcohol is flammable. But it's not like the movies where someone shoves a rag into a bottle of whiskey and throws it, and it burns down a house in seconds.

"The alcohol in any bottle of bottom-shelf to top-shelf whiskey acts as an accelerant, but in order to get the right bang for your buck, you need cask strength whiskey. For

Eggers to have burned himself alive, he would need something like Clyde Brothers' Whiskey, the cask strength version."

Shaw said, "Okay. So, this might've been his own bottle?"

"Not likely."

Tunney said, "A bottle of Clyde Brothers' Whiskey will run you about two hundred bucks in a liquor store. Eggers was homeless. He wouldn't have bought it."

Shaw said, "Unless he planned to burn himself alive."

Tunney asked, "You ever hear of a suicide done like that?"

Widow said, "Buddhist protestors do that in China."

Shaw asked, "What about the money? Did you mention money?"

Tunney looked at Widow. Then he explained to Shaw about the fifty million in stocks.

At the end, both Shaw and Kidman stared at Tunney with their jaws dropped.

Kidman asked, "What the hell was he doing sleeping on park benches? He could've bought a damn hotel with that kind of money."

Shaw asked, "Did he not remember that he had bought stocks that grew that much?"

Tunney shrugged.

Widow said, "He knew. He employed an estate attorney to handle his affairs."

Shaw asked, "When did he do that?"

Tunney said, "The attorney he hired is the one we're working for right now, but I don't know how long he's represented Mr. Eggers' estate."

Shaw took a breath and said, "We'll need to talk to him."

"Of course," Tunney said. He pulled out his thick wallet again, sifted through it, and pulled out another of the same simple business cards belonging to Aker that Widow already had.

Tunney handed the card to Shaw, who took it and thanked Tunney.

Tunney added, "Any questions you guys come up with about the money or anything, Aker will help you with. We just do as we're told."

Shaw thanked the two of them. Then he asked, "Is there anything else?"

Widow thought of the guys in the black Escalade again, but didn't offer the information because Tunney had instructed him not to, on the chance that he might sound crazy, Widow presumed.

Widow managed not to mention the Escalade, but he couldn't hold his tongue about the investigation.

"I gotta say that from my point of view. This whole thing was sloppy police work."

"Excuse me?" Shaw said.

"So, you didn't find the teeth. Okay. But you would have if you had looked closer. And the zip ties and the bottle of whiskey? You should've searched the bench, at least. That's where I found the zip tie. And there's broken glass all over the place. A little detective work would've led you to the same evidence I found."

Tunney said, "That's out of line, Widow."

But Shaw wasn't insulted, not the way Tunney had expected.

Shaw said, "I didn't investigate the crime scene because a fire investigator was called in. Our guys didn't look it over at all. The FI came, and he checked it out. He said it looked like an accidental death. Can you blame him? A homeless drunk lit himself up. Fell asleep with a cigarette in his mouth. We found the cigarettes and lighter. It looked like case closed."

The four of them looked at each other.

Widow asked, "This fire investigator, you've worked with him before?"

"Sure. Once. He's been around for years. He's reliable."

Tunney said, "Not here."

"We all make mistakes. How was he to know about the teeth?"

Widow said, "I found the zip tie underneath the bench."

Shaw shrugged.

"I guess he missed it. It's just a piece of plastic. Why would he even recognize what it was?"

Widow ignored that and asked, "Can we see the traffic cams?"

Shaw said, "Traffic cams? On the streets around Lincoln Park?"

"Yes. One of them might've gotten an angle of Eggers on the bench. We might see what happened. Maybe we can see who else was there."

Kidman said, "The cameras would've at least gotten the plates of any vehicles that might be involved."

Shaw said, "Let me make a phone call. We'll go look."

Tunney looked at Widow.

He said, "Nice job."

"That's Navy police work."

Tunney nodded along.

They waited as Shaw got on his desk phone and dialed numbers. He spoke to someone on the other line and told him the date and times he wanted to pull up on cameras on the streets surrounding Lincoln Park.

Widow interrupted him and told him about the specific camera on the specific cross streets that he wanted to see.

Shaw nodded along and relayed the information to the person on the other end of the phone. He followed it by waiting and making a few *uh-huhs* and a *yes* and, finally a *be right down*.

Shaw hung up his phone and said, "Okay. Follow us."

Widow and Tunney followed Shaw and Kidman back through the bullpen, past the other busy detectives.

Widow stayed in back.

They walked to the same elevators, but this time they took a different one down. They rode past the first floor to a basement level. When they got out, Shaw took a left and swung around to an office with a glass window on a door.

They went in and found a large office with multiple screens mounted on two walls, with three technicians at keyboards in front of them. Two were busy working on something together. They wore headphones. Occasionally, one would look up and nudge the other one, and they would talk, compare notes on whatever case they were working on.

As boring as technician work might be, Widow was struck with a sense of satisfaction to be back behind the scenes, on the hunt for a suspect.

A third technician was standing at the door when they walked in. He greeted them and gave out his name, which Widow missed because he was staring at the other techs working.

They followed the technician over to an empty terminal.

He spoke directly to Kidman and Shaw and didn't look twice at Widow or Tunney.

He glanced at Shaw and asked, "Okay, gentlemen. You asked to see the traffic cameras surrounding Lincoln Park?"

Shaw said, "Just the intersections around it."

The technician nodded and went onto his keyboard and typed away. He palmed a mouse along with a pad and clicked away there too.

Within moments, he was in some kind of search box. He unchecked some things and checked others. Then he clicked on a search bar and stopped.

He asked, "What dates?"

Shaw gave him the date from three nights previous and the times.

The technician keyed it all in, and the computer started searching. Only seconds later, it came up with the right streets and times, displaying multiple camera feeds.

"Which one you wanna check first?" the technician asked.

Widow intervened and stepped up closer to the guy's right shoulder. He pointed at one of the feeds with the right cross streets.

"That one!"

The technician moved the mouse and clicked on the tiny little box that displayed the camera he was talking about.

The box came up and filled the screen. The other four men waited, but the technician looked flabbergasted. He clicked the mouse again.

Shaw asked, "What is it?"

Tunney said, "Nothing's happening."

The technician clicked the mouse again. The screen was big. They could see a thumbnail of the camera's view, but nothing happened.

The technician said, "That's weird."

Shaw asked, "What?"

"The feed won't play."

"Why not?"

The technician clicked it again. Nothing happened. Then he sat back in his chair and took his hand off the mouse.

"What's going on?" Tunney asked.

The technician said, "It won't play. Let me try something else."

He double right-clicked over the video's thumbnail, and a little box of menus came up. He went into one called *Information*. It opened a box filled with stats about the camera's feed.

The technician reached up and tapped the screen on one section.

"It says zero?"

Shaw asked, "What's that mean?"

The technician said, "It means there's no video. It either didn't record..."

He trailed off.

Shaw asked, "Or what?"

The technician looked to the right at the other two technicians.

He said, "Or it was erased. There's no runtime displayed. That means there's no video to watch."

Shaw asked, "Is the camera broken?"

The technician tapped the thumbnail.

"There'd be no thumbnail if the camera didn't work. The thumbnail means there was a file."

"But now it's gone?"

"Yes."

Widow and Tunney made eye contact.

Shaw said, "Try the other ones around the park."

The technician tried the next camera up. The same thing. He tried four others; all had the same results. The feeds didn't play back.

The technician said, "I don't believe this."

Widow asked, "Who else would have access to the camera feeds?"

The technician said, "Well, really, anyone."

Tunney said, "Anyone?"

"Any cop, sure. Why wouldn't they?"

"For security reasons!"

Tunney grabbed the back of the technician's chair.

The technician said, "These cameras' primary job is to assign traffic tickets. We don't get a lot of requests for their footage unless it's for license plates. We share them with all of MPD."

Tunney released the chair-back and looked away in frustration. So did Kidman and Shaw. The technician stayed seated. He cocked his head back to look at the detectives.

Widow stayed forward, leaning over the back of the chair, and staring at the screen.

Widow asked, "Is there a way to find out who's accessed it?"

The technician said, "Not really. It could be anyone from anywhere in the department. It's all shared on a server. I can tell you I never emailed it to anyone. But maybe one of the other guys did."

Widow asked, "Email it to anyone?"

"Sometimes, we're asked for certain feeds by cops from all over the city. Like I said, the cameras can pick up plates of suspicious vehicles. Want me to ask the other guys if they've emailed it out to anyone."

"If you get requests for certain videos, then why does everyone have access to it?"

"A lot of the cops across the city aren't one hundred percent computer savvy. Or they've got too much else going on and can't take the time to search."

"What about other departments?"

"How's that?"

"You said the cops all across the city have access to this archive, right?"

"Right."

"What about other departments? Is it only available to the MPD?"

The technician thought for a moment.

He said, "I think some other departments have access to it. Like Secret Service, probably Homeland Security."

Widow asked, "What about the fire marshal's office?"

The technician nodded.

Widow looked at Shaw.

He asked, "You said a fire investigator came to the bench and ruled Eggers' death an accident?"

"Yes."

Tunney asked the question that was on Widow's mind first.

"What's his name?"

Shaw said, "Jay Haspman."

Kidman said, "He's posted up at the Office of the Fire Marshal Services. It's only about two miles from here."

Tunney nodded and glanced at Widow.

Tunney said, "If this Haspman guy is in on it, and he erased the video from the traffic cameras, then you guys should treat him as part of a murder."

Shaw said, "If there *was* a murder."

Tunney said, "Are you blind? We brought you enough evidence to suggest it was, and now, potential damning evidence has gone missing. That's enough to reopen this investigation as a murder, and you know it!"

"I'm just saying we don't know what we got yet."

Widow asked, "Can we get the fire marshal to suspend him? Until we can sort this out?"

Kidman said, "That'll be tough."

"Why?"

Tunney said, "They'll need a warrant to search his office. Plus, the DA has to agree to it. It could take time, but you guys can get that stuff."

"That's not the problem," Kidman said. "Haspman is the fire marshal."

SHAW THANKED THE TECHNICIAN, and the four of them left the tech office and went back to the elevators.

At the elevator, Kidman and Shaw talked between themselves in low voices, leaving Widow and Tunney out of the conversation.

No one hit the call button at first, not until Shaw and Kidman were done speaking in private. Then Shaw hit the call button and Kidman turned back to Widow and Tunney.

He walked them a few steps back. Shaw got on the elevator without them and hit the button to return up. The doors closed on him, and he was gone.

Kidman put a hand on Tunney's shoulder.

Tunney asked, "What is this?"

Kidman said, "Brigs, you're not a cop anymore."

"FBI. I was never a cop."

Kidman sensed some hostility in Tunney's tone and removed his hand.

Kidman said, "Look, guys. The Metro Police Department appreciates your effort and the evidence you've brought us. But we have to take over from here. Let us do our job."

Tunney said, "You're pushing us out?"

"I'm sorry. But that's how Shaw wants it. It's his case. We appreciate what you've done for us, but now he's going to take it."

"That's bullshit! If it wasn't for us, you guys would've missed a murder."

"I understand, but you're not FBI anymore. Criminal behavior is our bag. You're just supposed to be looking for an heir, not a murder conspiracy."

"You're telling us to butt out?"

Kidman walked forward, back to the elevators, and pushed the call button. He stayed quiet until the elevator dinged and came back to the basement floor.

He said, "We don't want you doing any outside action. We'll call you if we find anything that might lead to your heir. Or if we have any more questions."

Kidman put a hand up to hold the elevators open.

"Please," he said.

Widow walked past them and into the elevator. Tunney followed, along with Kidman, who pressed the button for the first floor.

Tunney stood between Widow and Kidman, fuming. He felt betrayed that an organization that he could once depend on had abandoned him. And he felt betrayed by his friend.

The elevator buzzed and lifted them up a floor. It dinged, and the doors slid open.

Kidman stepped off and led them back down the hall and through the metal detectors, where he pointed at a different desk cop than before, but at the same desk. They must've rotated or changed shifts.

"You can retrieve your weapon there. Thank you for coming."

Kidman put his hand out for Tunney to shake.

Tunney shook it reluctantly.

He said, "We've been friends for years, Tom. I can't believe you're shutting us out like this. We brought you guys a gold-mine of evidence."

"Sorry, Brigs. It's the way it is. It's Shaw's case. Not mine. Plus, the department won't let a PI work a murder case with us."

Tunney said nothing. He just pulled his hand away and walked over to the desk to sign his weapon back out.

Kidman looked at Widow.

"Sorry, Widow."

Widow said, "Don't be. Doesn't make a difference to me."

Widow left Kidman and joined Tunney, who had finished getting his gun back. He holstered it in his shoulder rig and motioned for Widow to follow him.

They left the police headquarters, back through the doors, across the square, and past the mural and statues.

They climbed back down the concrete steps and crossed the long field of grass until they got back to the car.

Tunney unlocked it remotely and hopped in.

When they were both inside with the doors shut and the engine still off, Tunney spoke.

"I'm sorry, Widow. I know you did all that work. Now, they're cutting us out."

Widow shrugged and said, "Don't be sorry. I figured they would do that."

"You did?"

"It was a fifty-fifty shot. Technically, there's probably some department regulation forbidding PIs to work hand in hand with police in a murder investigation."

"There is, but I've never heard it exercised before. Not when the PI in question is a former FBI agent and a friend of the detective."

"I wouldn't take it personally. It wasn't your friend's call. Plus, it had nothing to do with some department regulation. They did it because of Haspman."

Tunney nodded and said, "Yeah. You're probably right."

"I am right. We just learned that potentially the city's own fire marshal might have had a hand in deleting evidence."

Tunney nodded.

Widow said, "It seems to me the very best-case scenario is that Haspman mistakenly thought a murder was an accident, which still means he's incompetent."

"Worst-case scenario?"

Widow looked out the windshield and then over at Tunney.

"He erased those cameras on purpose."

Tunney started up the car. He gassed it; a couple of taps on the accelerator got the engine purring.

Widow didn't know why people did that. But he wasn't a mechanic. Maybe it helped to wake up the system.

Tunney asked, "Where to now?"

"They said Haspman's office was down the street. Let's pay him a visit."

"We really shouldn't."

"Why not?"

"The police might want to keep him out of the loop if they suspect him of covering up the brutal murder of a homeless man."

"We won't mention the police to him. He's the FI who called Eggers' death an accident. We're merely following up."

"He might blow us off. The fire marshal rarely meets with the public."

"He won't. Trust me. He'll be so curious and probably a little nervous about why we're there. We'll be on the top of his priority list."

Tunney reversed the car so he could make room in the front to pull out into traffic.

He asked, "What the hell are we going to ask him?"

"I'll think of something."

Tunney got the BMW out, and they were back on the move.

16

THE DISTRICT OF COLUMBIA FIRE MARSHAL'S office was at the fire department headquarters on Fourteenth Street.

The fire marshal's office was inside the building, top floor, nestled in one corner office that overlooked the street. If anyone inside had been looking for Widow through the window, he would've seen him because Tunney parked on the street diagonally from the building's main entrance.

The building itself was four stories. It was squashed between two other buildings double that size. It was mostly red brick with four huge red doors big enough to fit a fire truck through, which might've been how they were originally intended to be used. Widow wasn't sure.

On the building's rooftop, there was a white steeple with a bell inside, like on a church.

Widow didn't know how old the building was or how long the fire department had been there, but this building looked one, maybe, two hundred years old—maybe more.

He pictured, way back in the day, a time when the fire department headquarters was a functioning fire station. He pictured old-time fire trucks barreling out of those huge, red doors, carrying tanks filled with water and buckets to douse the fires. He pictured groups of firefighters forming a line at the scene of a fire. He imagined them running back for refills of water, and then running to the fire to throw it over the flames.

He wasn't sure if that's how it worked, but that was how he imagined it.

The building itself looked well-maintained, but definitely old.

Widow followed Tunney through a smaller door built into one of the larger ones.

The ground floor lobby had high ceilings with exposed brick and an industrial-looking air ventilation system. There was some security, but not like the MPD headquarters.

The only security people on-site were a couple of Capitol Police uniformed cops. Widow wasn't sure if they were actually on guard duty or had been there at the same time that he was, on official business maybe.

Widow and Tunney walked through the enormous lobby, bigger than the one at Metro, and over to a desk reception area. The reception desk wasn't manned by an armed guard, also different from Metro.

Tunney talked to a woman behind the counter. He offered her his business card that read *Brigs Tunney, retired FBI. Private Investigator. Licensed.*

Widow stepped back and waited, letting Tunney do his thing.

After a few minutes of banter, Tunney turned back and walked to Widow.

"Okay. He'll see us. Gotta say that was easier than I thought it would be. Without an appointment."

"Maybe it was your charm that did it?"

Tunney chuckled and said, "You a comedian now?"

Widow shrugged.

Tunney said, "Okay, let's go."

He went first, and Widow followed. They walked to the elevator, unescorted. Tunney kept looking around, expecting someone to stop them and tell them that there had been some sort of mistake. Someone who'd tell them that the fire marshal didn't take visitors off the street. But it never happened.

Tunney reached the elevator first and hit the call button. They waited.

The elevator came, and the doors opened, and Tunney stepped on first. The elevator was empty. Tunney clicked the button for the top floor.

They rode to the end of the elevator's route and waited for the doors to open, and then stepped off on the top floor.

The floor was carpeted. A sign posted across from them on the wall labeled the offices in both directions.

Tunney eyeballed the sign and saw the way to the fire marshal's office. He turned right and led the way. They started at the center of the floor.

Before following, Widow looked left and right. He inspected both directions of the hallway. It was another SEAL habit.

Widow needed to count exits, count doors, look for movement. He saw a couple of men in blue jumpsuits walking in the other direction. He saw a young woman walking toward him from the other end of the hall. She held documents on top of a black binder, pressed against her chest. She stopped at the elevators and smiled at Widow.

She gave him a casual, "Hello."

He returned it with a smile of his own. Then she turned and pressed the elevator call button, which only took a second because their elevator was still there. The doors opened, and she got on.

Tunney called back to Widow.

"Widow. Come on. It's this way. End of the hall."

Widow acknowledged him and followed.

They had to turn one curve in the hall, and then, they saw a closed door, black and heavy.

Tunney wrenched the knob and jerked the door open. They entered.

Through the door, there was another reception area, with a head secretary posted at the desk, as well as two more behind her, seated in another room.

It was the configuration that forced Widow to presume their ranks. Plus, the first secretary was older than the two behind her. And she had more of a professional tone and way about her that showed she was clearly in charge of the operations of the receptionist area.

Beyond the assistants in the back, Widow saw through two more open doors; each was on opposite sides of the reception desk. They both led down two different sides of the same hallway.

The hallway circled all the way to the back of the office and then swung back around to the reception area.

Tunney went to the desk and did the same thing as downstairs with the new secretary. He smiled and exchanged banter. He made all the same pleasantries and jokes that he made with the one downstairs.

Tunney had a routine he used on receptionists. Widow pictured the same basic chitchats being used in a long career in the FBI. It was something that Tunney had started three decades in the past and perfected to the script it was now, like a finely tuned routine.

The secretary reciprocated the chitchat. Then she told them both to have a seat. She told them that the fire marshal would talk with them as soon as he could.

Widow and Tunney nodded and sat down beside each other in a couple of chairs made of leather. They looked expensive, too expensive to be in a government waiting room, at least to Widow's liking. They belonged more in a cigar lounge at some country club that Widow had no business being in.

"This is a nice office," Widow said.

"Yeah. Kinda reminds me of the director's office."

"Director of what?"

"The FBI."

"You've been to his office?"

"Her office. When I was at the bureau, we had a female director for the first five years I started there."

"How many times you been to her office?"

"Several."

"Why?"

"I was constantly getting my balls busted about conduct. And so on. Nothing major. I just liked to do things. I get bored doing paperwork, and most of my job as a special agent was tons and tons of paperwork and reading and waiting around."

Widow nodded.

Tunney asked, "What about the NCIS? You guys do a lot of boring work?"

Widow barely ever had to do paperwork. That was what Rachel Cameron was for. She had been his director. She and her staff of support agents did all the paperwork and recon and intelligence analysis for Widow's missions. But there was no reason to inform Tunney about all that.

So he said, "It's the worst."

"Yeah. It must be the same for everyone. I bet the CIA has mountains of paperwork."

"This furniture though is so nice. Too nice."

"It's a boss thing."

"Guess when you get promoted to the executive level of all fire departments, then you get the royal treatment."

"I'll say."

They stayed waiting for longer than Widow expected, longer than he liked to sit in one place. They waited and waited.

Tunney was staring at his phone when the main receptionist finally spoke.

She said, "The fire marshal will be ready soon, gentleman."

Tunney said, "We know he's a busy man. Tell him to take his time."

She nodded.

Widow said, "Thank you, ma'am."

They looked at each other and ended up waiting half of the next hour. Widow noted the time by checking a wall clock that hung behind the main receptionist.

The waiting around felt like an eternity before the fire marshal called for them.

Finally, one of the underlings behind her stood up and came around the reception pen through one of the side doors. She came right into the waiting room through an open door. Instead of calling out to them, she greeted them at their chairs.

She said, "Gentlemen, the fire marshal will see you now."

Tunney nodded. But Widow was the first to stand up.

Tunney grabbed at Widow's Havelock sleeve and whispered to him.

"Let me do the talking."

Widow didn't respond, just noted that to be the second time that Tunney had put a hand on him. He didn't react to it, didn't threaten the guy, just noted it. It was a habit. He didn't like it, but it seemed to be part of Tunney's style. Lots of older guys who were retired cops had a way of touching and talking to people that wouldn't fly in today's culture of safe spaces. Tunney was one of those kinds of cops.

Tunney followed the lower-level receptionist back through the door and down the hall. Widow followed them both.

At the end of the hallway, they stopped and found a single black door, no window. The fire marshal's name and rank were posted on the outside skin of the door in gold lettering.

The receptionist opened the door for them and announced them like they were entering a royal court from four hundred years earlier.

The office was huge. It wasn't just another executive office. It was an executive suite.

It was set on the building's corner with two huge windows. One overlooked the street, and the other looked out to a tiny alley between the buildings.

The fire marshal sat behind an enormous oak desk big enough to float over crashing waves. The office was clean and organized, but cluttered with knickknacks. There were numerous awards and trophies and a little American flag on the desk.

Widow saw an open door. Beyond it was a private bathroom, shower and everything. There was another door. It was closed, but Widow bet that behind it was a bedroom and a closet.

The fire marshal's executive suite was basically a nice apartment.

On another side of the office, near the alley window, there were three leather lounge chairs and one leather sofa, all black. They faced each other. They must've been there for meetings that involved several people.

Widow wondered if policy talks went on in this room. He suspected there was a lot about government he didn't know. Maybe the fire marshal was a position heavy with duty and policy.

Sitting behind the desk was a bald black man somewhere in his fifties. Widow guessed it was closer to the end of the decade than the beginning. He wore a navy-blue jumpsuit with his last name printed on a nametape just above his left breast pocket. The jumpsuit's collar was plastered with insignias. It reminded Widow of an officer at sea.

He paid little attention to the insignias, as he had no idea what they meant.

A ball cap matching the jumpsuit uniform lay on the desk in front of the fire marshal.

The man wore dark frame glasses marked with an expensive designer brand Widow had never paid attention to before. He'd heard the name but just didn't register it. Fashion wasn't his thing. His only goal in that department was to match his socks every day.

The air nearly reeked of cologne. Widow didn't know the brand. The only time in his life he'd ever worn cologne was in the tenth grade when he went to homecoming with Cristina Sing, the prettiest girl he knew, way back then. His mom had made him wear cologne from one of his dead grandpa's bottles. He didn't recall the brand, only that it had a French name and came in a bulky, green bottle. It smelled of musk.

Not unlike a man who spends all day underneath the hood of a car in a mechanic shop down in Mississippi in the nineteen fifties, which wasn't what his grandpa had done, but that's what it smelled like.

The man stood up and stepped away from the desk. He came around and stopped in front of them and offered them seats in the leather chairs.

On the walk over, Tunney introduced himself and Widow—both as private investigators. He also mentioned Aker by name as his employer.

The fire marshal introduced himself, touching his chest with a heavy hand. He somewhat resembled a gorilla that had been taught how to talk.

"I'm Jay Haspman, the fire marshal above all fire marshals."

He spoke with pride in his voice and his demeanor. A bit too much—in Widow's opinion.

Widow wasn't sure if what he was saying was even true. He didn't know if whoever sat at the head of the fire department in DC reigned over all fire departments across the country. It might've been true, but then again, it might've been a lie too, a sense of self-grandeur.

The idea made him think of the postmaster general or the surgeon general. Both positions were over their respective departments.

Why not the fire marshal in DC? Why wasn't he called the Fire Marshal General? Widow wondered.

He wasn't going to dwell on the question because he figured that line of thinking could lead him down a rabbit hole he wasn't interested in going down. He had no time for that. Plus, he couldn't care less. All he cared about was getting justice for Eggers.

Haspman wore a gold Rolex on one wrist, along with a few expensive-looking rings.

Tunney explained to Haspman who they were and told him they represented Eggers' estate, which led them to question his death.

He told Haspman that they'd found some evidence that might alter the conclusions of how Eggers died. Beyond that, he didn't give Haspman any specifics. He left that up to Shaw and Kidman.

Tunney took a notepad and pen out of his inside coat pocket. The movement whipped open his coat, showing off the weapon in his shoulder holster, which Widow suspected he had done on purpose. It was an old tactic, used with suspected liars in an investigation. Showing off the weapon was an act of intimidation. You couldn't just take out a gun and threaten a suspect with it, but if they saw a glimpse of it real fast in a holster, it reminded them it was there. It put them on edge, where Tunney wanted them to be.

Sometimes it worked and sometimes it didn't.

Haspman asked, "So, that's what led you to me?"

Tunney said, "That's right. We have a few questions we'd like to ask you."

"Sure. But why? Are you guys investigating this as a crime?"

"No. Nothing like that. It's up to Metro to reopen this case as a homicide. Not ours. We're just PIs. Our interests lie in finding Eggers' heirs, if any."

"I don't understand. Heirs?"

"Eggers left behind a large inheritance."

"Really? A homeless man?"

"Yeah. It's weird. We know. But he did. We're trying to find his daughter."

Haspman folded his hands in front of his face and rested his elbows on the armrests of his chair.

"I'll take it," he said, and chuckled.

Tunney smiled back.

"Believe me; I'm sure we'd all take it if we could. But anyway, that's why we're here."

"Not sure how I can help you."

"We just have to follow every thread. We're not trying to solve a murder here. That's up to Metro. I'm sure they'll be calling you next."

Haspman looked at them, blankness on his face. He made no reaction to the news.

Tunney said, "So, I'm just going to ask questions. That okay?"

"Fire away."

"Is it normal for a sitting fire marshal to be called in to overlook a possible arson homicide?"

"Well, it was no homicide—first off. Not when I looked at it. I don't know what evidence you found, but when I was there, it was an accidental death. I saw the empty bottle of booze. And the cigarettes on the ground. Even found the one he smoked before he died."

"You found the cigarette that killed him?"

"Yes. It was right there on the ground with the others."

"The fire didn't burn it to a crisp?"

"It was hardly anything. Just the butt. Must've fallen out of his mouth when he fell asleep. He must've been piss drunk."

"Which explains the empty bottle of booze you found?"

"It was whiskey. A cheap brand."

Widow finally spoke.

"The bottle was whole?"

Haspman glanced at Widow, made eye contact.

"I'm sorry?"

"The bottle of whiskey you say was at the scene; it was one whole bottle?"

"Oh, yes. It was empty. Just lying there on the sidewalk."

"What brand?"

"Pardon?"

"Was the label still on it? What was the brand of whiskey?"

"It was a cheap brand. Not the kind I go for. It was what they call *rotgut*."

Tunney asked, "Remember the name?"

"Old Crow."

Widow stayed quiet.

Haspman said, "But to answer your earlier question, no. It's not normal for me to go to a scene like that. Usually, it's one of my guys. We have fire investigators who work with police and FBI all the time."

"So, why were you called?"

"That night, I was here. And it's only down the street."

Widow asked, "Anyone here with you?"

Haspman looked at him again. He looked stone cold. No reaction.

He asked, "Why does that matter?"

Widow said, "I'm just asking."

"You insinuating something? You think I'm lying?"

Widow stayed quiet.

Tunney said, "No one's saying that. He's just asking to confirm the times and all. Anyone else here to confirm the time the call came in for you?"

"You can check the call logs for that. You'll have to get them from the phone company, though."

Haspman looked away for a moment and then back at Widow.

"No one else was here. Not in my office. The phone rang, and I answered it."

Tunney nodded and wrote something down.

He looked back up at Haspman and asked, "You were here? The time of death was very late at night. Why were you here so late?"

"It wasn't late at night that I was called over. It was early in the morning."

Tunney wrote something else in his pad. Then he flipped back a page. He acted like he was reading something, but Widow could see there was nothing on the page. It was just chicken scratch, another old cop trick.

Tunney said, "The time of death was three a.m. You usually here at three a.m.?"

"The time of death might've been that early, but I wasn't called over till around five a.m."

Widow asked, "The fire burned two hours?"

Haspman shrugged and said, "It was out by the time I got there. Must've burned itself out."

Widow thought about Eggers burning alive. Obviously, he didn't burn for two hours straight. He would've been dead in seconds, but the thought of his body burning for some time up to two hours before someone came along to put him out enraged him.

Tunney redirected the line of questions.

"Isn't that pretty early to come to the office?"

"Fire departments all around the country are twenty-four hours. And so are we. Makes no difference the time."

"Still, that seems early for an executive to be in the office. Every director I've ever worked for didn't come in before breakfast. No way!"

Tunney chuckled a bit.

Widow realized Tunney was using him to play good cop, bad cop, the oldest trick in the book. It was a well-known trick, maybe the best known. But it lasted for as long as it had for a reason. It worked—sometimes.

Tunney was the good cop, and Widow was the bad cop—the carrot and the stick.

Haspman said, "Coming in early and leaving late is why I'm head of the entire department. And it's why I'll remain in this position."

Haspman lifted a hand and pointed behind his head with a thumb. He pointed at a wall of medals and framed certificates.

"That's why I have all of those," Haspman said. He dropped his thumb and hand, and placed both out in front of his face, touching fingertips like he was making a pyramid with his hands.

Tunney nodded along.

Widow said, "How long will you keep this job when word gets out that you made a wrongful determination of death? How long will people tolerate your complete miss of a homicide?"

Haspman moved his hands away from his face, breaking the pyramid. He sat up, agitation on his face. He pointed a finger at Widow.

"I did what any good investigator would do! That man fell asleep with a lit cigarette, covered in booze! He killed himself! Pure and simple!"

Tunney put up his hands.

"Okay. Okay. No one's saying you didn't do your job correctly here."

Haspman's composure was cracking, and Widow knew it.

Haspman said, "I'm a busy guy. If all you're going to do is grill me about your dead friend, I have better things to do."

Tunney said, "No. No. No one's doing that. We're just here for your side of it."

"How is this supposed to help find the man's heir, anyway?"

Tunney ignored the question because he didn't have an answer, and he didn't want to admit it because once he did, the jig was up.

"Can you tell us why you were called to investigate and not one of your guys?"

"It was very early in the morning. Our FIs don't work that late."

Widow asked, "I thought you were twenty-four hours?"

Haspman stared at Widow. There was anger in his eyes, which could've been fake, or maybe not.

"Not the arson investigators."

Tunney said, "Please continue."

"It was late or early, however you wanna look at it. And I saw no reason to bother one of the FIs with it. I thought it would be a quick look over. That's how it was pitched to me over the phone."

"A quick look over?"

"Sure. Metro called, asking for help. They said it was a homeless man in the park, on a bench. It was nighttime. The officer who called said it looked like he burned himself up. So, I figured it was your emblematic accidental fire."

"Emblematic?"

"Typical. Do you know how many homeless people die every year in this city from accidental deaths?"

"From fire?"

"Not fire. Usually, they sleep outside and freeze to death. Others fall asleep in the road and get themselves run over. Just last week, a guy was run over while sleeping in the middle of Independence Avenue."

Widow raised an eyebrow. Something he'd done before in a meeting like this, normally back when he was in the Navy. Normally it happened when he was in meetings with higher-ups who were talking out their asses. This wasn't much different.

But he stayed quiet.

Tunney asked, "Eggers was a veteran. Did you know that?"

"I didn't. Not till I read about it in the paper. I'm sorry for his death, but it *was* an accident."

"I wouldn't be so sure about that."

Haspman looked at Tunney and then glanced at Widow again.

Tunney said, "You hot, Haspman?"

"Fire Marshal."

"What's that?"

"It's Fire Marshal Haspman, thank you."

Tunney nodded

Haspman asked, "Why did you ask if I was hot?"

Tunney raised his writing hand, the pen tucked between his fingers, and pointed at Haspman's face.

"Got some sweat on your brow."

Haspman reached up and wiped it off. Afterward, he just sat there, quiet a long minute, like he was thinking.

Tunney spoke first.

"You okay, *Fire Marshal?*"

Widow stayed quiet.

Suddenly, Haspman looked at his watch. He held it in his gaze another long second. Then he stood up out of the chair, fast, like he might take off running right there, but he didn't.

"I'm going to have to call this meeting short, gentlemen. I've been more than cooperative. I have no more time for you."

Tunney asked, "Are you sure you can't tell us a bit more?"

Haspman stepped away from the chairs and over to his desk, leaving Tunney and Widow to face the wall of medals and certificates and the window that overlooked the alley.

Widow didn't stay like that for long. He suspected Haspman might go for a gun in a desk drawer. He jumped up and twisted around and faced Haspman at the desk. He locked eyes with him, in case he made a move for a drawer or anything else that was out of sight.

But Haspman didn't go for a desk drawer or a gun. Instead, he jerked his office phone out of its cradle and dialed one digit.

Someone must've gotten on the other end fast, because he spoke into it almost instantly.

"Grace, call downstairs and get the Capitol Police up here, now!"

Haspman slammed the phone down into the cradle.

Tunney folded the notebook and put it and the pen back in his coat pocket. He pulled himself up out of the chair and joined Widow's side.

He looked at Haspman.

"We say something you didn't like, Haspman?"

Haspman stared back at them. This time, he didn't correct Tunney with the whole *Fire Marshal Haspman* thing.

"I said, I'm done. That's it. You won't be wasting any more of my time today. And you can tell that lawyer you represent that I'll be talking to my attorney about a libel lawsuit if he tries to badmouth me with the press or anything else. I never want to see you again! Either of you! You have less than a minute to get out of my office before the Capitol Police come up here and arrest you!"

Widow stepped forward; his feet stopped just in front of the huge desk.

He stretched himself up tall, as tall as he could. He raised his head, extended his neck, and swelled every muscle and bone in his body, stretching himself out to look bigger and taller than he was normally.

In the wild, grizzly bears do this same thing when they perceive a threat. They stand up on their hind legs and stretch themselves out to full height in an effort of intimidation.

It works every time.

Widow was no different, and neither was Haspman.

Haspman shook and trembled. It wasn't a huge gesture, not like being dropped into freezing cold weather stark naked, but it wasn't far off either.

Widow stared him down for a long second, and then spoke.

"We got longer than a minute. No one's gonna make it up here that fast. We have plenty of time. Enough to do whatever it is we want to do."

Haspman spoke. His voice cracked like a teenage boy singing tenor and suddenly finding out that he's now a baritone, only in reverse.

"You can't come in here and speak to me this way! Threaten me! I don't know who the hell you think you are!"

Widow didn't move. He didn't step forward. He didn't grab Haspman from over the desk and slam his head into it. He didn't do any of that, but the thought crossed his mind, and Haspman knew it. He could see it.

It was in Widow's eyes. The only difference between Widow and the grizzly bear was that Widow stayed quiet.

Silence filled the room until Haspman spoke first.

"That guy burned himself up. Just like I said. The evidence is there."

Silence returned a long moment until the office door swung open, and Grace, the head receptionist, entered.

She looked at Tunney and then at Widow. She saw the stance. She saw the eyes.

She said, "I've called downstairs. The police will be up in a moment."

Widow recalled the cops in the lobby. They were armed.

He breathed in and breathed out, resetting the grizzly stance back to normal.

He looked at Tunney, who had his hands free. The pen and notepad were both back in his inside coat pocket. But there was something else in his stance. Widow hadn't noticed it before, but Tunney had his hands free, so he could go for his gun if he needed to.

Widow realized Tunney was also wondering if Haspman was going for a weapon somewhere in a desk drawer.

Tunney said, "Let's get the hell out of here."

Widow glanced back at Haspman. They made eye contact.

Widow said, "Know what SHG stands for?"

"What? No! I don't!"

Widow felt like he was lying, but not because he was intentionally lying, rather because Haspman didn't take the time to even listen to the question. He didn't think about it. He simply responded like someone trying to dust him off.

Tunney made the first move and walked out, passing behind Widow. He tapped Widow on the shoulder as he passed, indicating a request to leave. He didn't thank Haspman for his time, as he would've done under normal circumstances. He didn't even look back at him.

Widow followed but kept his eyes locked on Haspman, who still trembled.

17

TUNNEY WALKED out of the DC fire department headquarters in a hurry. Widow stayed close but walked casually. They had come with questions and were left with more answers than they'd expected, none of which were stated in Haspman's answers. Instead, they came from what he didn't say more than anything he'd said.

Tunney walked straight out the front doors of the fire department headquarters and beelined to the BMW. He moved fast, faster than Widow would've expected of him.

Tunney glanced back at Widow only once.

"Come on. Let's get going while we can."

But Widow walked at a normal speed, normal pace, normal tempo. He wasn't in a hurry. He wasn't worried.

Tunney got in the car and fired up the engine. Widow got in just after. As soon as the passenger door was shut, Tunney reversed the BMW, pulled out of the space, drove down the street and turned at the first cross street. He wanted to get away from the building as soon as he could. He didn't want any trouble with the Capitol Police, and Widow understood why. An entanglement with the cops could lead to more problems.

He drove fast, but not over the speed limit. A car in the other lane honked its horn like it was for them. He wasn't sure.

Tunney said, "That was constructive. We nearly wasted the entire day with this asshole."

Widow said, "He's hiding something."

"That's for damn sure. And not just something. It's something related to Eggers. I think we both saw that. It was like you said, he met us. I didn't think he'd meet with two guys right off the street like that."

"I knew he would. He couldn't help himself."

Tunney said nothing.

Widow said, "We should watch him."

"Watch him?"

"Yeah. Like a stakeout. You know the kinda shit you FBI agents used to do."

"A stakeout? Widow, have you gone crazy? I don't do stake-outs for murder cases. We're not here to solve a murder. If it was murder, we should just let the cops do their job."

"You think Shaw is going to come down hard on the fire marshal? This guy will just use his influence to get Shaw moved to crosswalk duty."

"No. We stay out of it now. It's not my job."

"Don't you want to see justice done?"

"I want to find Eggers' next of kin and get them their inheritance. That's my job. Not solving crimes. I didn't even do that in the FBI."

"What did you do for the Feds?"

"Not murder investigation."

Widow looked out the window for a second. Then he pointed a finger at a Starbucks up ahead.

"Drop me off there."

"Drop you off?"

"Yes. Pull over."

Tunney slowed the car, checked the rearview, and slid the car slowly to the curb.

Widow unlocked his door and opened it and climbed out.

"You're done now?"

"I'm going to see this thing through. You're not interested in that, so it's time for me to go alone. Thanks for everything."

Widow reached into his coat pocket and pulled out Aker's phone and handed it back to him.

Tunney waved it away.

"Hold on to it. If you get yourself into a jam and need help, call me."

Widow nodded, thanked him, and shut the door. He turned back to the street and walked to Starbucks to get the main item needed when doing a stakeout—coffee.

18

AT ABOUT THE same time that Widow and Tunney were called into the fire marshal's office, the same black Escalade that had followed Widow earlier drove onto the street in front of the headquarters and passed the entrance to the department. It drove past Tunney's parked BMW.

The driver was a heavily built guy, thick like a tree trunk. His head was shaved bald. He more resembled a Neanderthal caveman than homo sapiens. The only thing he didn't have in common was he didn't drag his knuckles, but they hung low by his sides when he wasn't driving.

The bald guy wasn't the best fighter in the crew, but the size of his fists matched with big boulder arms and relentless power made him deadly. That was why he was often assigned to wetwork duty. When someone needed shutting up, he did the shutting.

The passenger in the Escalade was the man with the forgettable face.

He rolled the window down as they drove and scoped out all the parked cars that didn't look like they belonged. He had his smartphone out. He video recorded all the cars he passed, getting their license plates on camera.

At the end of the street, the driver asked, "Which one is theirs?"

"Not sure. But one of them. Has to be."

"The guy from the church didn't have a car. Not the other day."

"Maybe he doesn't own one. But they got here in a car. Probably the other guy's. Whatever. We'll find it."

They drove around the block one more time. This time they searched for a parking space, preferably one that allowed them to view the big red doors in front of the fire department headquarters, but they couldn't find one with that view. They ended up parking in a lot down the street.

The bald guy asked, "How are we going to see them leave?"

The man with the forgettable face said, "Stay here. Watch the road. I'll go stand across from the entrance. I'll text you when I see them. So be ready."

The bald guy nodded.

The man with the forgettable face stepped out of the Escalade and left it. He walked back to Fourteenth Street. He saw a newsstand on the street corner up ahead. He walked over and bought a newspaper and continued to the fire department headquarters. He found a concrete ledge across the street with grass on the other side of it. He climbed up on it and perched himself there.

To passersby, he was just a guy reading the paper. Sometimes he glanced at the paper, turning the pages, moving his eyes up and down and across the page to make it look like he was scanning the paper, but he wasn't. He kept constant eyes on the doors to the fire department headquarters, waiting for Widow to step out.

19

As SOON AS Widow stepped out of the fire department headquarters, the man with the forgettable face saw him. There was no eye contact, luckily.

Widow followed an older guy that the man with the forgettable face had never seen before. But Widow was too close behind the guy for him to grab a photo.

The man with the forgettable face hopped down from the ledge, shoved his hands into his pockets, and started walking in the other direction so that Widow couldn't see his face. He was just a guy walking the streets—no big deal.

As soon as he was near the end of the street, he turned and saw Widow and Tunney get into a BMW. The man with the forgettable face already had the license plate in the picture he had taken earlier of the whole block.

He stopped and picked up his phone and called the bald guy in the Escalade.

"They're out now. Silver BMW."

"Want me to follow it?"

"Come pick me up first. Other end of the street."

"On my way," the bald guy said. He hung up the phone. He pulled out of a parking space and roared past a pedestrian walking to his car.

The bald guy pulled the Escalade out onto the street fast. A car honked at him as he cut them off.

He looked in the rearview mirror and saw the driver behind him wave a hand with the middle finger up. The bald guy looked past it and saw the brake lights of a silver BMW. It was the same one that he was looking for. The occupants were stopped at a traffic light at the other end of the street.

The bald guy turned his eyes back forward and saw the man with the forgettable face walking toward him on the opposite side of the street.

The bald guy hit the hazard lights on the vehicle to warn the pissed-off guy behind him he was about to make an abrupt U-turn.

Then the bald guy hit the brakes and spun the wheel. He came up on the opposite sidewalk and braked to a quick stop, just enough for the man with the forgettable face to open the passenger door and hop in. As soon as the door was shut, he peeled out and hit the gas.

"I saw them. The BMW, silver. It was up at this light ahead."

"Good."

The man with the forgettable face reached into his coat pocket and pulled out a Glock 19. He checked the weapon, made sure a bullet was chambered. He knew it was, but checking it often was second nature by now.

He rested the gun in one of the cup holders next to him. The bald guy's weapon, a Glock 34, was in the other cup holder.

The bald guy asked, "What you want to do?"

"Follow them for now."

"Then what?"

"First chance we have, we kill them."

20

THE STARBUCKS on the corner of Columbia Road and Eighteenth Street was perfectly fine. It had seating, and it had coffee, the two things Widow wanted in a Starbucks. But what it didn't have was a view of Haspman or the fire department headquarters or even one of the two ends of Fourteenth Street, so Widow could give himself at least a fifty-fifty chance of spotting Haspman leaving his building. Even that was no good because Widow had no idea what kind of vehicle the guy owned.

After Tunney dropped him off on the street corner, Widow entered the Starbucks, intending to buy coffee. He planned to buy it and drink it and regroup. What was his best next option?

But inside the Starbucks, he watched Tunney drive off, and he stood in the back of a three-person line. A fifth person came into the store and got in the queue behind him.

As he waited, he thought, strategized, contemplated. By the time it was his turn to order, he had come up with a solution.

It had been staring him in the face. Across from the fire department headquarters, there was a café or restaurant or bookstore—he wasn't sure which—but he remembered seeing it. It was called *Busboys and Poets*.

Widow had heard of it once before. And he knew who had told him about it. It was Rachel Cameron, his old boss. Exactly what she had said about it, he couldn't remember. It was years ago. He thought it was something in the vein of a recommendation to him.

He had no idea if the store was the only store or if it was a chain, and he didn't know exactly *what* it was. But he knew that with a name like that, there had better be some kind of coffee served there. And if that didn't work out, there was also a martini bar that had a decent view of those red front doors to the fire department headquarters.

The barista asked if he was ready to order. He apologized and told her he had changed his mind. He stepped out of line and walked out of the store just in time to miss the black Escalade passing by on the street.

Widow walked to the corner, crossed over to the other side of the street, and walked part from memory and part from his Navy sense of direction, back to Fourteenth Street and back to the fire department headquarters.

The whole trip turned out to be a grand total of one hundred fifty meters, give or take.

The first thing he did was walk to the parking lot for the fire department headquarters.

He saw a pair of Capitol Police standing around the entrance to the building. They were chatting. He was pretty sure they weren't looking for him and Tunney, but to be safe, he kept his distance and his eyes down.

The parking lot for the fire department wasn't under any kind of security other than a valet in a booth the size of a portable toilet. The guy was lounged back, reading a magazine. There was a mechanical arm out in front of his station. It stopped people from entering or exiting without him lifting the arm.

Widow passed him with little effort. He didn't walk past the arm. Instead, he walked along the sidewalk and waited till he was in the guy's blind spot. Then he took a big step over a long stretch of chain that acted as a barrier between the pedestrians on the sidewalk and the cars in the lot.

Widow entered the lot and walked around, looking for the fire marshal's car. He knew he would find it easily and recognize it without fail.

It only took about two minutes to locate it, but that was because he circled the long way around from the back of the lot. He did that just to be sure the guy in the booth wouldn't see him.

Part of the lot was near the fire department headquarters. There was a single door on the same wall that touched the parking lot. It looked like a fire exit.

Widow bet Haspman took the elevator down to the lobby and went through the back hallways and used the stairwell fire exit to enter the lot.

His suspicions were confirmed when he found Haspman's vehicle right there next to the door.

He knew it was the right vehicle for a couple of reasons. First, it was a huge Ford Raptor, black with black rims and a black bed cover to match. The second reason was that there was a sign posted on the wall in front of the space. It read: Reserved for Fire Marshal Haspman.

Widow shook his head. The guy he had met struck him as a man with no lack of vanity. The gold lettering on his office door, the expensive furniture in the suite, having not one, but three assistants, and the Rolex, were all signs pointing to a man with an ego big enough to cover the flight deck of the USS Gerald R. Ford aircraft carrier.

Widow needed no more verification that the Raptor belonged to Haspman, but just to be thorough, he circled the truck and stopped in front of the grille. He knelt and looked behind the grille blades, and found what he was searching for: embedded red lights.

The truck had no decals posted on it to show it belonged to a fire marshal, but there were the lights.

He was pretty sure it wasn't normal protocol, and potentially a violation of the fire department's policies, to not have an official vehicle marked. But who was going to turn in Haspman? Who would they turn him into?

Widow had no idea and didn't care to know.

He stood up and scanned the lot over the hood of the Raptor. He saw no one.

He walked back out of the lot the same way he'd come in and stepped over the same length of chain, back onto the sidewalk. Then he slid his hands into his coat pockets and walked back past the guy in the booth, who never even looked up at him. He nodded at the Capitol Police as they began walking

,

toward him. He had no choice. They made eye contact with him.

One of them was talking, but the other one looked him up and then down, and gave him a hard stare. But he said nothing.

Widow passed them and continued to a designated crosswalk and crossed the street. He walked to the place that Cameron had told him about. It turned out it was a coffee shop/bookstore configuration.

He entered and glanced around, and smiled.

He looked around at some of the other customers to figure out what the right sequence was to operate in a hybrid store like this.

It seemed the first step was to grab a book, then coffee, then a table.

Part of Widow kind of wished he wasn't there on business because he would enjoy hanging out all day and reading a book and drinking all the coffee his stomach could hold. But he was there on business. Personal, but business, nevertheless.

The first thing he did was scope out a table near the front window. He saw a couple of good candidates. The second thing he did was look for a clock. That didn't take long. There was a huge wall clock on one end of the store, above a bookshelf. The clock was inside a giant, opened book frame. The numbers looked like page numbers.

The time was later than he thought.

After Widow noted the time, he remembered he still had Tunney's smartphone in his pocket. Like all phones, it displayed time on the main screen.

He would've felt stupid for not realizing that, but he never carried a cell phone. He forgot about it.

Widow moved to the biggest book display. He didn't have time to sit around all day browsing. The display was one of those famous celebrities' book-of-the-month clubs. The top book he saw was called *Where the Crawdads Sing* by Delia Owens. He glanced up beyond the display and saw the *New York Times Bestseller List* of the top twenty books in fiction.

He walked to that wall instead. He wasn't interested in what celebrities thought about books. Not that whoever it was didn't have good taste, but Widow liked to make up his own mind.

Ironically, on the bestseller wall, the same book was also number one.

He grabbed the paperback version, flipped it, and browsed the summary on the back. It sounded interesting, but also like a heavy read. He wasn't so sure if getting a book that might jerk tears out of him was the right thing to get into while staking out a potential lead in Eggers' murder. So he put the book back.

What he needed was something lighter.

He skimmed the rows of books until he found something good, but forgettable.

In times like these, he found it best to stick to the golden oldies, the authors everyone knew, and everyone liked. The kind of author he needed was what he liked to think of as *airport reading*.

It was the kind of book that was a great, fast read while traveling through airports with long layovers. It was also the kind of book where he could skim it, set it down, and forget it.

He wasn't looking for Shakespeare here.

Widow let his eyes bounce from cover to cover until he found two viable candidates. Stephen King was always a good choice. Except that lately, his work had been really, really good. But it was also deep. Deep was not the right choice.

The second candidate was perfect. He picked up a copy of the latest Dean Koontz book.

Koontz was a famous author that everyone liked, but he could remember none of Koontz's titles. It was quintessential airport reading.

Widow grabbed the book and walked to the counter at the coffee shop setup. There was a short line of other people doing the same.

At the counter, he ordered his coffee, a large, and paid for it and the book. He took them over to the window table he'd targeted and sat down. He adjusted his chair so that he was facing the window.

That's when he realized his mistake. He was facing the big red doors, but he'd already established that Haspman would come out the side door.

Forgetting about the phone in his pocket didn't make him feel stupid, but this did.

He got his butt up out of the chair and took the book and stared out the window to see if there was a better table with the right angle on the side door. There wasn't.

He cursed himself under his breath, and then he took the book and the coffee and left the store.

He walked back outside and moved down the sidewalk until he found a spot that looked good. It was a concrete ledge.

It was better than he'd hoped for. From here, he could see the parking lot, Haspman's Raptor, and the fire door.

Widow hopped up onto the ledge and sat down. He set his coffee on the perch and opened the book. He started the book from the beginning, taking breaks every five to fifteen minutes to glance up at the fire door.

He knew he would probably be there the rest of the afternoon until Haspman left.

What he didn't know was that he was sitting on the same perch that the man with the forgettable face had sat on earlier, when he was staking out the place, waiting for Tunney and Widow.

21

THE MAN with the forgettable face and the bald guy followed Tunney's BMW around all day. They were a little confused because there was no sign of the stranger.

They followed Tunney and ran his plates through a contact at the FBI; their boss had contacts all over the place. That's how they got Tunney's name and occupation. Knowing what he did for a living told them what part he played.

Another confusing thing was that it seemed he had given up. There was no sign of Widow, but also Tunney wasn't doing any kind of investigation work. He spent the rest of the day running errands, and they were there with him every step of the way.

First, he went to the bank, stopped for gas, paid some utility bills, mailed a package, and picked up a dry-cleaned suit, along with some female garments. They figured those must've been for his wife.

They knew he was working for the lawyer, Aker, and they knew the stranger must've been too. Soon, they would have their answers because evening had rolled around.

They drove the Escalade slowly through Tunney's neighborhood. They followed him into a subsection of the neighborhood literally called *Friendly*, which made the guy with the forgettable face smile.

Tunney lived on Fort Hill Street in a two-story colonial, painted yellow. The suburb was quiet and peaceful, a real family-friendly place. The houses were far enough apart that if they raided his home, they could be in and out pretty quickly with little worry of witnesses. But there would be collateral damage; namely, they would have to kill his wife—if he were married.

They staked out the house for twenty minutes. Then they took a drive and studied the neighborhood streets. The only worry was that they saw a police car parked in one of the driveways on the street directly behind Tunney's house.

The bald guy said, "We should've taken him in the car."

"How? In the middle of the evening, traffic rush home on Three Fifty-Five? We'll do this the smart way. We've already caused too much exposure."

"Everything woulda been fine if not for the stranger."

The guy with the forgettable face nodded but didn't speak. He knew the bald guy wasn't wrong. They had the whole thing planned out. Even though he had never been a Navy SEAL, he still knew some of their mottos. One that he knew was: *Plans all go to hell once the first shot is fired.*

He said, "We've made enough mistakes. This time, we get it right."

"We still going to kill him? More bodies could mean more problems."

The guy with the forgettable face looked at the bald guy, said nothing.

Just then, his phone buzzed. He got a text message that he had been waiting for.

He looked at it and said, "Okay. We got his phone number. I don't think he's going anywhere. Let's drive. We need to find a better kill spot."

The bald guy smiled and took his foot off the brake, and they drove back through the neighborhood, back out to the main roads.

22

WIDOW READ his new paperback book until sunset. Then he glanced up, as he must've done a thousand times over the last few hours.

Haspman's truck was still parked, still in the same reserved space. He hadn't left yet.

Around five o'clock, the fire door to the parking lot opened, and a stream of office workers and firefighters streamed out, got into their cars, and drove away for the day.

Widow figured Haspman wouldn't be one of them. No way did a guy like that, with an up-front, close, reserved parking space go through the inconvenience of dealing with rush-hour traffic. And being the head of the department, he couldn't just leave early, not regularly. He had to think about the optics. How would that look?

Widow figured the guy wasn't lying about being the last to leave, but not out of some sense of duty to do the best job he could do. It was so he'd miss all the trouble of leaving when all his coworkers left.

Widow knew DC traffic at the end of the workday was a slugfest to get home. But after the sun went down, and after most of the workers from the city had already fought through traffic to get out to the surrounding neighborhoods, the city was a different story altogether.

Widow waited through sundown, and after most of the five to seven o'clock workers had all left, to make a move. He needed to do more than just sit there and wait all day for Haspman to leave his office. He wouldn't learn anything by simply watching the man leave.

Tunney had taken the only vehicle he had access to, which meant that he was going to have to get creative.

Widow left the book behind. He'd nearly finished it but didn't want to be stuck carrying it around. He liked to carry nothing, or as close as he could get. He finished his third refill of coffee from the coffee shop/bookstore and tossed the paper cup into a trashcan that was inside a metal contraption that kept people from stealing it off the street. And then, he looked up and down the street. There was no sign of anyone.

He crossed the street, keeping his hands in his pockets. He made eye contact with the parking attendant, who was now wide awake and at attention at his post. This was his time of day to be alert.

Widow made his way across Fourteenth Street and turned left. He walked casually, just a man going about his business. Then, when he was sure he was out of the parking operator's line of sight, he repeated the same actions as earlier—crossed the chain barrier and tried to stay low while he made his way to the Raptor.

It was a little more difficult this time because most of the cars he'd used as cover earlier were gone, but he made it pretty easily.

At the Raptor, Widow thought he would have to leave to find a crowbar, which might pose a problem. Luckily, Haspman was an overly confident man because the truck's tailgate wasn't locked.

Widow opened it and bent over to inspect how much room was in bed, when suddenly, the fire door opened behind him. He turned, expecting to see Haspman. In his head, he'd already pivoted to punch the guy straight in the solar plexus. Not a deathblow, just a hard, powerful strike, one that would put him on his butt. Then Widow could steal his keys, toss the guy in the bed, lock it, and drive away.

But Haspman wasn't at the fire door. It was two women. They came out, and they saw him because he was big as a house, and he was opening a vehicle that they knew didn't belong to him.

Widow froze.

The two women stared at him. Their jaws dropped and their eyes opened wide. They looked like deer in headlights.

Widow came back up. Thinking on his feet, he changed his accent to a Russian one. It wasn't very good, but believable enough. Only he didn't know why he'd gone that way. He figured it was something from his training that told him that lying and playing dumb worked best when you threw in an element that was unexpected by the person being lied to. It was kind of like walking with a limp and a cane to get through a security checkpoint. People are more easily fooled if they believe you are handicapped.

Widow said, "Good evening, ladies."

One of them, the one who appeared to hold rank among the office workers, spoke. The other one just started clutching her handbag, which reminded Widow of the mother from the apartment the day before.

The higher-ranked office worker asked, "Who are you? What are you doing to Fire Marshal Haspman's truck?"

She said his full title. Widow figured he made everyone do that.

Widow said, "Don't be alarmed. My name is Oleg. I'm the fire marshal's driver."

"I didn't know he had a driver."

"I'm new. Mr. Haspman is a very important man, as you both know. My job is to chauffeur him around."

"That doesn't sound right."

Widow glanced over his shoulder and then over the other one. He made the gesture big and obvious like he was seeing if anyone was watching him. He took a step closer to the women and put up a hand near his mouth like he was going to whisper a secret to them.

He said, "Truthfully, I'm more than a chauffeur."

The women both leaned in to hear him better.

"I'm working as his bodyguard. Mr. Haspman has some fear of certain powerful people who might harm him. He is the head of an important department, you know?"

The two women looked at each other and back at Widow.

The higher-ranked one said, "But look at your clothes. Why aren't you dressed like a bodyguard?"

"I'm dressed to blend in. These are street clothes. I'm not official."

"Not official?"

"Yes. Mr. Haspman pays me himself. Out of pocket."

Suddenly, the two women looked intrigued.

The quiet one asked, "Why?"

Widow leaned in closer. He tried to give the appearance that he had all the secrets.

"Mr. Haspman has gambling debts. He's afraid of action being taken against him."

They both nodded.

Widow knew he was pulling this whole story out of his ass, but they bought it. He expected they might because if they knew Haspman, then they knew he was not on the up and up. Having gambling debts to the wrong people, and being afraid of those same people, wasn't that farfetched.

The ladies nodded along, and the higher-ranked one said, "Well, you'd better get on with your work, Mr. Oleg."

"Just Oleg, ma'am. No need for formalities. You'll be seeing me around."

The two women laughed and smiled at him.

Widow asked, "But do me a favor. Keep it to yourselves for now. I don't want to blow my cover."

They nodded along and left.

Widow breathed a sigh of relief and looked back into the back of the truck's bed. There was some kind of canopy stuffed all the way to the front. It might've been a cover for the truck. Other than that, and a few shreds of plastic here and there, the bed was empty.

Widow looked around once again to make sure no one saw what he was about to do. No one was looking. The two women had walked away to their own cars.

Once they were a lot farther, Widow climbed into the bed and shut the tailgate. He didn't fasten the last panel down because he needed it open to climb back out again.

He waited for Haspman to come down and drive him away.

23

THAT NIGHT, Tunney was in his favorite chair with his favorite coffee mug; only it had whiskey in it and not much coffee. His second wife wasn't home. She was staying at her sister's for the week. It was part a family thing on her side and part they were taking some space, for the moment. Not a divorce thing, not yet. It was just a sort of vacation from each other.

It's nothing to be concerned about, she had told him.

I'll be back next week, she had said.

Tunney was trying not to think about it. He was trying to relax, but his thoughts kept drifting to Widow and Eggers.

Maybe he had made a mistake.

Maybe he should call Widow, and help the guy.

He drank little of the whiskey before he got a phone call from someone claiming to have information about Eggers and the fifty million dollars.

The number was set to private. The voice sounded muffled. The caller acted scared. It was a man's voice. He asked Tunney to come now and alone. He claimed he felt safer with just Tunney and no one else.

Tunney wasn't born yesterday, so naturally, he took his gun. And he texted Aker about the whole thing, which ended with Aker asking him to check in after.

Tunney changed into something more professional than his sweatpants. Then he fired up the BMW and drove to the address the caller had given him.

The address seemed safe enough. It was to a busy mall about forty minutes west. Tunney got on Two-Ten and headed north. When he got to Four Ninety-Five, he merged and headed over the bridge to Virginia.

It was after the bridge that he noticed a black Escalade. It tailed him for another few minutes. They were obvious about it, which made him wonder if it was a cop.

But if they were cops, then they must've been someone federal like the Secret Service. Escalades were too expensive for police departments to purchase for their detectives.

The other thing that made him think of cops was that the driver was tailing him, and it was obvious, which meant they wanted him to notice.

Only Feds did that. It was an act of intimidation, or they were trying to get a good look at his tags to check to see if they had the right vehicle and the right target.

Tunney wasn't sure who they were until he passed the third mile marker after the bridge and the road traffic waned. That was when blue lights flashed out of the Escalade's grille.

Tunney looked in the rearview, trying to get a look inside the windshield, but the headlamps were too bright. He blinked and changed his attention to the road. He saw a nice, lengthy section of shoulder ahead and he flipped on his hazard lights. He slowed and pulled off to the shoulder.

The Escalade followed him. He stopped. His brake lights shone out over the gravel behind him.

The Escalade pulled up directly behind him about four meters apart, nose to tail. The blue lights flashed. Blue light washed above the trees over a ridge to Tunney's right. He reached toward the radio and clicked a button to turn it off.

He used his gun hand to reach into his coat and unsnap a buckle on his holster shoulder rig. He brandished his gun and held it down below his door. His finger was in the trigger guard. Being left-handed would make it hard for him to draw it up and fire to his left, but he could fire at the passenger side.

When a Fed comes out of the passenger side of a vehicle, it's hard to tell which side they'll approach. The whole choice was fifty-fifty. But he'd also never slipped the BMW into park, which gave him the ability to slam the gas and peel out of there fast—if he needed to.

He watched in his rearview as the Escalade idled.

Dust rose and wafted in the headlamps' beams.

The driver didn't get out, but the passenger door opened, and Tunney saw a figure step out. It was a man. He walked out of the Escalade, out in front of the nose. He crossed between the two vehicles and cut through the wafting dust and the blue lights.

He crossed over to the BMW and around to Tunney's side.

He stopped at Tunney's door and knocked on the window.

Tunney hit the button, and the window streamed down.

The man knelt so Tunney could get a look at him.

The guy reached into his back pocket and pulled out a wallet. He flipped it open, held it out two-handed.

Tunney looked at it. He saw a badge and an official ID behind a milky plastic cover. He read the guy's name out loud. Then, he asked, "NCIS?"

The guy closed the wallet and returned it to his back pocket.

"That's right, sir. Are you Special Agent Brigs Tunney?"

"Former. I'm not with the Bureau anymore. I'm retired now."

"Of course. Well, it's nice to meet you."

"I didn't think you guys had jurisdiction out here in the civilian world. What's going on?"

"We do when it comes to sailors. We got jurisdiction anywhere when it involves the Navy."

"And the Marines?" Tunney asked.

"That's right."

"I've seen the TV show."

The guy made a face that ended with a little grin, like he was embarrassed.

"That stupid show. It's the worst thing to happen to us."

"Really?"

"It was better back when we were an enigma. When the public knew nothing about us."

Tunney nodded, kept his finger in his gun's trigger housing.

The NCIS agent said, "I'm sure you know. Hollywood is always getting shit wrong about the FBI."

"I'm not with the FBI anymore."

"Yeah. You said that. Still, they get shit wrong about private eyes too."

"That's true. So, what can I do for you?"

"We need to talk with you. It's about your client."

"My client?"

"Commander Eggers."

"He's dead, you know?"

"That's what we need to discuss with you. We think he was murdered."

"Murdered?"

Tunney eased up on the trigger.

He muttered to himself, "Widow *was* right."

The NCIS agent took a whiff of Tunney and asked, "You been drinking?"

"Just one."

The NCIS agent nodded.

"Well, that's okay. It's understandable. Can I ask where you're headed?"

"I'm headed to meet with someone."

"Is it about Eggers?"

Tunney paused a beat and decided to tell the truth.

"It is. Anonymous caller."

"Yeah. I was afraid of that."

"You know who it is?"

"I suspect it's the guy who killed Eggers. But listen..."

The agent paused because a cluster of headlights came up from behind them and shone across them. He waited till the cars passed and spoke.

"Listen, let's talk somewhere before you meet this person. I need to tell you something. Maybe we can help each other."

"Okay."

"Great! Follow us."

"Okay."

The agent backed away from the car window and returned to the Escalade the same way he had approached.

After his door shut, the driver switched off the blue lights. The Escalade backed up, the front wheels turned, and the vehicle merged out onto the road. It started out slowly, waiting for Tunney, who waited till they couldn't see inside the front cabin so he could holster his weapon.

The Escalade sped up as soon as Tunney was behind them.

They drove on, passing more mile markers and two more off-ramps, before the Escalade's turn signal flashed. The driver slowed and waited for Tunney to do the same before moving on.

Tunney followed them off the interstate and down a long, winding country road until they came to an abandoned gas station. The Escalade slowed and pulled into the gravel lot, kicking up dirt and grit.

Tunney was getting a bad feeling in the pit of his stomach.

He looked around.

At one time, the gas station had been a full-service place. But now it was just a ghost station. The pumps were long rusted over. The signs and posters were all faded away from years of weather. The cable that dinged was still there. It ran from the pumps up toward the main hub and vanished into the gravel.

The only sign anywhere that was still legible was for ice. It was above an old ice machine that was covered in dirt and mud.

The Escalade parked off beyond the derelict pumps and stopped.

Tunney pulled up behind the Escalade and slipped the BMW into park. He felt that pinch in the pit of his stomach again. He knew that feeling. He felt leery about cutting the engine off and getting out of the car. The Escalade's doors opened, and two men stepped out. They left their engine running as well.

The driver was a burly bald guy. He was thick, like a tree. The passenger was the agent he'd already met.

The agent stepped to the rear of the Escalade and leaned on the cargo door. He waved at Tunney to get out.

"Come on out."

The bald guy smiled.

It didn't feel right. He thought about texting Widow. He thought about calling him. But he didn't. Part of him felt paranoid, which made him feel a little stupid.

He left the keys in the ignition with the engine running and got out of the BMW. He looked at the agents.

The agent he'd met waved him over again.

"Come on. We ain't got all night."

Tunney nodded and approached.

The agent he'd met said something to the bald guy that Tunney didn't hear.

The bald guy stepped into the beams of the BMW and offered a friendly smile and hand for Tunney to shake.

Tunney took it out of social habit and shook it. But he realized his mistake after it was too late.

Tunney was left-handed. His gun was in a shoulder holster, adjusted to be drawn out left-handed.

Suddenly, the bald guy's big smile turned to a grin, and he clamped on Tunney's gun hand and jerked him into him. Tunney came up off his feet a little.

The bald guy slammed his head straight into Tunney's nose, breaking it.

Tunney's nose *cracked* in the stillness. All three men heard it. Tunney felt it.

It rocked him to his core. He felt faint. The blow was so hard he didn't even realize it had knocked him off his feet and onto his back.

A second after he realized it, the bald guy had already drawn his weapon and tossed it to the other agent.

Tunney's vision was blurry, half from his eyes watering over and half from the dizziness.

The bald guy stood over him.

The other agent said, "Get his phone."

The bald guy knelt and combed through Tunney's pockets until he found his phone. He pulled it out of Tunney's coat pocket and tossed it back to the other agent.

Blood streamed out of Tunney's broken nose; unlike any other wound he'd ever had before.

The bald guy stepped back into the beams from the BMW and watched as the guy with the forgettable face sifted through Tunney's phone, which was not password protected. Not that it would've made a difference. They would've gotten the passcode out of him.

After several long seconds, the bald guy asked a question.

"Anything interesting?"

"Not really. There's no communication with the stranger: Jack Widow."

They had finally gotten Widow's name, his Naval record, and they knew about Unit Ten, in parts. Bank accounts as big as their clients could buy any information.

The guy with the forgettable face slipped Tunney's phone into his pants pocket and looked at the bald guy and then down to where Tunney was, only he wasn't there.

"Where did he go?"

The bald guy sidestepped to see beyond the BMW's head-lamps and saw a trail of blood from where Tunney had been lying to the car's driver's side door.

Tunney was pulling himself up by the door handle.

"Where are you going?" the bald guy asked.

Just then, Tunney released the handle; his back slid down the side of the car. He reached down his pants leg and jerked up the cuff.

The guy with the forgettable face moved to the passenger side of the BMW. He was looking in through the passenger window.

He watched as Tunney pulled up his pants leg to grab a small firearm in an ankle holster.

He shouted to the bald guy.

"Milo! Gun!"

Milo Sathers was the bald guy's real name. He heard the guy with the forgettable face, and he sidestepped farther to the right.

Tunney drew a small gun and fired it in Milo's direction.

He squeezed the trigger in rapid succession. He blind-fired. Bullets hit the rear of the Escalade, shattering the taillights, slamming into the bumper. The rear window shattered after three bullets burst through it.

But none of the bullets hit Sathers or the guy with the forgettable face. Instead, Tunney's backup gun clicked empty.

Sathers stepped back into view and sauntered over to Tunney.

He reached down, knocked the backup gun away, and kneed Tunney square in the broken nose.

Tunney let out a scream. Sathers bunched up his shirt and lifted him, one-handed, off the ground.

He looked right into Tunney's battered and bruised face and spoke.

"That was a big mistake, my friend."

The guy with the forgettable face appeared from behind Sathers and stared into Tunney's eyes.

It was obvious to Tunney that he was the guy in charge.

Tunney asked, "Are you going to kill me?"

The guy with the forgettable face didn't answer that.

He said, "We've got some questions for you?"

"I don't know nothing."

"You know about the fifty million dollars in stocks. You know about Eggers."

"Yeah, but I know nothing about him."

"That's okay. My questions aren't about Eggers. My questions are about Jack Widow."

They questioned Tunney for over an hour before he gave up any information. And then they shot him in the head and left him for dead.

24

THE RIDE in Haspman's Raptor lasted only about fifteen minutes from start to finish. But once the Raptor was safely parked in Haspman's driveway, with the engine off and truck locked, Widow pulled back the panel cover over the bed and peeked out.

What he saw threw him for a loop at first because he had gone from DC to the middle of the English countryside.

All around him were acres of wooded fields and rolling hills and darkness.

At first, he thought he had been drugged and tricked and put on a plane, taken out to the New England countryside. But then he veered his view to the right and saw DC city lights on the horizon.

He scanned the terrain and saw a neighbor's house off in the distance. It looked huge. He pulled himself out of the truck's bed and stood up straight. That was when he saw the house that Haspman had stopped at.

It looked more like a large villa in the south of France than a house in DC.

The house was built of huge concrete blocks and brick. It looked to be around five thousand square feet. He guessed maybe it was five bedrooms. Widow hoped Haspman didn't have a family. He saw no other signs of anyone else living there. There was no other car in the driveway. And the house had a cold, empty look to it like it hadn't seen a woman's touch in decades.

On the front end, where Haspman presumably entered, was a large round section of house that on a small castle would've been called the keep.

"Jesus," Widow muttered to himself.

Widow was in a neighborhood called Massachusetts Avenue Heights. Looking around, he guessed the average house for sale there was skyward of a million dollars, maybe two million.

With the Rolex, the Raptor, and now this property, Widow figured it was safe to assume Haspman had another source of income. No way did he afford all this on his salary.

Widow turned his attention to the front door. It was a huge thing, solid wood. He wasn't busting it down; that was for sure.

He scanned the windows. They were small and all over the building. Most were dark, but there was a light glowing on the main floor.

The Raptor was parked on a driveway facing the entrance. To the left, the driveway veered off to a garage, also made of solid concrete and brick.

Widow approached the garage, but stopped in his tracks when he noticed an outdoor floodlight over the garage. He figured it had a motion sensor.

He looked to the right. The front yard was on a slope. The ground floor of the house was built into the side of a hill. The upper floors, which he wasn't sure numbered two or three because of the windows and the layout, were above the hill.

Widow circled the perimeter, staying more than sixty feet from the edges of the walls in case there were more motion lights.

He walked the landscape slowly and steadily, like the tortoise versus the hare. The grass was damp. The air was brisk.

He saw his breath as he exhaled.

Widow was unarmed, which was both good and bad. Technically, Haspman could shoot him just for trespassing. The good part of being unarmed was that if Widow sensed a gun pointed at him, his reflex was to fire back, and he didn't miss. But he wouldn't want to kill Haspman, at least not at this point.

The bad part was that if Haspman shot him, he'd be dead. And he didn't want that.

It was worth the risk because he knew Haspman wasn't clean. The missing video feed from the traffic cameras was enough to tell him that much. Throw in the Rolex, the Raptor, and this house, and he had enough evidence to get a warrant— if he were still in the warrant-getting game.

Widow needed to do a little recon before making his presence known. So he continued to check out the perimeter.

He climbed the hill alongside the house and entered into backyard territory. That was when he made his first mistake.

In the backyard, chained to a post, was the biggest Doberman pinscher mix Widow had ever seen in his life.

The dog had been resting his head in the grass when Widow was in view. Suddenly, it reared its head, stared in his direction, and jumped to its feet. It barked like a rabid dog. It took off running straight at him.

Widow hated seeing a dog on a chain, but this time he was grateful, because the dog ran to the end of its chain and stopped. It barked and raged like it was bloodthirsty.

So much for checking the rest of the perimeter.

A light flashed on through a rear window, and then a light came on over a back entrance.

Widow eased himself down the hill and back around to the front of the house.

He heard Haspman open the backdoor and yell at the dog to stop barking.

Widow came back to the driveway and decided to just go at this the easy way. He walked right up to the front door and rang the doorbell.

A flurry of sounds followed from behind the door.

Haspman cursed at the dog from the back of the house. He slammed the backdoor and walked through the house, down the stairs, and stopped at the front door.

Widow rang the bell again and stepped to the side and hugged the wall, staying out of view of the peephole.

He heard Haspman's voice.

"Who's there?"

Widow didn't answer.

Haspman unlocked the deadbolt and wrenched the door open fast.

Widow saw the barrel of a shotgun. It stuck out of the open doorway first. Haspman stepped out, following the weapon, still in his fire marshal jumpsuit, the matching hat, and dark-framed glasses. He still wore the Rolex and the expensive shoes and overpowering cologne.

Widow supported every responsible American's Second Amendment right. On paper, Haspman could shoot him, and he would be in the right. But Widow also was against the murder of his brothers and sisters, both in and out of uniform.

In a fast, violent explosion of force, Widow bounced off the wall and clamped down on the barrel of the shotgun with one hand. He jerked it forward and away, ripping Haspman's trigger finger out of the trigger housing, which was the goal. He didn't want the man firing the weapon, even if it wasn't pointed at him. The house was on more than one acre of land, maybe two, but the gun blast would've been heard by the neighbors.

And with the same explosion of force, Widow elbowed Haspman right in the jaw. Any fighter in the world worth his salt—boxers, MMA fighters, brawlers, street fighters, and SEALs—knew that being struck in the jaw in a certain way, with a certain amount of force and power, could rock a man to his core. It could disorient, discombobulate, disenfranchise, disembody, and disconnect a man from all his senses.

It could make you forget the day of the week. Make you forget where you were. It could make you forget who you were.

The elbow that Widow threw into Haspman's jaw wasn't full force. It wasn't powerful enough to make him forget. But it was enough to throw the guy's center of gravity out of whack.

Haspman stumbled backward and back into the open doorway. He slammed into a table in the foyer, knocking over some trinkets and knickknacks. One of them was a tabletop plant in a vase.

It shattered on the ground. Dirt and plant went all over the floor underneath the table.

Widow said, "Oops. I hope that wasn't expensive."

He took a quick glance around the street. It was still empty. No passing cars. No prying eyes.

Widow looked at the shotgun. He almost didn't recognize it at first. It was a modified Remington 870. Black. Pump-action. Reliable. But this one had some after-market modifications to it.

Widow two-handed it, one hand on the pistol grip, one on the pump. He pumped it. No shell ejected. He thumbed the breech bolt and saw a shell, and released it. The weapon was loaded, pumped, and ready to go.

He looked down at Haspman, who was gripping his jaw, moving it from side to side as if he was trying to set it back into place.

Haspman's vision might've been a little out of sorts because of the elbow to the jaw, but he recognized Widow from his size and height. Then he recognized Widow's voice.

Widow said, "You gotta pump the action to load a shell in it. Otherwise, it's useless. What were you planning to do? Slap an intruder with it?"

Haspman stared up at him.

"Widow?"

That was the first thing he asked before he panicked. He scrambled away, crabwalking to Widow's left, past the foyer, back into the house.

Widow followed him into the house. He trail-carried the shotgun in one hand. He didn't point it at Haspman. He didn't want the guy to say he had pointed a shotgun at him in front of a jury someday—if it ever came to that.

Haspman continued to crabwalk. Widow followed him. He was already a tower over most people, but with Haspman shrunk down to the size of a toddler, Widow looked massive from that angle.

Like a lot of tough guys Widow had confronted, Haspman shrank down to a coward's level.

"Oh, no! Please don't kill me! Please!"

"Why would I kill you?"

But Haspman didn't answer that. He just kept going on and on. The same plea. The same fear in his voice.

"Please don't kill me! Please don't kill me!"

Widow looked around the house for signs of life. There weren't any. A fire was burning in a gas fireplace. That he hadn't noticed from the outside, which made him feel a bit like he was losing his touch.

He saw no other signs of humans living in the house. No wife. No children. All the photographs scattered around the place were of Haspman and Haspman alone. No other family photos.

Suddenly, Widow felt sorry for the guy. Not that he had children or a wife of his own, but at least he wasn't stuck alone in a huge house. Widow saw it more like a prison than a thing to cherish.

From the looks of the place, the only living thing that Haspman shared his life with was a dog, and even that was chained up outside like a wild animal and not a companion.

Next, he scanned the house for weapons. Above the fireplace, he saw twin rifles. They were on display, and they looked like antiques from the Old West. They were well cared for. The wood stocks were clean and shiny. The metal was polished to a shine.

They looked like they cost a fortune. Haspman had probably bought them in a sumptuous collector's auction.

Once he stepped beyond the foyer, the main part of the house revealed a huge open floor plan. The main room was enormous. The twenty-foot ceiling had oak beams above his head. The furniture all matched, like it was bought straight out of a country home magazine for the rich.

The rifles above the fireplace weren't the only collector's items. The walls were littered with them. There were rapiers, old swords, more rifles, and old six-shooters. Even an eighteenth-century cannon was displayed on a table off in the distance.

In a den to the west, where a second fireplace lay dark, Widow saw hunting trophies all over the walls. There were mounted elk, deer, moose, pronghorns, and even one lion's head.

Widow looked back at Haspman and doubted with almost full certainty that he ever killed any of them. The possibility of it just seemed unbelievable to him.

By now, Haspman had stopped crabwalking backward because he ran into the back of a huge sofa, which was across from another matching sofa. At the end of both were a set of matching lounge chairs.

"Please don't kill me!" Haspman begged.

Widow said, "Get up!"

Haspman froze for a moment, but then he saw Widow's eyes, and he rose to his feet. He put his hands above his head as if Widow had been pointing the shotgun at him.

Widow asked, "Got any hidden weapons?"

"What?"

"Are there any other guns on this floor?"

Haspman was silent.

"Haspman! Guns?"

Haspman said, "On the walls."

"Any working firearms stashed around here for home protection?"

Haspman pointed at an end table near the fireplace, not far from a side door that led outside.

Widow kept his eyes on Haspman and walked over to the table. He jerked open the drawer and saw a Browning 1911 handgun. It was olive green, which meant it was special ordered. It burned him up a little.

Widow's color was Navy blue, always would be, but olive green was Army, not Navy, but still a part of his military brotherhood. Haspman was no military man. That was obvious.

Widow scooped up the 1911 and closed the drawer. He turned back to Haspman, who was still frozen in the same place, still had both hands up above his head.

Widow said, "Put your hands down."

Haspman put his hands down.

Widow said, "Take a seat on the sofa."

"Which one?"

Widow didn't answer that. He just stared back at Haspman.

Haspman took that as his answer and moved to the sofa that faced Widow and dumped himself onto the plush cushion. It was so soft that he sank into it.

Widow walked around to the other sofa. He stopped in front of it and faced Haspman. He stuffed the 1911 into the waistband of his jeans and two-handed the shotgun. He pumped it rapidly. Unused shells flew out of the ejection port. They bounced off a huge stone coffee table that rested between the sofas. Each bounced and rolled off the tabletop onto a rug underneath.

He pumped the shotgun until it was empty. Then he set it aside against the sofa.

He took out the 1911 and ejected the magazine. He racked the slide to eject the chambered bullet. There was none. The gun was completely empty.

He set the empty 1911 on the sofa and dumped himself down onto the sofa next to it. He faced Haspman. Widow sat up straight as best he could and tried to maintain good posture; slouching during an interrogation was never good optic. But it was hard because the sofa was about the most comfortable thing he could remember ever sitting on in his life.

Widow ran his hand along the cushion next to him, keeping his fingers between his thigh and the 1911.

He said, "This is nice. Where did you get it?"

"What?"

"The sofas. Where did you get them?"

"My interior decorator picked them out. I don't know where she got them."

"Interior decorator?"

"Yeah."

"Tell me, Haspman. How much does the leading fire marshal get paid?"

"What?"

"My stopping salary in the SEALs was eighty-five hundred a month. Which I didn't get to keep because my pay from NCIS overrode my SEAL salary."

Haspman didn't speak. He just stared at Widow, confused. It was more than confusion. It was a word that Widow had said. One of the words had gotten his attention.

Widow said, "I ended up making about ninety K a year when I finished my career with NCIS. And never in a million years, would I have earned enough to hire a decorator. So, I'm curious, how does a fire marshal afford a small castle in the most expensive neighborhood in DC? How did you pay for these antique guns? These sofas? That Rolex? The truck?"

Haspman said nothing.

Widow closed his eyes a moment and breathed in. He made it look like he was trying to hold himself back from unleashing on Haspman. It was a mental tactic. And it worked, because when he opened his eyes, Haspman was giving him his undivided attention.

Widow said, "I'm only going to ask you this once. If you lie to me, I'll know."

Haspman nodded.

"Where's the video feed?"

Widow watched Haspman's face. His eyes darted up and down. He stared at the stone coffee tabletop like he was reading from it.

Haspman was working out his answer in his head. He thought of the different scenarios, different lies he could tell. And Widow saw all of it. But in the end, he came back around to the truth.

Widow knew because he saw Haspman's shoulder slump down. His head dropped, and his eyes teared up.

Finally, he spoke.

"I didn't know he was a sailor. I didn't know he served his country."

Haspman pressed a hand to his forehead like he was relieving the pressure from a head-splitting migraine.

Guilt had appeared on his face, and not because Widow was there. It was already there. Widow saw it. Haspman was hiding something. He knew that not just because of the CCTV camera feed, but also because of the look in Haspman's eyes.

Haspman broke down. He didn't burst into tears, but he turned a shade of red. It had become hard for him to speak.

He looked away from Widow.

Haspman asked, "You know about the traffic camera?"

"I do."

"Do the cops know?"

"They do."

Haspman cried this time. Only a couple of tears, not a full-blown sob. Part of it was guilt, maybe most of it. But part of it was knowing his life was about to be over. His cushy life, his career, his reputation, all of it was about to be destroyed once the cops traced the whole thing back to him.

Widow added, "It's only a matter of time before they figure it out. Erasing the video was a mistake. You left a trail."

"I had no choice. I had to get rid of the video."

Widow nodded and asked, "Why?"

"Look around. I've got a good life. I like money. Things. I did it for the money."

"I don't give a shit about that. I mean, why the video? What was on it?"

"I didn't kill him! You know? I didn't know they were going to kill him. I only knew my part after the fact."

"I know you didn't kill him. But who did? Tell me."

Haspman swallowed hard.

"The day before they killed Eggers. That's the first I ever saw of them before. They came here."

"They just showed up?"

"No. It was prearranged—a meeting. I got a call from a guy I've taken money from before. Nothing major. Nothing like this. Once, I took money from a street dealer. A nobody."

"You took a bribe?"

"It was the first time. It might've been two years ago. It was just a guy who fixes things. He deals with many people who need things covered up. Some Congressman burned down some failing restaurant he'd invested in. It was an insurance scheme. They paid me to look the other way. To fix the evidence and say it was all an accident. I did, and they collected from the insurance company. No real victim. But once I took that one bribe, the guy started hitting me up for all kinds of new schemes."

"Were they all insurance schemes?"

"They were—all but this one. But I didn't know. You gotta believe me, Widow. I didn't know they'd murdered a man. Not until I got the call."

Widow stayed quiet.

Haspman said, "Day before it happened. Two guys came to my house."

"You ever see them before?"

"No. Never."

"Did they tell you what you would do?"

Haspman paused a beat, and then he nodded. Shame smeared across his face.

He said, "I refused to be a part of it. At first. But I couldn't refuse."

"Why not?"

Haspman stared into Widow's eyes and told the truth.

"They had badges."

"What badges?"

And then the word that had gotten Haspman's attention came back out at Widow from Haspman's mouth.

"NCIS."

25

"Bull shit!" Widow said.

Widow knew all about lies. He knew liars. He had been one himself, in a way. Because he had worked undercover for most of his Navy career and his entire law enforcement career, he knew about lies. He knew how to spot a lie. Being in deep cover, you must have a strong center, a strong code, a strong moral compass. It's imperative because many of the bad guys that Widow had put away all thought they were right. The most dangerous ones were the ones who thought that they were on the right side. Most of them believed in whatever horrible crime they were committing. And they could be very convincing.

Without a strong code of right and wrong, Widow could've been seduced by some of them. Anyone could.

The lies were a dangerous thing. Some people could be so convincing with lies. They were masters of lies.

Widow had become a master of lies. But he only used it to protect what was right.

In the same way that a firearm, in the right hands, can protect the innocent and uphold justice, Widow used lies to uphold Navy justice. But in the hands of the enemy, lies were more deadly than a firearm. More deadly than firepower. More deadly than many bullets.

Being a master of lies, Widow knew a master liar when he saw one. And Haspman was no master liar. He wasn't lying at all. He was telling the truth, but that didn't make it any easier for Widow to stop himself from calling bullshit.

"It's not!" Haspman claimed.

Widow was quiet for a long second, and then he said, "I know. Did you get names?"

"I did. But those are fake. They told me their names were White and Black."

"You didn't read the names off their badges?"

"They showed me the badges first. I got scared. How often does the NCIS show up at your door? You know? I just saw the badges and let them inside. Then, I got their names."

"They were here? At your house?"

"Yes."

"You got any hidden security cameras anywhere?"

"In my home? No."

Worth a shot, Widow thought.

Widow asked, "Tell me what happened."

"They rang my doorbell one night."

"When?"

Haspman's fear subsided a bit, and his eyes floated upward. He thought for a moment.

"It was maybe a week ago. Or six days."

Widow nodded.

Haspman continued, "They kind of pushed their way in. They were...scary, Widow."

"Scary? How?"

"They were very scary! I was terrified of them the moment I laid eyes on them—especially one of them. He was like an apparition. Like a guy who could be in a room, and you wouldn't know it. Or you'd forget it afterward."

Widow believed him. He could see the fear in his eyes, like a man who had seen a ghost.

Haspman paused a beat and breathed in and out.

He said, "I should've known better. I shouldn't have opened the door. NCIS badges? What do they mean to me? Nothing. They don't have jurisdiction over me. I should've said no, but I didn't. Once they were inside, that's when they mentioned the guy I knew by name. They said they were here on his suggestion. They told me I'd get a call to go to an arson scene. They said I'd have to declare it an accident. But I didn't know they were going to kill a guy. I swear to that!"

Widow believed him, but didn't tell him that. Why give his conscience the reprieve? He didn't deserve it. Plus, Widow wasn't in the game of making people feel better about their sins.

Widow asked, "When did you know they were going to kill Eggers?"

"When I got the call from MPD. That's when I knew. They told me that a homeless man was dead in the park. Burned alive. It was the right location and the right timeframe the NCIS guys had told me. But they didn't give me many details about what I was supposed to say. So I improvised. Once I got there, I knew he'd died horribly. But he was already dead. What was I supposed to do? I was already in too deep. I took their money."

"What did they offer you?"

"Money."

"How much?"

"Fifty thousand dollars was their first offer."

"But?"

"I got them up to one hundred thousand—their badges and coming to me, offering me money to lie. I mean. I knew they were crooked, which meant deeper pockets, which meant more money for me. So, I asked for a hundred. They accepted without batting an eye, like they had cash already waiting in the wings. If I had known what I was getting myself into, I would've asked for more. Much more. Believe me. Every day, I've been pissing my pants, waiting for the cops to show up and see through my lies. But they didn't. Not yet. It wasn't the cops who came to me. It was you."

Widow asked, "Did they call you and ask you to destroy the traffic camera feeds? Or did you figure that out on your own?"

"They called me. Afterward. Not sure why they didn't do it beforehand. If they knew where they were going to burn that poor bastard, you'd think they would've mentioned that. It might've been easier to find someone to just turn them off beforehand. But I don't think they had time."

Widow just stared at him.

Haspman continued, "Maybe they weren't exactly sure where they were going to kill him? Maybe they didn't know it until they did it? When they finally had him alone."

Widow didn't ask if Haspman had erased the footage because he already knew. The guys down at Metro had confirmed it was Haspman's login and ID stamp that was last used to view that's camera's footage.

But there was a question he wanted to ask.

"Did you make a copy?"

Haspman paused a second too long.

"No."

"Bullshit! You made a copy!"

Widow didn't raise his voice, but he used his cop voice, which came from deep down beyond the throat. It came from the diaphragm. It was the voice he'd learned way back from his mother, a small-town sheriff, and then from Quantico.

He said, "Where is it?"

"On a flash drive. Upstairs."

"Get it! Now!"

Widow rose from the sofa, scooped up the 1911 and put it and the magazine into his front jeans pocket. He didn't want to leave it out for Haspman to ditch him somewhere upstairs just so he could make his way back down to it.

Widow motioned with his hand for Haspman to get up.

Haspman remained seated and looked up at Widow like he was waiting for further instructions.

"Let's go!"

Haspman's shoulders slumped, and his head lowered. He got up off the couch and led the way to the far end of the room, past a large kitchen to the back of the house. He turned at a pillar and led to a staircase, tucked into one corner of the house.

Widow followed him up the stairs. They passed a landing and Haspman stopped, pointed to the right to an open doorway that looked like a bedroom.

Widow said, "After you."

Haspman nodded and entered. Widow followed.

It must've been Haspman's master bedroom, which was like his office in that it was a suite so big and lush that it looked more like an apartment than a bedroom.

The room was big. Near the middle, against the wall, was a huge California king bed. It had an enormous wooden headboard and footboard. Like the sofas downstairs, it was plush and covered with pillows. It looked like a bed suitable for a king.

Haspman was a walking cliché of arrogance and vanity. It almost put knots in Widow's stomach just to be in the guy's private bedroom.

Haspman pointed at a huge set of oak dresser drawers.

"It's there. Top left drawer."

"Is that your underwear drawer?"

"Yes."

"You get it."

Haspman paused and looked at Widow.

"You sure? What if I keep a gun in the drawer?"

Widow brandished the 1911, palmed the magazine back into the gun, and racked the slide, loading the chamber.

He held the gun down and out in front of him. It was ready to fire. He kept his finger out of the trigger housing and made eye contact with Haspman.

"Now, get it. One hand. No sudden movements, or you get a bullet."

Haspman shivered, not like a leaf in the wind. It was more like a twig near an oncoming train.

Haspman walked to the dresser and pulled open the drawer he'd pointed at. He did it all good and slow. He was sure that Widow wasn't bluffing.

He reached into the drawer, shuffling around his own clean underwear, and pulled out a flash drive. He held it up to Widow.

"This is it."

Widow waved the gun and said, "Close the drawer."

Haspman did as he was told. Then he turned back to Widow.

Widow asked, "Where's your computer?"

"Downstairs. In the den."

"After you."

Haspman carried the flash drive and led the way back out of the absurd bedroom. He led the way back down the stairs and turned toward the huge great room they had sat in earlier. Then, he stopped and turned right, leading Widow to the den with the dead animals lining the upper walls.

Widow hadn't noticed it before, but the den was at a sunken level. He had to step down a couple of steps.

"There," Haspman said and pointed at another obnoxiously large desk with a MacBook opened right at the center.

"Okay. Boot it up."

"Okay."

Haspman circled the desk and rolled out a chair and sat down. He tapped the keys, and the MacBook came to life. He inserted the flash drive and scrolled his fingers on the trackpad. He clicked and dragged, and a screen popped up on the computer screen.

"Here it is."

Widow walked to the desk, keeping an eye on Haspman's hands. But Haspman didn't move. He had complied completely—so far.

Widow stopped and stood over Haspman's shoulder. He looked at the screen. A video player was up on screen with a thumbnail. It was at an angle, the angle of the one traffic camera he saw at Lincoln Park. The view was as he had thought. Mainly, it encompassed the road, angled to see license plates, but the park, the bench, and the cars parked along the street were all in view.

Widow said, "Play it."

Haspman scrolled his fingers along the trackpad, and a small arrow traced over the video player's play button. He clicked it.

The video rolled. It was set on the exact moment that Widow needed to see. They didn't have to fast-forward through hours of footage.

"I thought you said you didn't watch it?"

"I didn't. I watched till I saw them arrive."

Widow watched the video. They both did. Seventy-five percent of the screen was footage of a still, nighttime street. But the top-left corner of the screen played like footage from a different film, spliced into a boring city street.

They watched the whole thing, the whole violent attack, from start to finish. There was no sound. They watched it all unfold like a macabre silent film. The first thing Widow noticed was the black Escalade that had been following him around. It pulled up along one of the exits and parked on the street. He couldn't get the plate number. It was out of view.

But it was the same Escalade that he had seen earlier—no doubt about it. He watched the four guys climb out. He saw them go through the park like they knew where their target was. He watched them make a perimeter like Special Forces guys would do. And he watched one of them pour whiskey all over Eggers as he slept on the bench. He couldn't see the guy's face. He was too far away, and the quality of the video was subpar.

He couldn't see any of their faces. The only distinguishing feature he could make out was that one of them was bald and burly, and that was about it. The video's graininess was so bad, with it being night that he couldn't even confirm that all four guys were white. He was sure about the main one, the one who stood over Eggers, but that was it.

He saw Eggers wake up, shaken, with the man standing over him. Then something strange happened. The man pulled something out and put it in Eggers' face.

"Pause it," Widow said.

Haspman clicked the trackpad, and the video froze.

"What?" he asked.

Widow stared at the screen.

"Okay. Play."

Haspman clicked play.

Widow saw the man standing over Eggers shove the object into the guy's face, and then it lit his face up.

Cell phone, Widow thought. The guy was Facetiming with someone else.

Eggers didn't seem to recognize the guy standing over him, but he definitely recognized the face on the phone. Widow couldn't quite see Eggers' facial expression. He was too far away and too far out of focus. But Widow knew body language, and Eggers' body language was of a man who was suddenly frightened to the core.

The video played on.

Widow and Haspman watched Eggers fighting back, and his attempt to run, and then the bottle thrown at him, shattering over the back of his head. The bad guys restrained him to the bench, and they burned him alive.

It was ghastly. He stopped the playback as soon as they saw the four guys return to the Escalade and drive off. Widow noted the direction they went and the driver behind the wheel, the bald, burly guy.

Haspman teared up.

In a hushed, shamed voice, he said, "Horrible. They didn't just kill him. They executed him."

Haspman's head fell into the palms of his hands. He wept.

Widow guessed seeing the horrific deed being done wasn't something that Haspman had the stomach for. It was one thing to take a bribe to cover up someone else's crime when you didn't have to witness it. It was another thing to see it play out.

Haspman's guilt got the better of him. He started pleading with his face buried in the palms of his hands, muffling what he was saying.

"I didn't know. I didn't know. You gotta believe me!"

He was quiet for a second. Then he looked up at Widow.

He said, "I think I'm going to be sick."

He swiveled in his chair and went for a trashcan at the side of the desk.

Widow backed away.

Haspman threw up in the trashcan.

After his stomach was empty, he sat back up straight in his chair. He just stared at the computer screen. He said nothing for a long moment.

Widow stayed where he was. He let Haspman have his moment to gather his thoughts.

Finally, Haspman stared at Widow's reflection in the monitor and spoke.

"I took their money. Sure. I've done that before. But I never signed up for this. I never signed up to help..."

He went quiet again, swallowed hard.

"I never signed up to torture someone like that. You gotta believe me!"

Widow stayed quiet.

Haspman composed himself, pulling himself back together. He sniffled and wiped tears off his face.

Finally, the guilt subsided, and he did what most of the criminals Widow had encountered in the past did when caught. It all became about him again.

He asked, "What will happen to me now? You gonna turn me in?"

"I'm not a cop."

"You're letting me go free?"

"You're not free now."

"How do you mean?"

"You've taken their money. You helped cover up a murder of a US Navy commander, a highly decorated hero. His blood is on your hands now. Whether or not you like it, you'll always be tied to this. You'll never be free of it. It doesn't matter what a judge and jury do to you. It'll always be there because you can't reverse it. If you had stolen money, you could've given it back. That would've been something like making it right. But you can't reverse this."

Haspman said nothing. His eyes stared at Widow in the computer screen, blinking, searching for forgiveness. But it wasn't a crime for Widow to forgive.

Then Haspman changed the subject and asked a question that Widow hadn't heard before.

"What're you, a vigilante?"

Silence.

"An avenging angel or something?"

Silence.

Widow didn't know how to answer that. At one time, he could've said he was an NCIS agent, but now what was he?

He said, "I'm just a guy who doesn't like to see bad people get away with doing bad things."

"Are you going to kill me now?"

"*I'm* not going to kill you."

Widow's inflection highlighted the *I'm* part.

"Why did you say it like that?"

"I'm not going to break a sweat over a crooked piece of shit like you."

More body language as Haspman seemed to relax his shoulders, like a threat had been lifted from them.

Widow said, "*I'm* not going to kill you. But they will. Whoever these guys are. They will circle back to you. If they think you're compromised, which you are, then they won't be forgetting about you. Trust me."

In the monitor, Widow saw Haspman's face change to one he knew better than guilt. It was pure fear as the realization dawned on him. He had taken their money, not just to cover up their crimes, but also for his silence. And he had just broken that.

He turned to Widow and pleaded again.

"No! Protect me!"

"Why would I do that?"

"I can help you."

"How? You know who they are?"

"I can contact them. I got a phone number."

Haspman dug into his pockets, frantic like he was searching for something that he'd misplaced. Finally, he stopped when he couldn't locate it.

"It's in my phone. I swear. We can contact them. My phone is over there. On the sofa."

Widow didn't turn around to look. He pointed at the flash drive stuck out of a USB port in the MacBook.

He asked, "That the only copy?"

"Yes."

"Don't bullshit me."

"It's the only one. I swear."

"Give me the drive."

Haspman jerked the drive out of the MacBook, and the video player on screen vanished. He handed the drive to Widow, who took it and slipped it into his pocket.

Haspman asked, "Now what?"

"If I were you, I'd go straight to the MPD. If the badges these guys have are real, they'll come for you. The cops are your best hope. Ask for a cop named Shaw or Kidman. Either one."

"No! Wait! You've got to help me!"

"Help you do what?"

Haspman stood from the chair and faced Widow. He reached out, fast and grabbed at Widow's clothes like he had a heart attack.

Haspman spouted, "Protect me! You can protect me! The cops will arrest me!"

Widow clamped down on Haspman's arms and pinned them to his sides so he could no longer grab at Widow's clothes.

Widow said, "Protect you? I'm this close to throwing you out the window myself."

Haspman looked into his eyes and saw he was telling the truth. And Haspman gave a big and obvious nod so Widow would let go. He did.

Widow asked, "Where's the money?"

"What?"

"Where's the money they paid you?"

"My bank account."

"In *your* personal account?"

"No. It's in an offshore account."

"How long would it take you to transfer it?"

"Not long. I have access to it online 24/7. Maybe it'd take the bank a day or so."

"I want you to log in and google the Wounded Warrior Project. Click on their website."

"What's that?"

"A charity for homeless veterans."

Haspman shook his head.

"No! No! You can't make me!"

"Yes! Donate it! That'll clean your soul. You'll feel better."

In a hushed voice, Haspman asked, "How much of it?"

"All of it! Then turn yourself in! Go see Shaw. Or Kidman."

Widow kept a hand clamped on Haspman's shoulder and led him back to the sofa. They found Haspman's phone. Widow got the passcode from him so he could unlock it anytime he wanted, no fingerprint required. Then he led Haspman to the backdoor.

"What are we doing here?" Haspman asked.

"I'm going to leave now."

"But why the backdoor?"

Widow ignored the question. He said, "I'm going to check up on you tomorrow night. If that money isn't donated, I'm going to come back. If you make me come back, you won't be walking out of here alive. Understand?"

Haspman nodded and asked again, "Why are we at the backdoor?"

"There's one last thing."

Widow looked down at Haspman and smiled.

Even though Haspman was afraid more than once during this visit, the smile on Widow's face scared him most of all.

Five minutes later, Widow was walking back down Massachusetts Avenue Heights, passing through the empty, quiet streets, feeling good about himself.

At a stop sign, down the street, he saw a couple in a car who had pulled over to the side of the road because they saw a beautiful Doberman pinscher standing there, looking lost. He was friendly with them. He didn't bark at all. He looked like a dog who was happy to have escaped from somewhere.

Back at Haspman's house, the fire marshal was in his own backyard, chained by the neck from the same chain that his dog had been on, chained to the same tree.

The key to the chain was on the ground, nearly in reach. Widow had left it inches out of his grasp. Eventually, if he kept clawing toward it, something would give, and he'd reach it. By then, Widow would be long gone.

26

It took Widow twenty minutes to walk back to civilization. He came to a service station that was close to Haspman's house, yet seemed like a different zip code because the street corner it was on was busy. It was a major four-way stop.

Widow took out the burner phone Aker had given him and sifted through the home screen until he found an icon that looked like an address book. He opened it and found only one programmed number. It was Tunney's. He dialed it and waited.

The phone rang and rang until finally he got Tunney's voice on a voicemail.

He hung up, pocketed the phone, and went into the service station. The attendant behind the counter stopped what he was doing, which was staring at a magazine with a half-naked girl on the cover, and he stared at Widow. He had a blank expression on his face.

Widow realized he was still carrying Haspman's 1911 in his waistband. The butt was sticking out. He made eye contact with the service attendant and smiled, and lifted the bottom of his shirt up and draped it over the weapon.

He said, "Sorry. Forgot that was on me."

The attendant shrugged and went back to his magazine.

Widow turned and breathed a sigh of relief. The last thing that he wanted was for someone to call the police on him. How would he explain the gun that didn't belong to him?

He turned and threaded through the aisles and headed to the back of the store. He was hunting for the coffee counter, where he expected to find brewed coffee and stacked cups and a trashcan.

He found the coffee station, with the cups and the trashcan, but instead of brewed coffee, he found a handwritten sign taped to an empty coffee pot. It read: *Out of Order.*

Widow raised an eyebrow. He wasn't sure how coffee was out of order. His guess was it was because they ran out, didn't want to brew any, or possibly the machine was down.

He returned to the front of the store and stopped in front of the same attendant behind the same magazine, only on a different page.

"Coffee is out?"

"Yeah. The machine's down."

Widow nodded. Not that the attendant saw it. He stayed standing there for longer than he needed to, trying to make the guy look at him. Finally, he got the hint and glanced up at Widow.

"There's Red Bull in the back. Next to the sodas. Left refrigerator."

Widow arched an eyebrow.

"Red Bull?"

"Yeah. Better than coffee. It'll jar you awake."

Better than coffee? Widow thought.

He shook his head, dismissed the thought of infidelity to coffee.

He asked, "Any taxis come out this way?"

"No taxis. Not here. I never saw one. But you should get an Uber, anyway."

Widow nodded. He knew what Uber was, but he had no idea how to use it. He figured it was an app on the phone. He had a phone, but not the app.

He shrugged and headed back outside. He redialed Tunney's phone number and got the voicemail again.

This time he left a message.

"Tunney. Where are you? I've got something. Call me back. I need a ride."

He clicked off the phone and stood in the service station parking lot. The place wasn't busy, but a steady line of cars came in and got gas. Many drivers paid at the pump and never went inside. The attendant was free to continue staring at his magazine.

A few minutes later, Widow called Aker instead.

He dialed the number from Aker's business card and waited.

Aker answered the phone. Widow recognized his voice, only it sounded like he was upset.

"Hello?"

"Aker. It's Widow."

"Widow. Where are you?"

"I'm in Massachusetts Avenue Heights."

"What? What are you doing there?"

"I'll explain when I see you. Can you come get me? I've got something."

"Widow, I'm at the hospital right now."

"What? Why? Everything okay?"

"Tunney is here. He's in ICU."

"What? Why?"

"He tried to kill himself."

"What?"

"Yeah. That's what the police are saying so far. Apparently, he drank himself into a stupor and put a gun in his mouth. Only he lived. He's in a coma."

"That can't be true."

"I don't want to believe it. But that's all they're saying for now."

A black Escalade appeared in Widow's mind.

"It's not. He didn't shoot himself. Trust me."

"How do you know that?"

"I just do. Listen. I'm stranded out here. I need a ride."

"I'm all the way at Inova Mount Vernon Hospital."

"How far is that?"

"It's probably fifteen miles south of you. Give me your address. I'll get you an Uber."

Widow looked around for an address marker for the service station. He didn't see one, but he saw the street signs for the cross streets and gave them to Aker.

Aker said, "Okay. I'll text you the info on the car and driver and time. Be waiting. They're usually only minutes away from wherever you are."

"Okay. Do I need to pay the guy in cash?"

"What? No. It's an Uber."

"Oh, right."

"Call me when you're in the lobby if they give you shit about getting in."

Aker clicked off the call, and Widow slipped the phone into his pocket.

He guessed that the Uber driver would pick him up on the corner, closer to the street. So, he walked through the lot and stood on the corner.

27

WIDOW WAITED for the Uber on the corner. While he was thinking about it, he thought he'd give Metro a call, let them know about Haspman. He took out Aker's phone and googled the MPD switchboard's number. He got it and dialed. The phone rang once, and a desk clerk answered.

"Metro?"

Widow said, "I need to speak to a Detective Kidman."

"Hold, please," the desk clerk said, and the phone went to silence. Then it rang like he was being transferred. After five rings, the call went to voicemail.

Kidman's voice said, "This is Detective Kidman. I'm away from my desk. Leave a detailed message and I'll get back to you."

Then it beeped.

"Kidman, this is..." Widow paused a beat and said, "an anonymous tip. Fire Marshal Jay Haspman has admitted to committing several felonies, including conspiracy to cover up the murder of Navy Commander Henry Eggers. He also stole the traffic feed from a camera near Lincoln Park. You'd better pick him up. You can find him in his own backyard. He's got a big house in Massachusetts Avenue Heights."

Widow clicked off the call and slipped the phone back into his pocket.

He waited for another three minutes for the Uber. It arrived but didn't stop for him at the street corner. It pulled into the service station he was already in and waited. Before getting in the car, he went through a couple of amateur security checks with the guy. He checked the license plate number and the make and model of the vehicle, all provided by Aker.

The driver had the same name as the name provided by Aker via text message.

All measures checked out, but all measures could be faked. He could've stolen the car from the real driver. Or he could've had the same car and made fake plates for it. He could've lied about his name. Easy enough. But what he couldn't fake was his face.

Aker texted Widow a screenshot that must've been straight from the Uber app. It revealed all the information he needed to confirm the Uber was legitimate.

Widow got in the backseat. As that's what he'd done with taxi-cabs and police cars his whole life. Then he realized he could've sat in the front seat. Uber had no backseat-only policy in place. Not that he was aware of.

The ride was pretty pleasant—a lot more than he had expected it to be. The driver was friendly, and there were free water bottles and gum in the backseat.

If the guy had coffee in place, he would've left him a big cash tip. He tried to leave the guy a cash tip anyway, but the driver refused it. He cited they didn't accept cash. It was all done somewhere remotely through the app and credit cards and processed directly by Uber.

Widow thanked him and got out eighteen minutes later, on the steps of Inova Mount Vernon Hospital.

He entered through the main entrance, not the emergency room one, and passed through the lobby to a reception desk.

Instead of an attendant behind the counter, it was a security guard. Apparently, hospitals had given both jobs to one person, at least this one did.

He didn't ask about Tunney by name or what room he might be in because he remembered Aker said he was in the Intensive Care Unit. So he just asked for directions to that location.

The security guard gave him the directions and even pointed the way.

It was on the first floor.

Widow thanked him and moved on. He passed elevators and hallways and busy hospital staff.

It turned out he didn't need the security guard's directions anyway, because there were plenty of signs hanging high on the walls of every corridor. All of them pointed the way somewhere.

He found the ICU.

There were two large doors with windows in them that blocked the way. They didn't have handles. Looking through the door windows, he saw another security station with one guard on post.

On the wall next to the doors was a black box. It looked like it was for staff to scan their name badges. He imagined each badge had some kind of chip in it that opened the doors.

Apparently, he had to be buzzed in.

Widow knocked on the door and waved at the security guard. The guard stood up from his post reluctantly and walked over to the other side of the glass.

Widow could see by the expression on the guy's face that he was going to have to argue with the man for a while before he was going to open the door.

Luckily, he saw Aker in the background. Widow banged on the window loud, and Aker heard him and peered up.

The lawyer was in his after-work attire and not a suit and tie. He wore a golf shirt and chinos. The shirt was tucked in.

Aker saw Widow and said something to the guard, who turned and nodded. The guard went back to his post and pressed a button somewhere out of sight. The double doors buzzed.

The guard waved for Widow to come on through.

Widow pushed both doors open and stepped into the ICU.

Aker met him, and they shook hands.

"I'm so sorry," Widow said.

He could see by the look on Aker's face that the man was genuinely hurt and confused. His friend and colleague were in the hospital for shooting himself in the head—supposedly.

Aker said, "I don't understand, Widow. Why would he do this? What happened with you two today?"

"I've not seen him since this afternoon."

"Why did he do it? I don't understand."

Widow looked around. He was expecting to see police around. It was a gunshot wound to the head of a former FBI agent. He expected the police to have questions, even if it had been assumed to be a suicide attempt. But there were no cops around. Not in his line of sight, anyway.

Widow leaned in and said, "We went to the cops, gave them the evidence we had. There was a camera feed that got the whole thing on video. A traffic camera. The video had been erased."

"Erased? I don't understand."

"Tunney got the name of the last guy to access the traffic camera."

Aker nodded along.

Widow said, "It was the head fire marshal. We confronted the guy. He helped cover it up."

"Cover what up?"

Widow glanced around again. No listening staff. No listening cops. No sign of any listening ears.

"There's more going on here."

"Like what?"

"I don't know the whole puzzle yet. But I know for a fact that Tunney didn't shoot himself."

"The cops said he stank of alcohol. It was all over him. They said he drank himself into a stupor and went out to some abandoned gas station and shot himself."

"He didn't shoot himself."

"They found him hanging out of his car. His gun in hand."

"What was the gun?"

"I don't know. A handgun."

"What's the make and model?"

Aker shrugged.

Widow asked, "Was it a thirty-eight?"

"A what?"

"Was it a Glock?"

Aker thought for a minute until he answered, as if he was trying to recall what the cops had told him.

"Maybe. What's the difference?"

"Was he shot with a nine-millimeter bullet?"

Aker's eyes lit up with recognition.

"Doctors said they pulled a nine-millimeter bullet out of his skull."

"They pulled a bullet out of his skull or fractions of a bullet?"

"It was in tiny pieces."

"That's a hollow-point round. The tip of the bullet is concave. The round flowers on impact, dumping its power into the target. It breaks into shrapnel, doing serious damage."

Once he had said it, he regretted it. He could see on Aker's face that it didn't make the trauma sound any better.

He asked, "Will he live through it?"

Widow thought back. His mother was shot in the head and left for dead.

"I don't know. But what I know is he didn't shoot himself."

"What makes you say that?"

"Tunney owned a thirty-eight. That's the weapon he carried."

"Tunney owned more than one gun. That I know just from being his friend. Maybe he used one of them, the nine-millimeter ones. The Glock you mentioned."

Widow shook his head.

"No. He wouldn't do that."

"How do you know?"

"Suicide is a personal act. Plus, Tunney knew weapons. He wouldn't want to survive it. Not like this. He'd use his most trusted firearm to do the job. He might've owned a Glock. Probably does. But he would've used the weapon that was his EDC."

"EDC?"

"Every Day Carry."

Aker nodded like he understood, but Widow could tell he didn't, not fully.

"If he didn't shoot himself, who did? Why?"

Widow paused and sifted a hand into his pocket and pulled out the flash drive.

"Because of this."

Aker stared at the small device. It was rectangular. Small enough to fit in the palm of a hand, to be concealed from body frisks, but large enough to hold secrets that could take down an empire.

Aker asked, "What's that?"

"The traffic camera feed above Lincoln Park. The one that pointed in part to the bench that Eggers died on."

"You watched it?"

"I did."

"And?"

"Eggers didn't burn himself up. It was no accident. He was murdered."

"Murdered? The video shows it?"

"Yes. The whole gruesome thing. It's all here. You can see a vehicle loaded with guys pull up, jump out, restrain him, and light him up."

"That's horrible. Are you kidding?"

"No. It's real."

Aker fidgeted nervously.

"No. No. This isn't my job. This is for the police."

"It's not your job, but it's your concern. Eggers was your client. My brother-in-arms. And now, they've shot your friend. We've both got skin in the game."

Aker slowly nodded. At first, it started as a headshake, but thinking about it, he saw the light.

"We need to give this to the police."

"I agree. But there's another element."

"What?"

"They've tried to cover it up."

"What? The police covered it up?"

Widow explained his visit to Metro with Tunney, the traffic camera feed gone missing, tracing it back to Haspman, and then his visit to Haspman, minus hiding in the back of the truck, taking Haspman's weapons from him, and not being invited in.

"What do we do? I'm not a criminal attorney. I only work on estates and contracts. This is way over my head, Widow."

Widow paused a beat. Aker was right. If these guys had this kind of reach, skill, and money backing them, plus the badges, then they would need help. And Shaw and Kidman were going to drag their feet. He knew that.

"We might need outside help."

"Like whom? The FBI?"

"No. Better. I have someone in mind."

"Who?"

"Better let me worry about it."

"What about me?"

Widow paused a beat.

Then, he said, "Listen, you carry?"

"What?"

"A weapon. A firearm. You got one?"

"Not on me. Why would I carry a gun?"

"Got one at home?"

"I do. Just for protection. I got a wife and kids at home."

"Good. I think you should be careful. In fact, I think you should go home, get the wife, the kids, any pets, and go out of town for a while. Take the gun with you. Maybe go to upstate New York or Delaware or New Hampshire or anyplace else. It's a nice time of year."

"What? Why?"

Widow looked at Aker's eyes, and then pointed at Tunney.

"That's why. If these people can do this, if they can burn a man alive in public and nearly cover it up, then they can come after you. And they will."

"Why? I know nothing."

"They'll come after you just to get at me."

"They know who you are?"

"I'm sure they do. Why do you think they did this to Tunney? This wasn't just an execution. It was an interrogation."

Aker turned away from Widow, staring at his friend lying there on a hospital bed with tubes and an IV drip, bandages wrapped all around his head.

Widow also stared. Images of his mother, lying in a similar hospital bed, with a similar gunshot wound to the head, came flooding into his mind. He felt the anger of what happened to her come back to him. He wanted these guys as badly as he wanted to kill the guys behind his mother's death.

Aker asked, "If we leave town, what about you? What will you do?"

"I'm going to find them and make them wish they were never born."

Minutes later, Widow said goodbye to Aker and left the hospital. He went back the way he'd come in.

Out in front. He checked the time on Aker's phone. It was nearing eight in the evening. He saw a sign on the way out of the hospital that posted the visiting hours. They would've asked him to leave. Visitor hours were over at eight. Then again, that probably didn't apply for ICU.

The first thing he did was go into the burner phone's main options and found an about page. It gave information about the phone. It listed memory, storage capacity, make, and model of the phone manufacturer. It also listed the phone number, which was the information he was searching for.

Next, Widow dialed a phone number he hadn't thought of in years, but it was one of two he'd never forget. The first was his mother's old phone number. This wasn't that one. This was the emergency line for his old, secret undercover NCIS: Unit Ten, a unit classified beyond classified.

The emergency line was the only number he knew by heart. He didn't know the reception number. Plus, there was no reception open right now, probably. There might've been someone sitting at a desk this late at night, but not likely.

He dialed the number and put the phone to his ear. He waited through a ring and then an automated response.

It was a man's voice, polite, non-robotic, but prerecorded. The message was ambiguous, but not like silly cloak and dagger, like in a bad spy movie.

The voice said, "You've reached a Navy line. If you've reached this recording in error, hang up. Otherwise, leave a message and phone number."

There was a beep.

Widow gave his last known military rank, his name, the serial number on his dog tags and his badge number, which was probably so long out of circulation they might consider reusing it someday.

He said, "Rachel Cameron. I need to come in. I'll be in tomorrow morning. Oh seven hundred. I need help, Rachel."

He hung up the phone and slipped it into his pocket.

A breeze gushed over him, and he popped the collar of his Havelock and slipped both hands in his pockets. He looked for a new hotel room. He thought it best not to return to the other one, in case the guys in the traffic video were as good as he thought they were.

His first stop was going to be the first convenience or grocery store he came across because he needed a new toothbrush.

He headed out east from there, on foot, ready for a hot shower, ready for a warm, clean bed.

28

WIDOW WOKE before the sun and showered and dressed and brushed his teeth with his new toothbrush, which was a regular, straight-handled brush. He stuffed it into his Havelock's pocket and not his jeans because the tip was curved, but still sharp enough to poke him in the thigh every time he stepped.

Before leaving his new motel room and grabbing a taxi out to Quantico, he palmed Haspman's 1911 in his hand and debated what to do with it. He could toss it down a sewer drain or into a random dumpster, hoping no one would go dumpster-diving. He couldn't leave it in the room, not without going to the front desk and paying for an extra night. And he couldn't just abandon it there. He didn't want the maid coming in and discovering it. He was pretty sure that hotel protocol was to call the police when a weapon was found in a room.

The most obvious thing was that he couldn't take it with him, not onto a military base.

NCIS headquarters was in the Russell-Knox Building, which was inside Marine Corps Base Quantico, not just any base. MCB Quantico housed a multitude of intelligence and military police organizations.

The Russell-Knox Building hosted NCIS, the Air Force Office of Special Investigations, and the Army Criminal Investigation Command, and probably more than that. That was just what Widow remembered.

He was walking out to the lot to wait for a taxi he had called earlier when his phone rang. He looked at the caller ID screen. It read *Private*.

He answered it.

"Hello?"

A female voice that he hadn't heard in years spoke.

"Jack Widow."

He instantly recognized the voice.

"Special Agent in Charge Cameron."

The woman on the phone sighed.

"It's just Rachel for you, Widow."

The caller was his old CO from Unit Ten, the undercover unit he'd worked with until his last day with the NCIS.

Her voice was the same that used to squawk orders in his earpieces or leave him coded messages during undercover missions. There were times, working for her, that she had frustrated him, but hearing her voice all these years later put a smile on his face.

"Nice to hear from you, Cameron."

"You're not military anymore, Widow. And I'm not your CO. I never was. I was your SAC. But I'm not now. You're a civilian now. Just call me by my first name."

"I always called you Cameron."

"You're never going to change."

Widow stayed quiet to that.

She said, "It's good to hear from you. But you know I have a personal cell phone. You can call me on that."

"Don't have the number."

"That's because I don't date my subordinates."

"I'm not your subordinate anymore."

"I don't date losers without jobs either. You still don't have a job, right?"

"No job."

"Still roaming the countryside, doing God knows what?"

"I'm doing that and stuff he doesn't know about."

"Oh, God! I bet! Well, Widow, I have to scold you for a second."

"Oh?"

"You know damn well the number you dialed is an emergency number for NCIS operatives. Not for ex-agents."

Widow looked up to the street at the end of the motel parking lot. No taxi yet. It was late.

He said, "I'm sorry about that."

"You should be. It's an emergency line only. You can get me in a lot of trouble."

"Did I?"

"No. Of course not."

"Of course not, because the guy working the phone works for you now?"

"What do you want?"

Widow took a breath.

"I'm sorry to say that I am calling about an emergency."

"What's up?"

"Not over the line."

"You want me to call you on a different line?"

"Not over the phone, I mean."

"How then?"

"I'm coming in."

"You're here? In Quantico?"

"I'll be there in an hour. Probably less."

If the taxi shows up, he thought.

"I need you to call the security gate and sponsor me so I can get on base."

"Okay. Sure. Can you give me some idea of what this is about?"

"It's about a murder."

"You didn't kill anyone, did you?"

Not yet, he thought.

"Never mind. Don't answer that," she said. "Sure. I'll call it in. You'll have to check in at the visitor center. Remember where it is?"

"I remember. I only worked there."

"Okay. Just asking. I'll see you when you get here."

"Cameron, wait."

"Yeah? I'm here."

"Can I bring a sidearm on base?"

Silence.

Cameron said, "Widow, don't bring a gun on base!"

"I won't. Just kidding."

She didn't wait for a response. She hung up the phone. Widow slipped his phone back into his pocket and walked the length of the parking lot, waiting for his cab.

He saw an opportunity to ditch Tunney's weapon. Just then, a city garbage truck pulled into the lot. It drove straight toward Widow because the motel's main dumpster was directly behind him.

No way anyone could dumpster-dive and find the 1911 before the truck emptied the dumpster. So he turned and ran toward the dumpster. He faced away from the view of the truck driver and took out the 1911. He wiped it quick with the flap of his Havelock and tossed it into the dumpster. He did the same with the magazine and the bullets.

He made it just in the nick of time. He turned around and the truck was right there, ready to take the dumpster. The truck used a set of huge metal arms to reach forward and latch onto the container. The arms slid into two long tunnels on the sides of the dumpster.

Widow heard the gears that controlled the arms. They grinded away and scraped metal. The dumpster lifted off the ground and up over the nose of the truck. The arms dumped the whole thing into an opening in the truck's roof and then did the whole process in reverse until the dumpster was back down on the concrete. It was completely emptied, gun and all.

Widow watched it. Then he turned away and headed back to the street.

The taxi he had called showed up thirty seconds later, and he was on his way.

Inside of thirty minutes, they crossed the state line into Virginia. The topography was spectacular. It was beautiful, just as Widow had remembered it. They drove down winding roads, passing thick clusters of sprawling trees on each side of the road. The ground and shoulders were covered in autumn leaves. Red and green and brown were everywhere.

Fifty minutes had passed since they left Widow's motel parking lot, and they drove by a line of cars trying to enter the base through the main gate. They lined up underneath a sign the width of the road that crossed over the top of the entrance. The sign looked like a long metal beam; the kind used in bridge construction. It was held up by two large brick pillars.

They couldn't enter the base, not through there.

Widow told the taxi where to go. The driver pulled into a parking lot nearby, and Widow stepped out into a world he hadn't visited in years. He was in the parking lot of the MCB Quantico Visitor Control Center, just outside the security checkpoint on Russell Road.

The line of cars entering were Marine personnel or vendors with preregistered IDs that gave them base access.

Beyond the gate was the town of Quantico, Virginia, a heavily fortified Marine base station. The town held secrets worth protecting. The FBI Training Academy was there.

This was the place where Widow was trained in law enforcement and undercover tradecraft.

Widow moved to the front passenger side of the taxi and pulled a wad of cash out of his pocket. With the fare, plus tip, the ride took all of it, leaving him only enough to buy a cup of coffee—maybe.

The taxi driver didn't say goodbye. As soon as Widow paid the fare and stepped a foot away, the driver and taxi were gone, back the way they'd come.

Widow walked into the Visitor Control Center. The building was all red brick and white pillars with a curved roof.

He entered and made his way to the end of a line and waited.

This was one of the few times he wished he had maintained a military ID card. It might've made this easier. But he'd never gotten one.

In the end, it turned out not to be such a fuss. Cameron had called ahead and sponsored his entry to the base.

As he got to the counter, he was greeted by a friendly desk worker. He told her of Cameron's sponsorship. She nodded and took his name and his passport, and keyed his information into a computer. A few moments later, she returned his passport to him and pointed him over to another counter, where another desk worker waited to take his photo. The camera setup was not unlike the DMV's driver's license photo setup.

He had to sit on a stool. There was a red stripe on the tile floor for him to put his feet. And there was a blue light the guy told him to stare at while he snapped a photo with a large machine.

Just minutes later, Widow had a printed paper day pass with his name and photo on it.

They pointed him to a walkway that led up through the same security station as the cars. He met with a friendly Marine guard, who took the printout and stared at him and then the photo, and then him again.

Finally, the guard waved him through the gate. And, like that, Widow was back where he'd never thought he would be again.

Luckily, Widow didn't have to travel far. The Russell-Knox Building, which housed NCIS headquarters, was right there close to the gate. He followed the walking path, passing more trees and grass and other civilians. He knew they were civilians by the way they dressed, walked, and carried themselves. Not to mention, they had badges displayed on their jackets and shirts.

Widow crossed through a maze of employee parking lots until he saw the Russell-Knox Building over a hill. He walked through additional grassy areas until he was standing at a second security checkpoint.

This one was the Russell-Knox Building Visitor Center. He went in and had to go through another check-in and security process. At the end, he was given a second pass; only this one came as an ID badge that clearly read: *Visitor*.

It dangled from a lanyard. Widow put it over his head and let it hang from his neck. He smiled and walked through a metal detector, passing guards, passing suspicious glances.

Eventually, he was on the other side of it all, but only to find he had to cross another service drive and grassy fields and pass by another parking lot areas.

He followed the walkway until he was inside the main building. But right there, he was stopped by a Marine armed with an assault rifle, his finger out of the trigger housing, but he looked eager and ready to change that with the right provocation.

The Marine was young, in his twenties. He looked tough in his Marine Corps Combat Utility Uniform. The Corps didn't build them any way but tough, and they dressed accordingly.

The Marine was from the security battalion. He was on guard duty. And he laid his eyes on Widow the moment Widow entered through the front doors. The Marine walked right in front of him and put up a hand.

"Stop right there, sir."

Widow checked the guy's black pin on his collar, which signified his rank.

Widow said, "What can I do for you, Lance Corporal?"

The Marine said, "Do you have your ID papers?"

"Got my visitor's badge right here," Widow said. He raised the badge off his chest to display it.

"I asked for your ID papers, sir."

"What's this about, Lance Corporal?"

"ID, please. Now."

Widow sighed and reached into the pocket of his Havelock and pulled out the paper that had been printed for him at the Marine Base's Visitor Control Center. He unfolded it and handed it to the Marine.

The Marine took it and reversed it and read it.

"Jack Widow."

He handed the paper back to Widow, who took it and refolded it and stuffed it back into a pocket.

"Can I be on my way now?"

"I'm sorry, sir. I have orders to detain you."

"Detain me?"

"Just temporary, sir."

Widow rolled his eyes.

"Do I have to wear handcuffs?"

"Nothing like that, sir. It's just temporary."

"So, what do we do?"

"Just come have a seat over there by me."

The Marine pointed at a set of concrete benches off against a wall in the lobby.

Widow nodded and led the way. He plopped himself down on the bench, confused. And he waited.

A half hour went by, almost to the second. He had seen agents from all the different sections in the building passing by. Most didn't pay him a first glance—all but one. A beautiful NCIS agent that he had never laid eyes on before walked out from the hallway he was trying to go to and stopped and turned right and stared at him.

She was half Japanese and half white. She had long black hair tied up in a bun. She walked over with a confident bearing.

She wore a navy-blue jacket. Underneath was a black top that was snug enough to distract him, which it did for a second. She might've noticed him staring as she walked over to him, because she smiled. Or maybe she was just being polite.

She wore gray chinos, with a comfortable pair of dress shoes. They looked like she could run a full sprint in them, but they were still stylish enough to wear to court.

In a holster, riding her right hip, was a SIG-Sauer P228.

Widow looked at it. It appeared better than well-maintained. It looked like it was right off the gun manufacturer's factory floor. He thought the gun was almost as flawless as she was.

The agent approached Widow and the Marine and nodded at the guard.

"I'll take him from here. Thanks, Lance Corporal."

The Marine said, "Yes, ma'am. Thank you."

The Marine pivoted and returned to his guard post across the lobby.

The agent gave Widow a big smile. It was all teeth. Then she offered a hand for him to shake. He took it and tried to keep his squeeze gentle. Her hand was swallowed up inside his.

"My name is Sonya Gray. I'm here to take you downstairs."

Widow knew exactly what that meant. There was no downstairs inside the NCIS side of the Russell-Knox Building. Not on any schematic or blueprint or building plans. The elevators didn't have a *B* for the basement button. There was no underground parking garage.

Only a small circle of people knew of a basement floor. An even smaller group worked down there.

Downstairs was where he had first been introduced to Unit Ten, a highly secret project that was created as an undercover unit, taking on crimes and investigations that no one, not even the Navy, wanted to acknowledge.

If Gray knew about the basement, then she knew about Unit Ten.

Widow asked, "Do you work downstairs?"

"I do."

They stopped shaking hands, and Gray looked up at him with stunning eyes.

She said, "Come on. This way."

She turned and led the way. Widow followed. He stared a little too long at her from behind and smacked his own forehead.

She heard the smack and glanced back at him.

"You okay?"

"Yeah. Fine."

They headed northwest, through the lobby, and around a corner. They passed the elevators and came to a security door. She swiped her badge across a scanner, and the door buzzed open. They walked through, passing more armed Marine guards, and continued beyond a maze of corridors until they came to a heavy door. She pulled it open and stepped inside to the top of a flight of stairs.

She led Widow down them and came to a security station with one uniformed Marine at a desk.

The Marine recognized her and buzzed her through another security door until they were inside the basement level.

Widow had been there before it was Unit Ten's headquarters.

Gray asked, "Is everything the way you left it?"

Unit Ten's headquarters was a single basement level with long concrete floors and walls of exposed brick. Numerous support staff desks were set up all along the main operations floor, which was one large open room. On the sides were offices and conference rooms.

Widow saw early-arriving NCIS agents standing around, drinking their coffees, and talking to each other, going over their cases. Seated at desks were support staff, also with coffees, and working hard. They were all starting their days.

Everywhere he looked, there were high-tech computer systems and machines. But the interior was all concrete, almost as dank as a dungeon.

At the end of the room was a set of metal stairs with only one arm rail. The stairs led up to a big block office made mostly of glass and steel.

Widow glanced up and saw a familiar face. It was Rachel Cameron, his old CO.

She was staring at a laptop monitor. The office lighting was dim. She had a thing about the dark. Unlike most kids, Cameron wasn't afraid of the dark as much as she was afraid of the light.

It put a whole metaphorical meaning on their work together in undercover work, on their work in the shadows. Cameron blossomed in the shadows. Often Widow wondered if the reason that Unit Ten's headquarters was in a basement was because that's what she had asked for.

Cameron must've sensed Widow was there, because she looked up from her laptop and stared down at him. She sat back in her chair, took off her reading glasses, and smiled. Then she stood up and walked to a heavy glass door. She exited her office and walked down the stairs.

Cameron was a secretive figure in the NCIS, a legend to some, but most details of her life and history were unknown. Her personal life was more secret from her team than the secrets buried in the Navy archives.

But Widow knew her well. Better than most. Better than everyone else in that office, he was sure.

Cameron was ten or fifteen years older than him. She'd let her hair grow out since the last time he saw her. It was blonde, but with thin gray stragglers here and there.

The one thing that stood out about Cameron physically was that she was short. He towered over her. His guess was that she was on the line of five one to five two.

She walked down the stairs, smiling at him all the way.

"Widow, you look like shit."

"Gee. Thanks!"

Cameron walked right up to him. He put a hand out to shake, but she dismissed it. She reached out her hand, arm extended all the way up, and she stroked the hair on his face.

"What's with this? You not keeping up with Navy regulations?"

"I haven't been in the Navy in years."

She smiled and wrapped her arms around him and hugged him.

The support staff, agents, and Gray all looked wide-mouthed. They had never seen her show affection for anyone before. And they didn't know who Widow was, not by sight.

Everyone seemed to stop in place to see what their glorious leader was doing.

Who was the guy?

Cameron hugged Widow, and he hugged her back. Her frame was tiny compared to his. It reminded him of hugging his own mother. Cameron was the only semblance of a family he had left.

After all the formalities, Cameron asked Widow to come up to her office. Gray followed. Inside the office, Widow sat at a chair across a huge metal desk from Cameron, who sat in her own chair.

Gray stayed standing beside the desk.

Widow arched an eye at her and asked, "Why aren't you sitting down?"

"I only sit when asked by my SAC."

Widow looked at Cameron.

"You're running a tight ship here."

Cameron smiled and talked about Gray like she wasn't standing there.

"Gray is like you. She came straight out of the Navy. She also rose through the ranks. Had stellar marks on most everything. Talented marksman. Great at detecting lies and great with deception. Especially with men."

Widow didn't look at Gray. He didn't respond, but he could see why Cameron said *especially with men*. She'd probably busted a lot of bad Marines and sailors just by asking them to confess. Widow normally had to use fists.

Cameron said, "And like you, she had a discipline problem."

She glanced at Gray, who stood at attention.

"You've changed a bit," Widow said.

"Widow, you were our first undercover agent. Our first to make it onto the SEAL teams. And our only. Still, to this day, no one has passed through SEAL training. Not even close. We've had two make it through Hell Week. But never like you."

Widow stayed quiet.

Cameron said, "Gray is unique. A brilliant investigator. Very promising."

Widow asked, "What's her role?"

"Right now, that's yet to be determined."

Now Widow understood why she was standing at attention. She was still on probation. She was new to the unit. She was freshly minted and untested. She hadn't proved herself yet. And she might've had a chip on her shoulder about it. Widow realized Gray was standing at attention like that by her own choice. She was trying to prove herself.

Finally, Cameron asked, "So, what the hell are you doing back here?"

Widow breathed out and laid it on her. He told her about Eggers, the fire, the bench, about Aker, the fifty million dollars of stock, which took repeating for her to realize that she'd heard him right the first time. And he told her about Haspman, the video feed, Tunney in the hospital, and the guys in the Escalade.

It took a long time, nearly a half hour, but it was fifteen minutes into the story that Widow asked if they had any coffee.

Cameron called in a subordinate from downstairs by clicking a button on her desk phone. Ten minutes later, the guy came back in with a coffee from Dunkin'. Widow realized that there must be one either in the lobby or in the building somewhere that he hadn't noticed.

He continued his story. By the time he got to the end, Cameron was speechless, Gray's jaw was on the floor, and he needed a refill of coffee.

He didn't ask for a refill.

He said, "And there's one more thing. The guys who did this..."

Both Cameron and Gray stared at him.

"They had NCIS badges."

"They had badges?"

Gray asked, "NCIS badges?"

"Yeah, but they were probably fake."

Gray asked, "Fake?"

Widow said, "Sure. How hard would it be?"

Cameron said, "It would be impossible to get a real one. Not without breaking into a locked drawer upstairs in one of the SAC's offices."

Gray said, "Armed guards everywhere. Not to mention, armed agents all over the place."

Widow said, "What about a field office somewhere in the world."

Cameron and Gray looked at each other.

Cameron said, "Conceivable."

Widow said, "At any rate. They got them. It could be from some guy on the internet, or they could be stolen. Whatever."

Cameron said, "So, now what?"

"I need help."

"Like what?"

"Can I see Eggers' file?"

"That's probably doable."

Widow said, "I need to see his NCIS file. Not just his Navy one."

Widow reached into his pocket to take out the flash drive. He pictured putting it on the glass desktop and sliding it over to her like in the movies. But he paused as soon as she said her next words.

"I can't do that," Cameron said.

Widow stared at Cameron blankly. He released the flash drive in his pocket. He wouldn't give it up if she wouldn't help him. There was a possibility that she would take it, and he would never see it again. He had to acknowledge the possibility that the guys in the Escalade really were NCIS. In which case, she might take the flash drive, and it might get buried in the system somewhere, which would do no justice for Eggers.

He held onto it.

She said, "You're no longer one of us. You're not an agent anymore. You're just a civilian now. I can't give you NCIS files. It violates NCIS protocol. Which means it comes with penalties. And not just to me, but to this unit. And these penalties come with sentences. Jail time. Not just terminations."

"Aren't you violating that now? By even having me down here?"

"No. As director, I can vouch for certain VIP visitors."

"But you can't let me see NCIS files?"

She shook her head.

Widow scratched his head and said, "Technically, you don't exist. Neither does Unit Ten. Since that's the case, then how're you violating any rules?"

"You always had a way of bending the rules."

"Isn't that what you paid me for?"

"True. I'm glad you were one of us. And not one of the bad guys."

"So, you'll help me?"

"I can't help you. Thanks for coming by though."

"You're not going to do anything for Eggers?"

"We'll look into it. That's all I can say."

Widow felt confused, and a little betrayed. His feelings were even hurt. But Cameron's word was final. It always had been.

Cameron reached over to a little tray near a desk lamp. She reached in and pulled out a card. She slid it over to Widow, across the table like in the movies.

He picked up the card. It was a business card—her business card; only it didn't list her title. It only said NCIS and Rachel Cameron.

Cameron said, "That's my direct number. Don't be calling the emergency line anymore. Understood?"

"Yes."

With nothing left to say, he stood up, ready to leave.

Cameron stood up and nodded at him. She walked around the desk and gave him another big, warm hug. She backed up and held his arms, stared up at his face like his mother used to do.

"You don't be a stranger. Call me sometime. Let me know you're alive. Okay?"

Widow nodded. The feeling of betrayal was on his face, but he said nothing about it.

"Yes, Chief."

Widow turned and walked out of her office. Gray followed.

29

Widow followed Gray out of the office and back through Unit Ten's workspace to the shared lobby, where they'd first met.

The walk gave Widow time to move from a feeling of betrayal to one of anger and disappointment. He was angry that Cameron wouldn't help him, although he knew her well enough to know that decision was made because it was the right decision for her unit and her people. There were forces at work that Widow wasn't privy to.

In the lobby, Widow saw the same Marine lance corporal who had stopped him earlier. The guy was standing tall near the same wall as earlier.

Widow headed for the exit, but he heard Gray from over his shoulder. She was still behind him—still on his tail.

"Wait up, Widow."

Widow stopped and turned back to her.

"Where are you going? I can walk myself out."

"Didn't you come here in a taxi?"

"How do you know that?"

"I checked on it."

"You checked on it?"

"I have a friend who saw you enter the Visitor Control Center."

"I came by taxi."

"Sounds like you need a ride."

"You taking me all the way back to DC?"

"Just follow me to my car."

Gray pushed past him and led him out of the building. He saw a sign that pointed to employee parking. But that wasn't where she went. She led him through more sidewalks and past more grass. They headed to a parking lot that was surrounded by barbed wire fencing.

She took him to a navy-blue Dodge Charger. She clicked a button, and the car doors unlocked. She slipped in and fired up the engine.

Widow walked around to the passenger side and dumped himself down on the seat. It was spacious. He had plenty of legroom.

"Seatbelt," she said.

Widow put his seatbelt on, and Gray gassed the vehicle like some people do when driving a sports car. The engine roared.

She said, "I love I get paid to drive this. You must miss getting a car like this."

"I'm not a car guy."

"Really?"

"Yeah. What?"

"You just look like the kind of man who is good under the engine."

"I'm not."

"Do you drive?"

"I can drive just fine. I took the same combat driving classes you took. Just not a car guy."

She backed out of the space and drove to the service drive. Within minutes they were out of the base and on Interstate Ninety-Five, heading north to DC.

Once on the interstate, Gray pushed the vehicle over the speed limit, which was technically a violation of NCIS protocol, when not in a high-speed pursuit or some kind of urgent business. But Widow wasn't going to tell.

After five straight minutes of silence, Gray finally spoke.

"Sounds like you need some help."

"Why do you think I came to you guys?"

"And Cameron turned you down?"

"Yeah. You were there."

"That seems unusual."

"How do you mean?"

"Aren't you the famous Jack Widow? The poster boy for our undercover unit?"

"I'm famous?" he asked.

"You are in certain circles."

"Good to know. But I'm nothing special."

"You were the first agent to infiltrate the SEAL teams. That's special."

Widow stared out the window at the green and red landscape whizzing by like he was seeing it from a train.

"I didn't infiltrate them. I am a SEAL."

"You spied on them, right?"

"It wasn't like that. I didn't spy on them. I was undercover. I hunted bad guys that were among us."

"You investigated them?"

"Yes."

"You arrested a bunch of them over your twenty years in? Didn't you? For us?"

"Sixteen."

"You arrested only sixteen? In twenty years?"

"I was only in the Navy for sixteen years. I don't know how many arrests came out of my investigations. I didn't count them all."

"I do. I know how many."

"How's that?"

"I studied them, all of them. Well, the ones I could get that weren't classified beyond classified."

"You studied them?"

"Yeah. I studied you. Only they don't tell us your name. Or any names. Just vague examples of operations."

"So, how do you know it's me?"

"It's you. We all know now. Everyone in the unit knows your name. Hell, even some agents not in our unit. You're kind of a legend."

"That wasn't my aim. I was just doing what was right."

"Putting away your brother SEALs? Didn't it bother you?"

"Only the bad ones. If they committed crimes terrible enough to be on my radar, then they weren't my brothers. They were traitors to the platoon, the Navy, the country. Besides, most of my arrests weren't SEALs. Most of the time, my investigations led me to external enemies."

"Such as what? Foreigners?"

"Sometimes. Sometimes it was SEAL flunkies or Marines or sailors or just other citizens. It all depended."

Gray was quiet a long second. Then, she said, "I'm a damn good investigator, myself. You know?"

Widow looked over at her. His anger at Cameron turned to sadness. By this point, he was feeling more hurt than angry.

He asked, "What was your rank?"

"I don't have one."

"You did. Cameron said you were out of the Navy, like me."

"I was an O3 on my last tour."

Widow nodded. It sounded right. She looked to be about thirty, maybe thirty-one. If she had gone straight into the Navy after high school, plus four years of university and twelve weeks of officer school, then she'd be the right age to have made it up to lieutenant.

The thing that didn't add up was how she had been recruited to Unit Ten. He couldn't figure it out. So, he just asked her point-blank.

"How did you make it into Unit Ten?"

"What? You already think I don't have what it takes?"

"Not that at all. Just you're so young."

"Just turned thirty-one in August."

He said nothing to that.

She looked at him and then back to the street. Her smile went flat, as if a painful memory was happening in her mind.

She said, "After my last tour ended, I signed up with NCIS. I was brand new. I was green. And they treated me that way. They discouraged me from shining."

Widow looked at her. He watched her cheekbones and facial muscles as she talked. She was a beautiful woman. He was trying to stay hurt about Cameron's rejection of his plea for help, but Gray made a fine distraction.

She said, "Cameron doesn't think I'll make it. I was pushed on her."

"By whom? Few people can force Cameron into something."

"By the director of the NCIS."

"The director? Are you his niece or something?"

"*Her*. The current director is a woman."

Widow stared at her.

"Bullshit! The NCIS has never had a female director."

"You don't think a woman can be director?"

"I didn't say that. It's just never had one. I know it's been all men. NCIS isn't that old."

"You're right. But there's a rumor that it might go to a woman this time. It's being run by an interim head right now. The female deputy director is in charge."

"Stop changing the subject. Why were you pushed on her? How did you make Unit Ten?"

"There was an incident," Gray said.

She stared straight. But Widow could tell she was reimagining it because her speed slowed to the limit, and she steered the vehicle into the slow lane.

"What happened?"

"In my first six months of being in investigation, I caught an officer red-handed committing a horrible crime."

"What was he doing?"

"He was trying to rape an underage girl. They stuck me on a task force that seemed hopeless. For five straight years, young girls were turning up dead in the regions around Camp Lemonnier. It's near Ethiopia."

Widow said, "It's in Djibouti."

"You been there?"

A particular SEAL mission he had been a part of came to mind. It took place in Yemen, but he flew out of Djibouti.

"Never," he lied. "But I know where it is."

Gray said, "Anyway, they set up a task force. It was there long before I arrived on post."

She said it in a certain way that told Widow she was indifferent to it.

"The rest of the team give you shit?"

"The rest of the team acted like I was some hotshot coming in and running all their police work. But I wanted to solve the case. So, I went back through five years of investigation, and I kicked up dust that was fully settled. I re-interviewed old witnesses and followed up every lead that had already been pursued."

"And?"

"The locals claimed it was a US sailor doing the killings. Every local witness claimed that was the rumor. But there was no proof. Eyewitnesses were too scared to come forward. It was a dead-end assignment, according to the agents on the ground.

"The brass believed it was just a group of pirates."

Widow asked, "But you didn't buy that?"

"It was no damn pirates."

"You know, because you caught the culprit?"

"I know because I shot him."

Widow asked, "Really? Did you kill him? Who was it?"

"No. He lived. He was a young officer. On his first command."

"That was enough to land you into Unit Ten?"

"The man's father is an admiral."

Widow stared at her. He already knew the story. It was on the news, at least in the *Navy Times*, which he still read from time to time.

"Really?" he asked.

"Yep. So, the pinheads in Washington wanted to stick me someplace where I would be forgotten. But they couldn't send me to a post in Antarctica. Not when they'd just recognized me for it in public."

"They give you a trophy?"

"Just an honor of recognition."

Which was big for an NCIS agent. It was like getting a new chevron on your uniform or a Navy Cross for distinguished acts of service.

"They tried to recognize me all at the same time they wanted me to vanish from the limelight."

"So, they negotiated with you?"

"They did. They dangled a better assignment for me. A better job. A better life."

"So, they offered you your choice of assignment? How did you know about Unit Ten?"

"They offered me a spot in Unit Ten."

"Really?"

"Yep."

"So much for secrets."

"I didn't want the limelight. I don't care about trophies or recognition."

"You just wanted to be where the action is?"

"I do."

"That's why Cameron doesn't trust you?"

"She trusts me. She just doesn't like that she didn't get to pick me the way she did you."

Widow nodded and looked at the clock on the radio. It read two minutes to eight in the morning.

He asked, "So, what was your first assignment with Unit Ten?"

"You are."

He asked, "What?"

"You're my first assignment. Well, Eggers is."

"What is this?"

"You need help, right?"

"Yeah."

"So, I'll help you."

"Is Cameron going to like that? She kicked me out."

"You didn't think she was going to leave you hanging out in the cold, did you?"

"She knows about this?"

Gray said, "I can't answer that. You know how it is."

Widow thought for a moment, and then he said, "That's why you were in the lobby? That's why you had me sidelined until you could get there. She called you in and told you to help me, off the books?"

Gray said, "Cameron's priority is protecting the unit. She can't have anything to do with this. Not on paper. But I've got nothing to lose. In fact, I've got an ace in the hole."

"Sleeve."

"What?"

"It's ace up your sleeve. Not in the hole. Least, I never heard that before except in poker."

"Whatever. So, where to? Where are we going first?"

Widow thought for a moment.

He asked, "Can you get a protection detail together?"

"For who? You?"

"For the lawyer who told me about Eggers. He's got a wife and a kid."

"Do they need protection?"

"They might. I told him to leave town. But maybe he has gone nowhere. We could get a team to protect him. That would be better than him going off on his own."

She repeated the question.

"They need protection?"

"Tunney, that PI I mentioned, someone shot him in the head and tried to make it look like suicide."

"Over what?"

"This," Widow said, and he pulled out the flash drive.

"What's that?"

"The video from the missing feed I mentioned."

"You have a copy?"

"No. The original. I took it."

"Well, that's obstruction of justice."

"I was planning on handing it over to Metro."

"But?"

"I haven't had the chance yet."

"Why didn't you give it to us?"

"I was about to before Cameron shut me out."

"Okay. Where's he? The PI?"

"Hospital."

"We should get a guy over there too."

"Agreed."

Gray asked, "You got any idea who's behind this? Who's the guy at the tippy-top, I mean?"

"Nope. Whoever it is must be connected, rich, and desperate to cover it up. This means it's someone with something to lose."

"Like what?"

"Money. Power, maybe."

Gray pressed some buttons on her steering wheel, and a dial tone came up over the car's speakers. She gave a voice command to her phone's computer, which answered her back in a soothing female voice.

She called someone from NCIS and gave her badge number and ordered two protection details. She stopped and asked Widow for names and exact locations. He gave the name of the hospital for Tunney and Michael Aker's name and the address on his business card along with his cell number.

The guy on the line said he would call him promptly and set the whole thing up. It was all done quickly and efficiently and professionally.

Widow's feelings of anger and betrayal and disappointment were replaced with gratitude and pride and the urge to drink another coffee. The last feeling came from his soul.

After it was all said and done, Gray clicked off the call and returned to her high-speed driving. She bumped the car over to the express lane.

She glanced at Widow.

"So where to first?"

"You got a computer?"

"At home."

"Got internet?"

"Of course."

"Got access to NCIS internal files from your home computer?"

"I do. For what I'm cleared for."

Widow paused a beat and asked the most important question in the world to him.

"Got coffee?"

"Of course. I was in the Navy for eleven years. My house has a fully stocked kitchen. Plenty of coffee in the cupboards. Why?"

"Sounds like we're going back to your place."

"Pardon me?"

"Your place can be our home base until we figure things out."

She paused a beat and said, "I've heard about you, Jack Widow."

"So you said."

"I mean, I'm not that easy. I'm not taking you back to my place that fast."

"Is that what you've heard about me?"

Gray glanced at him. There was a hint of a smile. She said, "I've heard things."

Widow said, "It's not like that. It's morning time."

"You never heard of morning sex?"

"I swear. It's not like that. We need to find the connection here. Who'd want to kill Eggers? And who hates him enough to burn him alive? Who's resourceful enough to get hold of that traffic camera's feed? Make it disappear? Who can bribe and murder and act like it's no big deal?"

"I'm just kidding with you."

"Okay. I know that."

"Okay. Okay. But we also have to ask ourselves, who's so bad at being a criminal that they bungle the whole thing?"

"How so?"

"You've got the evidence, right?"

"Yes."

"Then, they might be resourceful, but also they're not very good at crime."

"I wouldn't say that. They just didn't count on me."

"So, back to my place?" she said with suspicion in her voice.

"Yes. We have work to do."

"Why not *your* place?"

"I don't have a *place*."

"So, it's true then. What they say about you now?"

"What do *they* say?"

"I've heard you go anywhere, that you live nowhere. Like a homeless drifter."

Widow stayed quiet.

They drove on.

30

In North Bethesda, on a quiet suburban street, a black Escalade was parked in front of a mailbox for a house with a *For Sale* sign out front.

Sathers sat in the driver's seat, his usual post, and the guy with the forgettable face sat in the passenger seat. They watched through the windshield as a woman down the street nuzzled her two children into a minivan, parked in her own driveway.

She was loading up the kids so she could drop them off at school before heading to her own job.

She got them buckled in and paused a beat as a man came out of the house. He was dressed in a suit and tie, like he was going to head to work after. Dark circles were obvious under his eyes, as if he had been awake all night, which he had been.

They watched as Michael Aker kissed his wife and children goodbye.

The wife kissed Aker back. After that, she got into the driver's seat of her minivan and started the engine. She reversed it and backed onto the street. She looked both ways and drove off.

The guy in the Escalade watched her go.

"I guess he didn't tell them," the guy with the forgettable face said.

"Why do you think that?"

"They wouldn't be going off to school. They'd be running away."

"Maybe they're stupid."

"They are stupid."

Sathers asked, "Should we go in now? Grab the lawyer before he heads to his office? It'll be harder to get him there."

The guy with the forgettable face leaned forward and peered through the tinted windshield.

"Hold on a second."

He buzzed his window down a crack and leaned next to it. He put his ear out as if he was searching for a sound.

"What is it?"

"Quiet!"

They both listened hard. They heard tires on gravel. It was a car traveling fast through a neighborhood with children and families. It was a careless way of driving through a suburb. It was the kind of driving only a person who doesn't care about consequences would do, like a criminal or a cop.

Suddenly, a navy-blue Dodge Charger swung around the corner; it passed their Escalade and pulled right up to Aker's house. He was still standing in the driveway after his wife and kids had gone.

Two people got out of the Charger. It was two men. Both had military haircuts. Both had military bearing. Only something was different. They weren't military. They were something else.

They were law enforcement. They were former military.

Sathers asked, "Who the hell is that?"

"NCIS."

"Oh shit! Are they onto us?"

The guy with the forgettable face leaned forward in his seat and watched them through the windshield.

The two men parked half in Aker's driveway and half in the street. They left their doors open and walked up to him.

Neither Sathers nor the guy with the forgettable face could hear what they were saying, but they saw the two agents take out badges and show them to Aker.

"Now, we got a problem," Sathers said. "We should bail."

The guy with the forgettable face sat back and breathed like he was completely relaxed.

He said, "No. There's no problem. It just got interesting. That's all."

The guy with the forgettable face said nothing.

Sathers said, "NCIS is here. We take off, right? They're here investigating us."

"No they're not."

"What are they doing then?"

"It's a protection detail. Nothing more."

"What do we do?"

"Same as before. But we wait until nightfall. Late. Then, when the kids are back, and everyone is safe and sound in their beds, that's when we make our move."

31

LESS THAN TWENTY minutes from the base, Widow and Gray arrived at her house.

Gray lived in a small two-bedroom house that was painted gray. Pulling up in the driveway, she stopped Widow before he could make a crack about it. She clarified she had heard that before.

The yard was nicely landscaped. Love and care and skill had been put into it, and real talent was shown. It wasn't overdone to show off. It was just right. There were trimmed bushes in the front and level grass and cared-for plants.

From the outside, Widow saw the answer to an unasked question, which was, what does Gray do in her spare time? The answer was right in front of him. She was more than an unproven NCIS agent. She had a real knack for gardening.

They parked the car and got out and walked the driveway, then transferred to a short walkway up to the front door.

Gray led the way, and Widow followed.

At the door, she fished a set of keys out of her front pocket and unlocked the door. Widow noticed she had only three keys on a ring. He liked she didn't have a lot of keys because the more keys someone had, the more doors they had to lock and unlock.

Widow lived a simple life. The fewer keys he had in his life, the better. No keys were the perfect number because more keys meant more locks and more closed doors. Widow liked the open road.

Before Gray opened the door, they heard a dog barking. Gray froze and glanced back at Widow.

"You like dogs?"

"I do. If I lived somewhere, I'd probably have a pair of dogs."

"You'll love Milo."

She opened the door, and a small mutt escaped through the crack and ran up to her. He must've weighed ten pounds soaking wet. He was about the ugliest dog Widow had ever laid eyes on, but the kind of ugly mutt that made him unbearably adorable.

Widow was no dog expert. He didn't even know what that kind of expert would be called. But he knew there were dog shows and experts on dogs.

This mutt's breeding was a complete mystery to him. He imagined it would've been hard for anyone, even a dog-show professional, to guess what kind of dog Milo was.

Like Gray and her house, Milo was also gray, with wisps of silver and white fur.

The wind blew through the front yard and moved his fur around in multiple directions like blades of tall grass.

The dog pushed out past Gray and yapped at Widow's ankles. It got hold of his pant leg and started pulling with all its might.

"Milo! Stop!" Gray called to him.

But he kept on chomping at Widow's pant leg.

"I'm sorry. He's a little protective of the house."

"That's a good thing. He's got a lot of heart. He's lionhearted."

Widow knelt on one knee and put out a hand, palm up to let the dog sniff him. It released his pant leg and sniffed his open palm. After several seconds of that, he attempted to pet its head. The dog let him do it only briefly. Then it turned and ran back into the house—stalemate.

"I think he likes me."

"I think he's afraid you'll step on him."

Gray led Widow into her house. She set her keys down on a table near the door. There was a bunch of unopened mail in a basket on the same table.

Gray unclipped her gun holster, pulled it out of her waistband, and laid it on the table, gun inside, next to the keys.

She said, "Make yourself at home."

"Thank you."

She went over to a corner in the room and slipped off her shoes.

"Take your shoes off, please."

Widow nodded and stepped over to the corner. He kicked off his boots and walked in his socks to the living room, following Gray.

The house looked as small on the inside as it did on the outside. It was perfect for one person, or maybe two, if both people were small to normal in stature. Widow's stature wasn't small or normal. He felt cramped. But he didn't complain. He had been in tighter, more cramped spaces before, including submarines at sea for weeks on end. A cozy house with a beautiful NCIS agent wasn't bad, not by any sensible measure.

The cramped feeling wasn't a height thing. The main ceiling was pretty high. It was a square foot issue. The house had little space. It was small, but it had many attractive fixtures and good woodwork and lots of little details. Long beams were exposed on the ceiling, and the floors were real hardwood. They were dark and polished to a deep shine.

Japanese décor was everywhere. He saw an extra bedroom off to the left of the main room. The door had been taken off. The hinges were still there, bolted into the frame. The bedroom was exposed and wide open. Widow saw it had been turned from a spare bedroom into a Japanese Zen tearoom. Possibly Gray meditated in there. The sounds of a low, relaxing music hummed out of the room as if she had used it in the morning and left the music playing.

The whole house was stylized with Japanese decorations on the walls, oriental rugs on the floors, and the smell of incense in the air.

Everything was painted white until they hit the living room. The furniture was the first thing with color, and it was a lot of color. There were two comfy sofas with pillows stacked all over them. They looked cozy, not as comfortable as the sofas in Haspman's house, but Gray lived on an NCIS salary and wasn't taking bribes from criminals. She had done well for herself.

The furniture pieces faced each other. There was no TV in sight. Widow liked that.

Widow said, "Nice place."

"Thanks. It's expensive, but I love it."

"Expensive?"

"Yeah. Come on. I'll show you why. Let's go through the kitchen."

"Okay."

They walked through the main room into the dining room and kitchen. Both were small but efficient. There was no dining room table, just a rug where one would go.

Once in the kitchen, Widow saw why the house was expensive. Floor-to-ceiling picture windows lined the back of the house, next to a huge sliding glass door.

The view was the thing she was paying for. It hit Widow instantly. It overshadowed the empty dining room and the kitchen and the Japanese décor.

Through the slider and the picture windows, Widow stared at the Potomac River and a green Virginia vista beyond. She was right on the river. For the DC area, it was a spectacular spot to live.

Gray led him to the slider, glided the door open, and stepped out to her backyard. Widow followed. It was breathtaking. He walked past her and took in the sounds and the sights.

He heard the water; it rushed along at a brisk and steady pace. He saw a group of rowers across the river, packed into a boat like an Olympic crew team. It was a group of Marines in shorts and tank tops, all matching. They rowed past in unison, like one hive mind.

Widow turned his attention from the view to the backyard. The landscaping there was even better than the front.

There were containers with gardens of bonsai trees, pruned and trimmed and snipped and cared for, as much as the greenery in the front yard.

"Wow!" he said.

"Yeah. It's lovely out here, isn't it?"

"It's very nice," Widow said and pointed at the bonsai trees. "Did you do those?"

"I did. It's a hobby of mine."

"They're great. I bet they're worth some money."

"They can be quite expensive. But I don't sell them. I enjoy raising them. It's my place of Zen."

"Can you fish back here?"

"You can with a gaming license, I suppose."

"Do you ever fish?"

"Do I look like a fisherman?"

Widow wasn't a dumb man—slow maybe, but not dumb. He believed in seizing opportunity when it presented itself. When a beautiful woman with a badge gives you permission to check her out, you take it. He turned back and seized the day. He looked her over from top to bottom. Not slowly, but not fast either.

She had nice eyes, skin softer than a feather, lips red as a rose, and smarts like she was brought up on the streets of Tokyo or LA or New York; Gray was a total package.

"Not a fisherman."

She shook her head and smiled.

He asked, "What?"

"Nothing. We should get to work. You want coffee?"

"Does a duck fart in the woods?"

"What?"

"It's an expression."

"I don't think it is."

"I'll take coffee. Black. No cream. No sugar."

"I already knew you'd say that."

She turned her back to him and headed into the kitchen. She sifted through cabinets and pulled out a pair of coffee mugs, both the same standard twelve-ounce size. Then she looked sideways at Widow and reassessed her tactics, and returned one mug to the cabinet. She reached up to a higher shelf on tiptoes and pulled out a jumbo-sized coffee mug. It was big enough to bake a cake in.

Satisfied that she'd made the right choice, she went to a Keurig machine and slipped in a coffee pod. She set the large mug under the spout and tapped a button, and the machine started rumbling. She repeated the process in order to fill the cup.

Widow stared out the dining room window at a brown pelican flying over the river. He watched it go up and circle back and swoop down, gulping river water and a fish right out of the river.

Pelicans were among the dive-bombers of the bird world. Bird watching wasn't a hobby of Widow's, but he had grown to appreciate birds over the last several years. If you need to learn about danger ahead, learn about birds.

"Have a seat," Gray said.

Widow turned to face her and hopped up on a stool at a bar top that merged into the kitchen counter on the other side. More Japanese knickknacks were scattered all over the kitchen.

Waiting for the coffee, Widow asked, "Were you born in Japan?"

"No. I was born in the Regency Room at UC San Diego. Thirty-one years ago. My parents were born in Japan. They came to the US before I was born."

"They still alive?"

"They live in Florida. They're what you call retired."

After the coffee was made, Gray slid him the oversized cup. It was heavy and black, like oil. Steam piped out of the top. He took a sip, like putting a toe in the water. Then he took full swigs from it. It was perfect.

"It's good. Thank you. Tastes better than Starbucks."

"It is Starbucks."

Widow nodded and took another pull from it.

They sat and chitchatted for a long time, getting to know each other as newly minted partners do. At one point, Widow thought about his first day as a part of a SEAL platoon. It wasn't nearly this nice.

His first day, four of the SEALs came at him in the middle of the night.

Widow was unarmed. They were unarmed. They told him they were going to beat his ass. It was all part of a hazing ritual that went back to the beginning of the SEALs. It was unofficial, off the books, and the practice was denied by the brass. But it existed.

The unexpected thing was the four guys who came after him ended up being the ones in the dirt. One of them had to get stitches, which required him to lie about how he got them. The next day, five SEALs came at him. And five SEALs went down—two needed stitches.

The third day, six came at him. This time, they all went down, and he ended up needing two stitches, both on his fist right between the index and middle finger knuckles. His bone tore through the skin from three straight days of punching.

The seven of them, him included, called it a draw. Rituals were rituals until they were broken.

Gray and Widow talked small talk for a while. Widow didn't mention the SEAL hazing. An hour later, they realized time had gotten away from them, and they went to work. They had a long day of research ahead of them.

Just then, Gray's phone buzzed. She reached into her back pocket and pulled it out, and checked the screen.

She said, "Text message. Your friend is safe."

"Friend?"

"The lawyer."

"Aker?"

Guess he didn't leave town after all, Widow thought.

"Yeah. But the wife and kids went to school and work. But don't worry. They're all returning home."

"Okay. That's good."

Gray put the phone on the bar top and left the room. She returned a few minutes later with a MacBook in hand. She set it on the bar in front of an empty stool next to Widow and climbed up and sat down.

Widow said, "Thanks for putting a team on Aker. What about Tunney?"

"We got a guy posted there too. Plus hospital security."

Widow nodded.

Gray asked, "Tell me about these stocks."

"All I know is the trading letters are SHG."

"What does that stand for?"

"I have no idea. Been asking that all day. I can't seem to find anyone who knows what it stands for."

Gray looked at him sideways again. It was a look he thought he might get a lot from her. He understood that it was the look she gave when someone did something stupid or, in his case, didn't do something obvious.

She picked up her phone, unlocked it with her fingerprint, and tossed it to him, slower than a *think-fast* throw, but just as surprising. Widow caught it and stared at her.

Gray stared at him, waiting for him to catch on.

Finally, she said, "Widow, we have internet now. Everyone has it on their phones. When you don't know the answer to something, google it."

He looked at the phone screen. She stared and started giggling. It started like a low rumble and then turned into a full laugh, the kind that takes control and can't be tamed.

He looked at her.

"What?"

She held up a hand as if she was telling him to wait a beat while she caught her breath. She slowed her laugh down to a more manageable thing. Her cheeks blushed from the laughing.

She said, "Have you ever seen one of those commercials with the Stone Age man trying to figure out a modern device? Like a computer?"

Widow took a glance at his faded reflection in the sliding door.

"Hey. What's that supposed to mean? I look like a caveman?"

"You kinda do. Like a man out of time."

"I'm not that much older than you, you know."

"What are you? Forty?"

"Not quite."

"I'm sorry. It just hit me. I couldn't help it. I hope I didn't hurt your feelings."

A blow to his ego from a beautiful woman. It wasn't the first time. It wouldn't be the last time.

He clicked on the phone screen and the internet icon and googled *SHG* and the word: *stocks*.

Before he could read any of the search results, the phone rang in his hand.

Gray asked, "Who is it?"

She leaned in across the counter space between them. He showed her the screen. There was no name displayed for the caller ID, just a number.

"It's my guy. Answer it."

Widow clicked the talk button. Gray reached out and tapped the speaker button. They both listened.

A voice said, "Gray?"

"Yeah. It's me," Gray answered. "What you got?"

She mouthed to Widow, "It's one of my guys."

Widow nodded and held the phone out between them.

"The lawyer wants to talk to Widow."

Gray spoke to Widow.

"Go ahead."

"Widow here."

"Widow, there are armed guards here at my house," Aker said. There was fear in his voice. Widow figured he wasn't used to having armed men in his house. Then again, who was?

"I know."

"Did you do this?"

"Yes. There's no choice."

"Is this really that necessary?"

"It wouldn't have been if you'd left like I asked."

"We can still leave."

"It's too late now. Things have changed. Trust me; the protection is for your own good."

"Are these guys all that dangerous?"

Widow said, "Look what they did to Tunney."

"He shot himself."

"You still believe that?"

Aker was silent a moment as if he was processing the truth, trying to believe it not to be true. It was easier for a normal guy like him to see the lie as the truth. Violence wasn't a part of his reality.

"I don't know."

"Just do what our guys tell you, and your family will be okay."

"Okay."

Gray opened the screen to her MacBook and typed away on the keyboard, and swiped her fingers across the track pad. Eventually, she found what she was looking for and reversed it and pointed at the screen.

The screen showed a website. It answered the question that Widow had been asking for two days.

Aker answered the same question.

"Widow, I looked up SHG. It stands for Samson, Harwin, & Gaden. I think they make weapons for the government."

"Yeah. I got it. Thanks. Be safe. Do what our guys tell you. Talk to you later."

Widow didn't wait for a goodbye. He pressed the call end button and hung up the phone. He turned and looked at Gray's screen. She skimmed the website and started summarizing it for him.

"These guys are huge, Widow. Look at this. It says here Samson, Harwin, & Gaden is a corporate conglomerate. It started in the nineties and has grown to expand many industries. But it started as a weapons company. Now, they're into pharmaceuticals, vehicles, military and civilian, and still doing weapons."

"That's a lot of pies to have your fingers in."

Gray nodded.

Widow said, "And Eggers got fifty million worth of their stocks. Why? How?"

Gray said, "There must be a connection between them and his death."

"Maybe. I saw the guys who killed him from a distance, on a video monitor, but they're good. I recognized definite talent."

"They military?"

"Military-trained. This company has the money to employ guys like that. Certainly. Fake NCIS badges are expensive, I bet. But with money like this, they can buy anything they want."

"Maybe the badges are real."

"Could be. That'd cost more than fake ones. But if someone can afford it, it'd be these guys."

Gray asked, "Why would they want to kill him?"

"I have no idea."

Gray stretched out her back like a cat.

"Looks like we have homework to do. Let's move to the sofas," she said, and she climbed off the barstool. She scooped up her MacBook, grabbed her coffee, and led him back to the living room.

She said, "Don't spill that coffee on my stuff."

"I won't."

Widow followed her to the living room. She took the loveseat, put her feet out, and put her MacBook on her lap. Milo followed and hopped up on the loveseat next to her. He curled up into a ball and drifted off as if it was the easiest thing in the world for him to do.

Widow took the couch but didn't stretch his feet out because it was her house, not his. He just set his coffee on the coffee table and sat straight up.

Widow looked at the phone screen.

"Your phone locked up. Got a passcode?"

"Hand it to me."

Widow reached the phone over, and Gray took it and unlocked it. Then she went online and typed in a password to the NCIS private servers. She leaned up and stretched and handed the phone back to Widow.

"Here you go."

Widow reached over and took it back.

Gray said, "Just type in the search bar at the top. You can see any files I'm cleared for. Which should be all of them."

"Great."

"You start with Eggers' file. His history and family. I'll look into Samson, Harwin, & Gaden. See what I can find out. Bet you're not used to this."

"What?"

"Doing all your own research?"

"I don't mind it. I enjoy it. Part of the fun is uncovering what the bad guys don't want you to uncover."

"You ever miss just being out there? Undercover?"

"I do. I miss all of it."

"You can always come back."

"Not now. Not after experiencing freedom the way I've experienced freedom."

Gray said nothing to that. She just went to work, and so did Widow.

They worked through the morning and through lunch and into the late afternoon. Every so often, Widow had to tap the phone's screen because it would dim, some kind of power display setting.

For hours, he sifted through Eggers' Navy records and combed through his NCIS file and any known affiliations. Then he read about known affiliates and combed through their files. He read about missions he had never heard of. A lot of the details were redacted, even on the official files. Sometimes his mind filled in the blanks, and sometimes he just moved on. There was a lot of information, a lot of bureaucratic BS. After Action and Crime Reports are not page-turners. Many times he got bored and thought about quitting. He thought about catching a bus. Maybe he could head down south for the winter. But he snapped out of it and refocused on research.

Eggers had been active duty for nineteen years. He was a SEAL for sixteen, as many years as Widow's entire Navy/NCIS career combined.

Eggers had grown up in a small town in Nebraska, where he married his high school sweetheart. She passed away when he was in the service. His daughter, Maven, left for college around the time he jumped ship back in two thousand. He never contacted her after he dropped out of the Navy, and the NCIS and Navy records didn't show any known information about her current whereabouts.

Gray spent the whole morning and most of the afternoon searching through Samson, Harwin, & Gaden's website and reading articles about them posted on business websites. She spent a good bit of time learning about stocks and trading just so she could understand the lingo. She also looked through public contracts and any filed court cases related to SHG. Being a company worth so much money, they had the equivalent of a law student's nightmare of briefs to read through. But she sifted through them, searching for any connection she could find to Eggers.

As they approached the late afternoon, Gray said, "You finding anything?"

"Yeah. A lot. I found out about his daughter. She was born Maven Eggers."

"Maven?"

"That's her name. Don't look at me. I didn't pick it."

"What else?"

"She's like a ghost. It's weird. She's obvious for most of her life until twenty years ago when Eggers quit the Navy. And here's something interesting. He didn't quit. He went AWOL."

"AWOL?"

"Yeah, right when he was coming up on his twenty-year mark."

"He could've just retired."

"But he didn't. Something must've scared him away."

Gray asked, "What about the daughter?"

"She vanished. Her trail went cold."

"She marry? Change her last name?"

"Nothing here about that. There's no paper trail."

"That means nothing. Why would anyone follow her? Unless there was an investigation about him vanishing."

"There was an inquiry, but he was almost twenty years in. No one's going to kick up a fuss about a man quitting a month or two before he could retire, anyway."

They said nothing more about it. They went quietly again, back to their respective projects. Until twenty-one minutes later. Widow said, "This is interesting."

"What?"

"Back in two thousand, Eggers' last year in and about six months before he took off, he was in a SEAL platoon. And one of his teammates was gay."

"So?"

"He was murdered."

Gray sat up straight.

"Murdered? Did Eggers have something to do with it?"

Widow read off the phone's screen, glancing up at Gray and back down at the screen.

"No. They accused a sailor named Dwayne Shore. The whole thing happened right before Eggers dropped out. The next summer, Eggers was up for reenlistment, and he didn't reenlist. He just missed his retirement with that one. It all happened twenty years ago."

"There must be an NCIS file on the investigation."

"That's what I've been reading. Eggers had nothing to do with it. Other than they were in the same SEAL platoon."

Gray asked, "Did SEALs kill their own for being gay? I've heard rumors of that sort of thing, like killing their weakest link. I've heard of it in the Corps and Army too. What do they call it?"

"Code Pink. I've heard of it before too, from all over the military. But I've never heard of a SEAL doing it. Guess it's possible. But the SEALs I knew didn't care about being gay or straight or black or white or orange or purple. All they cared about was if you could shoot straight and follow orders and you had your brother's back."

"Still, it might be connected. Probably a long shot."

Widow said, "As ugly as it might get, we should turn over that rock, anyway. Until we get something more solid to go on."

"Agreed. Read me the rest."

Widow read the summary report and related news clippings about the whole story. Some were from the *Navy Times*, and some were from other news outlets.

In the end, he recapped it for both of them to hear.

Widow said, "A gay SEAL was murdered. An NCIS investigation concluded that he was killed by his lover, another sailor, Dwayne Shore. Shore wasn't on the SEAL teams. He was an E-3, a seaman."

Gray asked, "What happened to him?"

"Shore went to prison for the crime, where he hung himself. It's very detailed. He stuffed toilet paper rolls under the cell door so no one could break in and save him in time. And he hung himself from the bars on the window. He used bed sheets, ripped up and twisted and doubled to be strong enough to do the job.

"It also says that he pleaded his innocence until the day he died. Even claimed he was innocent in a suicide note."

Gray asked, "What's in the note?"

"It photocopied right here. He wrote: *I prayed to God that I would be found innocent. I guess the truth will be revealed in my death. Henry, I love you.* And that's all he wrote."

Gray stared at Widow. Her eyes were glassy, partially from staring at a computer screen all day and partially from the story he'd just told.

She said, "That's horrible."

"It is. Tragic."

"You think there's a connection?"

"Not sure. Fifty million dollars in stock from a weapons giant and now a dead gay SEAL."

"Any more details?"

Widow thumbed through the reports on screen. He read some more out loud.

"The dead gay SEAL had just gotten back from a mission with five others," Widow said. He looked up at Gray and asked, "Can you get their names? They're not listed here."

"Sure. That'll take some strings pulled. But I'm sure Cameron can get all we need. SEAL missions younger than thirty years old are protected under the National Security Act."

Widow took a pull of his coffee, which was the third jumbo cup he had so far.

Gray asked, "What was *his* name?"

"Henry Cho. Born in Los Angeles. He died right before his thirtieth birthday."

Gray stood up and moved to the sofa, next to Widow. She smelled like roses and incense. It was nice. Widow tried not to make it known that he liked it. She leaned up next to him, and they both looked at Cho's case and history.

Gray read out loud.

"Cho was stabbed to death. He was stabbed sixteen times."

Gray scrolled to the case evidence, which included photos of Cho's dead body and stab wounds at the scene of his apartment.

"Jesus!" she said. "Look at those wounds. They're deep."

Widow said, "And strategic."

"They looked chaotic to me."

"They are chaotic but strategic and tactical."

"They look more like a crime of passion to me, not tactical."

"They start out tactical. Look at this one," Widow said as he pointed at a deep wound on Cho's abdomen.

Gray looked.

Widow said, "See this one?"

Gray nodded.

Widow said, "It's up under the ribcage into the heart. And the killer twisted the knife in such a way that no paramedic could save him. He bled out and suffered a long, agonizing death. The rest of these wounds are done not out of passion, but they're frenzied, as if the killer started with a killing wound he had been trained to do, and then he went into a rage and stabbed the body over and over. But it was that first wound that killed him. Cho was never going to walk away from that one."

Gray was quiet a long minute. Then, she said, "Scroll back to the top. There should be a photo of him. I want to see him."

Widow scrolled up with one finger until they found a link. As Gray reached across him, her fingers grazed the back of his hand. She clicked the link, and the screen changed until they were both staring at Cho's face.

Like Gray, Cho was also Asian American. Widow wasn't sure which specific country made up the Asian part.

Cho had a wide smile. It was all lips. He didn't show his teeth. He had kind eyes, also like Gray. He looked youthful and vibrant. He had a tuft of thick black hair, even clipped a quarter inch from his scalp.

Gray said, "He was so young."

"Twenty-nine when he was murdered. I have no idea how old he is in this picture. He could be twenty-one or could be eighteen. The Navy takes them the day of their eighteenth birthday."

"Either way, he was just a baby in this photo, and when he was killed."

"You're thirty-one, right?"

"Yes. But I'm an NCIS agent now. I already did the Navy thing."

"True."

She turned her head and looked into his eyes.

"Remember my birthdate?"

"You didn't tell me the date. Just the month."

"Which is?"

"August."

She nodded and reached across him again and clicked the back button at the top of the browser. The screen went back to the file summary. She put her hand on the phone and scrolled through the pages until she found what she was looking for, which was a list of witnesses and Navy personnel and NCIS agents involved in the case.

She tapped on the screen over the names and looked up at Widow, into his eyes.

"We should talk to the agents who investigated. They can tell us more. That's them there."

"We should go see Cho's parents too. Maybe they can tell us something."

"Okay. Where're they now?"

Widow looked through the file.

"Looks like Cho's last known address was Los Angeles, in the Hollywood Hills. His mother's name is on a deed there. I guess we're going to Hollywood."

"Hollywood? We can just call her on the phone."

"Her son was murdered. You want to call her? Better in person."

Gray said, "He was murdered twenty years ago."

"Still, better in person. We're investigating here. We need to see, touch, smell, and taste evidence, not just hear it."

"You're going to taste evidence?"

"Sometimes. Like a narcotics cop might taste a suspected powder."

Gray shrugged and said, "Why do I get the feeling you're just trying to get a free trip to California out of the NCIS?"

Widow shrugged.

"Okay. So we're going to California."

Gray stood up from the sofa and stretched in another catlike action. She turned and looked out the window, and then she looked at her wristwatch.

She said, "It's getting dark. We won't get a flight out tonight. Plus, I'm tired from reading all day. You probably are too. I should take you back to your hotel."

"I don't have a hotel."

"Where are you staying? You got a friend in DC or something?"

Widow thought of Kelly Li again. She lived in DC. He could go see her. He could probably stop by unannounced. And she might be glad to see him. That's if she was even home. Secret Service agents worked a lot.

Then again, she might've moved on by now. She might be in a happy relationship. There was no reason for him to interrupt her life.

He said, "I'm staying nowhere."

"Nowhere?"

"I can check into a motel, though. Not a problem."

Gray turned her head and looked back out the window at the quiet street in front of her house. Then she looked at the sofa under Widow's butt.

She said, "You can stay here. But no funny business. That sofa pulls out into a bed. You can take it. We have more to do. You want more coffee?"

"Does a duck fart in the woods?"

Gray ignored that. She waited for him to take the last pull from his coffee mug. Then she took it and went back into the kitchen. Five minutes later, she returned with two fresh coffees. Widow took his cup and sat back down on the sofa.

Gray took the phone and called Cameron to report in. She shared everything that they had learned and put in flight request and the request for the list of names of Cho's SEAL platoon.

They worked into the night. Around eight in the evening, Gray ordered Chinese delivery. When it arrived, they stopped to eat. They ate right there in her living room, Widow on the same sofa he'd started on. His feet remained planted on the floor. His posture remained as upright as when he was in school. However, one thing changed. During the Chinese dinner break, Gray moved to the same sofa Widow was on, the one with the pullout bed.

Just then, a bell dinged on her phone and her MacBook at the same time. She received an email in her secure NCIS email account. She stopped eating and opened her phone. She had an email from Cameron.

She opened it and looked at it.

She said, "It's a list of SEALs in Cho's platoon."

"How many names?"

"Fifteen."

She handed the phone to Widow, and he took it. The list comprised full names and ranks and jobs of each SEAL. Widow saw Henry Cho on the list.

Widow said, "There's Eggers. Right there."

Widow looked it over. He started at the top and worked his way down and repeated the process, memorizing the names.

Widow grunted like an ape finding a problem.

Gray stared at him.

She asked, "Anything suspicious there?"

"SEAL Teams comprise six platoons, each with sixteen SEAL team members. There are usually two officers, thirteen enlisted, and one chief."

"So, what's the problem?"

"There's a name missing from this roster."

"There is?"

"Yeah. There are only fifteen names here."

"Is that something to worry about?"

"No. It's not a big deal because SEALs and SEAL teams are always in transition. So the number's not always going to equal sixteen. Could be that someone left the unit, and they were expecting a replacement. The weird thing is that it's the chief."

"Huh. But don't they get swapped and moved around all the time too?"

"They do. I suppose."

Gray and Widow stayed on the sofa and sat close together. Gray never moved closer to him than she already was. She was near the other arm, and she stayed there until it was time for bed. Bedtime procedures, for her, rolled around at nine-thirty at night.

Just before that, she got a call from Cameron, the last of the evening. Cameron informed her they could fly out the next afternoon. She relayed the information to Widow and told him goodnight.

Widow slept uncomfortably on the pullout sofa. He spent a good bit of time thinking of Gray in the next room, asleep in her bed, until he drifted off to sleep.

32

Widow had slept in his clothes on the foldout bed from the larger sofa. The night before, he had moved the coffee table out of the way in order to open it. The bed wasn't the most comfortable thing he'd ever slept on, but it wasn't the worst either. He lay on one side, avoiding the lump in the middle as best he could. His feet hung off the bed. Another thing he was used to.

In the morning, Widow woke because he heard Gray stirring in her room. A minute later, she opened her bedroom door. Milo ran out past Widow and ran through a doggie door in the wall in the dining room.

Widow sat up. The early morning sun beamed through the windows and curtains from the east.

Widow yawned once, stretched his arms out, and got up off the foldout sofa bed. He pulled up all the sheets and blankets and the pillows that he'd slept with, folded all of them up, and set everything in a neat stack on the other sofa. Then he returned the foldout to its sofa position.

He followed his first instincts, which led him into the kitchen, where he helped himself to his first cup of coffee for the day. He did all the same things he had seen Gray do the day before. He used the same big mug he'd drunk out of the day before. He rinsed it in the sink and set it under the Keurig and took out an old coffee pod and inserted a new one from out of a metal tree filled with them. He hit a button that read: *Full Cup*.

It turned out to be a false advertisement, but he took it and went to the sliding door and opened it. He stepped outside, walked to the middle of Gray's backyard, and stood there, letting the breeze off the Potomac blow over him like it was an old friend. He stood in the center of a row of bonsai trees. He surveyed the landscape and the river and the sky. All was good. All was peaceful.

Thoughts of owning his own property like that someday swept over him. A place to call home. That would be nice. But then he thought about property taxes and busted pipes and HOA fees and lawn care and mortgages and interest rates and staring at the same walls every day and neighbors. He thought about the freedom he had right then, and he breathed out a sigh of relief.

Widow saw more brown pelicans across the banks of the river. Milo came running by from out of some bushes at the edge of the shore and the property. He was wagging his tail like he was happy.

The dog's got the dream life, he thought.

He finished his coffee outside on a bench against the back of the house. Then he went back inside and saw Gray making herself a coffee. Her hair was all over the place. One of her eyes didn't seem to want to wake up. She wore pajamas with some cartoons on them. Widow didn't recognize the characters.

She turned and walked past him like she didn't even notice him. She stopped and turned back.

"I'm going to take a shower."

"I'd like to get in on that."

She froze. The half-closed eye popped open, and she stared at him with both.

Widow said, "I meant after you're done. If that's okay?"

She smiled and said, "You can join me."

He looked at her, blank-faced.

"Kidding! Of course. You didn't think I was serious?"

"No. I was thinking about what Cameron would think."

Gray smirked.

"She'd love that."

Widow said, "I can take one after. If that's okay."

"Sure. After me. I pay the bills. Therefore, I get first dibs."

"Understood."

Widow returned to the kitchen and set the Keurig to make himself another *Full Cup* of coffee in the big mug. Afterward, he sat at the bar and waited. He heard the shower click on and the pipes hiss. After a while, steam piped into the living room from underneath Gray's bedroom door.

Suddenly Gray's phone started buzzing. She had left it out on the bar top. The ringer was off, but the vibrate feature was on. Widow stared at it. He wasn't sure if he should answer it or not. On the one hand, it could be Cameron. On the other, it could be someone else. And Unit Ten wasn't supposed to be helping him. He might answer it and get someone who knew his name. Then the jig would be up, and Gray would get into serious trouble. Also, it might be her boyfriend or someone with equal reason to be concerned that a strange man was answering her phone. So he let it buzz until it stopped.

But ten seconds later, it buzzed again. He did the same as before and let it buzz until it stopped. Again, it started up, buzzing and getting louder and louder. He let it go to voice-mail like before.

The house phone rang from its cradle.

He heard Gray from the shower.

"Widow, would you get that?"

Widow got up from the barstool and walked to the living room. He scooped the ringing phone up from the cradle and answered it.

A voice on the other end said, "Sonya! Why the hell aren't you answering your phone?"

Widow recognized the voice. It was Cameron.

"She's in the shower, Chief."

"Widow?"

"Yeah."

Cameron was quiet for a moment, processing the fact that Widow was answering Gray's house phone while she was in the shower, which meant that he had stayed the night.

"Get her out of the shower!"

"I'm not sure she wants me bursting in on her."

"Widow!"

"Yeah?"

"Gray sent two guys to your lawyer friend's house?"

"You know she did."

"You'd better get over there! Now!"

"Why?"

"Something's happened. I don't want to get into it over the phone. They're asking for her to get there. Get Sonya and get over there—double time!"

"Yes, Chief."

"And Widow?"

"Yeah?"

"Don't call any police. Tell Gray not to inform anyone else. Keep this between all of us."

Reluctantly, Widow said, "Okay."

He hung up the phone and walked to Gray's bedroom door. He knocked on it, but there was no answer. He heard the shower running and nothing else. He turned the knob to her bedroom and opened it just a crack.

"Gray!" he called into her room.

Nothing.

He opened the door more and called to her.

Nothing. No response.

He opened the door all the way, putting one hand over his face in case she should walk out of the bathroom naked. He peered through the gaps in his fingers and kept his eyes on the floor. He made his way to the bathroom door and opened it ajar, and called out to her.

"Sonya?"

"Yes? Who was it?"

"It's Cameron. She wants us to get over to Aker's. Something's happened."

33

WIDOW WAS AN ADEQUATE DRIVER, not a great driver, but better than a mediocre one. He had gone through the same combat, evasive, and high-speed car chase courses that Gray went through. His were decades before hers, but still as good. Only they must've improved the curriculum because she qualified for Formula One compared to him.

After Cameron called to warn them about the Akers' house and the protection detail, Gray dressed, and they hopped in the Charger and took off. She drove onto Ninety-Five, where she lit up the lights and kicked up the speed to nearly ninety miles an hour, dodging and weaving in and out of lanes.

Eleven miles in, she moved to the Four Ninety-Five express lane.

The whole drive, Gray had her phone synced to the electronics in the dashboard. She called ahead to the highway patrol to let them know she would speed through their tolls, in case they had lanes closed or other road work, anything that might disrupt their drive to Aker's place.

Twenty miles in, she redialed her guys every few minutes using voice commands. She kept getting nothing but busy signals from both agents.

"What the hell is going on?" she asked out loud.

"Maybe they're on the phone with Cameron?"

"Both of them?"

"Maybe. It could be a conference line. Or maybe she instructed them to wait till you get there before answering."

Gray shrugged and kept trying and kept driving.

After several attempts to get one of her guys on the phone, she called Cameron's number. The phone rang and rang, just like the other lines. She got nothing and hung up.

Gray said, "Maybe she's on the phone with them now?"

"She said to go straight there."

Widow said, "We can call Aker direct. I know his number."

Gray glanced over at him and nodded and unlocked her phone and opened the keypad.

"Give me the number."

Widow recited the number from memory. Gray dialed it and set the phone down in the cupholder. The phone rang over the car's speakers.

She zoomed around a cluster of cars and continued driving.

There was no answer.

Gray hung up the call and drove on. Widow could tell that her mind was painting the worst-case scenarios for what they might find.

The drive from her house in Quantico to the Akers' home in North Bethesda would've taken an hour under the best of circumstances. Gray made it in fifty minutes.

They got off the interstate and drove through various streets into the suburbs. She slammed on the brakes on the Akers' road, and the car screeched to a stop out front.

Gray's two agents were leaning against another navy-blue charger, another car from the NCIS motor pool like hers.

Gray parked the car, left the engine running and the blue lights flashing, and got out. She marched straight for her guys. Widow followed behind, moving slower. He kept his eyes on Aker's front door and windows.

The curtains were all closed tight. He saw one of them whip closed fast, as if someone had been watching for them to pull up and then jumped back out of sight.

If Widow didn't know better, he'd say it looked like a hostage situation. Closed blinds and drawn curtains. The house was quiet and dark.

Gray stopped right in front of her guys. She stood dead center between them. Her hands clutched her hips. A stern look grazed her face.

She asked, "What the hell's going on? You guys aren't answering your phones!"

The protection detail was two guys. They both had buzz cuts and dressed like NCIS agents who were trying to get noticed. They weren't wearing NCIS windbreakers, but they were damn close to looking like cops on a bad TV show. The only visible difference between them was that one was black, and one was white. They both had that look of good soldiers who follow orders.

"We don't know," the white agent said.

The black agent said, "They won't let us in the house."

The white agent said, "They keep asking for some guy called Jack Widow."

Gray turned and stared at Widow. He shrugged.

Widow turned, glanced at the front door. They heard the deadbolt unlock, and the front door cracked open. Aker stuck his head out halfway, just far enough for Widow to identify him. There were smaller hands on his chest, as if someone were standing behind him, clutching him.

Widow saw the house was dark. He couldn't see who was behind Aker. He turned and walked slowly up from the driveway, easing his way across stone steps laid down in the grass.

Aker opened the door a bit more. The guy's hair was disheveled. His cheeks were flush. His face was red and dark. He had huge black circles under his eyes, as if he had been crying or hadn't slept or both. He was a far cry from the neat, trimmed lawyer Widow had met two days earlier in that church.

Widow stopped several feet from the door. The welcome mat was two feet from the toe of his boot. He put his hands up to show his palms like he was trying to approach a lion in the wild, calming it with his gesture, showing that he wasn't a threat.

Aker opened the door wide. He was dressed almost unrecognizably different from before. He wore a white T-shirt under a black sweater and jeans with holes in them. He had house shoes on. His face and his hair looked unwashed. Widow saw nothing but darkness behind him.

"Come in," Aker said.

Widow stepped closer. He saw a woman's face appear from behind Aker. It was his wife. She looked worse than he did. Her face was flushed crimson and her eyes were puffed to the point of bursting. She'd definitely been crying—no doubt about that.

"What's going on?" Widow asked.

Aker glanced over at the protection detail standing in his driveway.

"Come in," he said. He opened the door wide enough for Widow to step through.

Gray followed, but Aker put up a hand.

"NO!"

Widow spun halfway back to her and put his hand up in the air.

"I'll be back out," he told her.

Gray froze and shrugged.

Widow entered Aker's home. Aker shut the door behind him and locked it.

The house was dark, but Widow's pupils dilated, and his vision adjusted. He turned back to them.

"Aker, what the hell is going on? Why are you locking them out?"

Aker's wife stepped out from behind her husband and walked up to Widow. She was about the same age as Aker, maybe a little younger. She had short blonde hair and a frame near the same size of Gray's, only without all the muscle definition. She wore a housedress, all white. She was luminous, even in the dark. She looked like a picture-perfect mother. She had huge blue eyes, which stared right up into Widow's. They were glassed over and filled with turmoil, giving the appearance of oceans and crashing waves. She looked like she was fighting back a frantic version of herself, ready to blow, ready to fall off the edge.

Widow said, "What's going on?"

She said, "Our daughters. They're gone."

34

"LET me get my friend to listen to this," Widow said.

"No!" Aker's wife said.

Aker reached his arm around her and squeezed her, consoling her.

"We were told no cops," Aker said.

Widow said, "It's okay. We can trust her. She's not a cop. Trust me. We'll need her."

They didn't protest. Widow didn't wait for them to change their minds. He backed up through the darkness, into the foyer, and out the front door.

He waved Gray over. She came up the walkway to the front of the house.

She said, "Widow, what's happening? My guys are as confused as I am."

"Come inside."

He took her by the hand like lovers. He didn't do it on purpose. It just felt right. She didn't complain. He led her back through the open door and into the Akers' dark house. He closed the door behind them and released Gray's hand.

Widow led Gray into a living room. She followed close behind him. Her eyes still needed to adjust to the low light.

Widow presented her to Aker and his wife.

"Michael, this is Sonya Gray. She's with me."

Gray's eyes adjusted, and she reached out a hand to Aker. He took it and shook it. He didn't make eye contact. He just stared at the floor.

Widow looked at Mrs. Aker.

"Ma'am, I'm sorry. I don't know your name."

Aker's wife said, "Gill."

She offered a hand to Gray, slow, and feeble. Gray took it and shook it.

"It's nice to meet you, Gill," she said. "What's going on here? Why did you guys lock the doors on my agents?"

Widow said, "Why don't you two sit down and tell us?"

He pointed at a sofa against the living room wall. The Akers nodded and moved to the sofa. Michael kept his arm around his wife, leading her to the sofa like she couldn't be trusted to do it herself, like a caring husband would.

The Akers sat.

Gray and Widow moved to the center of the room and sat on two chairs opposite the sofa. Widow put his hands on his knees and sat up straight and listened.

Aker spoke while keeping his wife calm.

"We have two little girls."

Gray nodded along. She knew that. It was in her guy's report. Then she looked around the room and through open doors for the girls. She must've realized that they weren't there, because her eyes opened wide. She was about to jump out of her seat to get on her phone and call in a team to recover them. But Widow shot her a stare, asking her to wait. She caught on and stayed in her seat.

Widow turned to Aker and said, "Go on."

Aker said, "They're twins. Five years old. They're gone. We woke up this morning, and they're gone—no sign of them. We got the agents in here, but my wife called me from their bedroom. We can't involve the cops. We shouldn't be involving you now."

Aker paused a beat and swallowed and asked, "How could this happen? How could they have gotten past your agents?"

Gray said, "I don't know, sir. But we're going to get them back."

Gill Aker said, "How?"

Gray didn't answer that.

Widow asked, "'There's a ransom note?"

Aker said, "No note."

"How do you know not to involve the cops?"

Aker lifted a hand like it was the heaviest thing he'd ever lifted. He pointed behind them to a short hallway.

"There's a message scrolled on a mirror in the girls' bedroom. See for yourself."

Aker said nothing else. He just went back to holding his wife.

Widow stood up and glanced at Gray. She stood and followed him back to the short hallway. They walked through the darkness. Widow didn't go for a light switch. In case this whole thing came to an FBI investigation, he didn't want his fingerprints confused with any potential kidnappers.

He figured Gray was thinking the same thing, because she didn't mention it. And she also didn't go for the light switches.

In the hallway, she whispered, "Widow, we should call this in. I'm obligated."

"No. We say nothing until we have a look. If you feel you can't handle that, then you should step outside. I'm not obligated."

Gray said nothing to that. She didn't leave. She stayed with him. She reached into her pocket and took out her smartphone, turned on a flashlight app. The phone lit up the way in front of them.

Widow came to the girls' bedroom door. It was obvious because there were kids' drawings and small handcrafted art made stuck to the door. The door wasn't closed all the way. He used his boot to push the door all the way open. It squeaked on its hinges.

The Aker's house was all one level. The floors were dark hardwood throughout, with area rugs in all the right places.

The girls' bedroom was big, bigger than Widow had expected. There was a long floor rug covered in cartoon characters he didn't recognize. There were two sets of everything in the room. Two beds. Two little desks. Two chairs. There were two separate shelves with the same lineup of stuffed animals neatly placed in some kind of order. There was only one closet. The door was wide open. Inside, he saw the girls had split the sides up equally between them. Each side was an exact mirror of the other. The same clothes were all folded the same way. The same shoes were set out on the floor. There were two of everything, all neatly placed, all neatly arranged, and all mirroring the other side of the closet.

On the far-right wall were two matching desks. Above one of them was a corkboard with mementos strewn about. There were more kids' drawings and crafts. There were also several photos of the girls thumbtacked to the board. Widow could see they were two little fair-haired girls. They were smiling in every photo, like two happy little kids.

Widow was a good investigator. One of the secrets to being a good investigator was to stay cold, to stay unattached, but seeing their faces filled his veins with a furious blood rush. His teeth ground in his mouth. His temperature went up a degree. His heart started pounding in his chest. He knew that once he had them back safe and sound, there would be hell to pay for the man who had taken them.

Gray gasped when she shone the light, or did something else that indicated she was upset.

To the left above the beds was a large window with plantation shutters. Each bed had matching bedding. The beds weren't made. The blankets and covers were haphazardly thrown on the floor, as if the twins had been lifted right up from deep sleep and taken in the night, which was exactly what had happened, according to the Akers.

Gray moved the light back to the desks on the right.

She said, "They said there was a message on the mirror."

She shone the flashlight between the matching desks on a full-length wall mirror. Gray grabbed Widow's arm and squeezed it. Her nails dug into his forearm.

"Look!" she said.

A note was scrawled on the mirror. It was written in red paint from a kid's paint set. The tube was left open on one of the desktops. Red paint pooled under the nozzle onto the desktop.

The message read: *Get Jack Widow! Or they die! No cops! Or they die!*

That was it. There were no other instructions. No ransom. No trade. Just two demands.

"Are these your guys from the Escalade?" Gray asked.

"Have to be."

Widow stared at the message for a long time, seeming to read it over and over.

Gray said, "Widow? You okay?"

He turned and nodded and walked past her to the beds.

"Shine the light over here," he said.

Gray followed him with the light. He studied the beds and then turned to the shutters on the window. He reached up and grabbed the highest point of the opening cord and pulled it. The shutters opened with a swivel sound. Sunlight streamed into the room, illuminating the darkness with sudden white light. Gray shut off her phone light.

Widow studied the window without touching it. It looked intact.

"Let's check the rest of the house. Figure out how they got in."

Gray nodded, and they walked back out of the twins' bedroom into the hall. They went back to the living room. Because of the sunlight, the interior was much easier to see now.

Widow and Gray stopped in the living room and looked at the Akers.

"Did you guys touch anything?" Widow asked.

"No," Michael Akers answered.

Gray asked, "Any sign of a break-in?"

Michael Aker said, "The back door!"

He pointed toward the kitchen.

Widow asked, "Did you guys hear anything?"

Gill Aker said, "No! Nothing!"

Widow nodded and turned toward the kitchen. Gray followed behind him. The kitchen and dining room appeared normal. The Akers' kitchen was big. There was a large island in the middle. The light in the back of the house was better than in the front. Sunlight crept in between the shutters.

Widow walked right to the backdoor, which had panes of glass that connected to form one large window. The glass of one of the panels was busted out. There was broken glass all over a floor mat. There was dirt on the floor.

Gray said, "This is far from a clean break."

Widow stayed quiet.

Gray said, "I'm going to have to go over security protocols with my guys."

"I'd say so."

Widow leaned in and looked out the window. He stared down at a flower garden in the backyard. It was partially trampled.

He said, "Looks like the FBI can get a footprint out of Gill's flower garden."

Widow pointed at the dirt on the floor.

Gray said, "If we call them. We should call them now."

"No. Not yet."

Widow followed the dirt on the floor, and Gray stayed behind him. They walked back through the dining room, the living room, and back to the girl's bedroom.

Gray said, "Widow? What are we doing now?"

"We know they got in the house. And we know they got past your guys. I can accept that."

"I can't! I mean how did they get past my guys? They must've been slacking off."

"Not necessarily. Guards are not infallible. They have to pee just like everyone else. Maybe one stepped away for a second."

"We've got procedure for that."

Widow stayed quiet. He kept following the dirt crumbs over the floor to the kids' bedroom until they were back inside the room.

Gray asked, "What are you looking for?"

"I'm wondering something. How did someone take them out without the parents hearing?"

Gray thought for a moment and then said, "They drugged them?"

Widow stopped near one of the beds. He stared at part of the covers. They were off the bed, lying on the floor. He knelt over and sifted through the folds in the blanket and stopped cold.

From Gray's angle, she saw his shoulder's tense up.

"What is it?" she asked.

Widow reached down in front of him and found something. He pinched the end less likely to have been touched by the intruder, and lifted it up for Gray to see.

She stared at the object in terror. It was a small plastic syringe top cover, the kind used to cover the needle end of a syringe.

"They injected the girls with something."

"Poison?"

"No. I don't think so. It's probably a sedative. They must've done it in their sleep to keep them asleep and sedated so they wouldn't struggle. That's how they got them out without alerting the parents."

Gray asked, "Now what do we do?"

But the answer didn't come from Widow.

Right then, they heard a phone ringing.

Widow looked at Gray. They both start looking around the room.

"Where is that coming from?" Gray asked.

Widow dropped the syringe cap and left it where he'd found it, and stood up. He headed to one of the desks. He reached underneath and found a cheap burner phone. It was duct-taped to the bottom of the desk. He ripped it off, pulled it out, and showed it to Gray.

"Answer it."

Widow clicked the talk button and put the phone to his ear.

A male voice asked, "Jack Widow?"

35

GRAY STOOD BY WIDOW. She stared at him, stared at his face. She looked for signs of response, something that might tell her what the caller was saying.

From the other room, both Michael and Gill Aker came straight back to their daughters' bedroom after they heard the phone ring. They stopped in the doorway, standing together, holding each other like one parental unit.

Gill Aker said, "Is it them? Tell them not to hurt my daughters. Tell them we'll give them anything they want."

Michael Aker put a loving hand on his wife's shoulder. He pulled her as close to him as anyone could.

He said, "Let Widow talk."

Widow stood over the little desks. He looked like a giant compared to them. He closed his eyes and tried to listen to the background for any signs that could help him track the caller.

"You know my name. But I don't know yours. Who are you?"

The caller said, "I have to say, what bad luck it is that our paths cross like this again."

Again? Widow thought. *Does he mean from two days ago? The Escalade following him around?*

Widow asked, "Are they alive?"

"Straight to the point? That's not your style. Not really. Not what I've heard."

"What've you heard?"

"I heard you liked to pretend to be a Navy SEAL. That you used to rat them out to your bosses. Whoever the hell that was. I heard you're some kinda hotshot undercover operator. That true?"

"Meet me and find out."

The caller laughed.

"We have already met. What's the matter, Widow? Searching your memory for who I am?"

Widow glanced back at Gray. She shrugged. Quickly, Widow put a hand over the phone's receiver. He whispered to her.

"They know about me. About Unit Ten."

Gray stared back at him, with questions in her eyes like she thought there was a leak somewhere. Or maybe these guys had a contact, an NCIS informant.

Widow repeated his question.

"Are they alive?"

Silence.

"I saw you the other day. You know? At the park bench, where Eggers died."

Widow stayed quiet.

The caller said, "You're no fun, Widow. So, I'll just cut to the chase. Go there now. Alone. Tell your NCIS buddies to go home. I see one person wearing navy blue, or a car, or a guy on a cell phone I don't like. I'll kill these little girls. I'll send pieces of them to their parents. There'll be so many pieces that it'll take weeks to gather them to get enough to bury. You understand what I'm saying?"

The Akers couldn't hear the caller's side of the conversation, but Gill knew what was being offered. She sensed it. She read it on Widow's face. The frantic side she was trying to hold back wouldn't be restrained any longer. She covered her mouth and burst into screams. She screamed into her hands. Michael grabbed her with both arms wrapped around her tight. He used all of his strength to pull her back out of the doorway and into the hall.

Gray saw the same thing that Gill saw. She grabbed Widow's forearm with one hand and squeezed it. Her other hand covered her mouth like she was trying to cover up her gasps.

Rage filled Widow worse than before. He couldn't hide it. He clenched his fist tight like he was going to use it as a sledgehammer.

Gray felt his forearm expand and tighten under his coat sleeve.

The caller said, "And Widow?"

Widow breathed in and breathed out.

"Yes?"

"Bring the drive with you. You know? The video feed you got from Haspman. And make sure it's the only copy! Make sure it's original. We can check it. We got a guy who can tell if it's a copy or if it's been copied or even downloaded. It better not have been. If you got copies, bring them. You know what happens if you don't?"

The guy's voice sounded familiar. It had just hit Widow. But he couldn't place him. There was too much fury in his blood for him to think clearly, objectively.

"Yes."

"What?"

Widow stayed quiet.

The caller said, "Tell me what happens if you deviate from my instructions."

Widow glanced over at the Akers. He looked at Gill. They met eyes.

He said, "You'll kill them."

"That's not what I said. Tell me exactly what I said. Say it out loud. Repeat it verbatim. I want the parents to hear you say it. I know they're there. I imagine they're in the room with you now."

Widow paused and said, "You'll kill them. You'll send pieces of them to their parents."

"And?"

"There'll be so many pieces that it'll take weeks to get enough of them to bury."

"Close enough. Thank you, Widow. Keep the phone on you. See you soon. Don't take too long. I'm short on patience."

The caller hung up, and the phone went dead.

Widow pulled the burner phone away from his ear and stared at it. He slipped it into his pocket with the phone Aker had given him. He turned and looked past Gray and stared at Gill Aker. She was sobbing uncontrollably. He stared at her for a long second. Then he turned to Gray.

"He wants me to meet him."

Michael Aker said, "I'm coming with you!"

Gill Aker said, "We both are!"

Gray said, "No! Out of the question! You guys stay here! We'll get them back!"

Gill Aker said, "No! We're coming!"

Widow put up a hand.

"None of you are going. I have to go alone. He'll hurt them if I don't do exactly as he said."

Michael Aker asked, "Do you think he'll give them back?"

"Yes. I do. If I follow his instructions, he'll return them unharmed. He just wants something from me. That's it. I'm going alone."

Gray said, "Like hell you are."

Widow looked down at her. He stared into her eyes.

He said, "No choice. We're out of time. He said to meet him now. I have to do this. Otherwise, we might never see the girls again."

Gray didn't argue. They pushed past the Akers and into the living room and back to the front door.

Michael Aker asked, "Are you going to get them back?"

Widow stopped at the door and turned back.

"I'm going to meet the kidnappers right now."

Gill Aker had tears in her eyes.

"Please, get my babies back," she said.

"I will, ma'am," Widow said. He opened the front door and walked out into the sunlight.

Gray followed close behind him.

"Do you think these guys are telling the truth?"

"I don't know."

"Could be a trap."

"It probably is a trap."

"Who is it? Who's doing this?"

"The guys on the video. They want to meet where Eggers died."

"So, what do we do?"

"I go. Alone."

"What? No way!"

"I have to! You saw the message. You saw they snuck right in past your guys like it was nothing. They've bribed city officials. They seem to have a long reach. I can't risk the girls' lives."

"They already know we're involved."

"True. But I can't risk their lives."

"We're coming. That's final. We'll stay back. Don't worry. They won't know we're there."

Widow paused for a moment. Then, he said, "Agreed. But just you. No one else. You can drop me off and then fall back several blocks."

"Let's go."

36

THE DISTANCE from Aker's home in North Bethesda to Lincoln Park was less than the distance from Gray's house in Quantico to North Bethesda, but the traffic was worse. Gray drove faster and used the car's blue lights to weave in and out of traffic. Widow thought about complimenting her on her evasive driving skills, but let her concentrate on the road.

The heavy traffic was an issue. Gray was afraid they might miss their window. The kidnappers had only said "now." They didn't give a time limit. She mentioned it several times. Widow stayed calm, stayed collected. He knew they weren't going to miss it. The kidnappers were not out to trick them. They wanted to make a trade. They would be there when he arrived.

They arrived on a side street two blocks away from Lincoln Park about forty-five minutes after they'd sped off from Aker's house.

Gray hit the brakes and switched off the blue lights. She didn't want to draw unwanted attention. She parked in a fire lane and looked at Widow.

"You sure you want to do it this way?"

"What choice we got?"

Gray nodded and looked out the windshield like she was thinking. Then she pointed at the glove box.

"Open that."

Widow reached past his knees and popped the glove box open. Inside, the Charger's operational manual and some papers, probably the car's registration, were in a zip-lock bag. Then he saw a SIG Sauer P226 MK25, a beautiful firearm.

Gray said, "Take it."

Widow reached in and took out the gun. A Four Anchor symbol was etched on the barrel. He inspected the weapon. He ejected the magazine and studied it. It was fully loaded with nine-millimeter parabellums.

Widow set it on his lap. He checked the chamber. It was empty. He racked the slide and dry-fired it at the footwell. The metal *click* of the hammer was a fine sound.

Gray said, "That should look familiar. It's the official weapon of the Navy SEALs."

"It's not. This is the official weapon," Widow said, as he pointed a finger at his temple.

"Don't be so cheesy. Seriously, that's my personal gun. So only use it if you need to."

"Thank you. I love it. It's like coming home."

He smiled at her and inserted the magazine back into the gun. He racked the slide, sending a round into the chamber. The gun was chambered and ready for action. He tucked it into his waistband in the front and zipped up his coat to cover it.

Gray said, "You got a phone, right? Not their phone, but your own?"

"I have one that Aker gave me."

Gray nodded and said, "Program my number."

Widow said, "Just give it to me."

She smiled and recited her cell number to him. He memorized it and smiled back one last time. Then he opened the car door and got out. He walked the rest of the way.

Widow walked past two blocks, over to one of the side streets alongside Lincoln Park. Today was Monday and DC was up and active. He crossed busy streets and passed pedestrians headed in all directions. Most were busy-looking office workers, white-collar types. He passed some blue-collar workers, including a construction crew doing something at the street corner.

Once he was in Lincoln Park, he stopped and glanced up at the CCTV camera that the bad guys were interested in. Involuntarily, he reached into his coat pocket and squeezed the memory drive, the only bargaining chip he had to get the girls back safe and sound.

He entered the park and kept his hands in his coat pockets. He scanned everything he could, everything that moved. He passed the statues of Honest Abe and the other historic heroes. He passed a homeless woman sleeping on a bench. She was covered in blankets. He passed people enjoying the park, many killing time till they had to go to the office and punch in.

He walked toward the bench, the place where Eggers was murdered, hidden in a dark corner. He noticed the shadows getting more prevalent as he passed under the same huge trees and same colorful foliage he'd seen the other day.

Widow crossed through a clearing and turned onto the path with the bench. He slowed as he approached. Under the shade of the trees, he saw the yellow police tape dangling from the park bench. It had been snapped in various places and abandoned by the police and forgotten.

A man was sitting on the bench. His legs were crossed. His hands were on his lap. A Starbucks coffee was parked on the arm of the bench. It looked like a grande size. The guy must've been waiting a long time; he'd brought coffee. Or maybe he got the coffee because it made him look more like a guy who belonged there than a stranger sitting around on a park bench all day.

Either way, the coffee didn't make Widow hate the guy less.

As Widow got closer, he saw the man wore an M4 protective mask and heavy sunglasses to cover his face.

Widow scanned the terrain, looking for others, but there was no one else—just the one guy on the bench.

Widow kept going; his hands stayed in his pockets.

At about ten meters away, the man raised a gloved hand.

He said, "That's far enough."

Widow said, "Where're the girls?"

"You got the drive?"

"It's safe."

The man stood up from the bench. He left the Starbucks coffee where it was. He had a Glock 17 fitted with a silencer in his hand. He held it down by his side. He was dressed in a dark coat, dark sweater, and dark blue jeans. The Glock and the suppressor blended right in at his side.

He walked toward Widow.

He said, "Take your hands out of your pockets."

Widow took his hands out slowly. He showed the guy his palms.

Widow was worried, which was unusual for him. He wasn't normally afraid of a guy with a gun. He'd had a lot of guns pointed at him in his life. A guy with a hidden gun in a crowded park usually wasn't a credible threat. But a man with a gun in a crowded park, wearing a mask and with a silencer attached to the gun, was a different story altogether.

The man walked toward Widow and stopped about twelve or thirteen feet away.

Widow took a step forward, testing the boundaries, but the guy snapped at him.

"Stay back!"

Widow froze.

The guy paused a beat, calmed himself. He kept the Glock down by his side and pointed over his shoulder with his other hand. He twisted at the waist and pointed back at the bench.

He said, "See the coffee cup there? I want you to watch it closely now."

Widow nodded and put both eyes on the cup, keeping the guy in his view. He watched the coffee cup.

Suddenly, the wind changed, and he heard an echo bounce between the buildings around the park. It echoed through the trees. It wasn't a loud bang or boom. It was more like the sputter of an exhaust pipe from a car.

The Starbucks coffee cup exploded. A hole blasted straight through it. Coffee burst through the air and splashed all over the bench and the grass, like water bursting through a broken dam. The cup was in a thousand paper pieces.

One second it was there and the next, it was gone.

The guy in the mask looked back at Widow.

"My pal is an excellent shot. He was a sniper once."

Widow asked, "Who did he work for?"

"Wouldn't you like to know? Let's just say he's damn good. Now, where's the drive?"

Widow dropped his shoulders like he was defeated and reached into his pocket, one-handed, and took out the thumb drive. He held it up and showed it to the guy.

The masked guy reached out a hand, his palm open.

"Toss it here."

"Where are they first?"

"They're safe. Toss the drive, and I'll tell you."

Widow said, "How do I know you'll keep your end?"

"Guess we'll have to trust each other."

Widow tossed the drive to him.

The masked guy caught it. He inspected it like a precious piece of jewelry. Then he pocketed it. He stepped closer to Widow, but stayed out of reach. The guy had big blue eyes. Widow recognized the eyes, but couldn't place him from just that detail alone.

Widow asked, "Where are the girls?"

The masked guy said, "If you try to follow me, my friend will put the next bullet in your skull."

With that, the masked guy walked past Widow, staying six feet away. Widow turned and watched the guy leave. When he was ten meters in the other direction, he stopped and turned back.

"Widow, leave town. Today. We'll be watching. Leave town and let things be. Or next time, we won't keep the girls alive. Next time, we'll cut them to ribbons. And believe me, he'll do it."

Widow noticed he said *he'll do it*, not *I'll do it* and not *we'll do it*, but he'll do it. He said it like either it was a slip of the tongue, or he was delivering a message, warning Widow of someone else, someone worse.

The masked guy lifted his free hand and pointed in the direction Widow had come.

"The girls are with Lincoln. That way."

Widow turned to look back. He must've passed them. He turned again to look at the masked guy, but he was gone. He walked away in complete silence, like a ninja. Widow couldn't remember seeing anything like it outside of the SEALs.

Widow gazed up at the skyline and the windows of various buildings across the street. He searched quickly for signs that the sniper was gunning for him next. But there was no other muzzle flash, no second shot.

Widow turned back the direction he'd come, back to the Lincoln statue, and he took off running.

He ran and ran, dodging park-goers as he ran. He jumped over a low brick wall and ran past park workers emptying trashcans. He nearly slammed into one, but he didn't stop. He kept running.

He saw the Lincoln statue and stopped. He looked around frantically. He wanted to find them fast. He didn't want to spend hours searching only to find later that the masked guy had tricked him.

Widow looked everywhere he could think of for them. He looked under the statue. Nothing. He looked under bushes. Nothing.

He felt stupid. He felt guilty that he'd let them die. He'd let them become victims of some madman who was willing to slice them to pieces.

But then he stopped and turned to the homeless woman he'd seen earlier, the one sleeping on a park bench near the statue. She was covered with cheap coats and jackets. He saw blonde hair spilling out from under where her head should be.

Widow ran over to her. He reached down, grabbed one of the coats, and ripped it off the homeless woman only to find it wasn't a sleeping homeless woman, but it was one of the twins. He ripped and jerked the rest of the old coats until he found both girls lying on the bench. He put his fingers under each of their little noses and found them still breathing. Then he touched their cheeks.

He remembered the syringe cap he'd found in their room. It must've been a powerful sedative. They were still asleep. They were out cold, but they were alive.

Widow breathed the biggest sigh of relief in his life.

Widow flipped both of them over onto their backs. The first thing he did was he felt all around them to make sure they still had all of their limbs and fingers and toes. He wanted to make sure they had lost nothing. And they were both completely intact. Then he brushed the hair off their faces.

But he stopped on the first girl's face. He stopped because he saw something that sent shivers down his spine. It was a message, a threat. It was a threat directed at him. It was horrifying.

On each of their foreheads, the masked guy had left two messages, scrolled with the same kid's red paint that they'd found in the twins' bedroom.

On one little girl's forehead, a message read: *STOP*.

On her sister's forehead, a message read: *KAM*.

37

GRAY AND WIDOW took the girls to the nearest hospital to get them checked out. Halfway there, the twins woke up confused and groggy, lying in Gray's backseat. But they seemed okay. They seemed to recognize Widow instantly. Maybe their father had described him to them. Maybe he had been a bedtime story. At the hospital, Gray flashed her badge to get things rolling and to keep the hospital staff from calling MPD.

They telephoned the Akers and her guys that were protecting them. Forty minutes later, they were all in the twins' hospital room, plus a nurse and a doctor. There were lots of questions from the hospital staff and lots of tests and lots of sighs of relief.

Widow saw a whole day of more questions and testing ahead. He felt anxious. He felt ready to go. He felt ready to find these guys.

At one point, Michael Aker made it clear that he wanted nothing more to do with this whole affair. Widow understood.

Gray offered to protect them longer, but Aker protested, which was understandable. They had done a terrible job of protecting them.

Widow suggested Aker take his wife and kids and leave town. He suggested they travel any compass direction, just go far, stay long, and tell no one.

The last thing that Aker said to Widow was they would head north, and Widow could call him if he worked everything out.

38

AFTER THE AKERS WERE REUNITED, Gray and Widow left the hospital and drove her car out of the parking lot. They headed south several blocks and merged onto a freeway before Gray pulled over on the shoulder. She left the engine running and slipped the gear into park. The Charger's engine idled like a bull in a rodeo stall, snarling, raring to go, like it was barely under her control.

"What are we doing?" Widow asked.

"You know, Cameron's going to be pissed that you handed over the only hard evidence we had. You gave them the memory drive. And we made no copies."

Widow said, "Couldn't be helped."

Gray turned away from him dramatically, as if she was acting for a camera. She took a breath and then she turned back to him.

She said, "We should just give up."

"Why?"

"We lost today."

"We didn't lose."

"How do you figure?"

"We saved two little girls. They could be dead."

"But they got away with our evidence."

"We still got Haspman. He can testify to everything."

"We don't have him. He's probably changed his name and run off by now."

Widow said, "Doubtful. The Metro Police Department has him by now."

"How do you know that?"

Widow cracked a smile. He pictured Haspman chained to a tree in his backyard.

Gray ignored his smile. She said, "Plus the way you described him, he's probably not going to talk, anyway."

"He'll talk."

"Either way, the MPD isn't going to share him with us."

Widow shrugged.

Gray said, "We're losing, Widow. We should just give up, let the MPD handle it."

"I disagree. We're winning the war."

"How do you figure that?"

"They're scared. We kicked a hornet's nest. Someone out there was trying to murder one of our own, cover it up, and get away with it."

"Widow, they've already gotten away with it. How're we going to find them now?"

Widow paused a beat.

He said, "Someone along the chain of command is an amateur."

"You think they're amateurs? They snuck past two career agents and kidnapped two girls right out from under our noses. Not an easy thing. So far, they seem pretty damn competent to me."

"The mercenaries at our end seem very good. But I don't think they're permanent employees. At least, they're not at the top. They're getting their orders from somewhere. There must be someone else higher on the food chain than them. Someone who doesn't know what he's doing. Or out of practice."

"What do you mean?"

"Mercenaries are for hire. These guys are damn good. But they're doing someone's bidding. They're taking orders. Whoever is giving the orders is no criminal mastermind. He should've just had them take out the cameras beforehand. Then we wouldn't even know what we know."

"If these guys were just the street guys, and they're so good, why didn't they just take out the cameras beforehand themselves?"

Widow paused a beat and looked out the window. Just then, it started raining. Subtle for the first few seconds, but soon it started coming down pretty hard.

Gray clicked the car's headlamps and rear lights. She switched on the windshield wipers to a low setting, just to keep the road ahead visible.

Widow said, "If they're former Special Forces operators, they might've been used to someone else taking out CCTV cameras before they reached the operation. These guys are just the operations side. They're not the support."

She said, "I don't know."

"I wouldn't underestimate them that much. The whole plan to kill Eggers and cover it up would've worked. It was us who shined a spotlight on it. My being here was just bad luck for them."

Gray was quiet.

Widow said, "Don't forget the money. Eggers damned them out of the gate with having a huge fortune to leave behind to his daughter. If we ever find her. That amount would've raised some eyebrows at some point. We need to look closer at Samson, Harwin, & Gaden."

"There's not much we can do on that front. Not without the FBI. SHG isn't military or Navy. They're private sector. We'd need the FBI to question them."

"What about the military contracts part? Can't we question them on that basis?"

"Maybe. I mean, we can find the nearest headquarters and question them on any basis we want, but they don't have to comply. And they probably won't. Huge companies like that won't open themselves up to questions from a government law enforcement agency. Not with the teams of lawyers they have to advise them not to."

Gray sounded defeated, overcome, beaten. Widow was confused. That didn't seem like her.

"You sound like you're ready to give up."

Gray turned away from him and stared out the window at the rain. Her movements were big and dramatic, as if she was performing. Widow wondered what she was doing.

She said, "What if they're watching us?"

"They *are* watching us."

"I'm serious! What if they go after Aker's kids again or one of us?"

"That scares you?"

"I'm not scared of anything."

Widow believed her.

Gray looked into his eyes and lipped something to him, which took him off guard. He stared at her lips, not reading them, just seeing them. They were full and red, with white teeth underneath. He remembered she had a great smile.

She poked at his chest and lipped, *"Widow! Pay attention!"*

He nodded.

She lipped, *"The phone they gave you."*

Widow had forgotten about it. His eyebrows rose, and he reached into the pocket of his Havelock and came out with the burner phone. He showed it to Gray.

He lipped to her, *"It's the phone from them."*

Gray lipped back, *"Might be bugged?"*

Widow took it into the palm of his hand and examined it. He flipped it from side to side. Then he eased the battery cover off the back and studied it.

He replaced the cover.

Widow said, "It's not bugged. But they could trace it. I bet they are. A cheap phone like this is a great decoy for having some kind of GPS app downloaded onto it."

Gray poked at his chest again and said, "That's why I was doing all that! Didn't you pick up on my signals?"

"No. Guess I'm rusty."

"At least now we know they're not watching us, but tracking us."

"You had me going. I really thought you were throwing in the towel."

"No way! These assholes killed one of our own! Plus, they're threatening two innocent little girls! I say we take them down."

Widow asked, "Dead or alive?"

"I prefer alive, but I won't cry over dead."

He said, "Call Cameron. Let's get back on track."

"What do I tell her?"

"Tell her we're getting lost for a while. They'll track me, but they can't watch us in the flesh if we're not here. We need to get away from their boots on the ground. Throw them off."

"Where are we going?"

"I need to show a big sign that I'm leaving town. Let them think we're walking away."

"So? Where are we going?"

Widow looked at the clock on the dashboard. They had a booked flight to Hawaii. They wouldn't make it, not even with Gray's Formula One racecar skills.

"We can't fly. Not out of here. They'll suspect something. Plus, they can check the flight destinations. And I thought of something else."

"What?"

"The case file said that Cho's parents lived in Los Angeles, and Shore's are in Hawaii. We should talk with both. We need flights to LA, and then we can get one to Hawaii from there."

Gray said, "We should rent a car from LAX and drive down to San Diego since we're going to be there."

"Why?"

"The agents who worked Cho's murder case are out of San Diego. Remember? We should talk to them in person. I can set it all up. But what about you? What about now?"

Widow said, "We'll split up for now. Take me to a Greyhound station. From there, I'll call you on Aker's phone and give you a different airport for us to fly out of."

Gray nodded and pulled out her phone. She googled Greyhound stations in the area and set her map app to give verbal directions. She flipped on her signal and merged into traffic.

Within twenty minutes, they pulled into a bus depot. Gray parked the car in a drop-off lane, and they both got out. Gray left the engine running. She walked around the nose of the car and met Widow halfway. The rain pounded down on their heads.

Gray said, "Goodbye, Widow."

She said it loud like an announcement, and then she did something unexpected. She wrapped her arms around him and hugged him tightly.

She whispered, "In case they're watching now."

Widow knew the odds of them tailing her and watching them now were almost zero, but he didn't complain. He hugged her back. He wrapped his arms around her, swallowing her up. He stayed gentle. As tough as she was, she was tiny compared to him. He was afraid to squeeze hard. He was afraid he might crush her.

Gray let go and backed away, and smiled. She waved at him as she got back in the car and drove off, leaving him to buy a ticket and get on a bus. He considered his choices and picked Atlanta.

Widow bought the ticket and waited. When they called his bus, he took one last look around and boarded the bus.

39

THE ODDS that Widow's enemies were watching were almost zero, but not quite zero. At the same moment that Gray was hugging Widow goodbye, a black Escalade with tinted windows pulled up into a good perch in a parking garage across the street from the Greyhound bus depot. The engine hummed, the tires swelled, and the sounds of the rain pounding on concrete echoed all around them.

Inside the Escalade, Sathers and the guy with the forgettable face stared through the windshield and through the rain and down two floors to the Greyhound bus depot.

They followed far behind the GPS signal from the burner phone Widow had in his pocket. While Widow and Gray were parked on the side of the freeway, they got closer. They were afraid of being spotted, but then, as if the heavens were on their side, it started pouring rain. They passed them on the freeway, while they were parked, and went unseen by blending in with a cluster of cars and the advantage of the gray sky and the rain. They took the next turnoff and turned around and doubled back from the other direction. Following the GPS led them to arrive in the parking garage across the street just as Widow and Gray were hugging in the rain in front of the NCIS Charger.

They watched the targets hug. Then they watched Gray get back in her car and pull away.

Sathers asked, "Should we stay with her?"

"No. Let her go. We can't keep following a federal agent around. She's bound to make us, and then she'll have her probable cause to justify investigating further. Plus..." the guy with the forgettable face paused and smiled and said, "we know where she lives."

"What about Widow?"

"He won't be coming back. I think he got the message."

"What if he didn't?"

"He did. I saw it on his face."

"What if he was faking it?"

"You don't think I can see when someone's lying to me?"

"Haspman swore not to tell. Look at what he did."

The guy with the forgettable face stared at Sathers with a flat-tened smile. He didn't say it, but his subordinate had a good point.

Sathers asked, "Didn't he used to lie to his SEAL teammates? Part of his being an undercover rat? Which means he must be an expert liar."

The guy with the forgettable face thought for a moment. He stroked his chin with his fingers.

He said, "You'd better get on the bus with him. Just to be sure."

"Get on the bus?"

"Yeah. He's never seen you. Just stay back. Hang tight. Make sure he stays gone."

"Want me to retire him?"

The guy paused a second to think it over.

"If you get the chance, take it at a rest stop or bus transfer. Get him alone and take him out. But if you don't get the chance and he gets off the bus at his final destination, and you think he's going about his merry way, let him go. We don't need more of a body trail."

"Sure thing."

Sathers grinned and brandished his Glock 34. He racked the slide and chambered a bullet. He re-pocketed the weapon. He turned to the guy with the forgettable face and nodded. Then he got out of the Escalade and shut the door.

The guy with the forgettable face got out after him, walked around the back of the truck, and got in the driver's seat. He waited and watched Widow buy a bus ticket. Then Widow walked over to the platform and took a seat on a bench.

Thirty seconds later, the guy with the forgettable face saw Sathers down below on the street. He crossed with his hands in his pockets. Just a guy crossing the street. He watched Sathers walk past Widow. Then Sathers went to the bus depot counter to purchase a ticket. He pointed at the platform where Widow was seated like he was asking the attendant, "What bus is loading up there?"

Then Sathers bought a ticket and casually found a place to sit far from Widow, but kept him in view.

Twenty-three minutes later, the guy with the forgettable face watched both men get on a bus to Atlanta.

* * *

WIDOW BOARDED the Greyhound bus and did something he hardly ever did when given the choice. He took a seat just past the middle of the bus. He sat at a window seat halfway between the middle of the bus and the rear tire. He sat in front of an older couple, which was on purpose. He wanted to know who was directly behind him.

He said hello to them both and smiled. His smile was returned warmly with a pair of smiles from both.

The bus loaded nearly full in no time at all, but the driver had set parameters how long he had to wait before the final boarding call. It was a good thing he waited the full amount of time because right before he boarded and closed the doors, one final passenger got on the bus.

Widow watched a man step onto the bus. It wasn't the KAM guy. He knew that. But it was an associate of his. He knew that, too. For any good Special Forces operator, the giveaway wasn't subtle at all. This didn't tell Widow that the guy wasn't any good at what he did. It just told him the man didn't care if Widow spotted him or not. Plus the guy was most likely under the impression that Widow wasn't expecting him to get on the bus. So why would he even be looking for anyone to be following him?

He was both portly and muscular. He was built somewhere between Mr. Universe and an oil drum. He was closer to the oil drum. The guy had a cue ball head, completely bald, whether from shaving it or an unlucky draw of the genetic lottery, was unclear.

The guy wore black canvas pants and a dark button-down shirt under a gray bomber jacket. He might've been older than Widow by a little or by a lot. It was hard to tell because he had that rough, weathered look on his face, which could mean a younger man with plenty of rough-life experience.

He had broad shoulders like tire wells. He was shorter than Widow, maybe by just two inches.

At first, the guy boarded the bus and swiveled his head from left to right like he was seeking someone in particular.

Widow stared out the window. He was just a rider minding his own business, eager to get the show on the road. But he felt the guy's eyes find their target—him. He felt the guy stop searching halfway back as soon as he saw Widow seated.

Widow saw out of the corner of his eye as the guy slowed his pace and stuffed his hands into his pockets. He sailed past Widow and took a seat near the back of the bus.

Widow had taken a slight risk by allowing the guy to sit behind him, out of his view, but he figured the guy wouldn't make a move on a bus in broad daylight with dozens of witnesses.

The bald guy's seat was a few rows behind Widow.

Widow shifted in his seat and leaned his head against the window. Once the bus left the depot and started its trek down to Atlanta, he closed his eyes and went into a deep nap.

40

WIDOW WOKE several hours later when the bus slowed and pulled off the freeway. It exited an off-ramp and circled behind a long service drive until it came up along the back of a truck stop. Dozens of tractor-trails were parked in the rear. Some were way off to the back of the lot, and some were lined up to pump gas.

The truck stop was a chain thing; he recognized the name. Attached to the gas station section were a small convenience store and a diner. The diner was also a name-brand chain Widow recognized.

The bus driver pulled alongside the main building and parked the bus. He stood up from his captain's chair and announced a thirty-minute break. It was just enough time to grab a bite to eat and hit the bathroom. He mentioned the bus was leaving in thirty minutes on the dot and wouldn't wait.

The other passengers got up and started drifting to the front and unloading. Most of them just stretched their legs. Some headed straight to the toilets. Some pulled out snacks and ate them outside, staying near the bus. Others went to get coffee, and a few took the chance to grab a bite to eat at the diner.

Widow waited for his neighbor to get up and head out. Then he stood up, stepped out into the aisle, and stretched his legs.

The older couple sitting behind him were slow to get up. They seemed to have waited for almost everyone else to disembark first, as if they were used to letting the younger people go first.

Widow smiled at them and said, "Are you guys going to get out and stretch?"

Both of them were white-haired and glowing with cheerfulness.

The woman said, "Oh, you go first, dear."

The man said, "We're two slow old folks. We usually let everyone else go first."

The woman said, "We don't want to get in the way."

Widow said, "You'd better go ahead of me. I'm very slow."

They smiled at him and shuffled and moved and got up out of their seats. Widow offered a hand to the woman, who sat near the aisle.

"Oh, thank you, dear," she said.

The man said, "Be careful, son. That's my girl."

Widow smiled big, all teeth, like he was thoroughly amused.

He said, "I'm sure you're a better man than me."

He helped them both out to the aisle. The whole time, he could see that all but one of the other passengers who had sat behind them had already stepped past him and were off the bus. The one passenger left was the bald guy. Widow saw him from the corner of his eye. He stayed seated, looking out the window like he was trying to be inconspicuous.

Widow questioned his earlier assumptions that the bald guy wasn't trying to hide. Maybe the guy was just that bad at it.

After Widow had helped the older couple out of their seats and into the aisle, he turned back and took a long look at the bald guy.

The bald guy tried staring out the window like he didn't notice Widow staring at him, but then he turned forward and looked directly at Widow.

Widow locked eyes with the bald guy. It was only a second, but it was a long second.

Widow broke off the stare and the eye contact and turned away and stepped off the bus.

He walked to the store first, taking his time. He stuffed his hands in his pockets and strolled to the store like a man without a care in the world. He glanced back once he was at the store's front door and saw the bald guy had stepped off the bus and was headed in his direction.

Inside the store, Widow picked out the largest bottle of water he could find. Then he searched for something else. He walked the aisles with the water in hand until he found the automotive section. There he sifted through items that could be potential weapons. He was hoping to find a hammer or a screwdriver or even a pocketknife. Some gas stations even carried hunting supplies like a hunting knife, but there was none of that here. There was no hunting section. The automotive section looked like it had been cherry-picked of any sharp or blunt objects that could do any significant damage. The closest thing Widow found with a sharp edge was a key chain nail clipper with a pointy file on it.

He walked by the refrigerator aisle, hoping for a beer bottle that he could empty and break, making a jagged shiv, but the county he was in was a dry county. The gas station didn't serve beer or any glass bottles. Everything was in aluminum cans or plastic bottles.

Shit, he thought.

He took the nail clipper with him and walked away from the refrigerator aisle, and headed to the front of the store to pay for the water and the nail clippers. He paid with cash for both items. He pocketed the nail clippers and opened the bottle, taking a big swig.

The bald guy entered the store right then. He took a glance at Widow, checked out what Widow was buying. He saw no threat in a plastic water bottle. The guy stuffed his hands into his jacket pockets and turned and headed down the candy aisle.

The store had one of those curved mirrors over the back wall behind the register, so that the attendant, if he faced that direction, could just look up and see the entire store from that curved, fisheye view. Widow used the mirror to watch the bald guy.

Widow looked at the attendant.

He asked, "Where's the toilet?"

The attendant didn't answer. He just pointed to the other end of the store, near the entrance from the truck lot beyond.

Widow nodded as a thank you and turned and walked to the
toilet. He passed the truck-side entrance door and stopped.
He looked out the windows and saw a small building way out
farther, among the sleeping trucks. It had a single slight bulb
on the exterior, lighting up the entrance. Widow saw two
doors, the same size, same colors. There were signs on both. It
was a second toilet, probably for the truckers who were eager
and on the go. That way, they could just stop and pump gas
and use the toilets and leave. There were probably showers in
that building.

He ignored the bathroom in front of him and turned and
walked out through the trucker entrance. He headed toward
the other bathrooms.

Around the main service station building were vapor lights
way up on poles. He walked out of the cone of light and into
the dark parking lot beyond, between the service station and
the second set of bathrooms.

Tractor-trailers were everywhere, engines humming like they
were in hibernation. He passed one trucker on his way. The
guy nodded and smiled at him. He returned the same friendly
greeting and followed the guy for a moment with his eyes. It
gave him a natural chance to look back. He glimpsed the bald
guy about thirty meters back.

Widow continued on, picking up his pace.

At the satellite bathroom hutch, Widow stopped and entered
the bathroom marked for men. Inside, he checked around.
The bathroom was large. There were several cracked mirrors
with rusted metal trim and the same number of sinks to
match. More than one of the faucets dripped water. There
were half as many soap dispensers as sinks. They were tacked

up on the wall between sinks, for sharing. There were three metal paper towel dispensers. One was completely empty. Behind the door was a large trashcan.

Along the far wall, opposite the entrance, were a half dozen urinals. One of them was still running. Probably it was used by the trucker he'd bumped into. To his left, behind the sinks, were several toilet stalls. There were carvings of profanities and pictures all over the doors, inside and out. The walls in the bathroom were tiled white. There was more graffiti littered on the tiles. Some were chipped and broken. There was a janitor closet in the far corner of the room.

Quickly, Widow searched the bathroom. No one else was there. He ducked into one of the toilet stalls and locked it. On the outside of the door, a sign switched from *vacant* to *occupied*.

Several seconds later, Sathers caught up and stopped outside the bathroom hutch.

Sathers looked around, checked every direction on the compass, and saw no one. No one was coming. No one was looking at him.

He opened his jacket and brandished his Glock 34. He took a silencer out of an inside jacket pocket. He screwed it into the barrel and tucked his weapon hand into the open flap of his coat, concealing it in case Widow wasn't the only guy in the bathroom. He wasn't under orders to kill pedestrians. But he wasn't going to go out of his way to not kill anyone else, either. He would eliminate any witnesses; that was for sure.

Sathers checked right and checked left once more. He saw no one. He put out his empty hand and pushed the men's door open.

41

SATHERS HELD tight onto his Glock and kept it hidden inside the flap of his bomber jacket. He pushed open the door to the men's room and stepped inside armed and ready to kill Widow. The bathroom had fluorescent lighting above. A few bulbs flickered off-kilter and off-key and out of sync. It was all random.

He stepped through the door, quietly, and inspected everything in his first view. He saw the rows of sinks, the mirrors, the white-tiled walls, the toilet stalls, and the urinals on the opposite wall. There was a nook beyond the stalls that he couldn't see into. He stayed near the door and saw no one.

He spun around fast and locked a deadbolt on the outside door so no one could come in behind him and interrupt him.

After the door was locked behind him, he spun back around and pulled out the Glock. The silencer he was using was a bulbous, fat piece, but it was short, which gave him more maneuverability in tight spaces. He stuck it out and scanned the bathroom. He didn't know where Widow was.

He walked into the room. He heard the drip of one of the faucets. To his left, all the toilet stall doors were closed. Down the end of the room, he worried about that nook he couldn't see into. He kept his gun pointed ahead of him.

He made it to one sink and heard a new sound. It was streaming water, like someone was peeing. He looked left. The sound was coming from one of the toilet stalls. The sound was heavy, like Widow had drunk too much coffee.

Sathers inspected the closed stall doors and saw the one door with the *occupied* sign.

He walked over to it, kept his gun out, but pulled it in closer to him. He used his new position to check the farthest mirror. He used the reflection to check the nook around the corner. He saw a janitor's closet and shadow and nothing else.

He looked back at the locked stall door. The urine sound streamed continuously, like a broken faucet.

He knelt on one knee and checked under the stall to confirm that Widow was in there. He saw the bottoms of Widow's boots. His toes were turned toward the toilet. The stream continued.

He stood back up and stepped back a meter, and raised the Glock to point at the stall door. Bathroom stall doors are cheap and thin. The ones in a random truck stop in the middle of nowhere were double cheap and very thin. They weren't going to stop a nine-millimeter bullet. Sathers' Glock held nineteen rounds.

He aimed at what should've been Widow's center mass and smiled.

Sathers squeezed the trigger five times in rapid succession. The weapon fired. Firearm silencers don't silence firearms, not really. *Silencer* wasn't an accurate name. They're more like noise softeners. The five rapid-succession shots were quiet, but not silent, especially in the tight space. The gunshots echoed through the bathroom. They bounced off the tiles and the sinks and the metal dispensers.

The bullets Sathers fired through the stall door tore through the cheap metal like bullets through a sheet of paper.

His aim had been perfect. All those five shots should have made body contact. Any of them should've torn through the door and through Widow's back and filleted his organs and exploded his blood vessels and ricocheted around inside his ribcage, doing fatal damage to his lungs and heart. He should've been dead before his body slumped over the toilet in front of him.

Widow should've been dead. No question. But there was just one problem. The urination sound continued after Sathers shot five bullets through Widow's back.

He mumbled to himself.

What the hell?

Sathers took a step back and forward, fast and hard, and he kicked a boot into the stall door. It nearly burst into two pieces because it was already shredded by the bullets. The lock broke under his heavy boot, and the stall door slammed open. Widow's body should've been there, bloodied and battered and leaking out of five bullet holes in his back, but he wasn't there. Instead of a dead body, Sathers found an empty pair of boots stood upright on the floor and a large water bottle with holes poked in it so that water streamed out of it and didn't gush out too fast. The water bottle was lying across the toilet seat.

In addition, Sathers saw a pair of nail clippers on the floor. Even the toilet wasn't quite right. The tank cover was gone.

The next thing Sathers noticed was that he wasn't standing there alone, not anymore. He turned and looked over his shoulder and found Widow staring at him.

Widow stood there in his socks, and he held the cover of the toilet tank in his hands. He had it up, leaned against his shoulder like a baseball player holding a bat, waiting for the pitch.

Widow smiled back at him. Then he slammed the toilet cover across Sathers' face. At least that's what Widow aimed for. But the guy was fast on his feet, faster than Widow had expected.

Sathers dropped the weight off one foot and ducked into the stall. The toilet cover and swing were hard, as hard as Widow could swing it, which was pretty damn hard. But Sathers' quick dodge saved his life. He took the heavy cover on the shoulder and not the head.

The toilet cover *cracked* and shattered half on the guy's shoulder and half on the outer wall of the stall. It shattered in Widow's hand and scattered into smaller pieces all over the bathroom floor.

Sathers screamed in pain from the blow to his shoulder.

But he didn't want to let it slow him down. He spun around and countered with the gun. There was no time to aim; every second counted. He didn't wait. Sathers fired the weapon blindly into the open stall doorway, in Widow's direction.

Sathers was fast, but so was Widow.

Widow dropped the fragment of toilet tank that was left in his hand after the shattering blow. He dodged to the right, out of the stall doorway, and pressed his back up against the other door.

Sathers' Glock came out after him and fired three rounds, blindly. The bullets *cracked* through the air and shattered two mirrors over sinks directly in front of the stalls. The muffled gunshots echoed through the bathroom.

Sathers' wrist came all the way out with the weapon, turning and twisting to follow the direction Widow had moved.

Widow didn't wait for him to fire any closer in his direction. He clamped a hand down on Sathers' wrist and jerked the guy forward off his feet a little. Then he grabbed Sathers' gun hand with both his hands.

Widow rammed the back of his shoulder and back into Sathers' torso, putting the gun out in front of both men. He jerked and twisted, trying to rip the gun free.

Widow used his weight and the muscles in his legs and reared back as hard as he could. He rammed Sathers into the opposite stall partition.

Sathers continued to pull the trigger, violently, haphazardly, which was fine by Widow. Better the bullets fired in a direction he could control rather than at him.

The best thing for Widow was to get possession of the gun. Running it dry of bullets was the next best thing. But the guy wasn't giving up possession of the Glock that easily. With Widow's back turned to him, Sathers used his free hand, which was also better than his right because of the blow to his right shoulder, and punched Widow in the kidney.

It wasn't a full-force blow, not even close. The inside of the stall was too tight, and the distance was too short. But Sathers was a strong guy. Even a short jab could do serious damage.

He jabbed Widow once in the kidney. Twice. Three times.

It hurt like hell.

Widow squatted down fast and lifted full force and slammed Sathers into the partition again. He repeated it one more time, and the two men went busting through the metal partition. Like the stall doors, the partitions were weak metal and old. They crashed through the neighboring stall like two busting broncos running wild through a weak barn wall.

The Glock fired over and over. Bullets burst through mirrors and sinks and pipes. Porcelain from the sinks shattered and exploded into pieces. Glass from the mirrors shattered and fragmented and detonated, flying all over the tile floor. Water blasted out of bullet holes in the pipes.

Sathers kept jabbing Widow in the side every chance he got.

Widow stopped trying to wrestle the gun free for a second and returned Sathers' jab with a powerful elbow to the guy's shoulder. But it wasn't the busted shoulder. Still, it distracted Sathers for a moment, and the gun stopped firing because Sathers stopped pulling the trigger.

Widow's main concern was the gun. He jerked forward and towed the guy out of the wreckage of stall partitions and cheap metal, and spun them both around back to the front of the stalls.

Widow squatted again, low, and kept both hands clamped down on the weapon. Then he jumped straight up and back, taking Sathers off his feet. Widow reverse-body-slammed the two of them onto the floor and the broken glass and sink porcelain.

Widow was heavy, two hundred twenty-five pounds of solid muscle and bone. He landed hard on Sathers, knocking the wind out of the guy.

But Sathers didn't stop!

He kept jabbing in that same kidney. It hurt worse than before. Widow felt his side pounding and throbbing like the guy was beating on him with a claw hammer.

Widow stayed focused on the gun. He stayed diligent. He wrapped his hand around Sathers' trigger finger. He pointed the weapon away from him at the ceiling and pulled the guy's trigger finger in rapid sequence.

The gun fired over and over, round after round. Ceiling tiles burst from the bullet impacts. Fragments of tile fell on top of them like dust from the sky.

Sathers resumed punching Widow in the side.

Widow lowered his left elbow, wrenched his arm back, and pulled his arm in as tight as he could without letting go of the gun. His arm took most of the side blows.

Widow forced Sathers to fire the gun until it clicked empty. Sathers realized the weapon was empty about a second too late because Widow let go of his hands and grabbed a couple of Sathers' loose fingers. He wrenched them about a hundred degrees the wrong way. Two fingers on the same hand snapped and broke.

Widow heard the bones *snap!*

Sathers felt the snap. He cried out in pain and released the gun.

Widow released him completely and rolled off him and scrambled to his feet.

Sathers tried to follow, tried to do the same thing, but Widow wasn't having that. He slammed a knee right into Sathers' face.

This time, Widow wasn't confined to the tight space inside the stall. He leaped and throttled his body forward with his knee out.

The knee *cracked* right into Sathers' nose. It broke in two places.

Sathers fell onto his back, but that didn't stop him. He was on his feet fast. His good hand disappeared for a quick second into his bomber jacket, and he jerked out a blade, seemingly from nowhere.

Widow almost missed it. Sathers swiped at him.

Widow dodged it easily enough. He took a long step back and glanced at the blade. He recognized it instantly. It was an Ontario MK III knife, a great knife. SEALs were trained and equipped with many kinds of weapons, but the MK III was a staple of the whole organization. It was given to SEALs right out of the gate as a go-to knife.

It was black with a six-inch blade and a sawtooth edge on the top. The MK III could be used for cutting and sawing, and it was strong enough to be used as a hammer or a pry bar.

The MK III in Sathers' hand was as sharp as if it just came from the machine-sharpening stage at the factory. Widow saw that.

Sathers swiped at Widow once, twice, three more times.

Widow dodged and moved and danced around. He waited. He knew he couldn't dodge the blade forever, not unarmed. But he also knew that Sathers was busted up and bleeding and strained. He waited for the right moment.

It came. Widow moved to his left, Sathers' right. He stayed in that spot. Sathers lunged at him fast with the blade. Widow danced right fast and pivoted, letting the stab go right past him toward the stalls. Widow heaved a colossal kick right into Sathers' stomach, slamming him back into a stall door. Sathers fumbled backward into the stall. He came back up fast, but not fast enough to stop Widow from sliding off his Havelock.

Widow slid his Havelock off and flipped it and tumbled it fast. His hands disappeared inside it. One came back out to hold it, and one stayed in.

He pirouetted and paraded the coat out in front of him like a matador.

Sathers stopped slashing and stayed where he was, knife out in front of him. He took a long moment to catch his breath.

He said, "I'm going to put this knife under your ribcage, slip it into your lungs, and twist. I'm going to stare into your eyes as you bleed out."

Widow held the coat out, one-handed, in front of him. His other hand was behind it, out of sight. He also caught his breath, but he didn't make a full-court press about it like Sathers had done.

Widow said, "Then you won't mind telling me, why kill Eggers? Is it about the money?"

"Money? No! It's about protecting our client."

"Who's your client?"

Sathers said nothing.

Widow asked, "Why not tell me? If you're going to kill me, then what difference does it make?"

"I am going to kill you!"

"So, tell me."

But Sathers was done talking. His breathing slowed and regulated back to normal. He stood in an athletic position, which made Widow think of a bull the split-second before it charges, snarling and rumbling.

Sathers charged at Widow like the bull against the matador. Only, unlike a matador, Widow shot him through his coat.

The gunshot *boomed* in the bathroom's stillness. The sound was loud. It echoed throughout the structure and into the women's bathroom as well.

Widow fired Gray's backup SIG Sauer P226 MK25, and a single shot ripped a bullet-sized hole through his Havelock and blew out the back of Sathers' bald head. Brain gristle and skull fragments blew out the back of his head and smeared the stall door behind him. His head was flung back from the blow, but he didn't fall backward. Instead, his head whipped back violently, his legs took a quick step forward, and he toppled over frontward and crashed onto the tile and broken mirror glass and the ceramic shrapnel from the busted sinks.

His eyes stayed wide open, but they were completely empty by the time he hit the floor.

Widow paused a beat and watched the bathroom door. He waited for someone to come running in to check out the noise. But no one did. No one came. Maybe anyone who heard the gunshot assumed it might be one of the parked tractor-trailers backfiring. It wasn't likely that anyone was within fifty meters of him, but the truck stop parking lot was vast, and the bathroom hutch was in the middle of it. It was possible that no one was close enough to know right away that they had heard a gunshot.

Multiple gunshots would've been noticed and identified for sure, but a single shot? The brain likes to rationalize unidentified sounds. It automatically presumes the safest option when something is in question.

Widow stuffed the Sig into the waistband of his jeans and covered it with his shirttail. He took a long moment to catch his breath, to calm himself down. His adrenaline was spiking. He examined his coat and fingered the bullet hole. It was pretty noticeable. He shrugged and slid the Havelock back on.

Once he was all set, he glanced around, wondering where he could stash the body. Quickly, he realized how stupid that thought was. There was no point trying to hide the body. Not with the mess they had made. The bathroom was wrecked. Sathers had bled out everywhere. The blood pooled in one spot and ran off and slid down a drain in the floor along with water that sprayed out from all the busted pipes.

The second concern he had was evidence. Widow couldn't remember all the things he'd touched, other than the door handles, the door into the bathroom, the stall door, the water bottle, and the nail clipper. He took the time and wiped them all down and pocketed the Sig. He couldn't toss it or wipe it down, since it was surely registered to Gray.

Widow checked the dead guy's pockets and took his cell phone, his ID, his cash, and his knife, which he figured might come in handy.

He scanned the ID. It was fake, well done, well put together, but fake. He pocketed all the things he took, except the knife.

Widow used the knife and sawed off the guy's index finger, right hand, for its print. He washed the knife and the finger in the sink to get the blood off and then wrapped the finger up in several layers of paper towels and stuffed it into an empty pocket; he didn't want it bleeding out and soaking across his passport or his bank card or his toothbrush.

Widow spent the next several minutes cleaning himself off. Blood was all over his face. He wasn't sure from which of Sathers' injuries.

He went back into the empty toilet stall and slipped his boots back on. He took up the nail clippers and the water bottle and left. He thought about taking the silenced gun, but it was empty, and he didn't need it. He thought about disposing of it, but it was evidence that could help the cops or confuse them. He hadn't touched the actual gun; he'd only touched Sathers' hand. So he left it.

On the way out, Widow stopped in the janitor's closet. He sleeved his hand and gripped the doorknob and jerked it open, shattering the wood around a cheap locked door. Inside, he found an *out-of-order* sign. He snatched it up, exited the bathroom, and slipped the sign on the door on his way out.

Hands in pockets, Widow returned to the bus. The old couple was back on board before anyone else. They were last to exit and first to re-board; he figured they wanted to avoid holding everyone up, same as when they let everyone else get off the bus first.

The old lady smiled at him, and the old guy said, "Back with us, young man?"

They both got a good look at his face.

The old lady said, "My, you look flushed, like you just ran a marathon."

The old guy asked, "Everything all right, son?"

Widow thought for a second and gave them an excuse.

"Everything's great! More than great! I met a woman."

The old lady put a hand on her cheek and shot him a huge smile.

The old guy said, "A woman? Here? At the service station?"

"Yes."

"What kind of woman can you meet at a truck stop?"

The old lady hit her husband with a friendly jab in the ribs.

Widow said, "She's a truck driver."

"Truck driver?"

She said, "Jeb, nice women drive trucks too! Women can do whatever men can do, only better."

Widow thought of Gray and smiled and sat down for a moment. He casually took off his Havelock, like he was warm, and folded it up and stuffed it behind him in the seat.

The old lady said, "Well, are you going to keep riding with us or go with her?"

Widow turned around in his seat and looked back at them.

"You think I should go back and get a ride with her?"

The old guy said, "If you like this woman that much, I would! I don't let chances like that pass me up."

"Really?"

"That's how I got this one here!"

The old guy wrapped an arm around his wife and squeezed her close to him.

Widow smiled and nodded.

"You're right. I'm going to go after her."

He stood up from his seat and moved to the aisle. He left the burner phone in the seat with the GPS tracker in it, but he took the bald guy's cell phone. Then he got up and stepped back off the bus. He took one last look at the old couple and waved at them.

Off the bus, he passed the driver standing by the door. He was ready to go.

The driver said, "We're leaving in a few, sir."

Widow kept walked and waved back.

"Have a safe trip."

"Are you staying behind?" the driver asked.

Widow didn't respond.

He walked on, down the freeway, back the way he'd come, toward DC.

42

Two hours later, Widow sat at a table, finishing a cup of coffee, and eating the last of the fries from a cheeseburger and fries he had ordered. He faced the window of a fast-food joint in Greensboro, North Carolina, off a freeway cloverleaf.

That was when Gray pulled into the lot, off the freeway, in her NCIS-provided Charger. She pulled into a parking space right in front of the window and looked up at him and waved.

Widow finished the fries and crumbled up the paper from the cheeseburger, wrapping all his trash into it. He tossed it and his empty coffee cup into the trashcan on his way out. He walked out and over to the Charger and got in.

Gray looked him up and down and saw a cut on his cheek.

"Looks like you had some trouble?"

"You should see the other guy."

She asked, "Ditch the phone?"

"It's on a bus headed to Atlanta and wherever the bus goes from there."

"How far is that from here? Like five hours?"

"Yep. Plus one stop. Probably."

"Was there a guy following you like you thought?"

Widow nodded.

"How did you ditch him?"

"He's dead in a toilet two miles south."

Gray turned and stared at him.

"You killed him?"

"He was the *other* guy."

"Widow, you don't have a permit to kill! You're not James Bond!"

"License."

"What?"

"James Bond had a license to kill."

"Whatever! You can't just be killing people. Did you clean up after?"

"I wiped my prints. But I left him where he died, in a toilet."

More than he deserved, Widow thought.

Gray said, "I should get someone down there."

"For what?"

"We should tell the local police."

"Nah. Best to just let them do their thing. We got our own problems. Plus, we're trying to stay under the radar."

"So, what now?"

Widow said, "We need a fingerprint match so we can ID the guy who attacked me."

"You scanned his prints?"

Widow reached into his pocket and pulled out a wad of rolled-up bloody paper towels.

"No. I took his finger."

"Widow!"

"What? We need to know who he is. Can you scan for his print?"

"That's gross!"

"Can we get a print off him or not?"

Gray fished out her phone and unlocked it.

She said, "Here. Take my phone. There's an app on there. Just open the app with the green icon of a fingerprint and scan his print on that button. It'll automatically send the print to the database in Quantico and search for us."

Widow took the phone and unwrapped the bloody finger. He wiped off the print as best he could with the paper towel.

Gray said, "In the glove box, there are wet wipes. Wipe it before you scan it and then wipe my phone after. I don't want a dead guy's finger all over my phone."

Widow popped the glove box, found the wet wipes, and did as she had instructed.

After it was all done and sent, he asked, "What do you want me to do with the finger?"

Gray buzzed down his window.

"Throw it away."

"You sure? It's evidence."

"Yeah, that you murdered a guy and stole his finger!"

"Good point," Widow said, and he tossed it out the window.

They drove on in silence for a minute until Widow spoke.

"You notice any tails on you?"

"No one is following me. Don't worry."

Widow took a second and checked the clock on the dashboard.

"We already missed our flight out. It was out of DC, anyway."

"Don't worry; I canceled it."

Widow nodded and said, "Good. You got a spending budget from Unit Ten? Cause we're going to need more plane tickets. Plus, we'll need hotels."

"I can get one if Cameron approves. I'm still a newbie, you know."

"Don't worry. She'll do it. Let's find the nearest airport and get out of here."

"Where are we going first?"

"Let's do like you said. We'll head to see Cho's family. See if they'll talk to us. Then we can drive down to San Diego and talk with the agents who investigated Cho's murder and then Shore's parents in Hawaii."

Gray smiled inadvertently, like it couldn't be helped.

"Southern California in autumn and then Hawaii? Cameron's going to think we're hitting the beach."

"We might."

"What?"

"We're going to be there, anyhow. If we have time, we can hit the beach. You pack a bikini?"

She shot him a sideways stare that could level a SEAL platoon.

She said, "I packed nothing."

Widow glanced in the backseat and saw no suitcase. No extra clothes.

"You didn't? What took you so long to get here?"

"It didn't take me that long."

Widow smiled and looked out the windshield.

"Let's go," he said.

43

THEIR FLIGHT LEFT on time from an airport in Greensboro and landed in Dallas, where they had a brief layover until they were back in the air and finally landing at LAX in Los Angeles. To them, it had felt like nighttime, but the time zone differences made them see the sunset more than once in a single day.

They rode in premium economy because Widow needed the extra legroom, which he hadn't asked Gray to set up for him. And she hadn't. Cameron did. She had it all arranged for them. She knew Widow needed the legroom and requested it.

Both flights were good. No problems. No complaints.

After the plane, they left the airport terminal and went to a car rental counter, where Gray asked if they had any Dodge Chargers. Apparently, it was her personal favorite. It turned out they had one, only it didn't come in navy blue. They had two colors. One was Army green, and that was a hard no for Gray. The second one was all black, with black leather interior. It cost more, a lot more, than the other one. Widow saw her sign for it.

The weather in LA was much warmer than DC and Greensboro. Widow took off the bullet-holed Havelock, tossed it over a shoulder, and carried it with one hand. They got to the car and got in, Gray behind the wheel and Widow in the passenger seat. He didn't even ask to drive. He knew his place.

He said, "We should grab you a change of clothes."

"Not here. Airport clothes are crazy expensive."

"I know. I meant at a thrift store."

"Thrift store?"

"Yeah. Drive around; I'm sure LA has plenty of them."

"No. We're not going to a thrift store."

"Why? What's wrong with thrift stores?"

Gray stared at him with that same sideways look from earlier that could level a SEAL platoon.

"You can't represent the NCIS in thrift store clothes."

"So, what then?"

Gray looked at him and fired up the engine and smiled.

An hour later, Widow was in an expensive button-down shirt that was a little tight, in his opinion. He wore a muscle shirt under it. He didn't pick out the muscle shirt or the tight button-down. Gray picked out both. When he put on the muscle shirt, she told him that "muscle shirts were designed for guys like him—guys with muscles."

He wore black chinos and black Oxford shoes. She had forced both on him. She also got him a black sports coat, but like his Havelock, he didn't wear it. He just carried it around as an accessory.

Widow wanted to leave his old clothes behind, but Gray made him put them in the shopping bag alongside her own, which he ended up carrying.

Gray bought a stylish outfit that was becoming to any good female NCIS agent. She looked professional and tough and compassionate, all at the same time. She wore a black jacket, black pants, and a white top that stuck in Widow's mind like a tune he couldn't stop singing to himself.

Widow and Gray walked out of a store in Culver City and headed back to their car, which they had left in a paid lot. There had been no free spaces anywhere.

On the way back to the Charger, Widow looked at the sky. It was dark.

He asked, "What time are we going to see the Chos tomorrow?"

"Widow, we're going over there now."

"Tonight? Isn't it better to do these things in the daytime?"

"We already have a meeting with them lined up. Cameron set it up. They're expecting us."

"Are we eating dinner there?"

"I don't know. Maybe. It's not a social call, but they may offer us dinner."

"I doubt that. Where do they live?"

"Somewhere in the Hollywood Hills. I have the address in my phone."

"Okay. Let's go."

They made it to the Charger, got in and fired it up, and paid the valet for the parking. Soon they were back on the road and headed north.

* * *

DRIVING THROUGH LA, they had to deal with some LA traffic. But it wasn't too bad. Both Gray and Widow had been through worse.

They finally made it into the Hills, where they followed roads winding through them and around them. Widow marveled at the view from the drive. Almost everywhere he looked was some kind of spectacular view, some kind of vista. It all looked like the wallpaper that came with computers. He had never been to the Hollywood Hills before.

After twenty minutes of more driving and winding around the loops and getting a little lost, they made it to the address that the Cho family had provided.

Widow and Gray spent about ten seconds, jaws dropped, staring at the house in front of them. The driveway was short, and the street was empty, but the house was magnificent. It was two stories, all white and all windows. It was crafted like a work of art, the kind of house that was built with the first step having been hiring an architect who had probably been featured in magazines.

The house was built into the hilltop on Skylark Lane. In the front, leading up to the front door, was some kind of half greenhouse, half entrance.

Gray killed the engine, and they stepped out of the car. She looked back over her shoulder and paused.

"Widow," she said.

He looked at her. She pointed out toward the city. He turned and looked and saw a view so beautiful it looked like it was a fake background in a movie.

Widow saw downtown LA, the lower hills of Hollywood, all the way out to the ocean. It was breathtaking.

"Wow!" he said. "What do they do for a living?"

"They run some kind of production company. Film, I guess."

"Show business money?"

Gray said, "I guess so."

Gray saw Widow shutting his door, and she said, "Widow?"

"Yeah?"

"Forgetting something?"

"What?"

She gave him a sideways look again, and she put her hands on her hips.

"Your coat?"

Widow looked down into the backseat and saw his sports coat draped across the seat.

"Do I have to wear that?"

"Widow! Yes! You have to wear it!"

He shrugged, closed the passenger door, sidestepped to the rear door, opened it, and scooped up the coat. He put it on. Like the other items she had picked out for him, it was snug.

He closed the car door and joined her, and they walked up the drive to a stone walk that led through the greenhouse up to the front door. Gray hit the doorbell, and a loud noise was heard throughout the house.

Gray looked at Widow.

"I should've gone into movies."

"You could be a movie star."

"You think so?"

"I'd stare at you for two hours," he said.

She smiled, blushed a little, but resumed her tough exterior the moment the huge front door swung open.

They were greeted by an elegant woman in her late fifties or early sixties, but she looked much younger. The only reason Widow knew her age was from the math of Henry Cho being dead since he was in his late twenties, and that was twenty years earlier. She was short and Asian. She greeted them with a big smile made of porcelain veneers.

"Welcome. You must be Officer Gray?" the woman asked, and she put a hand out to Gray to shake it.

Gray took it and shook it.

"It's Agent Gray, ma'am."

"Of course. My apologies," she said, and she turned to Widow next. "And you are?"

Widow took up her hand and shook it gently.

"Jack Widow, ma'am."

"Nice to meet you both. My name is Jessica Cho. Come in."

They followed her into the house. She closed the door after them and led them into the first floor that opened up to huge windows in the back. The view from back there was as good as the one in the front. Plus, there was an infinity pool.

Jessica Cho led them to the main room and then turned to the edge of the kitchen. A short Asian man stood in the kitchen near a bar that sat six people.

He came forward and introduced himself as Henry's father, Jim Cho.

"Have a seat," Jim Cho said. He pointed at the seats at the bar.

Gray and Widow both huddled together at one end, and Jessica sat on the other side of Gray. Jim Cho circled around the bar and stood on the other side like a bartender.

Just then, Widow saw a woman about forty years old dressed in casual clothes. She was also Asian and also short. She entered from the hallway and went into the kitchen.

Jim Cho spoke to her in a foreign language that Widow recognized as Korean, but he had no clue what was being said. The woman seemed to hop to work as if he had given her an order. She went to a cabinet and pulled out a kettle and boiled water in it over a gas stove.

Jim Cho said, "This is Chang, our housekeeper. She's going to make us all some tea."

Of course, Widow's first thought was to ask for coffee, but then he remembered they were there about the Chos' dead son. Best to just take what they offered and forget about coffee.

After several minutes, introductions had been made. Expectations had been placed. And the tea was served in front of them. It was black tea, at least, so Widow sipped it and enjoyed it.

After small talk had passed, Gray said, "We're both very sorry about your son. The NCIS is sorry."

Both Chos nodded and accepted it, but said nothing back.

Widow said, "This is a nice house. How long have you lived here?

Jessica Cho said, "Thanks."

Jim Cho said, "This year will be twenty years."

Gray said, "So right after Henry passed?"

Jessica Cho said, "Yes."

Jim Cho asked, "Why are you looking into our son?"

Gray said, "We don't have a good reason. Just working another case."

"Involving my son?"

Widow said, "A man from your son's platoon died. We're just getting a sense of everyone who knew him."

Jessica Cho said, "Oh. What was his name?"

"Eggers," Widow said.

Gray asked, "Did you ever hear of him?"

Jim Cho said, "No. Can't say we have. Henry didn't speak about his teammates. He was all secret about it."

Jessica Cho said, "Guess he had to be."

Jim Cho paused a beat as if he was trying to stay composed, but he couldn't keep a grip, not totally. A single tear edged near the corner of his eye.

He said, "Henry loved it."

Widow and Gray didn't bring him up for a while. They were on the same page about that. They drank their tea and talked with the Chos for a long time.

Everything stayed casual and light until Jessica Cho got up and circled around to Widow. She showed him pictures of Henry on her phone. There were photos of him as a kid, a teenager, and the day he went off to basic. Then she had some photos of Henry from an unnamed desert country. He was strapped with combat gear. There was one photo of him with a platoon of guys. Widow scanned the picture and didn't see Eggers in it. Then she showed one last picture that was similar but with fewer guys. And there he was.

Widow said, "That's Eggers. Right there."

He asked for Jessica's phone. "Ma'am, can I show this to my friend?"

"Of course," Jessica Cho said, and she released the phone into his hand.

Widow crossed his hand over to Gray, who leaned in and looked.

"That's Eggers," she said.

Widow said, "That's him. A lot younger than he would've been now, but that's him."

Widow gave the phone back to Jessica.

Gray asked, "Ma'am, do you know that guy?"

Jessica looked at the phone and said, "No. Henry never introduced us to any of the guys in his squad."

Platoon, Widow's brain corrected, but he stayed quiet.

Gray asked, "When is this from?"

"Months before he died. He was in love. Talked about getting married, if it ever became legal."

Jim Cho said, "Which he never lived to see."

Jessica Cho pulled up a second photo. It was two men, both in Navy whites, both happy and smiling. They were out in public. It looked like a graduation ceremony. She held her smartphone out in front of her face and stared at the screen. She smiled at the photo.

After a long second, she leaned across the bar and showed it to Widow and then to Gray.

"That's my Henry!"

Gray said, "He was handsome, and he looks happy."

"He was happy. Very happy."

The face of the guy he was with looked familiar to Widow. Then he recognized him the second that Jim Cho saw the picture and said the name.

Jim Cho came up off his feet for a moment to reach across the bar. He tried to swipe Jessica's phone away from her, but she pulled it back. Suddenly, he became visibly upset. His heart rate picked up. His cheeks flushed. His temples hardened like he was grinding his teeth together.

"That's him! That's Shore!"

Cho paused a beat, trying to calm himself. It didn't work. He was visibly fuming after seeing a picture of his dead son with the man who had killed him.

Jessica Cho said, "Henry loved Dwayne!"

"He murdered our son!"

Jim Cho slammed his open palm down on the bar top.

Widow and Gray looked at each other. Widow knew there was some kind of paragraph somewhere in the NCIS field manual that referred to how to deal with upset parents, but he couldn't remember it. He had been out of the job for way too long.

Gray stayed quiet. He wasn't sure she could remember it, either.

Jessica Cho said, "He didn't kill our son! I don't believe that for a second! Dwayne loved Henry!"

Chang remained in the far reaches of the kitchen and stayed quiet, like she knew the drill. She knew the best thing to do whenever the Chos fought was to stay out of it.

Jim Cho stared at her with a look like he was bubbling up with anger. He stepped back from the bar and turned to walk away, and then stopped and turned back one last time.

He took a deep breath, and he kicked them out.

"I want you two to leave, please. I'm not angry with you personally, but seeing you guys has brought up stuff I'd like to leave buried. Finish your tea and get out."

Cho turned to leave the room, but Widow stopped him.

He said, "Before we go, mind if I ask about your business?"

Jim Cho rubbed his face hard with one hand. He looked back at Widow from across the kitchen.

"What do you want to know?"

Widow said, "This is a nice house. Hollywood Hills. It's an expensive area. Business must be pretty good?"

"It is."

"Has it always been this good?"

Jim Cho asked, "How do you mean?"

"How was it before?"

"You mean when Henry was alive?"

Widow nodded. Gray lowered her hand under the bar top and grabbed Widow's leg. She dug her fingers into his thigh and squeezed, seeming to warn him to be careful.

Jim Cho said, "When our son was alive, we struggled. For many years. The only good that came out of what happened was this."

Cho put his hands up like he was presenting his wealth to them.

"This house, all our money, it's all from when he died. We wouldn't have made it without his murder."

Widow looked at Gray. She dropped her hand from his leg and stared back at him, puzzled.

Widow asked, "How do you mean?"

"Our son is responsible for this place and our success."

"How?"

Jessica Cho said, "Henry left us a generous life insurance policy."

Gray asked, "You mean the Navy paid for all this?"

Jim Cho said, "No. The insurance money from the Navy was hardly enough to buy a one-room apartment here. We mean the insurance policy that Henry bought outside of the military."

Widow and Gray stared at each other again. They had the same question on their minds, as if they were totally in sync.

Widow thought, *Why the hell would a twenty-eight-year-old, unmarried, healthy SEAL buy an outside policy?*

Widow asked, "How much was in the policy?"

Gray put her hand back on Widow's leg. This time it wasn't to squeeze his thigh. It was tender but professional, like she might do to her partner just to get him to slow down a bit.

Gray said, "I'm sorry for the direct question. We're looking at all the information we can get. So how much?"

Jessica Cho looked at her husband lovingly and without judgment of his outburst.

"How much was it, darling?" she asked.

Jim Cho said, "It was five million and change. We used it to get our productions off the ground, paid all our debts, and purchased this house. It was truly life-changing."

Jessica Cho got up and walked over to her husband. She put her hands into his.

She said, "We'd trade it all back for our son to be alive."

Gray said, "Of course."

She stood up from her stool and tapped Widow on his lower back. He got the clue and stood up with her.

Gray thanked the Chos for their time, took Widow by the forearm, and led him back out of the house.

Widow saw more photos of Henry in the hallway that he hadn't noticed earlier. There were photos of Cho as a kid, doing kid things. They looked like a happy family before he died.

Jessica Cho walked them out, thanked them for coming, and closed the door behind them. They walked back along the stone walk back to the driveway and the Charger.

Gray said, "Nice people. What do you think?"

"I think we definitely should talk to Shore's parents."

"I agree."

Widow looked up at the night sky and over the city again. He doubted he would ever see this view again. He tried to take a mental picture of it. It was really something spectacular. He knew he could never afford a house like that with a view like that.

Finally, he asked, "Where to now?"

"We should drive to San Diego."

"Tonight?"

"No. First thing in the morning. Let's grab some dinner and then get some sleep. We have a long day tomorrow."

They drove back down out of the Hollywood Hills and onto Sunset Boulevard. It didn't take ten minutes for them to find rows of hotels and restaurants. They found a Best Western next to a Chinese restaurant and decided that both would do.

They checked into the hotel, all on Gray's credit card, and they got separate rooms. They ate dinner together at the Chinese restaurant and returned to the hotel an hour later.

They said their goodnights, and both went into their separate rooms.

Widow stayed up an extra hour, thinking about Eggers, thinking about the KAM guy, and thinking about Gray. It was the later thoughts that helped him slip into a good sleep.

44

GRAY WOKE up bright and early the next morning. She surprised Widow at his door with two hot coffees in paper cups with lids, stuffed in a carrying tray, and purchased from a gas station nearby. The coffees were in a carrying tray so she could carry them one-handed while she held a white plastic bag in the other hand.

The contents of the white plastic bag were for Widow. Inside were a new foldable toothbrush, a tube of toothpaste, a pack of disposable razors, a small can of shaving cream, and a comb—all travel-sized.

He thanked her, especially for the new toothbrush, because the new one he carried wasn't foldable. He preferred the foldable travel kind—easier to carry.

He washed his face, combed his hair, brushed his teeth, shaved, dressed, and joined her at the car. They checked out of the hotel, not knowing if they would be back, and they got on the road.

Southern California was famous for a lot of things, some good, some bad. The one good thing was the weather. And today was no exception to the rule.

They drove the speed limit along the Pacific Coast Highway. Gray pulled her hair back into a ponytail. When Widow got into the car with her, she pointed out a pair of sunglasses that she had also bought for him. She wore hers, and he wore his. They were matching aviator-style glasses. He was grateful; he needed them because Sunny California was indeed sunny.

They drove the whole way with the windows down and listened to what she called an *old rock station* on satellite radio. Only it wasn't old rock to Widow. It was all music from the nineties, with some eighties mixed in.

They drove like two people out on a short road trip, two friends, two potential lovers. They shared a lot of good conversation and a lot of laughing and a lot of smiling and a lot of flirting. Widow noticed all of it. He didn't complain.

Their conversations started with a question.

Widow asked, "Are we going to Camp Pendleton?"

"No. We're meeting Agent Reid in Little Italy in Downtown San Diego."

"Oh, great!"

That started them down the road of conversation that got them talking the whole drive. They got to know each other better. Widow learned more about Gray. She was a great addition to Unit Ten. He could see her ending up with Cameron's job in the end.

As they neared San Diego, Widow changed the subject, changed the focus in his mind from Gray and back to Eggers and the KAM guy, and he thought about the endgame.

He asked, "What are we going to do when we catch whoever these guys are?"

"What do you mean?"

"I mean, you're a cop."

Gray glanced at him.

"Yeah?"

Widow said, "I'm not. I've arrested no one in years. What are we going to do? We going to arrest them?"

"Of course. What would you do?"

He looked out the windshield at the road and the cars and the beautiful sky.

"I'd do whatever needed doing."

"What's that supposed to mean?"

Widow went quiet for a long beat, and then he changed the subject.

"Where exactly are we going?"

"We're meeting Agent Reid at a café. Would you like to drive?"

Widow looked at her.

"You want me to drive?"

"Yeah. I can navigate."

"Okay."

Gray slowed the car and pulled off onto the shoulder outside the exit to Mission Valley, and they swapped. Widow had to rack the seat all the way back and tilt the steering wheel and adjust the mirrors more to his height needs. Then they got back on the road.

They drove to Downtown San Diego and got off the freeway and merged into traffic. Gray used her phone to navigate the one-way streets and told Widow where to turn and where to go.

After about fifteen minutes of circling and turning and traffic lights, they entered Little Italy.

"Turn here," Gray said.

Widow turned the car, and she pointed up at a café on a street corner.

"Right there."

"Where do I park?"

"Good question. I wish we had a car from the motor pool. Then we could park anywhere."

They had to circle around the block several times before they found parking on the street. They parked and got out. Widow offered the keys to Gray, but she told him to keep them.

They walked side by side around a building and down the block back to the café. The café was just one small room with a counter and tables outside on the sidewalk.

Inside they only served Italian-style coffee and Italian-style food.

They were instantly greeted by a hearty smile belonging to the owner. He was a young guy with long hair. He greeted them and welcomed them and invited them to have a look at the menu.

Gray glanced around and didn't see the agent she was looking for. So they ordered coffees and took a table outside on the pavement.

Gray kept looking at her phone like she was patiently checking the time.

Widow said, "Why are we meeting the guy here and not at the local office?"

"I don't know. He just insisted on meeting here."

"He knows what this is about?"

"He knows. I sent him a workup of Eggers and that we're looking into his death as a murder."

"It *was* a murder."

"He knows that."

"He knows about the fifty million dollars in stocks?"

"He doesn't know that part."

A minute later, two men in a navy-blue Ford pulled up to the curb and stopped in an *Emergency Vehicle Only* space. The man in the passenger seat got out, said something to the driver, and the driver nodded and pulled away from the curb.

The man walked over to the café and saw Widow and Gray and waved to them. Gray stood up, and Widow stayed where he was.

"You must be Agent Gray?" the man asked.

Gray shook his hand.

The guy was about sixty years old but had a youthful appearance, indicating he was still bright-eyed and bushy-tailed. He had fair hair, losing it in some places, but not enough to cause worry, not yet.

He invited himself to sit next to Widow, across from Gray at the little table. He offered his hand to Widow, who took it and shook it.

"I'm Sonya Gray, from Quantico," Gray said. She gave no unit name, just the vague Quantico.

"Christopher Reid," the fair-haired NCIS agent said.

She said, "And this is Jack Widow, retired."

Widow and Reid exchanged nods, and nothing more.

Reid looked at Gray and said, "Your request to meet me must've come from high up? I have never gotten a direct request to liaise with another agent directly from the director's office before."

Gray smiled and added nothing else.

Reid asked, "Do you guys like coffee?"

Widow perked up just at the mention of coffee, even though he already had some in front of him.

"I like this place. I love coming down to Little Italy. I hope you guys enjoy it," Reid asked and looked at Widow.

Widow said, "I love coffee. This is pretty good."

Reid nodded and smiled.

"Yeah. I like it here."

Reid looked at his watch and gazed down the street and sidewalk to the west. At first, Widow thought he was glancing at the ocean view. It wasn't a direct oceanfront view, but the Pacific could be seen from where they were, partially because they were on a hilltop and partially because the ocean wasn't far away.

Gray asked, "How long have you been in the NCIS?"

Reid looked at her.

"I've been an agent now for twenty-one years."

Widow asked, "So, you had only been an agent for a year before you got the Cho case?"

"Yeah. That's right," Reid said and glanced again down that street.

Widow looked. He saw nothing but a regular San Diego street. There were cars and pedestrians. He saw a guy walking a dog up the street and a couple of office workers crossing the street and some tourists taking photos.

Only the man walking the dog was coming up the sidewalk toward them.

Gray said, "Reid, you waiting on something? You seem spaced out."

Reid turned and looked at them.

"You guys have called to meet with me about a case I worked twenty years ago. It was the one that stuck with me all these years. The Cho case was brutal. I figured the man you really need to talk to is that man."

He pointed at the guy walking the dog. It was an old German shepherd. The man was older, too. He looked early to late seventies, but still spry and wiry and full of life in his walk.

The guy walked up to them, and Reid met him in front of the table. They shook hands and hugged like two friends at a high school reunion.

Reid said, "Guys, this is my friend Andy Frost."

Frost held his hand out to both Widow and Gray. Both of them stood and greeted him.

Frost said, "Hello, guys. I'm Andy Frost, retired. I worked for NCIS for twenty years. I was a sailor before that."

Frost patted his dog on the head and introduced him.

"This is Bluto. He's an old sailor himself."

Widow asked, "Was he a Navy dog?"

"Retired."

The four of them all sat down around the little table on the sidewalk. Gray sipped her coffee while Widow took a few big gulps, finishing his completely.

Reid said, "Frost left us during the Cho investigation."

Frost said, "They fired me."

Gray asked, "Why?"

Reid said, "It was all bullshit!"

Frost said, "They gave me a choice. Either retire or get canned."

Gray asked a question she already knew the answer to.

"What did you choose?"

"They fired me," Frost said again.

Gray asked, "Is that why we're meeting here instead of the office in Pendleton?"

Reid said, "Yes. I thought you guys might want the truth. And you won't get it from the case files."

Frost said, "Not the entire truth."

"Which is...?" Gray asked.

Frost said, "On paper, the murder-suicide looked open and shut. The evidence was obvious. Cho was murdered by his lover, Dwayne Shore."

Reid said, "At the time, I was green. A new agent. Frost had been my partner for the first year I worked homicide. But Frost never bought it. He kept digging. The higher-ups didn't like it. He never stopped digging. He became obsessed with it. Eventually, they canned him for it."

Gray asked, "On what grounds?"

Frost said, "Drinking. They said I was drunk all the time after the case had been officially closed."

Reid said, "They found alcohol in his desk. And he smelled like it."

Widow asked, "Someone plant it?"

Frost said, "No. It was mine. I was drunk all the time. Almost for a whole year after. It was true. But that doesn't mean I was wrong."

Widow asked, "Wrong about what?"

Frost didn't answer that. He turned and looked away out toward the ocean and the sky. He stared out for a long moment.

Gray leaned in over her coffee. She studied him. She started to say something. She started to check on him. But Reid put up a hand. Then he reached across the table and touched his old partner's hand.

Frost turned back and looked at Reid with love in his eyes. It was the kind of love Widow had seen a million times in his life. It was a love built on brotherhood and shared experiences and friendship. The two of them had been NCIS agents together. They were friends, and they shared something else. They shared an experience.

Frost nodded at Reid that he was okay. He pulled his hand away and wiped a single tear away from his eye.

He said, "Someone else killed those boys. Murdered them both in cold blood and pinned it on Shore."

45

GRAY ASKED, "How do you know that?"

Frost said, "The Service identified Shore as the killer, but the more I dug around, the more pressure was put on me to stop digging."

Frost went quiet. Then he asked, "Did you meet with Shore's mother?"

Gray said, "Not yet."

"You should. She lives in Honolulu."

Gray said, "We plan to. Today, maybe."

Widow asked, "Is there anything you can tell us about why you think Cho was murdered by someone else?"

Frost looked at Widow. His dog was at his knee, and it also looked up at Widow.

Frost asked, "You got the names in Cho's SEAL unit?"

Gray said, "Yes."

"The official list from the criminal report?"

Gray said, "No. We didn't see a list in the file. We got one later."

"No list in the reports?"

Widow said, "No. Is that unusual?"

"It was back then. NCIS used to have clearance for everything involving a case," Frost said, "Anything strange about the list?"

Widow said, "It's missing a name."

Gray said, "But that could just be someone in transition. That's what Widow told me."

Frost said, "Yes. It could be. But it's not."

Widow asked, "Who is it?"

"I can't say."

Gray asked, "Why not?"

Frost said, "It got me fired. The name is the real reason I was fired."

Gray asked, "What's the name?"

Frost looked at Reid.

"Buddy, take my dog down to the corner there and let him do his business. Here's a bag," Frost said. He fished a doggie bag out of his front pocket and handed it with the leash to Reid.

Reid didn't argue. He nodded along and took the dog and walked off with him, all as if he had known it was coming, all like he was trying to avoid this part of the conversation.

Frost said, "The name of the SEAL that's missing is Nick Gaden."

Gray looked at Widow. They both knew the name but couldn't quite place it.

Frost said, "I've told you both too much already. That's all I'm going to say on the whole matter. I don't want Reid a part of this. He's still got his retirement ahead of him. They ruined me for looking at Gaden. I'm retired now, and I've been sober for years. I just got my chip two months back. I'm remarried and happy. Not going to risk it all over Gaden. Not again.

Widow believed him. He knew the look of a man who had lost everything, a man afraid of losing it all once again. Gaden was a big step forward. Before they had no leads and no name. Now they had both.

Widow had finished his coffee and was now looking yearningly at Gray's half-full cup. She smiled and asked if he wanted to finish it for her. He obliged. Reid returned with Frost's dog and handed the leash back over to him along with the doggie bag, unused.

The four of them shook hands.

Reid hugged his old partner and wished him goodbye. They watched Frost walk away with his dog, back down the street that he had appeared on, back toward the beach and the ocean.

Reid said, "Did he tell you anything you didn't know?"

Gray said, "He mentioned a name."

Reid put up a hand.

"Don't say the name. I already know it, but the less I know of what you guys are investigating right now, the better."

Widow said, "That's why you wanted us to meet you here and not back at the office. You wanted us to meet Frost. You wanted him to tell us what we weren't going to get in the file."

Reid nodded along.

"We got threats from that name. From his family. Let's just say they have a lot of clout in the military world," Reid said, and he looked off in the distance, back down the street where Frost had vanished.

He said, "I didn't back Frost up when he was on the job. Not like I should have. Like a good partner would have. The drinking was something I could've stopped. Maybe if I had backed him up before it got out of hand. I was new back then. Scared. I had a wife and a kid to think about. I needed my paycheck."

Gray and Widow stayed quiet.

Reid turned back to them.

"Can I tell you both something? Off the record?"

Gray nodded.

"Frost isn't wrong. He didn't buy it that Shore killed Cho. We interviewed Shore many times, as you know. I wasn't sure at first, but I knew in my gut that boy didn't kill Cho! He loved him like I love my wife and my kids. I saw it. Frost saw it. And we knew we had made a horrible mistake by following the evidence that led us to arrest and convict Shore of the murder. The evidence was so overwhelming; it seemed too good to be true. And I think it was. We found the knife in Shore's apartment. It was still soaked in Cho's blood. We found Shore asleep on his bed in clothes that were also covered in Cho's blood. Plus, Shore's fingerprints and DNA were all over Cho's apartment. But he claimed not to remember anything from the night before. He claimed he was drugged."

Widow asked, "Did you check his blood?"

"We ran tox screens on him."

Gray asked, "And?"

"Inconclusive. But there were signs of numerous sleeping pills, over-the-counter stuff. And we found a bottle in his apartment. Half empty. We guessed he murdered Cho and then was so ashamed of what he had done that he took half the pills, maybe to kill himself. But..."

Gray said, "But what?"

"I don't think he did it. I went along with it. Our bosses had said that was the case. We were to arrest him and prosecute him for murder. But I was wrong."

Reid looked at both of them. Then he looked around.

He said, "Frost told you about Gaden?"

Gray nodded.

Reid said, "He's evil. Pure evil."

Widow asked, "What got Frost to think of him in the first place? Why was he on Frost's radar?"

"Look into him. If you dig back twenty years ago, you'll find plenty of dirt that never stuck," Reid said. Then he stood up, signaling the meeting was over. He offered them both his hand to shake.

Gray and Widow both stood and took his hand and shook it. Reid turned away, shoved his hands in his coat pockets, strolled off down the street to the south, and vanished over a hill.

Gray said, "I can get Cameron to assign someone back at Unit Ten to put together a profile on this Nick Gaden."

Widow said, "Tell her to look for connections with Eggers and Cho, other than all being SEALs. See if she can find out why Gaden's name is missing from Cho's team roster."

Gray said, "We could go back now? Back to Quantico, I mean."

"No. I want to talk with Shore's family. Like Frost said."

"You believed him then?"

"I do. I know what it's like to have cases go unresolved. They can haunt you."

"Do you have cases that haunt you?"

Widow said, "I do."

46

After San Diego, Widow and Gray drove two hours back to LAX because they had to return the car before flying on to Hawaii.

They turned the car and the keys back in to the rental counter. They had carried their old clothes and the toiletry items that Gray bought all in one large shopping bag from the store where they bought their new clothes. They lifted it out of the backseat of the car and Widow carried it with them through the airport.

They had a flight booked by Cameron to leave for Hawaii on American Airlines. They got their tickets and passed through security with both of Gray's weapons. She had to flash her badge multiple times throughout the procedure, but eventually, they got to the gate all in one piece.

They ended up getting there right at the start of boarding. They followed their group and boarded the plane.

As Gray was figuring out whether to stow the shopping bag under the seat in front of her or up in the bin, a phone noise buzzed in Widow's old pants pocket.

Both Gray and Widow looked at the shopping bag, confused. She reached in and felt his pockets and pulled out two smartphones, both cheap, both in black shells. One was buzzing and vibrating with incoming text messages.

She climbed over Widow and dumped herself down in the window seat and stared at him. She handed the buzzing smartphone over to him. He took it and stared at the screen.

"Who's that? Your girlfriend?" she asked.

"I don't have a girlfriend," he said and smiled.

"So? Who is it?"

He read it out loud to her.

"It says, 'Is target retired?' and 'Where the hell are you?' and it says, 'Sathers, check in!' It goes on and on like that several more times."

"Who is it from?"

"It's the boss man. The bad guy."

"What?"

"I took the phone off the dead guy in the bathroom in Greensboro."

"You've had it this whole time?"

"Yeah."

"How do you know it's his boss?"

Widow showed her the screen. It read out the contact name for the sender of the text messages.

Gray read it out loud.

"Boss Man," Gray said, "Okay. There's a village missing its idiot."

Widow said, "Could be worse. He could've just written the guy's real name."

"The question is, who is the Boss Man? Is it the KAM? Or this Gaden guy? Because we're talking two different people here. Right?"

"I think so. Yes. I think KAM is the guy in charge on the ground in DC. But Gaden is the money, the man behind it all."

Gray said, "The head of the snake."

Widow nodded.

Gray asked, "Are you going to respond?"

"No. He doesn't know his man's dead. Let him keep texting and worrying. Besides, we're about to take off. They'll tell me to turn my phone off."

She nodded.

Widow turned off both phones.

Gray said, "I've never been to Hawaii before."

"You'll love it!"

"I think so! Kind of afraid I won't want to go back to Quantico."

"You can always put in a transfer later on. Work Unit Ten for a year or two and do a good job, and they'll send you anywhere you want."

After takeoff, Gray stared out the window at the end of the continental United States and at the Pacific Ocean.

Widow checked behind him and asked the guy seated behind him if he would mind if Widow reclined his seat all the way back. The guy nodded. Widow reclined as far back in his seat as it would, and closed his eyes. He napped the rest of the flight.

* * *

THEY LANDED in Honolulu at three fifteen in the afternoon. Widow woke just as the tires hit the runway.

Gray stared out the window at the blue skies, the white clouds, and the green and blue colors of the island state, which were so different from the trees in a New England autumn.

Widow sat all the way upright, surprised that a flight attendant hadn't woken him up with instructions to do that before. Usually, they were sticklers for that. He must've slipped under the radar.

The plane taxied up to a gate and stopped. They got off the plane with their shopping bag and followed the signs to the car rentals. At the counter, Gray asked for a Dodge Charger, which they didn't have. So she settled on a Ford Mustang. Widow recognized the sports car pattern for her. Not that he complained. She looked good in a sports car.

They drove out of the city to Mokulua Drive in Kailua.

The houses were amazing, but not as good as the view.

Widow said, "The Shores live here? Are we sure about this?"

"I spoke to Dwayne's mother on the phone. She gave me an address out here."

Widow buzzed down the window on his side. The sounds of crashing waves and birds and wind rushed into the car. Gray stopped the car. She stared at a driveway with a wooden fence covered in vines. There was a curbside security buzzer.

Widow said, "Is this it?"

"That's the address."

"Okay. Another millionaire family."

"Yeah," Gray said. She turned the car and pulled up to the security buzzer. She buzzed down her window and pressed the button.

A female voice came on over the intercom and said, "Come on in."

Next, there was a loud buzz. A mechanical arm on the interior of the gate started rising, and the gate opened up in front of them.

Gray took her foot off the brake and eased forward.

Beyond the gate, they drove along a short driveway past green grass and green palm trees.

As soon as they cleared the first set of trees, they saw a million-dollar view. The house was nestled back against the shore. They could see the blue ocean crashing into rocks beyond the house. Even with the night sky just around the corner, they could see how blue the ocean was.

Gray said, "Wow! I thought I had a good view!"

"This is something."

"Never in a million years will I make enough in the Navy to afford this."

"Maybe not. An admiral could pay this off in about fifty years when you include interest. Maybe forty, if the interest was dropped."

"Wow! Whatever this family does, I need to switch careers."

They drove up to the front of the house and parked, leaving the car in the driveway. Hawaiian music played from inside the house. It was low but audible. The bass echoed throughout the house, suggesting a good sound system was installed throughout the place.

They walked to the front door. Before they could knock, a woman with a martini glass filled with olives and vodka opened the door. She was about the same age as Jessica Cho. She wore colorful clothes that were good enough to go to a fancy restaurant but maintained a Hawaiian sense of casual wear.

She was a black woman, about five feet even. In the background, a much younger man was shirtless in white chinos and house shoes. He was built somewhere between a new sailor and a male model. He disappeared behind a wall as soon as he saw Widow and Gray.

The woman extended her hand to Gray.

She said, "You must be Detective Gray. I'm Sheila Shore. My son was Dwayne."

Gray took her hand and shook it, didn't correct her on the *Detective* title. Instead, she said, "You can just call me Sonya."

"Okay, Sonya. Just call me Sheila then," Shore said. She turned to Widow and looked him from bottom to top like she was tracing a tree from its trunk to the leafy summit high above.

"This is Jack Widow, ma'am," Gray said.

"Sheila, remember. It's just Sheila," Shore said. She extended her hand to Widow. But not for him to shake, rather for him to kiss the back of it as if they were now in some kind of high-society universe. And she was royalty.

At his birth, Widow had been a Southern gentleman by definition of where he was born. So, it didn't bother him to play along. He took her hand and kissed it.

He said, "Nice to meet you, Sheila."

"Nice to meet you too, Jack."

"Call me Widow, Sheila. No one calls me Jack."

"Oh, that's unique. Is that a sailor thing?"

"It's just always been that way. Started with my momma and continues to this day."

"I appreciate that, Widow. Are you and your momma close?"

"We were, once. She's dead now, ma'am."

Shore caught that Widow said *ma'am*, but she didn't correct him. Gray smiled at him. She saw what he'd done.

Gray said, "Can we come in, Sheila? We're not interrupting?"

Shore stepped back and left the door open.

"No. No. Come in."

Shore walked into a huge open-concept house. Everything was island-themed and colorful, calming and vibrant at the same time. She led them into a living room with a huge fireplace with colorful tiles going from the mantle to the ceiling.

She sat in a comfortable sofa and invited them to join her. Gray sat across from her in a lounger. Widow was about to sit on the opposite sofa, but Shore put a hand down on the sofa next to her.

"Sit here, Mr. Widow. Don't be so far away."

Widow stared at her for a second and then joined her on the sofa.

The shirtless man reappeared from another room, only this time he had put on a shirt. It was a Hawaiian shirt. Most of the buttons were undone, and the shirt was open.

Widow got a good look at the guy. He was twenty-five. The guy entered the room with a tray in one hand that had two more martinis on it. He set the martinis on a coffee table in front of both Gray and Widow.

Shore said, "Guys, this is Manuel. He works for me. Those drinks are for you. Drink up, please."

Neither Widow nor Gray touched the drinks, but they both thanked her for them.

Shore asked why they were there, and they told her, some of it. They left out the gory details and just gave her the basics. The dead man in the park and the money. They mentioned Frost.

Shore drank the rest of her martini and told them she was a single mother and had raised Dwayne on her own. She told them stories about Dwayne and the first day he came out of the closet to her. She told them about Henry Cho. She claimed Dwayne loved Cho and never would've done the things the NCIS claimed he did. She got upset, and she cried a little. Then she perked up when she mentioned Frost. She said he was the only guy to believe her.

Gray and Widow stayed with her for an hour, listening to stories about her son. Like Jessica Cho, she also showed them photographs of her son doing things and being happy.

At the end of the conversation, Widow asked, "Sheila, do you mind if I ask what you do for a living?"

Sheila wiped tears from her face and said, "I paint. But that's really more of a hobby. Are you asking how I can afford all this?"

Widow nodded.

Shore said, "This is a gift from Dwayne."

Gray said, "He left you this house?"

"No. He left behind a large sum of money in a trust for me. I guess it was some kind of insurance policy he bought."

Widow asked, "Insurance policy?"

"Yeah, in case he died. He loved his mother."

Gray said, "I'm sorry, Sheila, but I still don't understand."

Shore said, "After Dwayne died, one day this lawyer contacted me. He said there was a large sum of money in a trust that was paid out by an anonymous donor who claimed to have sold Dwayne a life insurance policy."

Gray said, "I don't think that's how life insurance works."

Widow asked, "What's the lawyer's name?"

Shore called out, "Manuel?"

Manuel came walking out of the kitchen.

"Yes, ma'am."

"Fetch me the name of that lawyer, please. It's in the top drawer in my study."

Manuel nodded and vanished back down a hallway. A few minutes later, he came out with a business card. He gave it to her and then she handed it to Gray, who took out her phone and took a picture. Then she showed it to Widow.

The name on the card read: *Sean Galt*.

Widow didn't recognize the name, but was surprised by it. He half expected it to say *Michael Aker*.

He handed the card back to Shore, who laid it on the coffee table.

She said, "Is there anything else I can do for you?"

Gray stood up and said, "No. The NCIS thanks you for your cooperation."

Shore nodded and also stood up. She eyeballed Widow as he stood. Then she led them out of the house back to their car and said one last thing.

She said, "If you find out something that exonerates my son, let me know. Please."

Widow said, "If we find something, we'll do that."

They got back into the rented car, drove out to the street, and headed back to Honolulu to find a hotel for the night.

On the ride back, Gray said, "I think Frost might be right. What do you think?"

"I don't think her son killed Cho."

"And what was that about an anonymous donation to her?"

"I think I know where it's from."

Gray shot him that sideways glance again.

She asked, "From where?"

"Eggers."

"How? Why?"

"Think about it. He hired a lawyer to watch over his estate. To make sure his daughter inherits fifty million dollars that he owns. Why not hire other lawyers to provide donations to Sheila Shore and the Chos?"

Gray said, "They said that they got a bunch of money from Henry's death!"

"It's from Eggers. Has to be. He definitely had the money."

"But why?"

Widow looked out the window at the last of the daylight before it vanished over the trees and the mountains.

He said, "What's the one thing that can drive a man, worth millions, to live like a homeless person, to eat garbage, to sleep on park benches, to give up a thriving military career? What would cause a man to do that?"

"I don't know."

"Think about it, Sonya," Widow said. He turned in the car seat to face her. "Why would a decorated war hero, like Eggers, let his life fall into desolation the way he did? Even though he was a multimillionaire? Why would he do that? Why would he donate millions of dollars secretly to the families of two dead sailors from twenty years ago?"

Gray stared straight ahead in silence for a long moment. She turned the wheel once to merge with traffic on a busy highway that headed back to Honolulu.

Finally, she said, "I don't know. What?"

"Guilt."

"Guilt?"

"Yes. Eggers knew something. He knew Shore didn't murder Cho. He must've. Maybe he saw something or heard something. Maybe he even took part in it."

"You think he killed Cho?"

Widow shrugged and said, "I don't know. But he might've been a part of it."

"When we get back to the hotel, I'm going to call Cameron. See if NCIS will reopen the investigation."

"Good idea. But wait on that. Let's wait to see where we end up."

"Are you sure?"

"Yeah. Hold off until we know more of what we have here," Widow said. He turned to the backseat. He fished into their shopping bags and through his old clothes and pulled out the phone that Aker had given him. He dialed Aker's number.

The phone sounded four long rings before someone picked up.

"Hello," Aker said.

"Aker, it's Widow. How are you? Are the girls okay?"

"Yes! Thank you for getting them back to us! We stayed with the guards. Armed guards are better than no armed guards. We've been moved to..."

Widow interrupted him.

"No! Don't tell me where. Best that I don't know."

"Okay."

"How's Tunney?"

"He's still the same. His wife is with him day and night at the hospital."

"Okay."

"What's your question?"

"You know anything about trusts being set up and paid out to two families called Shore and Cho?"

"Trust? From who?"

"Eggers."

"Oh. No, I'm not aware of that."

"Were you Eggers' *only* lawyer?"

"No. I don't think so."

"Do you know the name of the other lawyer?"

"Hold on a second. I have it on my phone."

Aker went quiet for a minute. Then he came back on the line.

"Widow, Eggers had another law firm on retainer. His lawyer's name there was Galt—Sean Galt. But I don't know him. I don't know what kind of lawyer he is."

Widow said the name out loud, so Gray would hear it.

"Sean Galt. Got it. Aker, do me a favor and contact him. Find out about Eggers and the Chos and Shore. We just need confirmations."

"Sure thing."

"Okay. Just text me here. I gotta go."

Widow hung up the phone and didn't wait for a goodbye.

Gray said, "Galt is Eggers' other attorney. You got to be right."

"I know."

"We should book a flight home."

"Not for today. Let's get a hotel and go out tonight."

Gray looked at Widow and smiled.

"Okay."

* * *

ON THE DRIVE back to Honolulu, Gray's phone buzzed from a text message. She opened it and glanced at it. She handed it to Widow. He took the phone and read through the text message.

She said, "It's from Cameron."

"It's the report on her findings about Nick Gaden," Widow said as he scrolled. He came to the bottom and found a link.

Gray saw him studying the link.

She said, "Just click the link, Widow. It'll take you to Unit Ten's secure servers. Cameron doesn't send out sensitive information across unsecured text messages."

"Oh. Right. Makes sense," he said. He clicked the link. It led him to another site. He opened it and waited for it to load.

"Well, what is it?"

"It's a workup on several guys. It looks like all military records. The first is Nick Gaden. And there's a photo."

He reached the phone over and showed it to Gray. She glanced at it and then back at the road ahead.

She said, "Don't recognize him."

"Me neither. But it says here that Gaden was a SEAL. Decorated too."

"What are the years he was active?"

"Looks like he was in twenty-five years, but he retired five years ago."

"What's he doing now?"

"No clue. The Navy doesn't record stuff you do after you're gone."

"True. What else?"

"A lot of confirmed kills on his record."

"How many?"

Widow said, "A lot."

"Was he a sniper?"

"Yes. A damn good one, too. And he retired as a one-star admiral."

"He retired at admiral? That's when you make the big bucks. Why would he retire?"

Widow shrugged and continued reading.

"No clue. Basically, his record is spotless. Lots of citations and medals. He's even got a letter of accommodation from the secretary of the Navy in here."

"Jesus. I wonder what got Frost onto him? See any connection to Cho or Eggers?"

"No. Nothing. No signs they even met. The only connection is the Navy."

Gray said, "And the SEALs. That might mean something. There are only so many SEALs."

"Twenty-seven hundred active duty, last I was on the team."

"What else?"

"Nothing more on Gaden. There are some other names here I don't recognize."

Widow scrolled on and stopped dead on a face he recognized.

Gray said, "Widow? What is it?"

Widow said, "That's him. That's the *KAM* guy."

"Let me see."

Widow flashed the phone screen at Gray, who took her eyes off the road for a second and looked at the photo.

She said, "I've never seen him before."

Widow looked back at the phone, and Gray watched the road.

Widow said, "Chris Fallow. He's younger than Eggers and Gaden. He's forty-five. But he served under Gaden before Gaden retired ten years ago."

Gray said, "Seems they stayed in touch if Gaden is the man behind it all."

Widow read about both Fallow and Gaden. They had multiple medals between them, multiple service commendations, multiple tours overseas, and multiple promotions. They were rock stars with rock star Navy records.

Gray asked, "What about the guy you killed in Greensboro?"

Widow scrolled through the file and found an attachment at the end. On it, he found a photo of fingerprints and a photo of the bald guy who attacked him.

He read it aloud.

"Milo Sathers. He wasn't Navy. He was Army. Green Beret. He's also got a bunch of medals and service commendations."

"Green Berets are tough."

"So are we," Widow said. He scrolled back to a photo of Fallow. He stared at it and clenched his fist. Then he turned and stared out the window.

47

WIDOW AND GRAY found a hotel on Kalakaua Avenue, not far from Waikiki Beach. They checked into the hotel, parked the car in a parking garage, and went out for some dinner in their newly bought NCIS-appropriate clothes. Widow took the jacket, since it was getting breezy and chilly outside.

They walked down to the beach, side by side, but not hand in hand. They found a beach bar with tiki torches and tiki wall masks of gods and goddesses with names of Hoaloha and Lono and Pele and Hina and Kuula. There were hula dancers in grass skirts, and they were both given leis to wear around their necks when they entered.

They sat at the bar and ordered. Gray had some kind of local creation drink called the *Islander,* and Widow had a Budweiser from the tap.

They ordered food and drank and ate and enjoyed each other's company. They began with going over the files, talking more about Gaden and Fallow, and learning all they could about them. They racked their brains to find the connection to Eggers, to the money.

That lasted through the early part of the evening, but later on, they switched gears and enjoyed their night on a Hawaiian beach. After the bar, they walked the shoreline and listened to the waves, the seabirds, and the sounds of the ocean.

They talked. Widow learned more about Gray than he had expected. She was more than just a beautiful NCIS agent and a colleague. She was a beautiful person: smart, funny, deep, and full of compassion.

Around nine at night, they were standing alone on the sand, five meters from the water. The moon was full. The sky was partly cloudy with soft, slow-moving clouds, and filled with stars.

Widow thought of kissing Gray. In fact, it was the only thing he thought of. He waited for the right moment. When it finally came, the bald guy's phone rang in his pocket.

Gray looked at him with disappointment in her eyes. She, too, was hoping for a kiss.

"Who is it?" she asked.

Widow looked at the caller ID, clicked the answer button, and put the phone on speaker.

A male voice said, "Milo, where the hell have you been?"

Widow said, "Is this Chris Fallow?"

Silence.

"Jack Widow. I told you what would happen if you didn't drop it."

"What're you going to do?"

"I'm going to kill those girls!"

"No. You're not."

Silence. No response.

Widow said, "I'll tell you what you're going to do. You're going to get off the phone and call your boss, the guy who's actually in charge. And you're going to tell him I'm coming for him. I'm coming for you both."

Gray leaned into Widow and whispered.

"What are you doing?"

Fallow's voice fumed. He sounded angry.

He said, "I'm going to find those little girls and tear them limb from limb! You think I won't do it? We've done it before! I've killed before! Men! Women! Children! We've killed kids in Iraq! It doesn't bother me! We don't give a shit about you or them! I'm going to do the same to everyone you ever cared about!"

"You've killed kids? You shouldn't have told me that. You're going to regret telling me that. I'm going to find you!"

"You won't have the chance! I'm going to find you and that pretty agent you've been canoodling with. And you know what I'm going to do?"

Widow stayed quiet.

Fallow said, "I'm going to kill you both! But first, I'm going to take my time with her! Think I'll get to know her real well! Make you watch! How do you like that!"

Widow looked at the phone and picked it up, reared back, and threw it into the ocean. It was swallowed up by the waves.

Gray shouted, "Widow! Why did you do that?"

"It doesn't matter at this point. You already doubled security on the Akers, and moved them to an undisclosed location. Tunney has more security on him. Fallow was going to find out Sathers is dead no matter what. It makes no difference, now."

"But why did you throw the phone? Might be evidence on it."

"Might be a GPS tracker in it, like the one they gave me."

She nodded and asked, "So what now?"

Widow stepped in close to her. He fanned his hand out across her waist, over her hips. He did the same with the other hand. He grabbed onto her by the waist and pulled her in close.

She whispered, "Widow? I'm not sure we should."

"We definitely should!" he whispered back.

"But, we're partners."

"Not officially. Officially, we're two people on a Hawaiian beach at night, under a full moon."

Gray grabbed at his jacket and pulled herself into his chest tight. She stood up on tiptoes and kissed him. It was slow and soft at first, and then it was harder and faster. The intensity grew and grew. It turned out that driving cars fast wasn't the only thing that she liked to do fast.

She reached up and combed her fingers through the hair on the back of his head. He slid one hand up her back and back down again to the bottom of her lower back. They kissed for a long time. Her lips were soft and wet. Their hearts raced. They both felt it.

Widow was the first to pull back. He stared down into her eyes.

He asked, "Did you already book our flight back?"

"I texted Cameron. She's got us going back tomorrow."

"What time?"

"At oh eight hundred, Commander."

"So, we got all night to kill?"

"We should sleep."

"We will. After."

They kissed again. Fervently. Vividly. Intensely.

They didn't make it back to the hotel, not right away. They lay in the sand, near the water, in the darkness and moonlight. Widow put down his new jacket, which was big enough to keep Gray's new clothes off the sand. That really mattered little, because she wasn't wearing them for long.

48

FALLOW CALLED the client known as The Chief.

"Chief, Widow is still on us."

"Does he know who I am?"

"Not yet. He and that agent are snooping around."

"What do they know?"

"They're kicking up old dirt, hoping they'll find something."

"What exactly are they looking at?"

"They've been snooping around the Cho thing."

"It's only a matter of time before they're on to me. Take care of it!"

"There might be a problem."

"What?"

"Widow."

"He's one man! Kill him!"

"I'll need some help!"

"What about your guys?"

"He's killed one already. Think we'll need more."

"That'll be easy."

"Think we'll need more than the usual guys. I think we'll need expensive guys."

"I've got a lot of eyes on me right now! The media's watching me, watching my spending."

"We need them, Chief."

"Fine! How much? And how many?"

"We got three left, counting me. I'd like three more."

"Do it. But no more talking for a while. We should do radio silence. I can't be suspected of being involved in this. Everyone's watching."

"That's why I'm here. I'll contact you after he's dead."

The Chief hung up the phone.

49

Widow and Gray got back to the hotel room, fully clothed. That changed quickly once they entered Gray's room. Widow never went to his room.

In the morning, they showered together, steaming up the shower, and fogging the mirror.

After, they cleaned each other with soap and water, which started things all over again.

Widow was the first out. Gray stayed in because she had more parts to clean.

Widow dressed in his old clothes because the new ones were filled with sand. He left the room, went down the elevator to the hotel lobby, and found a little café in the lobby's corner with a shared entrance to the street.

He ordered a couple of coffees and waited near the counter. He glanced over and saw a couple of guys reading a newspaper, not a Hawaiian paper, but the *New York Times*. Beyond that, there were tourists at every table in the place. He saw

Hawaiian shirts everywhere and people wearing sunscreen on their skin. He saw sun hats and ball caps, everything you needed for an island climate. No big deal. All around him, he saw ordinary people doing ordinary things.

A barista behind the counter called out his order for pickup. He walked over and picked up the two coffees. He popped the lid on one and took a sip. It was pretty great. Really great, actually.

He looked at the barista who had called out his order.

Widow said, "This coffee is pretty good! My compliments."

Widow smiled at the guy, who smiled back, and he turned to leave.

The barista said, "Thanks, Chief.

Widow froze in his tracks. The two coffees heated the palms of his hands. He turned back around and stared at the barista.

The guy looked at him weirdly, probably because he was just standing there staring at him.

The barista said, "Anything wrong, Chief?"

Chief. The barista had called him *Chief.*

Widow smiled and turned back around. But not to leave. He stared at the two guys who were reading the newspaper. They were finishing up.

One of them noticed him staring at them.

He asked, "Hey, buddy, you need this table?"

Widow walked over to them.

"Actually, I was wondering if you were done with that paper?"

"Sure," the guy said, "It's all yours."

The guy folded the paper and handed it to Widow. He set the coffees down on the table that they were deserting and took the paper.

The two men left. Widow followed them, abandoning his coffees back at the table.

He pushed past them and ran back to the elevator and to Gray's hotel room. He entered. She was out of the shower, but she was still in the bathroom and still naked. She was towel-drying her hair.

Gray asked, "Where are our coffees?"

Widow ignored the question. He went over to a little table in the room and laid out the paper. He picked up her phone and brought it over to her.

She wrapped her hair up in the towel and stared at him.

"What?" she asked.

He handed her the phone.

"Unlock it," he said.

"Sure," she said and took the phone and put in her passcode. She tried to hand it back to him.

He said, "Pull up the file on Cho's platoon. The one we went over at your place."

"Okay. Sure."

She went onto the NCIS secure servers and opened the file. She handed him the phone.

Widow took it and sat down in a chair and scrolled through it, searching.

Gray turned back to the bathroom mirror and started running the water out of the faucet. She took out a disposable toothbrush provided by the hotel, and she brushed her teeth.

With the toothbrush in her mouth, she paused and asked, "What's this about?"

Widow ignored the question and continued to scroll and read, like he was searching for something.

She repeated the question.

"Widow, what's this about? What's going on?"

He said, "SEAL teams comprise six platoons each with sixteen SEALs. Remember?"

"Yeah? We know that. One name was missing. You said that meant nothing. Maybe one guy was in transition?"

"There are two officers, thirteen enlisted..." Widow said, and stopped. He paused a beat, studying the list of SEAL names from the NCIS file. He went over the names.

"And? What, Widow? You stopped mid-sentence."

He said, "Six platoons each with sixteen SEALs: two officers, thirteen enlisted and one chief. There's no chief listed here. No chief listed in charge of Cho's platoon."

Gray walked over to him, stopped behind him, and leaned over his shoulder.

She said, "Every officer is called Chief. You know that. It's common. Chief just means the guy in charge. You were called Chief once."

"Right, but here in Cho's platoon, we have only one officer."

"Eggers," she said.

"Right. Which means the missing name is the other officer."

She said, "Maybe this was when they were in transition, without one. You said that happened, right?"

"Not likely. Not with officers. The team needs a leader. Cho was out on a mission just days before he was murdered. They had just gotten back from an op in Iraq. No way would they've been green lit without a chief in place already."

"And it wasn't Eggers?"

"I don't think so. I think it was someone else."

"The missing name?"

"Usually there's a promotion within the platoon or they have someone from outside brought in just before the outgoing chief leaves. But we don't go out on a mission missing one. There has to be someone in charge."

"So what? They went out on a mission without a chief?"

"No. The chief, the head honcho, is the name that is missing."

Gray said, "Gaden?"

"Yes. Has to be. That's how Frost got onto him in the first place. He figured out he was the missing name."

"Why is his name missing?"

"Maybe he was transferring to a different team."

"Or maybe it got covered up somehow?"

Widow said, "Could be. If he's got a reach like that."

"You said yourself that whoever is at the top of the chain must have money."

"That'd explain why he didn't stay in the Navy any longer, why he retired right at rear admiral."

Gray slid her hands to Widow's face and moved around him like a ballet dancer around her partner and she sat on his lap. She smelled sweet and felt soft.

She said, "Didn't you go downstairs for coffee?"

"I left it in the café," he said, embarrassed. That he abandoned coffee had just set in with him. He had never done that before.

"Why don't you go back for it, come back up here and we'll go over all this."

Widow looked at her, smiled, and nodded. She kissed him.

50

WIDOW WENT BACK DOWNSTAIRS for the coffees. Luckily, they were still on the table. He scooped them up and returned to Gray's room.

Gray was dressed in her clothes from before Los Angeles. Her and Widow's new clothes were folded up in the shopping bag. They sat on a little sofa in the room's corner.

They didn't have Gray's laptop, so they huddled together and stared over her phone at the files. They read Gaden's file.

Nick Gaden had been a Marine and then a SEAL. He was one of the few SEALs to pass the elite Marine sniper school as well. He had an impressive record except for one blip.

The blip was an investigation into Gaden that ended abruptly, which led them to read an unofficial NCIS report that had been filed away. It covered the whole thing. They switched over to it on a different page.

Gray read out loud.

"According to Unit Ten's own report, Gaden was the head of Cho and Eggers' platoon for six months, back in two thousand one, post nine-eleven. The reason his name wasn't officially on the list was that he *was* in transition. His trident and status were removed temporarily because he was under investigation by NCIS."

Widow took over, reading the rest out loud.

"There were accusations he sniped and murdered several children in the Middle East, calling them "piglets." And that's only the stuff noted here. That's not the only charge. It says he was being investigated for stabbing a prisoner to death."

Gray said, "This is horrible. So what happened? Why is it just gone after that?"

"It says here that Gaden was acquitted because of lack of evidence."

"That makes little sense. It says there were multiple witnesses."

"Six in total," Widow said.

"Six? No NCIS agent would arrest a decorated Naval officer without enough evidence already to convict him."

"I agree. And six witnesses are definitely enough. It's even a little overkill. To get that many witnesses is damn fine police work."

"So, why did they drop the charges?"

Widow said, "Look here. They dropped the charges because five of the witnesses retracted their statements."

Gray said, "Look at the date! It was the day after Cho died!"

Widow said, "And Cho was stabbed to death."

They looked at each other.

Widow said, "The other witness was Cho. According to this, he was *the* witness. He was the one who got the complaint out to NCIS. He was the one pushing for Gaden to be investigated."

"Are you saying that Gaden murdered Cho to stop the investigation?"

"Wouldn't be the first time someone's killed to cover up his crimes. It also wouldn't be the first time that the boys in the Pentagon would want to cover up a piece of nasty business like this."

Gray nodded. They both went quiet and read on through the morning, drinking their coffees, mostly in silence and shock. At one point, Gray stopped and canceled their flight home.

They hardly spoke until finally Gray said, "It says that Gaden was in confinement. How did he kill Cho?"

"He may have been in confinement, but Fallow wasn't."

Gray nodded. "He *was* a Marine."

"So was Dwayne Shore."

Gray stared at Widow.

She said, "SEAL Platoons are a bunch of guys who are very close. Like brothers. I bet they all knew Cho was gay. I bet Fallow was stationed with Shore."

Widow put his finger on the phone and scrolled back to Fallow's dossier. He stopped on it and read it out loud.

"Fallow is a graduate of Marine sniper school. The same months that Gaden was there."

Gray said, "They knew each other."

Widow nodded.

Gray took over the phone and scrolled back to a paragraph she was reading.

She said, "Here. They were all at the same base at the same time. That's our opportunity."

"And motive."

"What about the money? Eggers had fifty million in stocks? Is it tied to this?"

Widow said, "There were six witnesses against Gaden before Cho was killed. One of the other five was Henry Eggers. He was one of the five who recanted after Cho died."

"And he gave the Chos and Ms. Shore all that money. He was the life insurance. That's why he abruptly quit right after Cho died. And why he gave them all that money," Gray said. She paused a beat. Then she said, "He felt guilt."

"It's probably why he lived homeless, drank himself to sleep for twenty years. It's probably why his daughter is estranged from him. He couldn't live with himself."

Gray said, "He bore a horrible secret and could never tell. Why couldn't he tell after?"

"Fear. I guess he feared Gaden and Fallow and whoever else was involved. He feared they'd kill him, probably his daughter too."

"And the money?"

Widow pointed at the *New York Times* on the table.

"That's why I brought up the paper. I saw a guy down in the café reading over the stocks. Nick Gaden. I knew name was familiar."

Widow reached out to the paper and flipped a page to the stocks section. He put his index finger over the page and scanned it until he found what he was looking for.

He pointed at it.

Gray looked and read out the name of the stock.

"SHG."

Widow said, "Samson, Hardy, and..."

Gray said, "Gaden."

"Gaden is a junior. Nicholas Gaden, Sr. owns and operates as a partner in Samson, Hardy, and Gaden. I read about it the other day on their website."

Gray said, "They manufacture weapons."

"More than weapons. They manufacture battle vehicles. Big ones."

Gray said, "They have Navy contracts. Is that what this is about?"

"No. The father is in the company. Not the son," Widow said. He flipped the page of the paper a few pages over to the politics section.

He planted his finger on a small article about a Senate election.

He said, "And guess who's running for Senate?"

Gray stared at the article. There was no picture, but there was a name. She read it aloud.

"Nicholas Gaden, Jr. is running for a Senate seat in Alaska."

"That's right."

"So why did Eggers have so much money?"

"My guess is that Eggers and the other five witnesses left alive were both scared and bribed into retracting their statements. Maybe the other four were easily bought out. And Eggers wasn't. But he took the money. Maybe to prove to Gaden that he was loyal. Maybe to save his daughter's life."

"They bribed him with fifty million dollars? It seems a lot cheaper to kill him. Gaden already killed Cho. Why not Eggers too?"

"It wasn't fifty million dollars' worth of stock, not twenty years ago. Samson, Hardy, and Gaden didn't get those big Navy contracts until around twenty years ago. Their stock has been soaring ever since. The Chos and Ms. Shore never told us when they started getting money from this trust. I bet if we ask them, it'll be right around the time that Eggers' stock soared."

Gray said, "So, that's why they killed Eggers now. Gaden is running for Senate and feared all these old loose ends coming unraveled after all this time?"

"I'd say that's a good enough motive for this sadistic bastard to kill."

"This will be hard to prove. You're talking an old case and a vast conspiracy. Spanning two decades."

Widow said, "It's not my job to prove it. That's yours."

Gray said, "So, what do we do first?"

"Gaden is campaigning in Alaska. We should pay him a visit."

"I was afraid you were going to say that. I prefer the weather here."

51

Fallow called Gaden to tell him the bad news.

He said, "I'm sorry, Chief. But Widow got away."

"It was your job to manage this!"

"I'm sorry. There's more. They've been talking to Cho's family, and then they visited Hawaii. I guess to see Shore's mother. And they talked to Frost."

Silence.

"Chief?"

Fallow heard Gaden breathing heavy on the other line.

Gaden said, "Do they know about me?"

"My guess is by now they probably know your name. They probably see the dots. Not sure if they've connected them yet."

"You're not sure?"

"I'm sorry, Chief."

"You keep saying that! I don't care if you're sorry!"

Fallow said nothing.

Gaden said, "Okay, no point in dwelling on mistakes. What do we do now?"

"I think you'd better prepare."

"Where are they now?"

"Last, I could tell, they were in Hawaii. My guess is they're coming to you."

"Are you still in DC?"

"Yes. I can take a flight out, but I won't be there before them."

"Get out here on the double. I'll deal with them for now."

Gaden clicked off the line, but he didn't put the phone away. Instead, he put in a local call.

A voice answered.

"Yes?"

"It's me."

The voice sounded nervous and afraid.

He said, "Yes. I know."

"I need to cash in the favor you owe me."

The voice said, "Okay. What do you want me to do?"

Gaden explained about Widow and Gray and told him to check on incoming flights to Anchorage. He told him what to do. The man behind the voice wrote it all down and acknowledged that he understood the instructions.

52

Gray canceled their flight home and re-booked them on a flight to Anchorage, Alaska. They left in a Boeing 737 in the midmorning, and, because of the two-hour jump in time, they landed around eight-thirty in the evening. The flight was nonstop and comfortable enough.

Widow could tell that Gray was getting sick of planes.

At one point, she asked, "How are you okay with flying so much?"

He said, "I flew a lot in the back of cargo transport planes. All over the world. So, I'm used to it. Like second nature."

"C-130s?"

"All kinds. C-130s. I've also been in C-17s, CN-235s, and a bunch of others. Have you never flown on one?"

Gray said, "Not once. I flew commercial whenever I had to go somewhere."

Widow nodded.

Gray said, "I bet this beats flying in the back of a cargo plane."

"I wouldn't say that. In the backs of C-130s, we used to set up hammocks and lie stretched out. It was fun."

She looked at him with that sideways look again and smiled.

A bit later, they were on the ground. Widow carried their shopping bag. They were both dressed in their warm clothes from DC, which was good because it was cold outside. Widow had washed his clothes in the bathtub and sink at the hotel and he dried them off the balcony, all before they left. Luckily, he'd enough time to do that before they took off for Anchorage. He offered to wash Gray's, but she wanted to do it herself, which she did after watching how he did his.

They landed, disembarked from the plane, and walked to the gate. They were following the signs to the car rental office when Gray's phone rang. It was Cameron. She called to inform them they would have to liaise with a local FBI agent. Gray didn't protest. She'd expected something like this because the NCIS had virtually zero presence in Alaska at the moment.

After the call, Gray told Widow they would meet an FBI agent named Tyler.

They rented a car and got lucky; there was a Dodge Charger in stock. Gray asked for snow tires. The rental vehicles automatically came with snow tires, which they doubted they would need. Snowfall in October was just a few inches in Anchorage, Widow told her.

They walked to the Charger in the lot. It didn't come with a police battering ram on the front or sirens or police lights embedded in the grille, like the one she had back at home, but it was the same navy-blue color with black rims and tinted windows. Inside, it had a black leather interior with warming seats.

They got in, and Gray fired up the engine to let it warm up.

She pulled out her phone and went over the information that Cameron had texted her on Gaden.

She said, "Okay. Gaden is due to campaign the day after tomorrow. Right now, he should be in his home in a town called Anguta."

"Anguta?"

"That's what it says. What does that mean?"

"Anguta is the Eskimo god of death, or rather the English translation is the gatherer of the dead."

"Well, that's fitting."

Widow smiled and said nothing.

Gray said, "Okay. We have to meet with FBI Agent Matt Tyler before we do anything."

"Great."

"He's former Navy. He won't be all bad."

Widow said nothing to that.

He said, "We should go out there tonight."

"You don't think we should wait till tomorrow?"

"How far is Anguta?"

Gray looked at her phone and put in the town's name on Google Maps. Then she waited for it to calculate directions.

She said, "Three hours north."

"Better tell Tyler to meet us there in three hours then."

"Think we should go now?"

"Dark is best. Let's not wait for him to know we're here. Let's stop by."

"We have to announce it. We can't just show up at his house. He's running for the Senate. There is protocol. We're not arresting him."

Widow said, "Text Tyler and tell him we're here, and we're headed out to speak to Gaden tonight. This guy's slippery. We don't want to wait till tomorrow. What if he leaves early for his campaign? We have to assume he knows we're coming. Best to do it now."

"What are we going to do when we get there? We can't flat out accuse him of a conspiracy to murder Eggers and cover it up. Not to mention kidnapping, and possibly the murder of Cho."

"And Shore."

"Shore killed himself in prison."

"Did he?"

"You don't think he did?"

"I'm not sure. Either way, it's because of Gaden. So, let's go have a chat with him. If the FBI wants to be there, so be it."

Gray nodded and texted Tyler. Then she put on her seatbelt, told Widow to do the same, and they were off, following the GPS navigation to Anguta, Alaska. Most of the way was on Route Three, which changed road and highway names several times.

* * *

Two and a half hours later, they parked off the road at a local gas station that seemed to be in the middle of nowhere. As far as they could tell, theirs was the only car there, except for the attendant's truck. The only lights they saw were from inside the station.

Since they were already there, they gassed up the car. They parked in a space facing the road and waited. The car engine idled, and the heat blasted from the vents.

A thermometer gauge on the dash showed it was about thirty degrees Fahrenheit outside, which Widow thought was okay because it was Alaska at night; it could've been much worse.

They sat in their seats, waiting for a long time. Before they knew it, without realizing it, they were holding hands over the cup holders.

Finally, Widow said, "Where is he?"

Gray clicked a button on her phone to see if she had gotten a message from Tyler and hadn't heard it, but there was nothing.

She said, "Tyler said he'd be a little long because he's coming from Fairbanks."

"They didn't have an FBI agent in Anchorage?"

"They do, but I guess none of them wanted to be a part of this. I still don't know what we're going to do when we see Gaden."

"We're just going to ask him some questions."

"You think he'll cop to a murder twenty years ago and hiring some guys to kill Eggers in order to cover up that old murder?"

"He might. Think about it. He's been carrying this secret for twenty years. I've dealt with guys like that before. He's probably full of arrogance and superiority. He probably thinks he'll never get caught."

"Guess we're going to find out."

Just then, they saw a pair of headlights from a black truck pulling up. The truck turned into the gas station. It was unmarked but had government plates.

Widow said, "That's him."

They waited for the truck to pull up alongside the driver's side and park. Gray pulled her hand out of Widow's and rested it on her leg. The driver's side door opened, and a guy with fair hair, a tight frame, and a little gray in the temples got out. He wore a red winter coat and blue jeans.

He walked around the nose of the truck and greeted Gray at her window.

Gray buzzed down her window, and the guy bent down at the waist and stuck a hand out for her to shake.

He said, "Gray?"

"That's me."

Tyler reached into his coat pocket and pulled out a black object, which made Gray reach her hand to her Glock, which was in the holster but tucked between her seat and the center console. But the object wasn't a weapon. It was a badge in a black leather billfold. He showed it to her. She checked it, and sure enough, it was Matt Tyler, Special Agent of the FBI.

"I'm Matt Tyler, FBI. A deputy director over at NCIS in DC called us and told us some of what's going on. You're working a homicide and you've got interest in Nick Gaden?"

"That's right."

Gray moved her hand away from her gun, pulled out her own badge, and showed him. He glanced at it and smiled.

Tyler said, "That won't be pleasant for us if it turns to more than just interest. The Gadens are a very popular political family here in the state."

Gray nodded and didn't respond to that.

Tyler twisted at the waist and pointed north to Anguta.

"Well, the Gadens live up that way about twenty miles."

"Okay. Let's go."

"Not yet. We're waiting still."

"Why?"

Tyler leaned back down and put his head near the window. He looked in and saw Widow for the first time.

He said, "We gotta wait for the local sheriff before we go out there."

"We're not talking about arresting anyone," Gray said.

Widow thought, *Not yet.*

Tyler peered over at Widow.

"I was told to expect only one NCIS agent. Who's your friend?"

Gray looked at Widow, who smiled and tried to look as nonthreatening as possible, which wasn't possible, not really. But he tried anyway.

"This is Jack Widow."

Tyler said, "Nice to meet you, Mr. Widow. You NCIS too?"

"I was."

"So, what are you doing here?"

Gray said, "He's consulting with us. He's critical to our case."

Tyler said, "I see."

Just then, another set of headlights appeared from around a bend. A police cruiser pulled into the lot. It was a Ford Crown Vic, an older model with police markings all over it and a light bar on top.

The cruiser pulled in and parked on the other side of Gray's Charger, near Widow. The window buzzed down, and a heavy guy with a pretty big dark beard smiled at them. The sheriff was probably younger than Widow, but he looked ten years older. He wasn't the model of health.

Tyler called out over the roof of Gray's car.

"Sheriff."

The sheriff spoke with a rural accent that Widow guessed was local to the region.

"Hello, Tyler. It's always good to see you."

"You too, Sheriff."

Widow buzzed down his window so Gray could hear the conversation.

The sheriff said, "Hello, folks. I'm Sheriff Clark Daniels. You can call me Sheriff. Everyone else does. And who are the two of you?"

Widow said, "I'm Jack Widow, and this is Sonya Gray, NCIS."

Gray nodded from over Widow's shoulder.

Daniels leaned forward as far as he could, which put his belly into the steering wheel. He looked at Gray and smiled at her.

"Nice to meet you, Agent Gray. Okay. Now, Tyler warned you about the Gadens?"

Tyler said, "I didn't warn them. I just informed them we have to walk gently."

"Gentle as can be. They're an important family to the state. Randall Gaden, Nick's daddy, is a friend of the governor."

Gray said, "We're just here to ask some questions. It's important to our case. We're not here to point fingers."

She was a good liar. Widow thought she would make a good undercover agent.

Daniels said, "Okay. Good. Now, one more question. I was told there was only one of you."

Tyler nodded over the roof of the Charger at Daniels.

Daniels said, "I suspect that's you, Ms. Sonya Gray, and not Widow?"

Widow said, "I'm here as a consultant."

That was the first time he'd said it out loud. It was a lie, technically, because he was there unofficially. They both were. Still, the thought occurred to him that NCIS consultants usually got big, hefty paychecks for consulting, and he was getting nothing. It was just a thought, like remembering a song lyric from out of nowhere. It was meaningless, and it vanished as fast as he had thought it.

Daniels said, "Well, I'm real sorry to ask this, but are the two of you armed?"

Gray said, "Of course."

"And you, Mr. Widow. Are you armed as well?"

Widow looked at Daniels and nodded.

Daniels asked, "Is that a yes?"

"Affirmative," Widow said.

"But you're not officially an NCIS agent, correct?"

Gray said, "He's retired."

Daniels said, "I'm real sorry to say this, but I'm going to have to take possession of your weapon."

Gray said, "What?"

"I'm real sorry. It's just for the time being. Widow can get it back after we've talked to Gaden. It's a security thing."

Tyler bent down again and looked at Gray.

He said, "It's okay. He's within his rights to request that. Widow isn't officially an active-duty law enforcement officer."

Gray said, "It's my gun; he's carrying."

Tyler said, "You'll get it back."

Gray turned to Widow. He stared back at her. Then he reached down into the waistband of his jeans and pulled out her backup SIG Sauer P226. He ejected the magazine and racked the slide. A chambered bullet hopped out of the ejection port and into the air. He caught it one-handed. He did all of this within seconds.

Widow opened his car door, slid out of his seatbelt, and stood up. He handed the gun to Daniels along with the magazine. Daniels took the weapon and the magazine and stuffed them into his glove box, which was an ordeal because he had to reach across the center console to do it and his belly made it a chore.

He closed the glove box and came back into his seated position. He looked up at Widow.

"Thank you, Mr. Widow. You'll get it back after we leave the Gadens."

Widow nodded and pocketed the extra bullet. No one seemed to notice. He got back into the Charger.

Tyler said, "Okay. Sheriff, do they know we're coming?"

"No, but I had my dispatch call ahead and see if Nick was even home."

Tyler said, "And?"

"He's there. Randall isn't."

Gray said, "We aren't interested in the father, just Nick."

Daniels nodded and said, "Okay. Everyone ready? Tyler, why don't you ride with me?"

Tyler said, "Yeah, sure. That's fine."

Tyler locked his truck and joined Daniels in the police cruiser. He sat in the passenger seat. As he crossed out in front of the car's lights, Widow saw a Glock in a hip holster under Tyler's jacket.

Gray reversed the Charger and backed up into the parking lot, turned the nose to face the road. Daniels and Tyler drove out alongside.

Daniels peered past Tyler and looked at Gray.

"Follow us."

Gray said, "We're right behind you."

Daniels and Tyler pulled out onto Route Three and sped up. Gray and Widow followed close behind.

* * *

GRAY AND WIDOW followed behind the sheriff's police cruiser up Route Three and into the night, into the darkness of a lonely stretch of Alaskan freeway. They followed, expecting to go straight to Gaden's house in the town of Anguta, but that wasn't exactly what happened.

About halfway into their drive, Widow and Gray saw the police cruiser veer a bit to the right, as if Daniels hadn't been paying attention, and almost ran off the road. Then the cruiser did something they hadn't expected.

The lightbar on top lit up like a Christmas tree, and the cruiser slowed and then took a sharp right off the freeway. The tires kicked up dirt and gravel from off a dirt road.

Gray stared at her GPS on the dash and said, "That's weird."

"What?"

"They're going a different direction."

"Follow them."

Gray turned the wheel and followed the cruiser. Widow watched through the windshield. They saw the cruiser fishtail a bit to one side and then the other.

Widow asked, "Are they going faster?"

Gray looked down at her speed and said, "Yeah."

They followed close to the cruiser. It stopped fishtailing and sped up. The route ahead was covered in darkness and trees. They stayed tight behind Daniel's cruiser. He looped around tight paths, barely dodging trees and ditches.

Dust spiraled behind them, smoking up the roadway.

Gray said, "What the hell is going on?"

Widow's primate brain fired up and primal instincts, buried down deep in his DNA from a million years ago, from the open forgotten plains of North America, from some prehistoric ancestor, kicked in.

He said, "Careful. Stay back a bit."

Right then, Gray's phone rang.

She said, "Get that for me."

Widow picked up.

It was Tyler on the line.

He said, "You guys, all right back there?"

Widow said, "We're okay. What's going on in there? It looked like you guys almost went into a ditch."

"Everything's fine."

"Where are we going?"

"We have to make a pitstop."

Widow said, "Why? What's going on?"

"Daniels got a nine-one-one call. We have to check it out. He's on duty. Hopefully, it's nothing."

Widow stayed quiet.

Tyler said, "Tell Gray to get her weapon ready."

Widow thought for a moment. Gaden was from Alaska. He'd lived there most of his life except during his stint in the military. Tyler lived in Alaska. He had been in the Navy. It wasn't inconceivable that they knew each other.

Widow said, "I'll let her know."

"Good. It should be nothing, but just in case. Better safe than sorry. Just keep on us."

Tyler clicked off the call.

Widow set the phone down between them into a cup holder.

He asked, "Didn't you say that Tyler was in the Navy?"

"Yes."

"Any chance he would know Gaden?"

Gray glanced over at him from behind the wheel. Then she looked forward, keeping up with the cruiser, trying not to slam into a tree.

She said, "I'm sure he knows of him. He's stationed here. Alaska is just one big, small town, isn't it?"

"Gaden was in for twenty-five years. I think it's possible that Tyler knows him."

"No. I don't think so. That would be an insane coincidence."

"Not that insane."

"Maybe."

Widow said, "Maybe they know each other. We should proceed with caution."

Gray said, "Daniels took your gun."

"I know."

They continued down long, winding roads covered with sleet, gravel, and dirt, turning right, veering left, until finally they come to a dead-end road with what looked like an abandoned shantytown on the end.

They dead-ended in a cul-de-sac and parked behind Daniels' police cruiser. The sirens were off, but blue and red lights from the lightbar rotated, washing the empty structures with the colors. The Charger's headlamps followed and washed over several rundown, derelict structures like ruins from an Old West town. There was one large building still standing, and mostly all in one piece. Several others were only fractions of buildings: missing staircases, missing roofs, missing entire sections of wall.

Gray said, "What the hell is this?"

"Looks like a ghost town."

Gray said, "I don't like this. You might be right. Something's going on."

"We're about to find out."

Gray and Widow waited for Tyler to step out of the cruiser. Sheriff Daniels stepped out next. Widow was a little surprised to see him. His primate brain had pictured Tyler bushwhacking the sheriff and leading them all to their deaths, but there he was and all in one piece. Maybe there was nothing to worry about.

Apparently, Gray had been thinking the same thing.

Daniels had a Glock stuffed into a belt holster.

She said, "The sheriff is okay."

Widow said, "Might still be a trap. Keep your head on a swivel."

They climbed out of the car. Gray was first and then Widow. They met the sheriff and Tyler at the back of the police cruiser.

Daniels' belly was even bigger than Widow had thought previously. He stood at about six feet. His belly was built like an oil drum.

Daniels popped the trunk open and waved them over to the back of the car. Widow and Gray joined Tyler and Daniels at the trunk.

Gray said, "What the hell is going on? Why are we here?"

Tyler said, "Sorry, Agent, but duty calls."

"What?"

Daniels said, "A nine-one-one call came over the wires."

He pointed out over the structures.

He said, "This is what we call a hornet's nest."

Gray asked, "What does that mean?"

Tyler said, "It's slang for a meth house."

"Meth house?"

"Yeah. Look around. This is the sticks, middle of nowhere. People out here, you know, the homeless kind, the kind with nothing to do, get bored and usually find employment cooking and selling meth."

Daniels said, "They're the less fortunate, the less civilized of our state."

"Anyway, they can be dangerous. They don't like outsiders."

"And they hate cops," Daniels said.

Widow asked, "So why are we here?"

Daniels said, "I told you, nine-one-one call."

"But why?"

Tyler said, "Someone called nine-one-one and said their kid went missing and was seen with some boys who live here."

Daniels nodded and said, "Don't worry. I deal with them at least once a month with no violence."

Widow looked into the trunk and saw police gear: a bullhorn, bulletproof vests, ammunition, and similar gear. One item interested him, a Remington 700P, a police special sniper rifle. Widow glanced at it and then at boxes of ammunition lined up in a crate. The Remington 700P was chambered for .308 Winchester cartridge, but it could also fire other rifle rounds, including the .300 Remington Ultra Magnum bullet, which was a big bullet that could do colossal damage.

Widow saw an opened box of .300 Remington Ultra Magnum bullets right there with the others. He made a mental note of it and looked away.

Widow asked, "What about backup? Where're your deputies?"

"Unfortunately, this is a large, rural county. And I'm sheriff of all of it. It might take my closest deputy thirty minutes to get all the way out here. We can't wait. A kid's life is on the line."

Tyler said, "We're the backup."

He looked at Gray.

He said, "It's our duty."

She nodded and looked at Widow.

She said, "What about Widow?"

Tyler said, "He's got no gun."

Daniels said, "He's not a cop."

Gray said, "He's liaising with NCIS."

Daniels said, "The NCIS has no jurisdiction here."

Tyler said, "He's right. Widow is just a civilian. Best if he hangs back. With the cars."

Widow looked at the cruiser and into the trunk. He saw shotgun shells in a box.

He said, "What about your shotgun, Sheriff?"

Daniels stepped back away from the trunk lid and stared into his cruiser at a shotgun locked upright in the front bench.

He said, "Sorry, Widow. You're still a civilian. It'll be okay."

Tyler said, "Besides, the shotgun is mine."

Daniels looked at him, fished his keys out of his pocket, and handed them to Tyler.

"That's fine."

Tyler took the keys, walked back to the front of the cruiser, and got in. He unlocked the shotgun and took it, and came back out.

He asked, "Got shells?"

"Right here in the trunk," Daniels said.

Feeling his primate brain screaming and pounding in the back of his head, Widow tried to stay calm, cool and collected as if he didn't suspect a thing, but he feared the worst.

He stood back, leaned against the hood of the Charger, and watched the others gear up, as prepared as if they were going into a war zone.

He counted the bulletproof vests in the trunk. There were four, one left over for him if he could get to it. He watched as Daniels came out with them and divvied them out. Widow didn't get one.

His primate brain was telling him to act now while he had the chance. He could club Tyler over the head and try explaining to Daniels that the whole thing was a trap. But Daniels was armed, and he wasn't. No way was Gray going to pull a gun on a sheriff, not even for him. Would she?

His brain started running scenarios, calculating the best course of action. In the end, it came back with two options. Club them both over the head and leave them handcuffed in the back of Daniels' cruiser. Let the FBI sort it out tomorrow. Or he could just sit back and do nothing, hope for the best.

But the choice was made for him because Tyler handed the keys back to Daniels, who locked the car.

Tyler loaded the shotgun and pumped it, loading a shell into the chamber. He held it ready to go, and then he did something weird, like he was psychic. He stared at Widow, locked his eyes on him the way a Secret Service agent locks onto a suspect in a crowd. And he never took his eyes off him, not while Widow was within clubbing range.

His opportunity was gone.

Daniels closed the trunk and moved to the driver's side, rear tire well. He pointed at the main structure, the one that could still be identified as a house. All of its walls and stairs and concrete and roof were intact. A large wraparound porch went all the way around the front of the house before it stopped dead on the sides. Most of the windows still had glass. All the doors were there. They looked like they still opened and closed and locked.

There was a huge fireplace with a chimney made of thick stone. It looked strong enough to take a rocket and still stand afterward.

Widow stared up at it and thought, *A whole man could fit in that thing.*

Daniels said, "I'll go to the front door. You two go around back, different sides. And check the windows. Be careful."

Gray asked, "What about the other buildings?"

"We might have to check them. Usually, they're in this one. And they're usually cooked out of their minds at night. So, I expect little resistance. Or even much speech from them."

Gray asked, "Then why are we all geared up?"

"You never know. Middle of the night like this, these folks have Second Amendment rights the same as the rest of us. They may mistake us for ghosts come back from the dead. Who knows?"

Tyler said, "Let's clear this one first, and if we don't find the missing girl, we'll check the others."

Gray said, "Okay."

Widow pulled Gray by the arm over to him and hugged her tight. He whispered into her ear.

"Don't let them get behind you."

She nodded and turned and joined Daniels and Tyler.

Widow thought of the twins and Fallow and killing him for taking those two little girls. He shook off the thought and watched Gray and the others walk past the police cruiser, out into the blue and red lights. He watched her intently like it might be the last time he ever saw her again, alive at least.

53

DANIELS LED Gray and Tyler up the walkway toward the main house. They all had their guns out. He pointed the two of them around to the back of the house. He paused and waited for them to disappear around the outer wall and into the backyard.

Widow watched Gray's small frame vanish around the side of the house into the darkness. He clenched his fists.

Widow was back with the vehicles a good sixty-five feet from the front porch. He watched the sheriff climb the front steps onto the porch. The boards on the porch were old and worn. They creaked under Daniels' weight.

At the front door, Widow heard him bang on the front door, identify himself as law enforcement, and call out for the occupants to come to the front door and open it.

Widow watched the windows. There was no movement. No lights came on. The curtains didn't move.

Daniels called out again, same as before. Nothing happened.

Daniels shouted, "Open up! Or I'm coming in!"

Nothing happened.

"Police! I'm coming in the front door!"

Daniels was a heavy guy, but he was limber, a lot more so than Widow would've guessed. Daniels stepped back on one foot, pulled his Glock in tight to his chest, heaved his other foot out, and kicked in the front door.

The door busted open. The lock plate busted through the weak wood, and Daniels disappeared into the darkness in seconds.

Widow was not the kind of guy to stand back and do nothing. He wasn't the kind of guy who stood down.

As soon as Daniels vanished into the house through the front door, Widow tried to break into his police cruiser.

He felt it was better to be completely wrong about Tyler and have to apologize to Daniels for breaking a window, than being right about his gut feeling.

Police cars are built tough, and the windows are also built tough. The windows in the back seat are double tough. They're virtually unbreakable. The last thing cops wanted was to have a criminal in the backseat able to bust out their window. But the windows in the front weren't as strong.

If he had a certain emergency tool, also known as a window breaker, it would be easy to break out the front window or the windshield, but he didn't have one. He thought for a moment, and then he remembered a trick, not a Navy SEAL trick, but something he had learned somewhere in life, an emergency escape hack.

He returned to the Charger and went inside and pushed the passenger seat backward. He was facing the back seat. He gripped the headrest and pulled it, extending the metal bars in it all the way up. Then he jerked it, and the whole headrest came right out, bars and all. He hopped back out of the Charger and over to the driver's side window of the police cruiser. He aimed the pointed ends of the bars at the window and rammed the headrest into the glass. The window shattered, and pieces of glass fragmented and exploded all over the seat.

Widow tossed the headrest onto the hood of the car and reached in and unlocked the door. He wrenched the door open. Fragments of broken glass poured out onto the gravel. He reached in and did two things. He released the trunk mechanism. Then he jerked open the glove box and recovered Gray's back-up SIG Sauer. He got out of the cruiser and tucked the Sig into the waistband of his jeans. Then he ran around to the back of the car and opened the trunk.

First, he took the last bulletproof vest and slid off his Havelock with the bullet hole in it and strapped the vest on. He shivered in the cold night air. Next, he put the Havelock back on over the vest. He looked back into the trunk at the sniper rifle. He doubted he would need a long-range weapon, but the more firepower, the better, he always said. And maybe there was a ravenous, dangerous group of meth heads living here.

So he scooped up the sniper rifle and checked it. The Remington 700P was a bolt-action rifle. He took the box of the .300 Remington Ultra Magnum bullets and loaded one into the weapon. The bolt action went back so far that the manufacturer had to design a groove in the top of the stock in order to fit one of the bullets inside. The .300 Remington Ultra Magnum was a large bullet.

The rifle came with a shoulder sling. He stuffed the box of bullets into one of his pockets. It almost didn't fit. It bulked out as if he had an actual full-size gun stuffed in there.

Widow slung the sniper rifle over his shoulder and scanned the trunk for anything else that might be useful. He saw a couple of smoke grenade canisters. Like the sniper rifle, he thought, *Why the hell not?* He scooped them up, too. The grenades had belt clips on them, which made it much easier to carry them. He clipped them to his belt.

Widow closed the trunk and went after Gray and Tyler. He wanted to catch up to them and keep an eye on Tyler.

The house was longer and deeper than it appeared from the front.

He edged along the side of the house, keeping an eye on the windows. So far, he heard nothing. No sounds came from inside the house, not even Daniels. Everything was quiet.

That changed as he neared the back edge of the house.

Gunshots erupted and *boomed* through the air. He saw quick bursts of muzzle flash, but couldn't pinpoint them.

Widow picked up the pace and started running toward the back of the house.

He heard Tyler's shotgun. He heard Gray's SIG Sauer.

Widow ran full sprint. The Remington 700P slammed into his back over and over as he ran. One of the smoke grenades almost fell off his belt.

He ran until he reached the back of the house. He slammed his body into a wall on the corner and peered around the edge of the wall.

More gunshots rang out, one after the next. Then it was several at once. Then he lost count. He heard gunfire being exchanged from one hundred eighty degrees. He heard single shots, and automatic fire, and rifle shots, and shotgun blasts. It sounded like a ground battle of countries at war.

Widow had the SIG Sauer out, ready to go. He peeked around the house, but then he saw something in the corner of his eye. Ten meters to his right, in the woods, he saw movement. He looked, aimed the Sig at the movement. He saw swaying branches and then a muzzle flash and gunshot *boomed* across from him.

Wood splintered and exploded just behind him, about two feet from his head. Someone had shot at him.

Widow dropped to a crouch and aimed and fired.

But he was firing into the dark. He must've missed the shooter because, he saw another muzzle flash and heard another *boom!* Then a third and a fourth. Someone was shooting at him. Rotted wood from the house shattered and exploded all around him.

The shooter was firing and missing. Either the person was firing blindly because Widow was also covered in darkness, or he or she was just that bad a shot.

Widow didn't fire multiple shots the way the shooter was doing. He aimed and waited for the first and last mistake of the shooter. The muzzle flash on its own could be misleading in a nighttime firefight, but this guy was shooting rapidly.

Widow saw the figure behind the bursts of muzzle flash. It was a grown man dressed in tattered garments. He was thin and pale and dirty like he hadn't seen a shower in months.

Widow returned fire with one, and only one, shot.

He aimed and fired. He saw red mist puff out in the air around the guy's head, and he saw the back of the guy's head explode. The next thing he saw was darkness, but he heard the guy hit the dirt like a sack of rocks.

Widow stayed in the crouch position and aimed at the direction of his shooter, in case there was more than one. No one else fired back at him—no sounds of rustling leaves or footsteps on gravel.

Widow turned toward the backyard. He heard more gunfire. He took a peek around the corner. The backyard was more visible because of stars in the sky and vast stretches of emptiness and muzzle flashes. There were dozens of flashes. They were all firing at the back of the house. It was hard to get a headcount of assailants, but Widow counted at least six.

Widow tried to peer all the way around the corner and see if he could locate Gray, but he couldn't. Then he heard her SIG Sauer fire from behind the house. She was firing back at the shooters in the backyard. She must've found cover because she was still alive.

Widow saw several structures in the darkness out in the backyard. Then he realized they were ambushed. Had to be. Whether or not Tyler had something to with it, he didn't know. But the meth heads were there waiting, already armed. Had to have been. They were too fast getting into position.

Widow saw half a tree that was more than a stump, but not a grown tree, between him and the back porch.

In an explosion of force and speed like a sprinter, he took off for the tree and ducked down behind it. One of the meth heads saw him and shot at him. Bullets sprayed and exploded off the other side of the tree. Dead bark flew into the air.

Widow could smell gun smoke everywhere.

He waited and looked at the back porch. He saw Tyler and Gray huddled together behind a solid rock pillar. Then he saw there were several pillars on the back porch, like the house had two front porches instead of one. He thought maybe the front where they had come in at was actually the back. It was hard to tell in the dark.

Behind Tyler and Gray was a pile of old logs for the fireplace. They exploded and splintered from the gunfire coming from their assailants.

While Widow waited, several more bullets exploded on the other side of the tree. He could tell the weapon firing at him was an AR-15.

He crouched and hugged the tree and peered around the edge with one eye. He saw the muzzle flashes from all over the place. But he waited until he saw the one firing at him.

He saw it burst into automatic fire.

Widow aimed and fired. *One! Two! Three!* times at the assailant shooting at him. He saw one more muzzle flash from returning fire, but that was the last. In that last muzzle flash, he saw another meth head. He was virtually identical to the one he'd just killed. He had the same skin-and-bones look, the same tattered clothes, and the same unshowered appearance.

Widow saw the guy's chest explode from three rounds, all from his SIG Sauer.

This got the attention of the other shooters. More than one of them fired at Widow's tree. He ducked back behind it.

He looked over at the back porch.

"SONYA?" he called out.

"WIDOW? HOW DID YOU?" she said, but never finished.

He called out, "SONYA, GO INTO THE HOUSE! I'LL COVER YOU GUYS!"

She called back, "IT'S LOCKED!"

"TYLER?"

Tyler called back, "YEAH?"

"USE THE SHOTGUN! BLOW THE LOCK OFF! I'LL COVER YOU!"

Tyler didn't respond; he just turned back to the door and aimed his shotgun and fired and pumped and fired and pumped and fired.

Widow hopped out from the other side of the tree and started firing blindly at every muzzle flash he could see, which was good because it got every meth head's attention. But it was also bad because it got every meth head's attention.

Suddenly, he was under fire from all of them. Widow ducked back behind the tree and heard so many gunshots he could no longer distinguish them individually or tell how many shooters there were.

The other side of the tree exploded and rocked and splintered. He felt the impact of each bullet rattle through the nearly dead tree. Now he was worried. It was only a matter of time before they cut through the tree.

He called out, "SONYA?"

"YEAH?"

"HURRY! GET THROUGH THE BACK DOOR!"

Widow saw Tyler turn away from the back door and pop out from cover. He started firing and pumping at the meth heads. He was trying to buy Gray time. Maybe he wasn't a traitor after all.

Two seconds later, Widow heard Tyler shout to her to go, and he saw Gray's small figure hop up and burst into a full sprint at the back door. The door was still shut, but the lock and the knob were completely blown out from Tyler's shotgun blasts.

Gray ducked her head down, pulled her Sig close, and rammed into the door with one shoulder. She busted through it. The door flew back on its hinges. And she was in.

Tyler kept firing and pumping and moving. He stayed low and tried to remain behind the railing of the porch. He was moving toward Widow's position.

He called out, "WIDOW! GET YOUR ASS UP HERE NOW!"

Widow got up on his feet to dash for the porch, but before he did, he saw Tyler take two hits to the chest.

Tyler flopped back onto the pile of logs. He kept his grip on the shotgun.

Widow hoped his vest had taken both rounds.

Widow didn't wait any longer. He ran at the porch. He leaped right over the railing, didn't touch it. He landed on the floorboards, tucked the Sig in close to his body, and bolted toward Tyler's position.

Half of the meth heads fired at the tree where he had been, but three of them saw the change in position, saw his burst of speed, and fired at him. Bullets whizzed past him and slammed into the house's exterior wall. One bullet shattered a window, barely missing his shoulder.

Widow got to Tyler, grabbed him by the corner of his vest, and hauled him up to his feet. Tyler gripped the shotgun.

Widow scrambled to the open back door and hauled Tyler with him. He was afraid they wouldn't make it because the meth head with the AR-15 realized he was firing at the tree for no reason and started shooting at Widow.

Just then, another window exploded from gunfire; only it came from inside the house.

Gray was firing back at the guy with the AR-15. She probably saved Widow's life.

He got in through the open back door, and he hauled Tyler with him.

They burst through the open door, and Widow dumped Tyler down on the floor. He spun around and grabbed the back door, and slammed it shut. The lock and knob were destroyed, but he wrenched it closed.

Gray stopped shooting and ran over to Widow and Tyler. She leaped on Widow and hugged him tightly. Then she started feeling all over his body with her free hand.

Widow did the same back. He wasn't shy about it. He ran his hands all over her, checking everything, looking for damage, but she was all there.

She said, "Are you shot?"

"No. I'm okay. But Tyler was hit."

They both moved over to Tyler. He was still on the floor.

Gray knelt by him and inspected his vest.

She turned to Widow and said, "He's been shot. It went through the vest."

Tyler said, "I'm okay."

He tried to move, tried to lift himself up to his feet, but he fell back down again. He let out a scream.

Gray said, "No. Don't move."

Then she looked around. They could all see well enough inside the house because their eyes had adjusted to the dark. And there was enough starlight through the windows to shed some dim light into the place.

Widow called out into the darkness for Daniels.

"Sheriff? Where are you?"

No answer.

Gray said, "Daniels?"

No response.

Tyler joined them in calling out.

"Clark?"

No answer.

Widow got to his feet, pointed the Sig out in front of him, and swept through the first floor of the house. He saw nothing or nobody. He passed the huge fireplace he had seen from the outside. It was enormous. It was big enough to cook a pig in.

He moved on to the front of the house and still saw no one. The only thing weird was he smelled something. It was faint, like it was soaked into the wood. He ignored it and moved on.

He saw a half-crumbled staircase and nothing else but a bunch of broken floorboards and exposed brick and rotted wood. The guys in the woods were definitely meth addicts because he stepped on broken needles and old, bent spoons. They were all over the place.

He didn't find the sheriff until he got to the front door.

He stayed in the shadows because he heard voices out front. He looked out a window and saw Sheriff Daniels standing back by his police cruiser. He was staying behind it like it was cover from gunfire, only he wasn't alone. He stood there with three more guys. They were more of the meth heads. They stood there like old hunting buddies gathered around a camp-fire, only they were all armed.

Widow's mouth dropped. It wasn't Tyler who had betrayed them. It was Daniels.

Just then, a face appeared in the window. Another meth head was on the porch with a hunting rifle. He raised it fast to shoot Widow.

He wasn't fast enough.

Widow bounced back and shot through the glass, shattering the whole window. He squeezed off two bullets; both tore gaping holes through the meth head's gut, and he tumbled back violently and broke the porch railing. He tumbled back onto the dirt beyond.

The hunting rifle fell off the porch and out of sight.

The meth head's gut was black with blood. He screamed out in agony. He was gut shot, which was a horrible way to die. Widow could've shot him again, in the head or the heart. It would've been the merciful thing to do, but Widow wasn't feeling merciful.

Besides, Daniels and the other three meth heads all raised their guns and fired at him. He dodged right, out of the line of fire. Bullets sprayed through the open window and slammed into the huge rock fireplace, doing virtually no damage. The fireplace was built like it was the main attraction. It was built to last. It was money well spent.

Widow ducked down and scrambled past the window and back to the kitchen.

In the kitchen, Tyler was bleeding badly. His head rested in Gray's lap. She was on the floor, on her knees. Tyler's vest was off. She had taken it off him so they could get a better look at his wound.

Widow saw that like the meth head he'd just shot, Tyler was also gutshot, and it was bad. Blood was everywhere. His clothes were soaked in blood. His hands clenched the bullet wound, but blood was all over them.

Gray was on her phone and cursing it.

Widow stopped dead in the doorway and stared at her.

She looked up at him and shook her head.

Tyler said, "There's no phone reception out here. Not this far out. Our only chance is to get Daniels to call for backup on his radio. Where is he?"

Widow shook his head.

"Daniels is with them."

Gray looked up at him.

"What?"

"Daniels betrayed us. He set us up. There's no missing kid here—no nine-one-one call. At least, it wasn't real. It was probably one of his meth buddies out there."

Gray asked, "Are you sure?"

"He's outside right now with them. I saw him. He shot at me."

Tyler held his gut tight and said, "Whaaa...what're we going to do?"

"Right now, we need to fortify the house. We're sitting ducks here."

Just then, Widow listened.

Gray said, "What?"

"They stopped firing and they're not coming in."

Widow walked to the shattered back window and peeked out.

He saw the meth heads in the backyard, all covered in dark shadows like haunting figures. They were in a big circle around the house, surrounding it.

Suddenly, he realized what he had smelled earlier in front of the house. It was gasoline. He knew because he saw the meth heads light up fast. Each of them became visible nearly in unison.

They were lit up by firelight. They were each lighting Molotov cocktails.

Widow turned around fast and ran to Gray, grabbed Tyler by his arm, and lifted him up to his feet. He put one of Tyler's arms around his own neck and grabbed the back of Tyler's pants and hauled him up. He carried the guy as fast as he could out of the kitchen.

Gray was shocked.

"What are you doing?"

"RUN!" Widow shouted at her.

She listened and followed him and Tyler back into the front of the house. They all heard windows shattering in the back of the house as Molotov cocktails burst through them.

At the front, the same thing happened. More Molotov cocktails came bursting through the windows and slamming into the outside of the structure.

Within seconds, the whole first floor of the house was up in flames.

54

THE HOUSE WAS ON FIRE. From the outside, the meth heads and Sheriff Daniels surrounded the house, giving each other a wide berth. There were five meth heads in the back, still alive, and three in the front, still alive, but one was dying an agonizing death from being gutshot.

Sheriff Daniels barked orders at them to stay vigilant, to stay ready for anything.

Inside the house, Widow led Gray and carried Tyler to the second floor of the house.

Before the Molotov cocktails contacted the gasoline-laced floors and walls, he had grabbed Tyler and lifted him and led Gray back to the staircase. They walked through the second level, searching for any meth heads or for a way out. They found neither.

They passed through rooms. Some had holes in the walls. Some had holes in the floors. In one room, there was a huge hole in the floor. Widow saw the garage below. The floor and wall of the garage were on fire, but there was a metal tool table, still standing, untouched by the flames. It wasn't flammable, apparently. At least, it wasn't flammable yet.

Widow noted the tools that lined the walls. One tool, in particular, was a heavy sledgehammer. It was laid across the wall like a rifle on display.

He wasn't sure why he noted it. It was his primate brain that liked what it saw.

Finally, they found a bathroom with an old claw bathtub. Widow laid Tyler down in the tub and put his hands back on his gunshot wound.

"Keep pressure on that!" he said.

Tyler stayed quiet. He just nodded back that he understood.

Widow and Gray stepped into the other room.

Gray said, "I guess you should've stayed behind after all."

"No, because I would be dead right now. Daniels set us up. This was an ambush. These meth heads are everywhere."

Gray said, "Did I hear an automatic rifle out there?"

"It was an AR-15. Maybe more than one. I have no idea."

Gray said, "I wish they had bows and arrows."

Widow nodded but didn't smile.

He said, "We have little time. This house is old as dirt. Eventually, everything will come tumbling down."

"How the hell do we get out of this?"

Widow stayed quiet for a long, long second. Gray holstered her Sig and wrapped both arms around him, hugged him tightly.

She said, "Thank you for not staying behind."

He hugged her back.

They heard a wall somewhere in the house crumble from the fire.

Widow pulled back. He kept thinking, and she knew it. She saw it on his face.

Suddenly, he nodded, like a plan had been formed, and a decision had been made.

She said, "What?"

He told her. He had a plan. It wasn't a great plan, but it was a plan. She listened intently.

He laid it all out for her.

He turned, and they both searched until she found what they were looking for, which was a door to an attic. Widow went over to it, reached up, pulled a cord, and a ladder came down out of the roof.

He spent the next few minutes helping her and Tyler up into the attic. Tyler was bad, but he did most of the climbing himself. He knew he had to pull it together if he was going to live.

After Gray and Tyler were safely in the attic, Widow went to the front of the house.

He found a second-floor window, one that overlooked the front yard. He pulled the box of rifle bullets out of his pocket and tore the lid off it. He busted out the window and aimed the rifle at Daniels.

One of the meth heads shouted, "Sheriff! Look out!"

Daniels was a fat guy, but he could move. He dodged right and ducked down behind the tire well of his cruiser, which was fine by Widow because he wanted Daniels alive for now.

But the meth head who had shouted the warning gave out another warning. His head exploded in a puffball of red mist and brain fragments and shards of skull. *A Remington Ultra Magnum bullet*. It was more bullet than Widow needed, but he smiled at the results. He racked the bolt back and took out the brass from the spent shell. He loaded the next one and racked the bolt home.

The meth heads at the front of the house returned fire to his position. Bullets sprayed all over the exterior of the house. None of them came through the broken window.

Widow took aim and exploded another meth head's chest wide open. He racked the bolt back and dug out another .300 Remington Ultra Magnum bullet and fired at Daniels' police cruiser. The bullet busted out the windshield. It exploded worse than the driver's side window had. Glass was all over the front bench of the cruiser.

Widow repeated the process.

Daniels snuck around to the trunk and used his keys to pop it open. He scooped the bullhorn out of it and crept up the side of the car, staying down. He clicked the button and called out through the bullhorn.

"IT'S SHERIFF DANIELS! GET YOUR ASSES TO THE FRONT NOW! THIS MANIAC IS SNIPING US!"

Widow smiled.

* * *

IN THE ATTIC, Gray and Tyler located a broken window that led out to the roof. Gray hauled Tyler over to it, leaned him against the wall, and took a peek out the window. She could see into the backyard because of the fire on the ground floor. She saw dark figures as they approached the back of the house.

In fact, the whole backyard was a lot more visible than before. She counted the meth heads. They numbered five alive, just as Widow had told her. Then she waited for his sniper shots. They came. She heard them. One. Two. Three.

Then she heard Daniels over the megaphone, calling out to the meth heads, which confirmed what Widow had told her, that Daniels had set them up.

The meth heads in the backyard all looked at each other like idiots. When they heard Daniels call for them, they all ran off to the front of the house. All of them went but one. One guy stayed behind, but at the far corner so he could see to the front.

Gray went back to Tyler.

"Okay. Here we go!"

"I can't make it," he said weakly.

"You have to!" she said, and she slapped him across the face.

He looked at her like he was suddenly awakened.

"Okay," he said.

She hauled him up, and he stood on both feet, resting his armpit on the butt of the shotgun. She pushed open the window and crawled out. She took his arm and led him out onto the roof with her.

On the roof, Gray took the smoke grenade that Widow had given her and pulled the pin. She threw it to the ground beneath them and waited. The grenade ignited, and smoke streamed out. Within seconds, it was all over the place, so even the firelight wouldn't help give away their position.

Then she took the shotgun from Tyler and tossed it below. Next, she helped him to the edge.

"On the count of three, you gotta jump," she said.

"I don't think I can make it."

But she didn't count to three. She didn't even count to one. She shoved him off the roof. He landed hard on some shrubbery, which broke his fall, and he rolled off to the side.

Tyler was tough. The impact hurt, but he broke nothing, and he didn't scream.

Gray went next. She landed on the ground not far away. She also hit hard, but was lucky not to break anything. She sprained her ankle, however. She found out the moment she tried to get up and run over to Tyler.

Together, they stayed in the smoke and darkness and took off half-running, half-stumbling, for the structures beyond.

55

THEY STAYED HIDDEN in a small structure that had once been a cabin, fifty meters from the house that was on fire with Widow still inside it.

Once Gray hauled Tyler all the way there, she hid him inside. Then she did what Widow had told her not to do. She went back for him.

She ran back, staying low, staying hidden in the darkness and behind the other structures. She saw that two of the meth heads were now in the backyard. They looked like they were staring at something on the ground. As she closed the distance, she realized they'd found the smoke grenade canister. They were walking in and out of the smoke, which was dissipating.

She kept going. She would kill as many as she could to get Widow's back. But as she got closer, she saw her worst fear come true.

The house exploded!

* * *

GRAY STAYED WHERE SHE WAS, watching the fire, seeing the house's outer walls crumble and fall over. Tears streamed down her face.

Widow was dead. She couldn't believe it. She couldn't!

He can't be dead! she thought.

After five long minutes, she tried to move forward to get closer; maybe he wasn't dead. Maybe he was still alive. It looked impossible. Everything was on fire. The more time that passed, the more parts of the house collapsed in on itself.

She got closer, but then she saw more of the meth heads coming back from the front of the house. Then more came, until she counted seven. Then she saw Daniels. He was pointing in her direction like he could see her. He barked orders at the meth heads to search everything. Five of them turned and headed her way, headed toward where she left Tyler.

She had to go back. She had no choice.

Gray backed up into the darkness and turned and took off, running back to Tyler.

She got to where he was hidden and burst in. She looked down at him. He was huddled against a back corner. The shotgun was at his side, lying across the floor. His hand spanned out over the butt.

She said, "I think Widow's dead."

Tyler stayed quiet.

She moved in closer. She wiped the tears off her face, and she stopped at Tyler's feet.

She said, "Tyler? Widow's dead."

He stayed quiet.

"Tyler?"

Nothing.

She reached into her pocket and pulled out her phone. She turned on the flashlight and shone it across Tyler's face.

His eyes were wide open, but he wasn't blinking. His mouth was wide open, but he wasn't speaking. His chest was completely still. He wasn't breathing. The hand that plugged up his gutshot was now laid out, palm open, across his lap.

He stared back at her with lifeless eyes. He was dead.

56

DANIELS STOWED the bullhorn and took out his phone. It wasn't a regular smartphone. It was a satellite phone. He had minor cuts all over his face and one major gash on his forehead that would need stitches. He had dodged Widow's bullets, but he couldn't dodge the exploding windshield glass from his car.

He dialed the number from the last call he'd received, which was from Nick Gaden.

Gaden answered the phone.

"Yes? Is it done?"

"They're all dead."

"So, you've recovered their bodies?"

"Not yet."

"I want their bodies! Especially Widow's!"

"Understood. He's burning right now. But once this fire goes out, we'll find him."

Gaden said, "Don't leave until you've recovered the bodies! I want a photo!"

"Okay."

Before Daniels finished saying okay, Gaden had clicked off the call.

Daniels slipped the satellite phone back into his pocket and started barking orders at the meth heads again to let the fire burn out and locate the bodies.

* * *

GRAY LEFT THE SHOTGUN BEHIND. It was used up and heavy, and she wasn't as proficient as she was with her own Sig. She tried her phone again and got no signal. She texted Cameron in all caps, but the text message wouldn't send until she had a signal or Wi-Fi. She returned the phone to her pocket and snuck around the outer edges of the backyard, staying low, trying to keep within the trees. She was nearly spotted once by one of the meth heads, but she ducked behind a tree, and he passed her by.

She made it to the north side of the house, near where she and Tyler had jumped off the roof. The whole house burned like nothing she had ever seen before. It was bright red, like blood.

She got as close as she could and searched for Widow's body. She saw that some of the meth heads were doing the same while others searched for her and Tyler as if they suspected they'd escaped the fire because of the smoke grenade.

Gray waited and looked for a good ten minutes from the shadows, hoping to glimpse Widow's corpse. She couldn't stand that he had died this way. And after sitting there for ten minutes, her worry turned to anger, which quickly escalated to rage.

She had known his plan was stupid. She'd tried to protest. She'd even asked him how he was going to get out if the fire got worse. And he'd only smiled at her.

Gray decided it was enough. She was ready to take on Daniels. She moved on, creeping through the trees until she was at the front of the house. She stayed low, passing between two of the meth heads that were five meters apart. They didn't notice her because they were searching the ground for dead, charred bodies.

Then she saw Daniels. He was leaning against the hood of his cruiser, wiping blood off his face with a handkerchief.

She went along the passenger side of the cruiser and snuck right up behind him and stopped.

She said, "Hey."

Daniels heard a woman's voice and turned around to see Gray standing there holding a gun, only she wasn't pointing it at him. Instead, she wrenched it back fast and pistol-whipped him right in the face.

She heard an audible *crack* as his nose broke in two pieces. Blood sprayed out and dabbed across her face.

She wrenched the weapon back a second time and aimed to pistol-whip him right in the jaw. She hoped she would break that, too.

She never made it to his jaw. At the same moment, she was spun around, nearly coming off her feet. A meth head stood behind her with a hunting rifle. He smiled at her with a mouthful of part rotten teeth and part craters, where teeth used to be.

He punched her with a vicious right hook, and she went down. Her lights were out before she hit the ground.

57

DANIELS SAID, "WATCH IT, DUMBASS!"

The meth head was pointing his rifle down at Gray, who looked unconscious.

"Lemme shoot her, boss?"

"No. Just hold on. I'm thinking this is better than dead."

Daniels gripped his nose with one hand. Then he shoved the meth head out of the way with the other. He bled all over the place, but he had broken his nose before, twice. He was a fat guy. He knew that. And he knew people looked at him like he was a backwoods, fat sheriff, but that was a deception. He was fat, and he was backwoods, but he wasn't a weakling. He knew how to get down and dirty.

That low-bar opinion of him was how he surprised people all the time.

He slumped down over Gray and kicked her gun out of her reach. She wasn't moving. He reached down and turned her over. He felt her pulse. She was alive and breathing. He inspected her face. She was going to have a shiner, that was for damn sure, but otherwise, she was intact.

"She alive, boss?" the meth head asked. "I clocked her pretty good."

Daniels looked at him.

"Clevis, you're a hundred twenty pounds soaking wet. You couldn't kill a house cat with that punch. Now, help me get her up."

The two of them struggled to lift her up because she was out cold, which made her dead weight. They brought her to the hood of the car and bent her over it. Daniels stepped back.

Clevis sidestepped and leaned his rifle up against the car. He grabbed the drawstring that held his pants up and undid it.

He said, "Oh boy, boss. Can I go first?"

Daniels looked at him.

"Clevis, what the hell are you talking about?"

Clevis' pants fell to his ankles.

Daniels shouted, "Clevis! Put that away! Nobody is doing nothing to this little starlet. Not yet, anyway."

Clevis nodded and pulled his pants back up, retied the drawstring.

Daniels slid Gray's jacket off and tossed it into the cruiser. Then he unsnapped the bulletproof vest and added it next to her jacket. He took out his handcuffs and cuffed Gray from behind, tight.

He laid her back across the hood, whipped the hair out of her face, and turned her face, so it was clearly visible. He took out his satellite phone and aimed it at her and snapped a picture. He texted it to Gaden with the message: *One lived. What do you want to do with her?*

Just three seconds later, he got: *Keep her alive. She can tell us things we need to know.*

He texted Gaden back: *You got it.*

After that, he lifted her up and shoved her into the trunk of his cruiser and closed it.

AT THE SAME time that Gray was getting stuffed into the trunk of Daniels' cruiser, Chris Fallow and the other guys who had helped him kill Eggers, minus Sathers, stepped off a private plane at Ted Stevens Anchorage International Airport.

Fallow breathed a heavy batch of Alaskan air and stared off to the west-northwest and saw the Tordrillo Mountains, which were seventy-five miles away, but huge and white and grand under the night stars.

Fifteen minutes later, they were grabbing their bags from baggage claim. Five minutes after that, they were firing up a black Chevy Tahoe left for them in short-term parking earlier in the night by one of Gaden's assistants.

They drove out of the airport and merged with traffic, and drove to Route Three to pick up Sonya Gray before heading to Gaden's estate.

From the Gaden family estate, one of them anyway, Nick Gaden called Sheriff Daniels one last time.

Daniels answered.

"Yes, sir."

"How's it going? Find any more of them?"

"We've recovered the FBI agent. And the woman is in my trunk."

"I know that. What about Widow?"

"Nothing. But, sir, both the FBI and the NCIS are going to investigate the disappearance of their agents."

"Let them. It's not a problem. Money can buy anything."

Daniels said, "I wouldn't know."

"Of course, you wouldn't. You're a peon. Listen. Just get rid of his body. Make sure no one ever finds it. And you'll have nothing to worry about."

"Okay."

"What about Widow?"

"Nothing so far. But there's a lot of burned ash here. Hard to tell what's what."

"You find any bones?"

"Don't think so. There's a lot of debris. We burned a whole building down with Widow inside it."

"Get your boys to stay there till you find his bones. Tell them to save his skull for me. I want you to take the girl and meet with Fallow. Hand her over to him. He'll take her and bring her to me."

"Where?"

Gaden gave him the address.

60

Before he got into his police cruiser, Daniels told the meth heads what to do, instructing them to stay and sift through the ashes until they found Widow's dead body.

Daniels got into his car, brushed as much of the broken glass as he could out onto the gravel. A lot of it fell into the cracks of the front seat and down into the footwell.

He fired up the engine and revved it up. Then he backed out and K-turned so that he faced the way they had come in. He drove around Gray's charger and headed back down the winding dirt roads to the main highway.

He could hear Gray thumping around in the trunk, kicking and slamming her fists into the backseat. She wasn't screaming because he had duct-taped her mouth closed. And she wasn't going to escape. He had his trunk reinforced so that nothing could get out. He did it a long time ago with a mechanic buddy. It only cost him a six-pack and a onetime look-the-other-way kind of deal, which the mechanic had already called in. He got busted one night with a bag of marijuana, and Daniels had to get him out of it by making a trade with the arresting state trooper. This was all long ago, way before legal weed ever became a reality.

Eventually, Daniels bumped off the dirt track and back onto Route Three. He turned right and headed south to meet with Fallow and hand off the woman in the trunk. On the way, he smiled, thinking of what they were going to do to her.

* * *

BEFORE THE HOUSE EXPLODED, Widow was on the second floor, in the master bedroom, which had been a grand thing, once upon a decade. Now, it was nothing but ruined furniture, derelict floors, and exposed cracked brick.

Widow waited by a rear window and looked out over the backyard to get a glimpse of Gray and Tyler. He saw the smoke grenade canister on the ground and the dissipating smoke and several meth heads back there combing over the area, searching for Gray.

He would have shot them with the Remington sniper rifle, but he was out of bullets. It turned out the opened box of Remington Ultra Magnum bullets had been used before, and a lot were missing. There were only a dozen bullets in it. He'd already shot them all.

Widow saw the smoke from the grenade and the canister on the ground, which told him that Gray had gotten away.

The meth heads started throwing more Molotov cocktails at the house, which was like throwing dynamite on the sun. It was already burning. There was no real point to the extra fire.

The house all around him was coming down. He heard parts of the outer walls crumbling and collapsing. He knew it was only a matter of time before the whole house came down around him.

The smoke was getting worse. The fire was getting worse. The second floor was filling with smoke and fast.

Widow got down on his hands and knees and crawled below the smoke, back the way he'd come, to the room he saw with the giant hole in the floor. Once he got there, he monkey-climbed down to the garage. He hung from the crumbling boards from the floor above and stretched out a foot, and planted it on the metal tool table in the garage below. He felt heat through the bottom of his boot. He shimmied down carefully and balanced himself on the tool table. It held him. He slid his feet to the edge of the table. Flames ignited and erupted all around the garage walls and floor and ceiling.

Sweat drenched out of his pores from the immense heat.

Widow looked at the wall filled with tools. He eyeballed the sledgehammer and reached his hand out as far as he could. He could almost reach it, and then he almost slipped off the table and fell into the fire.

Widow stepped back abruptly to regain his balance. Then he edged back to the end of the table. Somewhere behind him in the house, he heard another section of wall crumble and collapse.

Widow came up on one foot and then one tiptoe and leaned forward like he was doing a yoga pose. He reached out as far as he could and got his fingers on the sledgehammer. He edged forward all the way to the end of the table; half his toes hung off the side.

He grabbed the sledgehammer's handle and scooped it up off its hooks and leaped back to the table. He grabbed a long, dark cloth off another rack and set the hammer down. He wrapped his face with the cloth to keep him from passing out from the smoke. Then he snatched a pair of work goggles and put them on to help him see.

Widow climbed back to the second floor and made his way back to the master bedroom.

He went over to the rock fireplace and picked up the sledgehammer. He wielded it like a lumberjack with a heavy ax. Widow bashed the rock with it. He slammed the rock over and over, as hard as he could.

He slammed and hammered and crushed the stones. Bits and pieces came flying off the stone fireplace. He bashed until there was a big hole left behind. Smoke billowed around him and went up the chimney and out the top.

None of the meth heads noticed the smoke pluming above the chimney outside.

Widow dropped the hammer and went back into the room. He gathered together all the old, dirty bed covers he could and went back to the hole and squeezed himself up above the fireplace in the lower part of the chimney. He dragged the covers in behind him and plugged up the hole as best he could, preventing smoke from filling up the chimney and killing him.

The inside of the stack was a lot roomier than he had thought. He shimmed himself up as high as he could and waited.

The whole experience was grueling. There were several times he feared suffocating to death, but he didn't.

THE COLD NIGHT WENT ON, and the meth heads searched through smoke and flames for Widow's body. They never found it. They found Tyler's body back in one of the structures behind the main house, which led them on a wild goose chase through the dark and the woods.

Eventually, they determined that Widow never escaped the fire, and they returned to the main house and waited.

They waited nearly all night for the flames to die down. In the early morning fog, they saw nothing was left of the old house except for the large stone fireplace and chimney, the concrete slab, the metal tool table in the garage, and the stone steps that led up to the house. The rest of the structure had bowed and crumbled to ash and broken wood and rubble.

There were still large sections on fire, but mostly, it all was over. The time was very early in the morning, but the sun didn't fully rise until around eight-thirty, so the sky was still dark.

There were seven meth heads left. The gutshot one in the front was dead. The others searched through the fog and remaining smoke for Widow's body. They were all still armed with AR-15s and hunting rifles and shotguns. They were exhausted, and each of them was on some level of meth withdrawal from not shooting up all night.

Widow had stayed in the chimney through all of it. He was uncomfortable and afraid to fall asleep because of the position and the fear of smoke inhalation. But he was dog-tired and got a few hours here and there throughout the night.

Now was the time to act. He didn't want to wait any longer. The flames and heat seemed to have died down. So he shifted his weight and scooted back down the chimney. He shoved the bedcovers back out the hole he'd come in through and waddled his way back out. He stopped at the hole and saw that the entire house had collapsed. He had to step out onto the framing that remained. He got all the way out of the hole and stood upright and scanned the terrain below. He saw a few of the meth heads through the dark and fog, but none of them were looking up at him. They were occupied, searching through the rubble for his dead body.

He cracked his joints and stretched all the way out. He had a crick in his back from being folded up inside the chimney for hours.

He crouched low to keep his profile small and climbed down to the rubble below, which was mostly shingles from the roof. He snuck down to the ground and scanned around him. No one was looking at him.

He saw a meth head twenty feet to his right, facing the other direction. The guy was lifting rubble with the muzzle of a

Mossberg shotgun. It was old and worn, with a brown stock and black frame.

First, Widow searched his waistband for Gray's SIG Sauer. It wasn't there. He had lost it somewhere. He needed a weapon, preferably something silent.

Widow slowly knelt to the ground and reached for a loose brick to use to club the guy over the head. He picked up a brick and stopped. Underneath, he saw the head of the sledge-hammer. It was covered in dust and ash, but it was all there in one piece. He dropped the brick and lifted the sledgehammer out of the rubble and smiled at it.

He crept over the roof shingles and the rubble as quietly as he could. He had gotten five feet behind the meth head when the guy heard him.

The meth head said, "I can't find him, Flint. Where's that body?"

Widow reared the sledgehammer back all the way like a base-ball bat.

He said, "Not Flint, asshole."

The meth head heard his voice and spun around fast with the shotgun ready to go, but it was too late. Widow crashed the hammer right into the guy's face. It crushed and caved in under the blow. And if that hadn't killed him, his neck wrenching too far too fast would have.

The meth head spun around with the blow like he had been hit in the face by a train going full speed.

Widow set the sledgehammer down and picked up the shot-gun. He checked it. It was out of shells completely. He checked the meth head for ammunition and found nothing in his pockets but lint and a dollar and thirty-five cents in change.

Widow left the shotgun and took up the sledgehammer and looked for the next meth head. He saw him thirty feet north. He was also digging through rubble. He had no gun on him, just a big stick. Then Widow saw another meth head nearby. This one had a hunter's recurve bow and a quiver of arrows on his back.

Where the hell were all the guns? he wondered.

Widow sneaked up on them, slowly, but the one with the stick heard him coming and looked up fast.

"Jeb!" he called out to the one with the bow and arrows.

Jeb turned and saw Widow as a smoky figure standing in the mist appearing from out of the fog like a ghost.

Jeb pivoted to one foot and got the bow up in his hand, and reached for an arrow. He got his fingers on the tail of the arrow, and that was it. He got no farther.

Widow pulled the sledgehammer over his head all the way back and aimed and threw it full force straight at Jeb. The sledgehammer spun through the air fast and hard like it had been slung by a catapult.

The sledgehammer flattened Jeb's skull in a fast, violent blow. Jeb came up off his feet and was flung backward, into the fog.

"Jeb? Jeb?" the other meth head cried out. There was a certain inflection in his voice like Jeb had been more than a friend.

None of that mattered much because the next thing that happened was he turned back to face Widow with his stick.

He never had time to make a single move because Widow grabbed him by his tattered shirt collar and clamped down on the guy's chin. He grabbed his other shoulder for leverage and broke his neck. It was one quick wrenching, and the neck snapped like a twig. The sound was audible.

Widow dropped the dead meth head like tossing a garbage bag into the bin.

Widow turned and scanned the scene for anyone who might've heard the commotion. Someone did.

He heard two other meth heads rustling behind him. They were coming up on him fast. He heard their footsteps over shingles and broken boards.

Widow turned right and scrambled over to the dead one called Jeb. He didn't go for the sledgehammer, despite the fun he had with it. Instead, he scooped up the bow and grabbed two arrows. He stuck one into the dirt and set one into the bow and drew it back on the string all the way. He aimed and saw one of the meth heads coming into view through the fog.

The guy said, "Jeb? Mikey? You guys find something?"

Widow waited until he saw the whites in the guy's eyes, and then he released the arrow. It flew about as fast as it could and covered the distance between them in seconds. It arced straight into the meth head's eye socket. He let out half a scream before the arrow split a gaping hole through his brain and he fell back, dead.

The next meth head was right behind him. He had a hunting rifle and raised it fast to aim at Widow. But Widow was faster. He scooped the second arrow out of the dirt and pulled it back on the string, aimed, and released it.

The arrow stabbed right through the guy's chest. The guy jerked the trigger once, and the hunting rifle fired. The bullet went loose through the air and vanished into the woods behind Widow.

That was five meth heads down, leaving two more.

Widow scrambled to get the hunting rifle. He took the bow with him and stopped at both dead bodies and jerked the bloody arrows out of each. Then he went for the rifle, but he heard the two remaining meth heads coming at him. He stepped back into the fog and crouched.

He waited.

Seconds later, both of the other meth heads were back. One had the AR-15, and one had a revolver. They stopped cold over their dead friends. They looked at each other, completely confused.

Widow came out of the fog. The bow was slung over his shoulder. He held both arrows, crisscrossed in one hand. The bloody arrowheads came out of his fists like duster knuckles with spikes. He snuck up behind both meth heads.

Two feet back, he stood up tall, towering over their scrawny frames.

He said, "Hey."

They both turned around toward him. He slammed his fist, arrowheads and all, straight into the throat of the one with the AR-15. Blood splattered across his face. He jerked the arrows out, and the guy dropped to the ground. He choked and gurgled on the blood pooling in the holes in his throat.

The last meth head trembled in terror. Then he raised the hunting rifle to shoot Widow in the gut, but he was too slow. Widow clamped the front stock with his free hand and jerked it out of the guy's hand.

He took it away and flung it out into the fog. Then he grabbed a handful of the guy's shirt and bunched it up and pulled him in close. He raised the arrowheads with his fist and showed them to him.

The meth heads said, "Oh Jesus! Oh, no! Please! Don't kill me!"

Widow said, "That all depends."

"On what?"

"What do you know about Gaden?"

"Who?"

"Nick Gaden?"

"Never heard of him."

"I heard he's some kind of big shot in this state?"

"What state?"

Widow shook the guy once.

"THIS STATE!"

"Sorry. I need my fix. I haven't had my fix. You holding, mister?"

Widow didn't answer that.

He asked, "Where's Daniels?"

"He took off with the woman."

Widow jerked the meth head in close, which he instantly regretted because the guy's breath stank.

Widow said, "What woman?"

"The cop. Your friend. The pretty one."

"Where did they go?"

"I don't know."

"WHERE DID THEY GO?"

"He put her in the trunk and then took off to hand her off to some guy."

"What guy? What's his name?"

"I don't know. I swear!"

Widow said, "Was it Gaden?"

"I done told ya. I don't know Gaden."

Widow paused a beat.

He said, "Was it Fallow?"

The meth head's eyes widened like he recognized the name.

"That could be it. That could be what he told us."

"Why are you helping him?"

"Sheriff made a deal to pay us with the police lock-ups entire batch of Yaba."

"Yaba?"

"Crank, man! You know? Chalk? Glass?"

Widow stared at him blankly.

The meth head said, "Meth, man!"

"Guess you're no more use to me."

The meth head stared at Widow. Fear filled his eyes.

He said, "No! Wait! Don't kill me!"

"Better tell me something I don't know!"

"The sheriff. He'll be back."

"When?"

"He was just exchanging the girl with that Fallow guy. Then he was coming straight back."

Widow smiled at the meth head and lowered his fists with the arrowheads. The meth head smiled, showing off his three or four teeth.

Widow head-butted him straight in the face. Lights out.

Widow left the guy lying in the ash and dirt. The guy was still alive, just knocked out, probably for the rest of the morning.

Widow searched the rest of the bodies and the grounds and the compound. He found nineteen dollars in ones and a handful of change. He found one old burner phone. Inside it, there was a string of text messages from the sheriff. He'd tried to call out, but the phone didn't work, like Gray's hadn't.

He continued searching and found two AR-15s, three hunting rifles, a shotgun, a revolver, and the bow and arrows. He left them all in a pile. Both AR-15s had empty magazines. The hunting rifles were so ancient he didn't want to mess with them. And the shotgun was empty. So, he took the quiver and gathered all the arrows and shouldered the bow.

He considered keeping the revolver, but he didn't, although it still had five bullets. He left that as well because he found Gray's backup SIG Sauer. He pocketed it and faced the stone ruin left behind by a structure that was long gone. He sat on the stone remains of a wall and waited for Daniels to return.

62

Daniels took Gray about an hour south and waited behind a closed strip mall. He parked near a dumpster. Gray rocked and clawed at her restraints the whole time. She never quieted. He heard her banging around in the back.

Fallow had shown up with two other guys and they made the exchange.

Afterward, Daniels drove behind them on their way to Gaden's. Once they got to the turnoff, Fallow continued on. Daniels turned off road and followed the winding dirt track until he came to the abandoned meth head shantytown and finally back to the pile of rubble.

The sun was still down, and he yawned. He was ready to go home and crawl into bed.

At the house he had watched while Widow burned inside, he parked and left the engine running. He got out of the car and looked around. He couldn't see any of his guys.

"Where the hell are y'all?" he called out.

Suddenly, a huge hand clamped down on his shoulder from behind and jerked him around. Daniels spun about-face and stared into Widow's eyes.

Widow was covered in blood and ash and soot. But his eyes were ice blue and big and filled with anger.

Daniels trembled. His jaw dropped.

He said, "You?"

"Me," Widow said, and he head-butted Daniels square in the face. Not enough to kill him, but enough to break his nose for the second time in one night. Blood splattered out of it and all over Widow's already blood-covered face.

He held onto Daniels and pulled him back up to him. Daniels went for his gun, but Widow grabbed it first. He ripped it out of his holster and let go of Daniels. He backed away and pointed the gun at him.

Daniels raised both hands up and out, palms open. His nose gushed blood from a new crack in his skin. He stood completely still and stared at Widow.

He said, "Okay! I know where the girl is."

"Good. Take me there."

"Let me call them. They'll bring her to us," Daniels reached for his satellite phone.

Widow shot him through his gun hand. Daniels hunched over and grabbed his hand. He squealed once. He held the hand up quickly to inspect it. His ring and pinkie fingers were gone. Widow saw them on the ground in a small pool of blood splatter.

"You son of a bitch!" Daniels shouted.

Widow said, "Make another move. Do one thing wrong. Do one thing I don't tell you to do, and I'll put the next bullet in your head. Understand?"

Daniels looked up at him.

"Yes!"

"Good! Now, get in the car. Let's go."

They got in the car—Daniels behind the wheel and Widow in the passenger seat. Widow put on his seatbelt. Daniels tried to put his on, but Widow slapped it off him and told him to drive.

Ten minutes later, they were back on Route Three headed to Gaden's estate in Anguta, Alaska.

63

Widow and Sheriff Daniels pulled up to a large metal gate with a guard hut, and one guard in the hut. He wore a baseball cap and a brown button shirt.

The guard saw their lights as they drove up and stepped out of the hut.

The Gaden estate was out in the middle of nowhere, on its own private drive. They were far enough from the town to shoot guns all day and have no complaints because no one would hear the sound, which was exactly what Widow was thinking about.

The gate was a large iron thing with bars and pointed tips on the top. The estate was surrounded by a ten-foot stone wall: thick and intimidating.

The guard stepped past the bright headlamps and over to the driver's side window. He stopped and stared as he got closer to the missing windshield and the broken windows.

He leaned down and stared at Daniels, who gave him a big smile. Daniels wore a strand of duct tape across his face, covering his double broken nose, a courtesy from Widow. The guard moved his eyes over to the passenger seat to see Widow looking back at him. No smile. He looked back at Daniels.

The guard said, "Sheriff? Everything okay?"

"Yeah. I need to pass through," Daniels said.

"Is Mr. Gaden expecting you?"

"Yes. Now, open up!"

The guard looked at Widow and then back at Daniels.

"Let me call it in then and check."

Daniels said, "No! Wait! I meant he's not expecting me, but he's going to want to hear what I have to tell him."

"I still have to call it in."

Daniels nodded along.

The guard turned back and walked back to the guard hut. He picked up a wall phone and dialed.

Widow looked out the hole where the windshield used to be and saw a security camera. He exploded into movement and elbowed Daniels square in the face, breaking his nose a third time. Plus reopening the old chasms in his bones, which filled the duct tape with blood. Some of it was old and dry, and some of it new and fresh.

Daniels' head crashed back into the headrest from the blow. Then he toppled over forward. Widow reached over and turned off the engine and took out the keys. He reached down into the footwell and came up with the bow and some arrows.

He got out of the car and strung up an arrow, pulled it back, and launched it at the security camera. The arrow fired right through the lens and the camera sparked once and went dead.

The guard in the hut saw it and heard it and dropped the phone. He came out of the hut with a Glock drawn from a hip holster. He aimed it at the cruiser where Widow had been standing, but Widow was gone.

He looked left, looked right, traced the outline of the cruiser, searching for him.

He walked around to the passenger side, around the nose, and saw nothing but an opened passenger door and the spot where Widow had been. Then from behind the tail, Widow popped up and over to one side. He was in a crouch around the rear of the car. He shot an arrow straight through the guy's wrist, and the guy dropped the gun and clamped down on the arrow.

He cried out in pain. Blood squirted out around the edges of the wound.

Before he realized he should grab his gun with his other hand, Widow was on him. Widow kicked the guard right in the groin, and he toppled over onto his knees and puked.

Widow grabbed the guy by a tuft of his hair and punched him with a full fist in the back of the head, square in the brain's base, where all the circuits are kept. It wasn't a fatal blow. It could've been. But why kill the guard for doing his job? Widow couldn't pin him as some kind of accomplice. He might just be some local working for a paycheck.

He didn't kill the guy, but he switched the guy's lights out.

Widow dragged the guy back to the guard hut and laid him against the wall in a seated position. Then he grabbed the wall phone's cables below the machine and ripped them out. He went to a computer and clicked on a button to open the gate.

The gate cranked to life and started opening inward.

Widow went back to the passenger side of the cruiser and scooped up the guard's dropped gun. It was a Glock. He checked it. It was in good working order. He chambered a bullet and tucked the Glock into his coat pocket. He now had a Glock and Gray's SIG Sauer. Both great weapons.

He returned to the passenger seat of the cruiser and closed his door.

"Drive," he said, as he tossed the keys at Daniels' face. They bounced off and landed in his lap.

"You broke my nose again!" Daniels said.

"Drive!" Widow said. He took out the Glock and pointed it at Daniels.

Daniels' hands shook, but he picked up the keys, started the car, and drove through the gate.

They continued for over a minute until Widow saw the house in the distance around a bend in the driveway.

Widow said, "Look at this place! It looks like something Oprah would live in."

Daniels said nothing.

The estate was enormous. There were clusters of trees on all sides, a huge fountain with various colored lights lighting up the water, and huge column pillars at the front of the house. The drive was lit by lights dug into the sides of the road. The trees were illuminated by ground lights. Widow heard sprinklers going off somewhere in the distance.

Widow said, "Pull off here."

He pointed at a dark area in the grass, behind some trees. Daniels listened and turned the wheel, and they drove off the road. Daniels parked the cruiser and cut off the engine and the lights.

"Pop the trunk," Widow said.

Daniels popped the trunk.

Widow took the keys and got out of the car. He escorted Daniels around to the trunk.

He said, "Put your hands together."

Daniels put his hands together.

"Close your eyes," Widow said.

Daniels closed his eyes.

Widow put the Glock back in his pocket, scooped up the duct tape from the trunk, and taped Daniels' hands together at the wrists. Then he shoved him back, and he tumbled into the trunk.

Daniels opened his eyes. He was in the trunk.

He asked, "Are you going to kill me?"

"I'm going to lock you in here," he said, "I don't kill unarmed men."

Daniels got all the way into the trunk, tucking his legs down against the back of the tire well.

Widow stood over the trunk and left it open. He vanished from sight. Daniels heard one of the backseat doors open, and Widow leaned in and then back out, closing the door.

Widow returned and stared down at him. There was something in his hand. It was the last of the meth heads' Molotov cocktails. Widow had found it and hid it in the backseat.

He looked down at Daniels and showed the Molotov cocktail to him.

He said, "Then again. Agent Tyler would be alive if you weren't a piece of shit!"

Widow slammed the trunk. Daniels shouted at him from under the metal lid.

Widow went around to the nose of the cruiser and lit the wick on the Molotov cocktail with the cigarette lighter from the car. He tossed it into the car.

The front bench lit up fast.

He turned, took the Glock, the Sig, the bow and arrows, and headed toward the house.

The police cruiser went up in flames in minutes.

64

WIDOW CREPT through the darkness and trees. He stayed near the tree line, not sure if Gaden's property had motion lights or not. He wasn't sure if they had guard dogs, which would be worse than the lights. Lights didn't have teeth.

He walked as close to the house as he could and waited. He saw the fountain a lot better from here. It was on, and the water was flowing. It kept changing formation and colors. Even in the cold, the thing was on. Widow figured it was heated and set on a timer to go all night, which was technically over, but Alaska in the autumn didn't have sunrise till eight-thirty in the morning.

The sunrise was just beginning. White light peeked over the edge of the world.

Just then, Daniels' police cruiser exploded. The fire must've hit the gas tank. The explosion was loud and powerful and distracting, which was what Widow was betting on.

He stared straight ahead and saw guards dressed in the same uniforms as the one back at the gate. They came running from behind the house and the other side. He saw a garage door opening on the other corner of the house. He saw two golf carts come out with guards on both. He watched them drive off, chasing after the first round of guards, to the fire.

Once they were out of the way, he started to the house. Then he stopped. He saw movement at the top of huge stone steps that led to the front door. It was two more guards, only these weren't dressed in uniforms. They wore casual clothes. And they were armed with serious firepower.

They came out armed with MP5s. They weren't a part of the regular guard unit. That was for damn sure. These two guys looked like they had clocked serious battle time. They both wore all black, including winter coats, but Widow could see them in the light from the front of the house. Their faces were suntanned like they'd just gotten back from the desert.

They were private military, mercenaries—no doubt about it. They came down the steps and walked straight for him like they knew his position.

They both clicked on flashlights attached to their weapons. Widow scrambled for the nearest tree. He ducked down behind the trunk. He waited.

They got closer. He peeked around the side to get a look. He saw them using hand signals. They were searching for him. They must've figured his path up from the gate and the fiery police cruiser. That's how they guessed his location.

Damn, he thought. It was stupid for him to take a straight line up from the car.

Widow wanted to maintain stealth as long as he could, so he took out the bow and set an arrow in the nock until he heard the *click*. Then he came around the tree and aimed at the guards. He was out of their flashlight beams, but only for now. If they were as good as he figured, they would spread apart before the tree line, which they did.

One went right and one went left. Widow was dead center between them and about thirty feet away from the one on his right. He waited, stayed low, kept the bowstring on his cheek. He followed the one closest to him. He saw the flashlight beam wash across the trees, just missing him.

He breathed in and breathed out, slowly. He waited. He pressed the bow with his left hand and felt it pushing back. The pressure built.

The mercenary in his sight went farther and farther. He took another step to the north and another.

Widow relaxed his fingers, drew and released the bowstring. The arrow went flying out of the bow. It glided through the air silently. It hissed and then slammed straight into the merce-nary's neck. He dropped the MP5 and stumbled back into a tree. He grasped at his neck and the arrow in it. Desperate, he clutched at it, trying to pull it out.

Widow sidestepped around the tree and came out on the opposite side, taking up another arrow and sliding it into the knock. He heard the *click* and drew the string back. He steadied his stance and drew the string all the way back to his cheek and aimed at the second mercenary.

The second mercenary heard the other one hit the tree. He turned and started scanning for him. He pointed the MP5 in the sound's direction and washed the flashlight beam right over his dying friend. He missed Widow.

Widow released the arrow. It hissed through the air and caught the guy right in the shoulder. He dropped the MP5 and clutched at the arrow and his shoulder. He let out a scream.

Widow ran at the guy, taking out an arrow on the run. The second mercenary saw him coming at him in the dark and went for the MP5. He squirmed across the ground and got his hand on it and rolled onto his back. He aimed it at the dark figure running at him.

Widow had an arrow in the nock as he ran, and he aimed it. Not a recommended course of action. Running with a loaded bow was like running with scissors. You never know who could get hurt. But in this case, it was his target.

Widow released the string, and the arrow hissed through the air. It was an insane shot. The arrow burst through the guy's left nostril, cutting straight through cartilage and weak bone until the tip lodged into his brainpan.

The second mercenary stared back at Widow over the shaft of the arrow. He stopped moving. He just stared, cold and dead.

Widow got to him. That was his last arrow. He pulled it out of the guy's face, but the hilt came out without an arrowhead. He stared at it. It must've broken somewhere when he was scrambling around, maybe. He took out the arrowhead, which looked like a tiny spear now. He shrugged and kept it. He stuffed it down deep into his front jeans pocket.

Widow tossed the quiver, and the broken hilt and took up the MP5. He checked it: fully load. He searched the guy and found a knife and a radio. He took both and switched the volume on the radio all the way down, so it didn't crackle and give away his position. He clipped it to his belt. He put the bow back around his shoulder, in case it came in handy later, and used the MP5 instead.

The knife was the same as Sathers'. It was an Ontario MK III, same black steel, same sawtooth top edge as Sathers'. He took out the sheath from the dead mercenary and pocketed the knife in the sheath. He didn't want to be running around with the blade exposed.

Widow left the dead mercenary and checked the first one. He was still alive, but he would be dead soon enough. Widow took up his MP5 as well and ejected the magazine. He pocketed the extra magazine and tossed the weapon too far for the mercenary to crawl to it.

He left the guy there to die and took off for the house.

Widow ran to the garage and entered. The garage was massive. He looked around and counted twenty parked cars. They were all expensive, all washed, and all buffed to sparkling shines. There were SUVs and sedans and trucks and sports cars. There were Mercedes and Bentleys and Lamborghinis and Ferraris and Porsches. One red Lotus sports car stuck out. The sticker price for each vehicle was more than he'd made in a year at NCIS. He used the MP5 as his point weapon and passed the cars. He saw a long built-in worktable. Above it, there were regular garage things: tools, cabinets, and stored plastic containers with more tools. Then he saw the car keys for each car hanging from hooks in an open metal case.

He entered the house through a door in the garage. Normally, he would go slowly and steadily, but he wanted to find Gray fast, so he moved fast. He entered the house and cleared it room by room.

The inside of the house was grand and huge. The ceilings were twenty feet high, even higher in the main room. Crown molding and expensive fixtures and handcrafted details were everywhere. From the outside, he had guessed that it was owned by a multimillionaire, but now he was sure a multimillionaire couldn't afford it. The Gadens must've been billionaires. They had to be. The light bill alone was probably a hundred thousand a month. The inside of the house was built and designed and maintained at no expense spared.

There was gold trim everywhere. Widow stared at it, and he couldn't rule out that it wasn't real gold. Every room had a grand chandelier of some massive size and more lights than he had time to count.

First, he cleared the kitchen. No one was there. Then he cleared a hallway and a bathroom and a downstairs guest bedroom. No one was around so far. Back in the hallway, he barely heard faint noises coming from a closed door. The door was extremely heavy, like a bomb shelter door might be. It was reinforced hardened wood and metal. It was seriously out of place. He went over to it and pushed it open slowly. He aimed down the MP5's sights and saw a staircase that led down to a basement. There was light coming up from the basement.

Widow entered. A metal arm closed the door behind him slowly. He eased down the stairs and got to the bottom and saw something that both horrified him and enraged him in that same, singular moment.

Gray was lying on a tabletop. She was zip-tied, hands and feet. Her hands were in front of her. She was stripped down to her bra and panties. And she was covered in water. Her hair was drenched. Her head was drenched. Her breasts were soaked.

Her head was hung off the table's edge. She looked like something out of a torture movie.

She wasn't alone in the room. There were two big guys in there, more of Gaden's crew. Both of them had their backs to Widow. One of them was holding a wet towel. And the other held a large bucket of ice-cold water.

The first one grabbed Gray by her hair and tossed the towel over her face.

He said, "You're going to talk, bitch. There's no getting away from it."

The second one stepped in over her and was about to pour water over the towel as the first held her head up by her hair.

They were waterboarding her.

The second guy said, "You're going to talk after this, or we're going to remove the last articles of clothing you got."

Widow did something he always tried to avoid. He shot them both in the back.

First, he flipped the fire selector switch to a three-round burst. Then he aimed and fired.

He aimed high. He didn't want to chance a bullet hitting Gray, in case any of them were through and throughs. None of them were.

There were three loud pops and a split-second later, another three loud pops. The six bullets left three bullet holes in each

man's back, lined up vertically like triple portals in a
birdfeeder.

Both guys slumped forward from the blasts and clumped into
each other and fell backward. They dropped the wet towel
and the bucket of water. Water spilled all over them, and the
bucket rolled away.

They grabbed at their backs in unison, both with extreme pain
on their faces. They both made sounds and said something,
but Widow couldn't hear them because the gunshots echoed
through the basement. That was when Widow noticed the
soundproofing foam, stuck up all over the place.

Widow realized it wasn't just a basement they were using as a
makeshift torture room for Gray. This hadn't been a onetime
thing. There were knives and blades and all forms of weapons
all over the room, stuck up on hooks like tools from the garage
in the meth head house.

And there was a sledgehammer on one wall. It was much
newer than the one he had used earlier. It was stainless steel
with a black rubber grip.

The soundproof foam was installed to keep houseguests and
probably the staff from hearing things they weren't supposed
hear.

No one came down the stairs to check on the gunshots
because no one had heard them. The room was soundproofed.
Maybe audible, brief pops could be heard just outside the
basement door, but that was it, and that was all.

Gray strained to lift her head to see what had happened. She
squinted in the bright basement lights and saw him standing

there. Water in her eyes blurred her vision, and he looked like an apparition.

"Widow?" she asked.

He lowered the MP5 and ran over to her. He set the weapon on a counter and turned to her and cradled her head with one hand.

"I'm going to get you out of here," he said.

He unsheathed the knife and cut through her zip ties. She didn't rub her wrists like in the movies. She grabbed at him and pulled herself up, and he scooped her up in his arms. She kissed him like she had never kissed any man before, then stopped and hugged him tightly.

She stopped and hugged him tightly. He held her in his arms off her feet for a long time. She grabbed hold of him and didn't let go. She didn't want to let go. He didn't want to let go.

She whispered in his ear.

"Thank you! Thank you! Thank you!"

* * *

GRAY HELD onto Widow for a long, long minute. He disengaged first and looked into her eyes. Her face was now covered in soot from hugging him for so long.

She said, "You can put me down now."

"Are you okay?"

"I am now."

He set her down on her feet.

"Anything broken?" he asked.

"No."

He looked her over anyway. He looked her top to bottom and then spun her around and looked her over from bottom to top. The zip ties had bruised her wrists and ankles. Her body looked fine. A dark shiner was welling up around her eye.

He reached out and touched her chin and moved her face from side to side, checking out the shiner.

She said, "Widow, I'm fine. They didn't hit me. This is from one of those yahoos back at the shantytown."

He let go of her chin.

He asked, "What about these guys? They assault you?"

He pointed at the dead bodies on the floor.

"No. They stripped off my clothes, piece by piece. I thought they were going to rape me. I was so scared," she said and paused a long beat.

She said, "But it never got that far. I'm fine. Really."

"Okay. Where are your clothes?"

She looked around. Then she went over to the metal counter and opened up a cabinet on the bottom. She reached in and came back out with her clothes in a pile. She held her pants, her top, her jacket, and even her gun, still in its holster. But there were no shoes.

She dressed in everything she could and walked barefoot.

Widow escorted her up the stairs and back down the hall and through the kitchen to the garage. He opened the door and walked her out. He snatched a set of car keys off the rack and clicked the button. The red Lotus beeped to life.

He clicked the button to start the engine, and the car fired up like a beast waking from a deep hibernation. He walked her over to the car, opened the door, and plopped her down in the driver's seat.

"Widow, what are you doing?" she asked.

"You're getting out of here."

"No! Not without you!"

Widow didn't respond to that.

He said, "Take that drive all the way out. Stomp on the gas the whole way. The gate should be open, but if it's not, crash through. Drive fast! Stop for no one! If a guard gets in your way, run him down! I mean it!"

She clawed and grappled at his Havelock and pulled him down.

"Get in, Widow!" she cried. "Get in! Now! We go together!"

He grabbed her hands, gently, and leaned in and kissed her passionately, like it was the last time he might see her, which it probably was. Then he backed out, removed her hands from his coat, and put them on the wheel. He tossed the keys onto her lap.

He said, "I can't. I have something left to do."

And he closed the door. She pressed a button, and the window jetted down.

She said, "You're not a one-man justice department! Get in! Come with me!"

"I can't. I've got a score to settle with Gaden and Fallow. They murdered Cho. They murdered Shore. They murdered Eggers. My brothers-in-arms. They're the reason Tyler's dead. And they threatened those little girls. I can't let that stand. I just can't."

"But they'll kill you!"

He said, "I'm sorry. You go. Go now!"

She begged, "Let it go, Widow! Come with me!"

"If I leave them alive and someone else dies, I'll never be able to live with myself. No. This ends here and now. My way," he said and took a step back. "Now go. Keep going till you find a town. Don't trust the local cops. Call Cameron and the FBI. Get them here."

She looked down at the steering wheel and then back up into his eyes.

She said, "You're a great man, Jack Widow. I like you! And I want to see you again! Come back to me! Come back to me alive!"

He leaned down and kissed her. Then he shifted to stand back up again. She grabbed him by the collar. They kissed one more time.

Widow smiled and said, "I got your number."

Gray hit the gas and peeled out of the garage. The tires squealed and smoked the air, and she was gone like a Formula racer. The Lotus left black tire marks.

She raced down the driveway and the long winding road and past the fiery police cruiser and the guards and the golf carts. She crashed through the gate.

Widow heard the gate and metal crash in the distance. He watched as the Lotus's taillights faded away.

65

WIDOW WENT over to a utility box in the garage. He wrenched it open and shut off the power to the house. Then he walked back into the kitchen. He skipped the kitchen and went straight to the main room. It was a huge, grand living room with a double staircase to match. He waited and saw no one. He walked up the stairs and saw no one.

At the top of the stairs were two long hallways; each led into darkness. The halls had more gold trim and crown molding and high ceilings and expensive everything. He saw a dim light down the left corridor. He followed it, keeping the MP5 out and ready to kill. He checked every door and every room that he passed. Everything was empty: empty bedrooms, an empty home theater, and an empty closet that was the size of a bedroom.

The left corridor led to the west wing of the house. He followed it until he heard voices. He ended up at a heavy oak door. It was ajar, and a light came out of the crack. He kicked it open, and it creaked on old hinges.

He entered a massive study or library or den or a whole other apartment. He wasn't sure.

Inside the room was another twenty-foot ceiling. There was a massive stone fireplace with a large fire roaring in the pit. It crackled and buzzed with life.

A stuffed grizzly bear stood in a far corner, next to a set of French doors that led out to a massive balcony. There were taxidermied animals of all types mounted on the walls. In one corner, he saw a huge striped tiger. It was as big as the bear. It was stuffed in an attack pose like it was about to leap on the back of an elephant and maul it to death.

There were elk heads and deer heads and pronghorns and moose and wolves and all kinds of big game animals. A stuffed lion stood up in the opposite corner from the tiger.

There were massive bookcases and a huge antique telescope. A massive open skylight was directly in front of the telescope. The telescope was pointed up at the brightening sky, but the skylight's glass was tinted, making it still seem dark inside.

On another wall, opposite the bookshelves, were tons of military items. There were photos of Gaden all over the place, in military uniform and out. Medals and antique rifles and pistols were displayed in cases. There were various war uniforms. One large American flag was strung up on the wall above it all.

Widow stepped into the room. The MP5 was out in front of him. The room was so large it took him a minute to scan it all. There were shadows everywhere. The only light was from the crackling fire and the morning sunlight that was dimmed by the skylight and curtains over the French doors.

There was furniture everywhere: a massive table—embedded with an ancient map of the world—lounge chairs and sofas, and a huge stone and marble desk. It looked like something he had seen Saddam Hussein sit behind, in a news spread once.

Behind the desk was Nick Gaden. He had a lit cigar in his mouth like he was celebrating a victory. He stared at Widow with the biggest expression of dumbfoundedness that Widow had ever seen in his life. Gaden was thunderstruck.

Widow stepped farther into the room. He pointed the MP5 straight at Gaden.

Gaden reached up slowly, took the cigar out of his mouth, and set it down in an ashtray. He raised both hands, showed them to Widow, and stood up out of the desk chair. He stepped around to the front of the desk.

He said, "Jack Widow?"

"That's me."

"I'm utterly impressed. You should come work for me."

"I don't think so."

"Why? The pay is really, really good."

Widow said, "Where's Fallow? And the other two?"

Gaden stepped forward, slowly, and kept his hands up.

"Well, Fallow is out somewhere. And by the other two, I assume you mean the two left from his guys?"

"The other two who murdered Eggers?"

"They're not here. They're somewhere else. With your girl-friend. You had better put down that gun, or you'll never find her."

"Good. Then they're already dead."

Gaden paused a beat. Widow stepped closer so he could better see the guy's features. Gaden stood six feet tall. He wore a wool sweater and dark chinos and house slippers. He looked comfortable, like a man about to pose for a *Vanity Fair* cover in a gaudy den, like the one they were standing in.

He was neatly dressed and neatly trimmed. He was clean-shaven with gray hair, buzzed short. He looked like a man about to run for the Senate, which he was planning to do.

The only leftover reminder on his body from his military service was a vicious old scar across his forehead and cheek. It looked like a knife wound. It was white and hardened, appearing to have come from an injury decades ago.

Gaden smiled and said, "So you got her out. That's good. You really are impressive."

Widow stayed quiet.

Gaden said, "You know what room you're standing in?"

"A latrine?"

"Funny. It's a replica of the Oval Office. All except for the animals, of course."

Widow glanced around and realized he was right. The room was oval-shaped, but it was far larger than the Oval Office, not that he had ever been inside the real deal before.

"Not exact. There are pictures of a douche bag all over the place in this room."

Gaden said, "You think you're so smart."

"I did pretty well on my SAT."

Suddenly, Widow felt something like a brisk wind. Something moved with little noise and little energy, like a ninja.

Then he heard the click of a slide being racked, and the metallic start of a trigger pull. He felt the tip of a cold barrel brush against his ear. He felt a muzzle jammed hard against the back of his head, right behind his ear.

Gaden lowered his hands and said, "How smart are you now?"

Fallow stood behind Widow; his Glock 19 was jammed against Widow's head.

Fallow said, "Drop the gun!"

Widow stayed where he was, keeping the weapon pointed at Gaden's center mass.

Fallow said, "Go ahead. Shoot him. But then you'll be dead. And I can pay that girlfriend of yours a visit. I feel like we didn't have enough time to get properly acquainted."

Gaden said, "You can't kill us both. You're beat, Commander. Drop the weapon."

No choice. Widow dropped the MP5. Fallow shoved Widow forward, and then he scooped up the MP5, tossed it to Gaden, who caught it and ejected the magazine, ejected the chambered bullet. He tossed both into opposite directions in the room.

Fallow reached out and took Widow's other guns, unloaded them all, and did the same, tossing them into the farthest shadows in the room. Next, he took the bow off Widow's shoulder. He tossed it over to the stuffed tiger.

Gaden reached behind him and pulled out another Colt 1911 from his desk. It was gold-plated with an ivory handle. It was the kind of gun that Widow had only seen rich dictators possess, a collector's item.

Gaden and Fallow circled Widow with their guns in his face. They forced him back deeper into the room. He ended up with his butt against the massive desk.

Gaden said, "Empty your pockets."

Fallow holstered his Glock and moved and shoved furniture out of the way like he was making room for something, some kind of spectacle event. He pushed everything that wasn't bolted down or heavy all the way against the walls.

Widow emptied his pockets in front of Gaden, setting his belongings down on the desktop. It included his passport, bank card, the Ontario MK III knife, the nineteen dollars and change he took from the meth heads, and the nine-millimeter bullet he caught from Gray's SIG Sauer before handing it over to Daniels. He laid it all out in a pile.

Gaden barked, "Lose the coat!"

Widow took off the Havelock and draped it over his belongings.

"Want me to lose my pants next?" he asked.

Gaden smiled and said, "Lose the shoes. Kick them off."

Widow kicked off his boots. They went flying against the grizzly bear's feet.

Fallow kept pulling and pushing things out of the way, making a huge space in the room like a boxing ring.

Fallow finished moving things out of the way and then joined Gaden. They motioned for Widow to move to the center of the room.

Fallow and Gaden circled him again, like two predators circling their next kill.

Gaden asked, "Commander, have you ever heard of vale tudo?"

Widow said, "It's Brazilian boxing."

Gaden said, "Not just Brazilian. It's an underground thing."

Fallow said, "Men fight to the death."

Both Fallow and Gaden smiled at Widow.

Fallow said, "Ours is knife fighting to be accurate."

Gaden said, "Two men enter a ring, like this room, and they knife each other to death. See, we've been doing vale tudo for decades. In Iraq, we'd take prisoners and make them knife fight to the death. We promised them the winner got his freedom and his life."

Fallow said, "They never did."

Widow thought for a second. Something clicked in his brain, the more civilized brain. Henry Cho had been stabbed to death. Thirty-one years old. He never lived to see another birthday. He never lived to marry his partner.

Widow said, "Is that why you killed Cho? Is that why you blamed it on Shore?"

The two men laughed.

Gaden said, "Hardly. No Cho and Eggers and most of the others weren't in on the vale tudo. We only did it when we had the right guys in our unit—like-minded kind of guys. Once we did, we'd go out and make it happen. During the war, it was easy. Easier than you'd think."

Fallow said, "It got harder after Saddam was caught. But in the beginning, it was easy and fun."

Gaden said, "We gave them knives. We watched the blade combat until they were both stuck pigs. And then we'd stick the winner."

Fallow said, "I miss those days."

Gaden said, "No, I killed Cho because he was the one who ratted me out. He started the investigation into me. He got some of the other guys to go along with it. They all knew the things we were doing. My daddy had a lot of money, as you can see. From our family business."

Gaden pointed around the room with the Colt, like he was showing off his wealth.

Widow asked, "Weapons?"

"Right. My being investigated woulda led to an arrest and court-martial and prison time for the rest of my life. I have no doubt. I was sloppy back then. I had to scare Eggers and some others into submission. I couldn't kill them all. That would've gotten noticed. So, we needed a target," Gaden said.

Fallow said, "We killed the butt pirate and his boyfriend. That was fun. We made it look like what it looked like, and that was that."

Gaden said, "Eggers was the weakest link. But we bribed him with stock in my daddy's company. We bribed all of them with stock."

Widow asked, "Fifty million dollars of stock?"

They laughed at him.

Gaden said, "Nah. It wasn't worth that much back then. It was under a million. How was I to know that Congress would grant my daddy's company those huge contracts for Naval weapons and equipment? The stocks skyrocketed after that. We had unbelievable growth for twenty years, even through the stock market crashes. Weapons sales always remain high. All my guys got a cut. All the guys who knew got a cut. It was a way of ensuring their silence. Some of them didn't agree with it. So we had to silence them."

Widow asked, "Why murder Eggers? He was a nobody. A drunk. He was drinking himself to death already."

"Don't you know? Don't you see it?"

Widow thought for a long second. He glanced at the medals, displayed like trophies. He glanced at the flag.

He said, "Because you wanted to ensure he kept your secret. You wanted a guarantee that he'd never tell anyone that you murdered Cho. Because you're running to be a Senator from Alaska? But who gives a shit? He probably would never even have known?"

"Look around you."

Widow glanced around.

Gaden said, "My Senate seat will be vacant a year after I get in. Know why?"

Widow stayed quiet.

"Because once I'm a senator, I'm going to announce my run for the big office."

"You want to be president?" Widow asked. He couldn't help it, but he burst into laughter.

Gaden's smile receded, and his voice broke and rose.

He said, "I will be in the White House! I had to erase all who might stand in my way!"

Gaden took a slow, deep breath.

He said, "Eggers was out there with an enormous bank account. He left me alone for years, but as soon as he saw my face on national TV, he'd spill his secrets. And I couldn't have that. But you came along. You couldn't just leave it alone. I read about you. Everything that I could read. You have some sealed files. High-priority clearance required. You must've been some hot shit, Widow. But now you'll never leave this room alive."

Widow said, "Gray got away already. She'll go right to the FBI. She's probably already halfway there. She probably has already told NCIS. You'll be ruined. No matter if you kill me or not."

Gaden nodded.

"Maybe. Or maybe a has-been SEAL, someone that nobody ever heard of, and a rookie NCIS agent invaded my home without cause and killed a bunch of my guys."

"That's horseshit. In an hour, you'll either be dead or in handcuffs."

Silence.

Widow looked around. He knew what was coming. It was vale tudo, a gladiator match, a deathmatch.

Widow said, "Pick your poison."

Gaden said, "Know what Cho saw to make him betray me?"

Widow stayed quiet.

Gaden said, "I killed a kid. I'm sure you saw the accusations about the towelhead kids. Those were schoolgirls. No one cared. But it was a teenage boy I killed. That was the one. He was nobody. Just some kid. I claimed he was one of the insurgents, but I didn't know. Who knows? Maybe he was."

Gaden lowered his Colt 1911.

"I gutted him with my knife. Know what I whispered to him before he died?"

Widow stayed quiet.

Gaden said, "I asked, 'How you like my knife work?' And I stuck him till he bled out. And to be honest. I said the same thing to Cho."

Silence.

Gaden ejected the magazine from the Colt 1911. Then he ejected the round in the chamber. He tossed the bullet at Widow's feet, and then he tossed the magazine off in the shadows. He circled behind Widow, forcing him to the center of the room. Gaden laid the Colt 1911 on the desk.

Fallow kept his Glock out.

Gaden stepped behind the desk and went into a drawer. He came out with a display box of military knives. He opened it and took out three knives. He handed one to Fallow, kept the second for himself, and offered the third to Widow, only it wasn't a knife. Not like the others. The third knife was a fake wooden knife for practicing.

He said, "Take it."

Widow reached out and took the wooden knife.

Gaden said, "Enough talking. Now, you can fight us in a match of vale tudo."

Fallow emptied his Glock of bullets. He tossed it. Then he took the magazine and tossed it off hard into a corner.

Gaden said, "Any of the guns are fair game. If you can find them, load them before we kill you."

Fallow said, "This is going to be fun."

Widow stood there; his feet planted firmly. His waist and arms and legs were all loose and ready to dance.

Fallow came at him first. He swiped right and swiped left. Widow danced and maneuvered and parried the knife blows with the wooden blade. Then he did something neither guy expected. He dug deep into his pocket and jerked something out of it.

Gaden didn't see what it was, but he saw the move. He came at Widow's empty side. Fallow retreated and stabbed at Widow's center mass.

In one fast move, Widow made two moves. First, he threw the wooden blade hard and straight at Gaden like it was a real knife. The wooden blade jabbed him straight in the forehead, right on the old scar. It was hard and powerful. The wood didn't cut him or stick him or knock him off his feet, but it startled and rattled him, and it hurt. He stepped back several paces as if Widow had planted a powerful uppercut in his chin.

The second move: Widow danced right. Fallow came at him again. The knife missed Widow's center mass, but Fallow was already in the move, in the stabbing motion. His weight moved him forward and fast. He passed along Widow's ribcage, and Widow stuck Fallow in the back of the neck, in the medulla oblongata, the brain box, the central power box to the brain.

Widow stuck Fallow in the back of the head with something long and sharp and broken at the hilt.

Fallow's expression froze. And it never changed again, not for the rest of his life.

Widow had plunged the broken arrowhead from the bow right into Fallow's brain stem. He held it there for a long, long second. He made direct eye contact with Gaden, and he twisted the arrow hard, first clockwise and then counterclockwise.

Gaden stared on in horror. He saw his friend's body go limp and lifeless.

Widow jerked the arrow out. Clumps of brain matter extracted with the arrowhead.

Fallow's body collapsed like a crash test dummy. Widow showed the arrowhead to Gaden and stared at him and smiled.

He said, "You should've had me turn my pockets inside out."

Gaden screamed at him. It was some kind of primal indiscernible noise. There were no words in it.

Gaden flipped his blade and reversed it and threw it at Widow. Widow slapped it away in the air.

Gaden turned around and looked at the tiger and then the lion. He ran to the tiger and searched for one of the weapons, one of the thrown guns. He found nothing. He bolted to the lion. He got down on his hands and knees and searched frantically.

He was too slow and too stupid.

Widow came up behind him and grabbed a tuft of his hair and slit his throat with Gaden's own knife.

Before he slit his throat, he let the sharp edge press against his skin, and he pulled Gaden's head as far back as it would go, and he whispered to him.

"How you like my knife work?"

Then he slit his throat.

Blood gushed out and sprayed all over the long-dead lion. The claws, the teeth, the mane were all soaked in deep red blood by the time Gaden died.

66

An hour later, Gray lay in a bed in a hospital room in Anchorage. She was fast asleep.

She had cleaned herself up and showered and dressed in a hospital gown at the request of the nursing staff. It was all protocol. Her chart had read that she was healthy, but needed to be kept overnight for observation.

She still had to get checked out. It was all procedure, all by the book. She was glad because she was dead tired.

She slept through the rest of the day and most of the night.

Around noon, she got a visitor. It was Widow, showered, cleaned up, and stitched up. He had a couple of cuts. Both of them were from the knife fight with Fallow and Gaden. He hadn't even felt them when they happened. It was no big deal —two stitches in one cut and one in another.

He ended up sitting in a lounge chair against the window. He fell asleep there until that night. When he looked up, it was midnight. He saw the time on a wall clock. He looked at Gray; her eyes were closed.

He got up quietly and smiled at her, and headed out the door. His instincts were pushing him. The open road was calling.

At the door, Gray spoke.

"You trying to sneak out?"

Widow turned back to her and smiled.

"I can't. You're my ride back to DC."

OVER THE NEXT SEVERAL DAYS, inquiries were opened, and arrests were made. Gaden's old teammates who had taken the bribes were brought to justice for their silence. Many people were fired or indicted. Fire Marshal Jay Haspman was both.

Careers were made. Promotions were handed out. Pats on the back were given all around.

Andy Frost was offered the chance to be reinstated to the NCIS, but he declined. Michael and Jill Aker remained in DC with their daughters. Brig Tunney recovered from his wounds, though it was a long and arduous path. In the end, it saved his marriage because his wife helped him every step of the way, which brought them closer together.

The strangest part took place in Nebraska. In a small farming community, a nearly penniless elementary school teacher, who was a single mother of two children, received a phone call one day. She was on the verge of having to move because her school was losing funds and cutting programs. That all changed when the caller told her that her father, Henry

Eggers had passed on. He had left her a sizable fortune. She was told that she needed to sign some documents and sell all the stock by the next day, which she did, right in her small-town lawyer's office. She did it all by teleconference with a law firm in DC.

By the end of the day, she was worth fifty million dollars.

By the end of the week, a corporate conglomerate that she had never heard of had gone out of business because the FBI stepped in and indicted owners and the CEO and other figureheads.

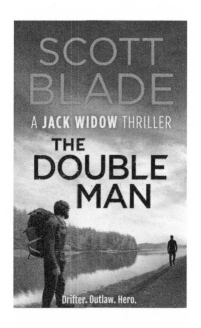

Out Now!

THE DOUBLE MAN: A BLURB

A face he recognizes.

Is it a wanted murderer?

Or is Jack Widow seeing double?

Tired of people, Jack Widow takes a break. He camps out in the Alaskan wilderness on Kodiak Island, relying on nothing but his survival skills. It's everything he wanted: quiet terrain, plenty of fishing, sleeping out under the stars, and no people. It seemed like the perfect vacation until Widow meets a man with a familiar face.

He recognizes a total stranger, but from where? The stranger goes by one name but has the face of another.

In a riveting, new thriller by International Bestseller Scott Blade, Jack Widow investigates a man who is either a cursed lookalike or a deadly criminal.

CHAPTER 1

THE HELICOPTER WAS a Sikorsky MH-60 Jayhawk, a twin engine rescue aircraft capable of reaching speeds of two hundred and seven miles per hour—for maximum short distance missions. The United States Coast Guard depended on it for deepwater rescues. It was the workhorse of the US water and mountain rescue operations. The bird was designed to fly three hundred miles out to sea loaded with a crew of four but could hoist six people from the ocean and carrying them all back to shore. It could hover over a rescue site for up to forty-five minutes before needing to return home to refuel.

The man was called Gary Kloss. Although no one would know that because he didn't have a wallet on him. No identification. Nothing. The only way to know who he was, was to ask him. The only way to know *anything* about him was to ask him, which was why he was out here.

Kloss was strapped into a CMC Rescue Disaster Response Litter, a highly durable stretcher fused together with powder-coated steel, metal wire, and mesh. The US Coast Guard used it to pluck up survivors from disastrous situations, like capsized boats stranded in the ocean or injured climbers on the side of a mountain. It was an essential piece of equipment for any rescue unit. No doubt about it. Without it, hoisting people out of choppy waters after their boat capsized was near impossible, especially for survivors with broken limbs. And Kloss had two broken limbs. Both of his legs were broken at the kneecaps. He felt the pain. It wasn't numb. No way could he survive treading water for long, not on his own, not without a life vest, which he wasn't wearing. Under normal circumstances—normal weather and sea conditions—the Coast Guard helicopter would be a welcome sight. But these weren't normal circumstances—far from it.

Kloss's stretcher dangled from a retractable cable rigged outside the helicopter to a winch. Nylon cloth belts strapped him into the stretcher tight. His movement was completely constricted, and he couldn't move his legs. The straps were so tight that he barely had room to breathe and wriggle, but that was about it. Since his legs were broken, he could only squirm from the waist up. Not much good that would do him. He couldn't swim, not with the broken legs. He wasn't much of a swimmer, anyway. Even if he could swim, even if his legs weren't broken, he still wouldn't escape the litter. The straps were too tight. And his hands were pinned underneath them.

The only thing he could do that mattered was he could take deep breaths, which was good. He needed them.

Gales of cold wind howled and bayed and bawled all around him. A lightning bolt flashed and electrified the sky for one long, bright second. Kloss dangled in the stretcher. The wind swayed him from side to side under the helicopter. He stared up and saw the undercarriage of the Jayhawk. He saw the rotor blades whopping fast like the wings of a dragonfly. He stared past the aircraft and the blades and saw the underbelly of enormous storm clouds above. They hung in the sky like massive creatures. In comparison, he felt like a bug.

A lightning bolt flashed, brightening the sky. Then it vanished and faded, and the skies died back to near darkness. All except for the Jayhawk's exterior navigation lights, but not for long. More lightning crackled and coruscated above the Jayhawk. It continued like a light show in the sky. There was no pattern to it. The lightning was completely random, as lightning is. He knew that, but it seemed to spark the sky every five seconds. Thunder rumbled above. Armaments of rain drenched and decanted and pounded around the helicopter. Wind beat and punched huge wafts at him, making the rain worse. Rainwater gusted everywhere. It slapped across Kloss's immobile body, across his bruised and battered cheeks.

Kloss's legs were broken, but that wasn't all. His face was a wreck. He had two black eyes, one of them was mashed shut. His nose was broken. There were bruises on his arms and chest. He was sure he had a fractured rib or two.

The Gulf of Alaska was thirty feet below the helicopter. The water below swelled and crunched. Huge waves rose and fell and gulped below him. Whitecaps crashed into each other in a chaotic rhythm that only the sea understood. The water was dark and gray. It was just as terrifying as deep space, but far more alive. Below the surface lay the unknown. Below was everything meant to kill him. There was no escaping it, not for Kloss. He couldn't swim to shore, not even if the conditions were calm. It was too far. And again, his broken legs wouldn't allow it. The only thing that waited for Kloss below the water was death.

Kloss, the gurney, and the basket dangled in the harness from the Jayhawk about fifteen feet above the crashing waves. The waves splashed and wallowed up. The spray slapped across his cheeks and into his eyes. Saltwater stung his face. He tasted it on his lips and in his mouth. He swallowed some of it. He inhaled some of it. It couldn't be helped.

The Jayhawk's rotors spun, whipping wind and rain back out into the rotor wash. The night was cold and wet in every direction. Rainwater ricocheted from the rotor wash and spat back out away from the helicopter. The cargo cabin doors were slid all the way open. Two men leaned out. Their hands held onto grips near the door. They didn't want to fall out. One guy wore a ball cap. He operated the winch. The other stood over and peered down at Kloss like he was supervising a deep water rescue.

The man supervising wore a leather jacket in place of a blazer over a crinkled dress shirt and tie and black chinos. His tie whipped in the violent wind gusts, hugging tight to his neck and shoulder. His gray hair was slicked back from the rain.

Behind him were three other guys, all built like human pit bulls, only taller. All of them wore casual, warm clothes, minus the pilot, who was the only one wearing a flight suit. The pilot was the only guy out of the six who didn't have broad shoulders underneath his suit. He was more of a desk type than the others. Even though he didn't sit behind a desk all that much. His life was sedentary. The other five were different. They were built like former football players. They were built like former Special Forces Operators, only bigger, not far from some coastguardsmen.

If someone could see them from shore, it would appear that the US Coast Guard was rescuing a man from drowning, but they weren't. That's not what the guys in the Jayhawk were doing at all. Not that it mattered, because the shore was too far away for anyone to see them. Even in daylight, they would've been a speck in the sky, a dot on the horizon. But there was no one onshore watching them. No witnesses. No onlookers. Not in this weather. They were closer to a passing cargo ship than anyone standing on the beach. They knew that because the pilot had logged the ship from radar. He told his leader, the guy in the leather jacket, about it. But the cargo ship was far away. They knew of the helicopter presence— probably. They could see it on their own equipment, but they didn't know who was onboard or why it was there. The pilot monitored the radio just in case the ship's crew tried to be Good Samaritans and offer help. But they didn't. They never radioed.

The Jayhawk hovered fifty miles from the south shores of Kodiak Island—Alaska's biggest island and the second biggest under the umbrella of US territory. Only Hawaii was bigger. No one could see them, not from the ship, not from shore. Maybe the helicopter's navigation lights would've been visible on a clear, dark night. Maybe they could've even been seen with a high-powered scope, like a telescope or a camera lens. Maybe it was possible to see the lights with the naked eye as a faint, distant twinkle. Maybe, from the nearest ship, sailors on deck could catch a faint whisk of the beacon light that blinked from the Jayhawk's undercarriage. But this was no clear, dark night. And no one was looking at them with a high-powered scope or camera lens. No one was looking with thermals. No one was looking out at them—period. Why would they? Not during a storm like this. Not at the end of an Alaskan September.

Kloss stared up at the man with the whipping tie leaning out of the helicopter. Lightning crackled again. Even without the instant flash of light, Kloss saw the man with the whipping tie. The Jayhawk's interior cabin lights illuminated his face. There was one distinguishing feature about the man with the whipping tie. It was his expression, the look in his eyes. It was horrifying. A malicious smile cracked across the man's face. It resonated like pure evil, the kind seen once in a lifetime.

Kloss would never forget that look. He would remember it for the rest of his life.

"Who did you tell?" the man with the whipping tie yelled down to Kloss.

Another large swell crashed below him, and water sprayed up across his face again. The swells continued like relentless drumbeats, constantly pounding below.

Kloss shouted, "No one!"

"You're lying," the man with the whipping tie said, and he paused a beat. Then he called out, "Take a deep breath!" He glanced at the guy controlling the winch and said, "Do it."

The guy controlling the winch smiled under the ball cap and hit a button on a control panel. Instantly, the cable slacked, and the winch released, and Kloss and the rescue litter went crashing down into the waves below, into the black water. The guy controlling the winch pressed the button again and stopped the slack. The helicopter hovered. The man with the whipping tie stared down. Glee danced in his eyes like dancing candlelight. He watched. He was impressed because even though Kloss was old and his legs were broken and he was strapped into the litter, he thrashed and flogged and flayed about from the torso as best he could. He tried to free himself, tried to get loose.

The man with the whipping tie could see the water splash violently from Kloss's struggling. It was impressive. The man had been impressive all around so far. He'd given up some information, like his name. But the man with the whipping tie knew he was holding something back. There was more to get. And so far, he'd been unable to get it. The man with the whipping tie couldn't remember the last time a subject held out on him. It had been decades, probably.

Kloss wanted to live, so he squirmed and wriggled under the weight of the water, under the tight straps. But it did no good. His efforts changed nothing. He was fighting against immense undertow while his legs were broken, and his arms were strapped down. He didn't stand a chance.

The man with the whipping tie watched. The glee in his eyes continued. The thrashing continued. He didn't know how long Kloss could hold his breath. Not long, he bet. But that didn't stop the man with the whipping tie from keeping Kloss down there. If the guy died, then he died.

The man with the whipping tie waited. *Thirty seconds. Forty-five seconds. One minute.* The thrashing continued.

The guy controlling the winch asked, "Now?"

The man with the whipping tie said nothing.

One minute, thirty seconds.

The guy controlling the winch repeated, "Now?"

Silence.

One minute, forty-five seconds.

The thrashing slowed like the drip from a loose faucet until it stopped.

The man with the whipping tie said, "Okay. Now."

The guy controlling the winch hit the button, and the winch cranked, and the cable retracted and reeled back up. The litter surged up out of the water. Seawater dripped off the sides. The litter came back up several feet out of the crashing waves. The man with the whipping tie peered down from the Jayhawk and waited to make sure Kloss was still alive, which he was.

Kloss coughed and wheezed and spat up seawater violently. His lungs hurt. His throat hurt. His body ached, but he couldn't tell the difference between pain that came from his broken legs and pain that came from the barbaric water-boarding.

"Stop," the man with the whipping tie said.

The guy controlling the winch hit the button again, and the winch stopped cranking, and the cable and the litter froze in place. Kloss and the litter swayed to one side from the wind.

The man with the whipping tie called out, "Who did you tell?"

Kloss coughed and gagged and breathed. *Did he already tell them? Didn't he already break?* He couldn't remember. The last twenty-four hours had been the longest of his life. All the pain and torture made a lifetime of memories run together.

He shouted, "No one! I swear! No one!"

Didn't I tell them already, he asked himself. The answer was no. He never broke. He told them nothing that they couldn't find out on their own. But he lied about who hired him. He never gave them a name. At least, he hoped.

The man with the whipping tie called out, "Who hired you?"

"I don't know," Kloss lied.

The man with the whipping tie paused. The wind continued to push the litter to one side. The man with the whipping tie looked at his wristwatch. Then he tucked it back under the leather jacket sleeve.

He spoke under his breath. "I don't have time for this." Then he called back down to Kloss. "How do I know you're not lying?"

Kloss spat seawater out of his mouth. He lied, "I'm not! I swear! It was anonymous."

The man with the whipping tie said, "Dip him again."

Kloss didn't hear the order, but he read the man with the whipping tie's lips and understood the gesture. He shouted back in protest, shouted up into the noise of the rain and wind and thunder and rotor wash, but it wasn't heard.

The button was pressed, and the winch cranked once, and the locking mechanism released the cable, and the litter dropped several feet at once, and it went back into the water. Kloss vanished under the swells.

The man with the whipping tie stared down and smiled. The same glee danced in his eyes. But the same thrashing in the water wasn't the same at all. This time, it was barely a struggle. It was more apt to a death rattle than a man fighting for his life. It was like Kloss was defeated. It took all the joy out of it for him to watch. It was pathetic. Kloss had given up. They always do.

The man with the whipping tie's smile faded, and the glee in his eyes died down to nothing. He was disappointed. Kloss had been an army veteran. He knew that from a simple background check. Anyone could discover that about Kloss, but the man with the whipping tie's resources was a lot more than what most people could access. Not that he needed to do a background check because Kloss had already told him enough, all but who hired him.

Every man has a breaking point, even a retired army veteran. When breaking a man's legs gets you nothing, injecting them with narcotics often will. The man with the whipping tie hadn't injected him with any narcotics, however, because he had neither the time nor the proper equipment, not on Kodiak Island. The island itself wasn't the middle of nowhere, but it was remote enough. Having the proper equipment on standby took time to prepare. He didn't have that time.

Taking Kloss out on a dip from a helicopter seemed to be enough to get the job done. Sometimes it was the crude measures that worked best. Plus, the man with the whipping tie enjoyed the hell out of it. But that sensation had passed. And he had better things to do. If Kloss hadn't told him by now, he wouldn't tell him at all.

"Pull him up," the man with the whipping tie said.

The operator nodded and hit the button, and the winch cranked to life again and reeled the cable up. Kloss and the rescue litter came up out of the water.

The man with the whipping tie looked over at the operator controlling the winch and nodded at him again. The operator nodded back and hit the button again. The cable stopped cranking, and Kloss was left dangling again several feet over the water.

The man with the whipping tie gave it one last go and called down. "Who did you tell?"

Kloss coughed and gagged and nearly vomited, but didn't because there was nothing left to vomit. His stomach was empty. His abdomen muscles were beyond the point of straining.

Kloss shouted up, "No one! I swear! Please! Let me go!"

The man with the whipping tie stared down and yawned. He felt tired, partially from the long flight to Alaska just to deal with this guy. Partially, he was tired because he had been awake and a part of the long torture of Kloss. He called out, "Okay. I believe you." Though he didn't.

The man with the whipping tie stepped back and stood straight and tall. He stretched his arms out and looked at the guy controlling the winch. He yawned again.

He said, "Bring him back up."

The operator nodded and did as he was told. Once again, he pressed the return button. The winch motored and cranked. The cable took several seconds to lift all the way.

The guy controlling the winch stopped it as soon as Kloss and the litter were within grabbing distance.

The man with the whipping tie turned to the pilot. He said, "Take us up higher."

The pilot said nothing. No affirmative response. No nod. No look. He just did as he was ordered. The Jayhawk climbed.

The man with the whipping tie got back into the cabin and dumped himself down in an empty jump seat behind the cockpit. His tie stopped whipping. He looked at his watch.

Without eye contact, he barked an order to one of his guys. "Help him."

One of the large guys, the one closest to the doors, unbuckled his safety belt and stood up. He clambered over to the open door and helped the other crew member drag the litter in and unharness it from a large hook at the end of the cable.

Kloss breathed in and breathed out. Rainwater and seawater drenched his face. There was saltwater in his stomach and lungs. No doubt about it. His skin was pale blue. The bruises on his face were wrinkled and had turned purple. But he said nothing. He felt lucky to be alive.

The helicopter climbed higher and higher.

Kloss stared at the man with the whipping tie. The two large guys dragged the litter into the cabin set him down in the middle of the floor. They checked the straps on his hands, made sure they were fastened tight. He didn't struggle or thrash about like he did before, because he didn't want to piss them off. They were letting him go. He had told the man with the whipping tie enough.

Kloss thought he convinced the man with the whipping tie to let him live, and that was victory enough. His broken legs would heal in time. His bruises would heal. Now they were going to let him go. They'd probably dump him at an emergency room somewhere, probably in Kodiak or Homer.

Whatever, he didn't care. He just wanted to be rid of them. He could regroup later. He could get the FBI involved after he was safe and sound.

The helicopter climbed.

The man with the whipping tie stayed quiet. The two large guys that set Kloss down stayed near him. One unhooked him from the cable. The cable whipped back out into the night. It dangled from the side of the winch. The operator stayed near the open doors but did not close them.

One of the large guys kept a massive hand laid across Kloss's chest like he was keeping him restrained with it. The hand was the size of a shovel, but heavy as a rock. Kloss looked them all over casually like he was taking notes about them. He recorded their faces for his statement to the Feds later. Then he paused a beat and glanced back over his shoulder out the open doors. Lightning cracked the sky again. He stayed fixated on the rough sky beyond the doors until a question popped into his mind. It was a question he couldn't ignore. So he asked it.

He asked, "Why is the door still open?"

No one answered him.

A fear crept up on him. Kloss's heart raced. He asked, "Why is the door still open?"

No answer.

"Guys, close the door," he said.

No response.

"Close the door," he begged.

No answer.

Kloss asked, "Where are we going?"

He got nothing but silence from the men and the howl of the wind and rumble of the thunder and the hum of the rotor blades. No talk. No speeches. Nothing else.

The man with the whipping tie turned in the jump seat and looked back over his shoulder at the pilot. His tie started whipping violently again. It was from a draft that blew through the open door.

The man with the whipping tie asked the pilot, "Where are we?"

The pilot called back, "Fifty miles out from the island."

"How high?"

"Over three thousand feet."

The man with the whipping tie turned back and faced his crew. He glanced down at Kloss. He said, "Okay. We're going to let you go now."

Kloss stared at the man's eyes. He saw that evil glee return.

The man with the whipping tie looked at his guys. He said, "Do it."

The two guys standing over Kloss, including the one with his shovel hand on Kloss's chest, stood up from their perches. They both grabbed a hold of opposite sides of the litter and hauled him up off the floor. The litter was in the air. They shuffled him over to the open doors. A third guy unbuckled his seat and reached under it and came out with a heavy object. He stumbled over to the stretcher. He lifted the object into Kloss's view. It was a fishing boat anchor. There was no chain attached to it. There was only the hole where one would go. The third guy hooked the anchor onto the stretcher's railing and dropped it on Kloss's lap.

Kloss's heart raced faster, like a fast telegram pulsating an urgent message. He squirmed and struggled and whipped his head back and forth. He asked, "What're you doing?"

No answer. No one listened. The large guys hauled him to the edge of the helicopter and the empty sky. They wrenched him back and then started swinging him forward like they were about to throw him out. They swung him forward and back repeatedly. At the end of each swing, he feared that would be the last one until they tossed him out.

"No! Wait! I told you everything! Wait!" he cried out.

It was no use. On the fifth swing, they tossed him out the open doors. Kloss and the litter went out into the storm, into the darkness, into the night.

A WORD FROM SCOTT

Thank you for reading PATRIOT LIES. You got this far—I'm hope you enjoyed this installment of Widow.

The story continues...

To find out more sign up for the Scott Blade Book Club and get notified of upcoming new releases. See next page.

Next is **The DOUBLE MAN**, out now!

THE SCOTT BLADE BOOK CLUB

Building a relationship with my readers is the very best thing about writing. I occasionally send newsletters with details on new releases, special offers, and other bits of news relating to the Jack Widow series.

If you are new to the series, you can join the Scott Blade Book Club and get the starter kit and other exclusives: free stories, special offers, access to bonus content, and info on the latest releases, and coming soon Jack Widow novels.

Sign up at ScottBlade.com.

THE NOMADVELIST
NOMAD + NOVELIST = NOMADVELIST

Scott Blade is a Nomadvelist, a drifter and author of the breakout Jack Widow series. Scott travels the world, hitchhiking, drinking coffee, and writing.

Jack Widow has sold over a million copies.

Visit @: ScottBlade.com

Contact @: scott@scottblade.com

Follow @:

Facebook.com/ScottBladeAuthor

Bookbub.com/profile/scott-blade

Amazon.com/Scott-Blade/e/B00AU7ZRS8

Made in the USA
Las Vegas, NV
17 September 2022